TALKING MAN

www.johnmbroadhead.com

Cover art and design by Joseph Donovan

ISBN-13: 978-1-7323591-0-9
ISBN-10: 1-7323591-0-5

JOHN M. BROADHEAD

TALKING MAN

CONTENTS

"Behind me tread one thousand men and ever there are more. We men who walk before them are the men they must adore."

PROLOGUE

Commencement speech, given to the graduating class at the
Aurora Technical Institute.
Presented by Dr. Abrahim Misleh, PhD.
May 9th, 2167

*Good morning. Congratulations to all of you. It's very exciting to see
so many eager young people moving through this wonderful process of
being educated in the sciences, especially during these changing times.
They asked me to say a few words to you about my own career, I suppose
with the intention of inspiring you. I don't want to talk about my own
career, however. Hours, days, years worth of studying, crouched over
books, telescope images, data sheets – that isn't something I would find
inspirational to listen to, if I were you. Instead I want to talk to you
about the nature of the journey on which you are embarking. I know, I
know your journeys will not all be equal, and they will not all lead you
to the same place. But all your journeys are those of science, and that is
what I want to address.*

*This is both the best time and the worst time to be a scientist. Best,
because today's technology, our reach into outer space, has made our possibilities truly endless. Worst, because more and more people every day
are not believing in what we do. If any of you has not yet been mocked*

or persecuted for the choices you have made, it is only a matter of time until you experience that. Your family and friends may tell you that you are betraying our species. They will tell you that you should be paying attention to other things that are more tangible. They will talk about our failures, like the terminated Mars project, the lost ships, and the harmful impact our early missions had on our own atmosphere. Of course, you will answer by reminding them of our research that has produced the cancer cure, the ocean-cleaners, habitable zones around our cities, and synthetic nutrition, things that our world now depends on. But the detractors won't listen. You will become frustrated because you believe that, through all our failures, science will save us in the end. But you won't be able to communicate your belief to those who don't share it, to those who are more short-sighted.

I once heard an argument that technology doesn't matter, but that it is communication that will save our species — communication between people, between cultures. I don't disagree. But let me suggest something to you: science and communication are the same thing, and to stifle science is to make mankind mute. We are born to communicate, to transmit, whether that is transmission of our words, of our poetry, or of our genes to our children. Sometimes our communication is simple, as a newborn baby squeaks in fear and questioning, unsure whether to trust the mysterious giants around it. Sometimes the communication is more complex, as when we, like the newborn babe, reach out to the mysteries around us to learn whether they will feed us or crush us.

Now, we could choose to be silent. We could lie still and tend to our own needs as best we can. But then we will never get an answer, and we will certainly never grow. Before we take a first step we must commit to falling a few times. Yes, we are a species that is still a baby. Will we lie here quietly and ignore the business of the universe around us? Or will we learn to talk?

CHAPTER ONE
S.A.S.H.

"Space is a dead end."

He didn't lean forward in his chair, but he didn't need to. The burning blue eyes and percussive voice provided the intensity that was only increased by his casual posture.

"Science – it's gone the way of religion.

"In the old days, people used to look up at the sky for answers, and you know what they came up with? Mythologies. That's right. Stories fueled by imagination, but inspired by what? Space. And now, look. You've got these smart, supposedly brilliant individuals who are *still* looking up at the sky for answers. Sure, they can go farther than the fellows who came up with the astrologies and the polytheistic creation myths, but in the end they're just interpreting signs the best ways they know how. They're still running into a wall of darkness that asks more questions than it answers. How much farther do they have to go before they realize the answers aren't out there? I say they'll never come to that realization, not on their own. They're going to keep coming back with new *discoveries*, new *information* about the universe that'll help *solve* the mysteries about how you and I came to be, what we're *made* of, *why* we are here. As if any of that matters to you and I, to our children and to the hungry children in unglobalized nations!

"The scientists will ask us to believe them but why should we? Why should we let them dictate how we interpret the signs in the stars?

"How is their work any different from an old Mesopotamian looking up at those same stars, seeing shapes same as a little child might see, and using those to determine the course of the future? Maybe it was enough for them, thousands of years ago. Here in the twenty-second century, those distant shapes won't reduce our poverty rate. They won't stem overpopulation or overcentralization, won't make the World Government more palatable, won't do away with the death sentence, won't stop the Eams epidemic, won't make trees grow again. We search for answers to our crises and I tell you the answers aren't out *there*; they're around us and inside us, and that's where they always have been. The world has been distracted by outer space exploration for long enough, and if we're ever to make real progress as a species, we need to put a stop to it!"

He didn't need to hear the billions of shaking breaths that now exhaled in excitement and agreement. Nor did he need to see the wide eyes and sweaty foreheads, palms rubbing together and heads nodding ever-so-slightly. He knew they were out there. They always were.

"And we're down," piped the producer. The red blinking lights around the cameras and scanners shut off, and four assistants scurried in to remove the sensors from Traver's head, shoulders and arms. "Good show, Mister Graff."

Traver Graff sat for a moment longer without moving, closing his eyelids over those hypnotizing irises. His hand rose slightly as if to make a point, but he pursed his lips and hesitated – then he went on: "'Science has gone the way of religion' – I should have closed with that."

"I think it was great the way it was. It sounded good to me and, according to the ratings report, to two point seven billion other people." Weston, the head producer, patted Traver on the back – Traver hated the feel of that cold, flabby hand, but smiled nonetheless. He opened his eyes and gifted Weston with a glance.

As he emerged from the studio hallway and into the big front lobby of the building, the talk show host felt an uncharacteristic sense of unease. To all appearances this was just another day at the Secular Alliance for Social Humanities, and outside the glass double doors was expected to be the usual crowd of over-excited interviewers, media-men, and zealots, with some protesters thrown into the mix. Today's crowd would be a little bigger, though – a little wilder. He'd thrown the world a few bones today, given them a reason to listen. He wanted more eyes and ears attentive to him when he stepped out of those doors on this day in particular. He just hadn't expected to be nervous about it.

His bodyguards opened the big doors. The hot outside air rushed in, and Traver paused for a moment to pass a hand over his jet-black, neck-length hair where the wind had disturbed it. Then he nodded and walked out.

Applause, first – it awakened like a fast-kindled flame upon his setting foot on the top step. There were some shouts of angry disagreement, but this crowd was mostly supportive. The SASH's opposition couldn't come out in full force every time a spokesperson finished a show – that would have made them look desperate.

Then through the applause came the questions. Twenty to thirty media mongers struggled to get within talking or at least shouting distance of Graff. A few, failing to get close, tossed their drones into the air, driving them with a soft whir toward where the gentleman was walking.

"Hey! Were you authorized to use drones today?" The bigger of Graff's bodyguards belted with an outrage that might have served just as well during a political assassination attempt. "I'm not going to ask you again – get these out of his face!" He swatted at one of the drones and it fell to the ground, where it rolled instantly into an insulated, slightly bounceable ball and made its way back to its owner.

"It's alright" Traver whispered to the bodyguard. "Let it slide today." Then he whispered a few more things to his men. A few moments later, the bodyguards were working their way through the crowd. "Interviewers front and center. You hear? Media to the front, everyone else back." It took some pushing, but once it became clear what was happening, the crowd cooperated.

The interviewers wasted no time in barking out their obnoxious queries: "Do you have a comment on the new entertainment censorship regulations?" "We know you support noncentral regrowth, but how can you honestly suggest we bring back the suburbs without rural food sources?" "How does the public knowledge of your recent extramarital affair affect your relationship with your family?" "Mister Graff, do you believe in aliens?"

Traver Graff held up his hands and shut his eyes. A religious silence fell over the crowd.

For an introspective half-moment, he realized that his nervousness was gone. Being surrounded by other people gave him a supreme confidence in himself, and it was a confidence he knew how to use.

The whir of the traffic hundreds of feet overhead, echoing down the Manhattan skyscrapers, would have made the crowd's hushed anticipation seem even more hollow and strange to an onlooker expecting pedestrian hubbub. But on this particular Friday afternoon there were no onlookers to give judgment; every soul gathered in front of the SASH building was there for Traver, and each one of them eagerly awaited his words.

Perhaps longer than was needed Traver held his hands up, basking in the silence for which he very well knew he was responsible. Then he said the words that he knew would be heard instantly by even more billions of people than attended to him weekly:

"I'm not going to answer any of your questions today. There'll be plenty of time for that later. Instead, I'm going to pose you all a question. *Who is the enemy?*"

Murmurs bubbled through the crowd – confused murmurs.

"The truth is, you don't know. *We* don't know. *I* don't know."

Ignoring the rhetorical nature of Traver's question, an excited voice in the crowd shouted "it's the Aurora Corporation" before the big bodyguard silenced the voice with a terrifying stare.

"And that's exactly where we're wrong!" Traver's eyes snapped back open and the hundreds of gathered spectators could feel his energy. "We're so eager to assign blame to some corporation, some name, some face, that we forget what the problem is in the first place. The Aurora Corporation is a symptom of a much greater problem. Now, I've always stated, in my broadcast, that the answers to humanity's questions exist here" (he put a hand over his heart) "in ourselves, and of course in the people around us. So let me ask you this: why should we alienate the people around us, call them the enemy? Doesn't that make us a part of the problem?"

The gazes were more confused, and the silence was total. Nobody knew what he was getting at, or where this would go, but not a soul wasn't breathless to find out.

"It's the goal of the Secular Alliance to fully understand all view-points so that we can distill a solution for the benefit of all humanity, without discrimination and without demonizing. So, in that same spirit –"

His hand went back unconsciously to that part of his hair that had been touched by the breeze.

"– this has been my final regularly formatted broadcast for the near future. There's going to be a hiatus of three months –"

Gasps. Disbelief. Wonder. Why?

"– and the next two years' worth of shows, I will be transmitting from space."

The gasps and the murmurs dropped off.

Traver himself was shaking. The confidence he had mustered had done its job, but now it was gone. His eyes swam, the buildings and the people blurred and spun. He could neither see the eyes of the crowd nor interpret what they were feeling toward him.

A quick nod at the bodyguards, a soft "thank you" to the interviewers and the drones (which now hovered indeterminably in place, looking just as bewildered as the rest), and Mr. Graff stepped down from the doors of the SASH.

The crowd didn't part for him, but it didn't need to. The bodyguards maneuvered him expertly and the people offered no resistance to their nudges. He reached the company aircar in a matter of minutes and then he was gone. The crowd he left behind, made up of dedicated fans, media hawks, protesters and a few public safety officers, were on this rare occasion all united, sharing a common state of being confused.

....

New York Now, April 3rd, 2153
"COMMUNICATIONS GIANT PUSHES UPWARD"
By Raymond Frenter, staff writer

The Aurora Company is going to outer space.

Months of speculation and unofficial reports paid off last night when Daniel Gladstone, Aurora's spokesman, held a press conference during which he confirmed the company's acquisition of S.T.A.R.S., a purchase that came with a price tag exceeding 40 billion unidollars. Already the move has sent shockwaves through major tech-based cities, many of which are suddenly turning their backs on smaller companies in preparation for the industry shifts that are certain to follow. "An industry tsunami like this hasn't happened in my memory," said Hans Weidner, a financial analyst among those who predicted the world market crash of 2121. "Aurora had already set a precedent through their other acquisitions but nobody honestly believed them to make such a big move so quickly."

Aurora Company, known in the mid-century for their revolutionary slidescreens and other personal communication devices, began expanding just a decade ago with their rapid-fire purchases of upstart tech companies. Their industries have come to include A.I. design, airmobiles, city weatherproofing and food manufacture among others.

Criticism against the Company has become more and more popular as they've grown in size. These criticisms include accusations of monopoly and of failure to utilize environmentally-friendly energies. Increased criticisms are sure to surface now with the purchase of S.T.A.R.S.

The space-travel dynasty first found its feet in the 2090s, in the wake of NASA's dissolution during Globalization. Their privatization of space travel was one of the most controversial movements of the turn of the century, though it yielded some spectacular discoveries along with devastating failures.

Most noteworthy as both success and catastrophe was the mission to ZL-24971, nicknamed the "Zilly" mission. Alien plant life, the first (and only, so far) of its kind, was famously found to exist on the planet. A solo manned mission was sent six years ago to orbit and observe Zilly, only for the space station Virgil and the astronaut Eve Abaddon to both disappear without a trace. S.T.A.R.S. did not come forward to the public with any details, a fact that was not overlooked by the organizers of the Pilots' Strike two years later.

Those failures along with a myriad of financial setbacks may have finally proven too much for the company, which seemed unhesitant to liquidate in its entirety at Aurora's first offer. Staff, facilities, copyrights, vehicles, and all documentation will belong to the Aurora Corporation as of Tuesday.

Aurora's only involvement in space travel previously had been its contribution to inter-spatial communications, with their transmitters becoming standard for all ships and stations built to leave Earth's orbit. "Our work on transmitters isn't going to stop, whether we're talking about interstellar communications or the screens in your pockets," promised Gladstone toward the end of the press conference. "You have *our guarantee that Aurora's focus on old projects isn't going to dissipate. Our gaze is going to broaden, and the benefits of that broadening are going to be felt in every one of our industries."*

....

Traver Graff had first been visited by the Aurora man six months prior.

It had been just after New Year's, with 2176 being so far much the same as 2175. Business at the SASH went on much the same as usual. The *Traver Talk* broadcast of the day consisted of its host reading off a list of all the astronauts who had been declared "missing," from Abaddon to Zweicker. Traver followed up his list by ranting about how the word "missing" indicated some kind of nonexistent middle ground between life and death, and since these "missing" people never actually ended up coming back alive, it was just a sugarcoated way of saying they were "very much dead." What a waste of life and effort and intelligence. And money.

He'd had no comments for the media people. No stops on the way home. He had his driver Karl call ahead to the house for a martini to be ready and waiting (Karl could have predicted this without prompting, but he'd long ago learned that Mr. Graff's ego was gratified by giving the order). The car was soon docked in the third-story garage, and Traver took the quicklift into the main living room where he tossed his jacket onto the couch (it didn't touch down before it was caught by one of the maids) and fell into the easy chair, the martini being ushered into his hand not twenty seconds later.

"Dana" he said flatly. No answer. A tiny purple light in the living room ceiling seemed to blink at him.

He rolled his eyes. "I wasn't calling for Dana, I was asking where she was."

"I'm sorry, I misunderstood your question as an imperative," came the programmed voice in response, as the purple light brightened enthusiastically. "But Missus Graff did not log a destination upon her departure."

"When did she leave?"

"Two hours twenty-seven minutes ago."

"Alright. Let me know when she's on her way back. And call Lucy."

Half a minute passed. Then: "Lucy is on the line."

Traver's palm-sized slidescreen, docked into the A.I. table-top mount beside his chair, activated, sliding open by itself and tilting toward him. A woman's voice came loud and clear through the living room speakers. "Hey Trave."

"Hey, yourself! Just voice? Turn on your video – if you get to see my pretty face then I want to see yours."

"C'mon…I'm at work right now."

"Still? It's after five."

"Yeah, remember how I told you I was picking up a few hours overtime that one day? Well the restaurant owner Randy comes in the evenings sometimes. Anyway he saw me and apparently fell in love with my work ethic. I've been doing twelve hour days all month long."

"Take off early today."

"I didn't think you'd want to meet after doing an episode. You have a few hours free?"

"I do if you do."

"I'll be throwing away overtime. Buy me dinner?"

"Is that a rhetorical question? When have I not?"

"Just making sure. I'll get out of here in an hour. If you send an aircar I can be over there quick after that."

"It'll be waiting for you. And so will I."

Traver smiled the wistful, empty smile of a man who is victorious over nothing, who has earned for himself a few more hours in which to indulge in meaninglessness before reality comes home.

"End call." He hoisted himself out of the chair, martini untouched.

"Let the cook know that we'll be having dinner for two tonight, at six thirty."

The house A.I. was only concerned about what it perceived as a failure in basic arithmetic: "But your children will be home by six. If Missus Graff is also home, with the guest in attendance, that will require dinner for five."

"Just dinner for two. Have the bus drop Allie and Damian off at the Langs'." He knew the kids would be more than happy, and less than suspicious, to have an evening away from their tiresomely uptight home life.

Just like that, with a few words spoken to his home computer, Traver had put everything in order, and now he just needed to wait.

In some ways he found himself missing the less comfortable times before he'd been immeasurably wealthy, when he still could feel that he earned things. *Earning* wasn't even a concept he thought much about anymore. Everything he possessed – the house, the cars, the perfect family, the show – it was all just hanging about, vaguely present in his consciousness as being stuff that he *had*. The way his life was going, it was just *going*. He still thought of himself as a happy person, but perhaps a little bored. Maybe that was why he'd intentionally left to chance the possibility of his wife coming home during his dinner for two. His life needed some excitement, or at least the distant eventuality of it.

He hated to sit around and wait, so he took the quicklift down to the second story, where the household recreation room was stationed. The rec-room-including-gym had come cheaper than buying the two separately, a fact he had used to justify to Dana the installation of the newest, best A.I. driven rec room. At the time of purchase, it had been exciting. The kids loved it for the interactive games, Traver for the gym, and Dana would only ever switch it on when she wanted to relive her years growing up on the Pacific beach. An undetected hint of bitterness was all that Traver felt about that.

Already that morning he'd spent two hours in the rec room, as he did each day after his half-hour of breathing exercises. But with nothing better to do than wait, he used the next forty-five minutes here again, alternating between the dumbbells and the rolling-runner. He didn't turn on the lifelike virtual display, instead opting for the blank, featureless room in which to work. Unlike Dana, he was just fine with reality being the way it was.

The latter twenty-one of Traver's years had been no worse on his body than the first twenty-one. He would never publicly admit it (and the SASH lawyers had done a sensational job of hiding the fact), but he had made his first million unidollars as a male underwear model. That was a long time ago, but now even at forty-two, he probably could get away with doing it all over again. The perfection of his body was one thing he earned, he often thought to himself — one thing he still was earning, every day. That felt good.

The pleasant voice of the A.I. interrupted him four kilos into his run. "Mister Graff."

"What?" He shouted breathlessly. He didn't like being angry, but it happened sometimes when his routines were cut short. What's more, he suddenly felt a little light in the head and weak in the legs, which was strange.

"You have a visitor. He's waiting at the front door."

This gave Traver pause, as he tried to recall the people who might possibly be calling on him. "Do I have any appointments?"

"No."

"Do you know who it is?"

"He doesn't have an ID that's registered with my manufacturer."

"Well, have Karl show him inside. I'll be up in ten minutes."

Ten minutes later, punctual to within five seconds, he stepped out of the lift and into the living room, groomed and wearing one of his better sports coats, top two shirt buttons undone so as to reveal a bit of his chest. He believed in dressing himself in such a way as to impress his confidence on others, particularly when approaching an unpredictable social situation. And the situation he was entering was certainly unpredictable.

The stranger was sitting in the living room, looking neither comfortable nor uncomfortable. He was just there. Upon Traver's entrance, he looked up from the couch with a smile that was amiable enough.

Traver believed in visual first impressions – indeed, how else is one person supposed to estimate another, prior to conversation, except with a hasty but thorough surface judgment? However the only thing he could tell by a quick study of the stranger in his living room was just how *average* the man was: neither good-looking nor notably ugly, his smile was inviting but bland, and his suit well-cut but not stylish. His face sported a five-o'clock shadow that might have been a few hours or a few days old. The absolute unmemorableness of the stranger was the terrifying thing about him, since there was not a single judgment Traver could make.

The man stood up. His height was about average.

Traver smiled ferociously. "I'm sorry to have kept you waiting."

"That's not a problem. I hope this isn't a bad time."

"Not at all."

As Traver lied through his teeth (it *was* a bad time), they shook hands. The man's grip was comfortable but not too confident, and his voice was smooth, but neither nasal nor very deep.

Stop noticing what's unnoticeable, Traver's consciousness screamed at itself.

"Will you have a seat?"

"Thank you."

They sat facing one another, and the stranger folded his hands calmly onto his lap. *He didn't introduce himself, but it's better if I don't insist, at the risk of appearing needy,* went Traver's bewildered thoughts.

"You are Mister Traver Graff?"

How could he not know who I am? Of course he does – he's playing.

"Yes, I am."

"I will make this brief. The Aurora Corporation has taken notice of you and your society. It may, at some point in the future, be in your best interest to adopt a more open mindset when it comes to the benefits of space discovery programs."

The ticking of the clock resounded through the room like a gong for what may have been a century, as the two men stared at one another.

Traver broke the silence. "Is the freedom of speech of the SASH and its broadcasting partners under attack?" He was once again confident; he hadn't expected for the newcomer to lay out his entire hand so bluntly.

But the man didn't respond. He stood up, tilted his head in what passed for a respectful nod, and strode out of the room at a casual pace. A moment later he was gone.

Despite all the mental anguish it caused him at that time, Traver later thought very little of the visit, because there was very little to think about. He tried his best to put the encounter out of his mind so that he could simply enjoy an evening with sweet, hopeless romantic Lucy.

Lucy, it turned out, had been planning for "weeks" to break things off since she was no longer "comfortable being in an affair" and, what's more, had "met someone." The dinner lasted twenty minutes, and that was that. Traver prided himself on always having a cool head about these things, and over the course of that last supper he neither argued nor lost that coolness. He'd liked Lucy, but he'd also liked other people before.

He did lose that cool after Lucy said goodbye. As soon as she left he stretched himself out in his couch, shutting his eyes and thinking of other things. But *what other things?* There was nothing to distract him. Lucy's words repeated in his head: "I've met someone. I've met someone." She had been so meek and unassuming, kind even, when giving him the news, but now his memory dressed her up with a mocking smile and unfeeling smirk.

By the time Traver could see clearly again, he had thrown the couch across the room where it knocked over a bookshelf, and kicked the slidescreen's table-top mount repeatedly and violently until it was not much more than a compressed ball of metal and plastic.

"Would you like me to summon the house staff?" asked the helpful, unfazed A.I.

"No," replied Traver, recovering his breath and running his fingers through his hair. "I'll clean it up." He did, and by eight o'clock had purchased a replacement slidescreen mount courtesy of the Aurora Instant Delivery Service. Traver prided himself on always cleaning up after himself.

He didn't know why he felt exhausted and a little nauseous, but Traver slept well that night.

The next day he received a call from the office of Brucker and Bruckner, of whom Brucker was his personal attorney and Bruckner was one of the many scurrying lawyers working for the SASH.

"Chad Brucker here. Am I catching you too early?"

Dana was snoring beside him, but Traver had been just moments away from throwing off the sheets for his morning run. "Nope. What's up?"

"I think we should continue this conversation somewhere you can be private."

Traver moved away from his wife and into his personal office, where Brucker briefed him.

Months worth of images and videos of Traver and Lucy, some innocent enough but most quite damning, had been sent to the SASH's Public Relations Department. No notes or demands accompanied the images, so nobody could make out whether this was a blackmail or just someone trying to stir the pot.

"Do you know if there is anyone who might be wanting to blackmail or threaten you?" asked Chad.

Yes, there were thousands. "No, there are none."

"Would you like me to advise you on how I think you should

proceed?"

Traver considered hearing his lawyer out, but quickly realized he'd known what action to take since the beginning of the conversation.

"I'm going to get out in front of this. If the information goes public, it's not going to catch my audience, my peers, my wife off guard. I'll talk to them all about it, and sooner rather than later."

And he did.

* * *

The next three weeks found him preoccupied with the backlash. Political enemies of the SASH had a field day with the scandal, making Traver their straw man so they could directly associate infidelity with any number of non-marriage-related ideals espoused by the Secularists. The media went about their usual circus, and the SASH Public Relations spent many hours pondering what to do with him. The only person in the world who didn't cause any fuss was Dana. She was there for him; that was why, whomever else Traver might like, Dana was always the one he loved.

But Traver didn't lose his job. No, he was never in danger of that. When he broke the news to the public during his show, he did it with showmanship and grace. Dana appeared as a guest and joined her husband in a discussion about the disadvantages of monogamy. The timing could not have been any better, since SASH was currently sponsor to several law proposals before the World Government in Oslo to allow the Americas to follow an increasing number of other nations in doing away with monogamy laws.

"I knew about it, of course," Dana broadcast. "This has been a lifestyle choice with which we've agreed to experiment. Traver and I support each other in whatever pursuits our hearts demand." It was a lie, but it didn't matter because Traver had saved face. The public was thrilled, the ratings soared and the SASH received an unusually high number of contributions.

....

The American Monthly Report, May, 2163
"THE S.A.S.H. LAUNCHES ANOTHER EMBARRASSING LAWSUIT"
by Carolina Vargas, contributing writer

Last month Auroramatics, a European subsidiary of the Corporation, pledged a donation of 10,000 slidescreens with Network access to the starving citizens of Cairo. In response, the Secular Alliance for Social Humanities attacked the Aurora Corporation with a class-action lawsuit.

Karen Tiplins, a spokesperson for the Alliance, had this to say about the lawsuit: "We don't believe a few thousand little electronic screens are going to help a few million hungry children. Send them food, send them clothes, send them shoes; don't send them slidescreens! What are poor families going to do with those anyway? It's not as if they'll know how to use them. Those electronics are going to end up unused, falling apart and contaminating the river."

Tiplins' quote continues: "Thank you, Aurora for 'solving' Cairo's problem by ruining our planet a little more. But while you're busy escaping into space, I'm going to actually do something about it. The SASH is organizing a food drive. We are asking for food donations, as well as monetary contributions to help us transport the food to its destination in North Africa. Please, instead of discarding your food, send it here to the Secular Alliance, and we pledge to pass it on to a starving child."

As of the writing of this piece on May 3rd the SASH has succeeded in gathering just under two tons in donated synthetic food [source: SASH public network]. A method and schedule for transportation of the goods has not yet been announced.

Meanwhile the Aurora Corporation has been providing a stable supply of rations and medical care to the citizens of Cairo, while their workers labor day and night to maximize the output of the city's food manufacturers while repairing the factories that had broken down last summer. Slidescreens are hardly the extent of the Corporation's contribution.

From this writer's window in a hovel in Cairo can be seen no less than five Aurora airvans attending to the citizens. Three are unloading crates of food supplies while the other two seem to be medical stations.

An interview with one Aurora doctor, Galina Shurovsky who is overseeing the medical care, provided this excerpted quote: "I do call America home and have for most of my life, but being brought halfway around the world to take care of these people is really a pleasure... Aurora sees what it means that we're no longer a divided world, and to turn our backs on another suffering nation is to turn our backs on ourselves." The doctor went on to add that Aurora is planning to build three more food plants here, though construction will need to delay until after next month's projected meteor impact, which is predicted to hit near the Nile Delta and bring even harsher environmental conditions to an already suffering region.

Tiplins and the SASH made no comment pertaining to Aurora's relief efforts. They mean to press forward with their lawsuit despite the likelihood of its being thrown out of court.

Is this really the best the Secular Alliance can do? As an opponent of mega-corporations like Aurora and a proponent of social justice and human rights, the SASH is an invaluable organization for this day and age. We are rooting for them, but we wish they would be wiser about choosing their battles.

But perhaps they are learning, if slowly. The Secular Alliance's change of methodology, moving away from failing class-action lawsuits and focusing more on inspiring media presence, could not have come at a better time. Perhaps the organization will finally learn from failure and let go of its illusions that it can go head-to-head with a giant like Aurora without first winning the hearts and minds of the public. The enlistment of the popular Traver Graff, former actor turned political commentator, may be a step in the right direction. The first episode of Traver Talk *debuts next Friday. Only time will tell whether SASH can pull itself out of the rut it has dug for itself, and find a way to be relevant again.*

....

"I've got them running," Traver had to yell through the live music at the *Downed Eagle*, his favorite anachronistic dive. Equipped with barstools, beer, faux-wood paneling and dim orange lights, the place harked back to a time before sleek liquor lounges were the drinking man's choice.

"They're nervous. Aurora sent a man to my house the other day. To my house! And I'm not even mentioning the blackmail, which *had* to be them. Who else? That's how I know they're desperate."

"Desperate how?" Callie Vargas sat beside him at the bar. She was a professional acquaintance, a journalist who ran a small network-based report that, while reaching a small reader base, tended to agree with the SASH broadcasts on principle but never on specifics. She and Traver had developed a friendship after a heated public forum several years before, and still made time for one another on an irregular basis. "What do they think you're going to do to them?"

"If you'd asked me that last week I would have told you they didn't know we even existed. But now I'm wondering if the mighty stone isn't starting to crack. It's a long road ahead but we're making progress."

Callie was distracted for a moment as she smilingly shoved away a drunk factory worker who was trying to push up against her. She picked up the conversation where Traver had left it: "What progress are you talking about? You're not realistically hoping to beat them – to actually kill space travel?"

She received a long stare from Traver that almost made the latter look sad. He had seemed to forget about the drink in his hand. "Yes."

Callie tilted her head and opened her mouth in surprise that might have been sarcastic. "Wow. Space travel. The pinnacle of human ambition. Traver Graff is going to bring it all to a grinding halt."

"We're just people, Callie – animals who learned how to talk, and we should consider ourselves lucky we got that far. We have everything we need, right here. Hubris, that's the thing that keeps people looking for more. We don't belong up there. Even if there is something out in space, why should we think it's there for us?"

Callie looked back down at her own drink and smiled. "You surprise me. Every time I think I understand your brand of idealism, I always end up standing corrected."

"What's wrong with my brand of idealism? Don't you think I believe what I say on the broadcasts?" Traver remembered his beer and stared at it. The truth was, he hadn't been feeling too well and drinking wasn't doing him any favors.

"I'm not questioning you, Traver! It's just that your public persona is so…big!" She stretched her arms wide, herself a little way beyond tipsy. "When I communicate – when most people communicate – it's for the sake of making a good impression, usually. You're no exception, since you seem to spend a lot of time making good impressions. After all, nobody really takes everything seriously that comes out of their own mouths."

Traver took a deep breath and shot down his beer. "I do."

CHAPTER TWO
EAMS

O*slo, Norway, Global Government Seat –*

ANNOUNCEMENT FOR PROPAGATION THROUGH ALL NATIONS AND TERRITORIES:
The International Department of Health has declared a STATE OF EMERGENCY.

<u>*Protect yourself against EAMS!*</u>
—Eams is a deadly bacteria that spreads via ingestion, but here's how YOU can avoid it:

> *Take all purchased food [ESPECIALLY that which is unsynthesized] to a designated Health Department Center or Aurora Treatment Plant. These facilities are set up to quickly test your food and beverages for the offending bacteria. Testing is free, and is strictly mandatory for EVERYONE until the state of emergency has ended.*

—Knowledge is power, so here is some history about Eams:

> *It first appeared during the 2163 Cairo Food Crisis, during which several major food factories malfunctioned. This event concurred with a rush of refugees into the capital from the surrounding areas,*

which had held back from Centralization for as long as possible until the Dry-up forced them to abandon their farms. During the resulting lapse of cleanliness, the deadly bacteria first surfaced among the destitute population before rapidly spreading, via the sharing of rations, throughout the city. Containment was unsuccessful.

—*Eams is still relatively rare in First World nations but new cases are reported daily.*

If you are reading this posting, the bacteria has either been detected in your city or we need your help to prevent it from appearing.

—*Eams makes its home in bone marrow.*

It subsists on calcium and causes severe deterioration of the bone structure. It is nearly impossible to detect in its early stages, so GET YOURSELF CHECKED.

—*Currently there is NO CURE.*

If you think you have been infected, see a health specialist immediately and stop sharing food. Don't lose hope; there IS treatment available to reduce the pain and give you a full life. The best treatment is prevention.

Eams is scary, but it will not get the better of us. As with cancer and AIDS before it, we're going to keep working tirelessly until we beat this.

[This statement was assembled with contributions by the Aurora Corporation.]

....

On a morning in February, Traver shook off the cold as he walked from the parking tower into the back entrance of the big glass SASH building. The bodyguards (recently assigned to Traver after the business of his affair) shut the door behind him and walked with him down the bland, echoey hallway toward the studio.

Weston the overweight producer appeared at the far end of the hall. Lungs heaving for air while his rolling stomach bobbed, he was doing something that vaguely resembled running.

"Hey, Mister Graff."

"Good morning Weston. Everything alright?"

"Yeah, everything's…well, everything's alright except that when I came in this morning, I found someone sitting in the studio. I don't know him, but he says he's waiting for you."

"How did he get in?"

"I asked Security, and they said he'd shown them a clearance badge."

The bodyguards, excited to make themselves useful, both stepped in front of Traver and put their hands to the clubs hanging from their belts.

"Oh, I don't think he's dangerous," panted Weston. "He's just… just…" and his words petered off as the producer found himself at a loss for adjectives. That's when Traver knew exactly who was there waiting for him.

The bodyguards opened the door and saw the Aurora man with the five-o'clock shadow in the studio, sitting comfortably in Mr. Graff's broadcasting seat. "Can we help you sir?"

"I told your producer already, I'm waiting for Mister Graff."

"Are you a friend of his?"

Traver spoke up: "This is the man who harassed me last month. I don't know him, so feel free to remove him."

The bodyguards were practically rejoicing at the opportunity, beneath their angry Easter Island Statue faces. They moved toward the calmly seated stranger. As if he'd been expecting them, the man reached into his shirt pocket and produced a letter. Wordlessly, he handed it to the furiously enthralled guards, who stopped in their tracks. "What's this?" He flicked his finger as if to say *just read it*, and then turned his steady gaze onto Traver.

"Mister Graff, we can't make him do anything" said the bigger bodyguard, after opening the letter and reading the contents.

"For god's sake, why not?"

"Well…" The guard paused, embarrassed. The other, no less embarrassed, took the initiative to speak up. "This letter is from our contract company, and it says we can't."

Traver snatched the letter from him. Sure enough, it was marked by the seal of Leeman Securities, and contained explicit instructions for the bearer of the letter to remain untouched, undisturbed and unharassed by any of its employees.

"Alright. Step outside please," Traver ordered, sighing. The bodyguards bowed their heads, devastated at this turn of events, and walked out into the hall.

Traver leaned against his desk and faced the five-o'clock shadow man, who still sat. "What are you hoping to win? Threatening me, blackmailing me weren't enough, so now it's intimidation?"

Now the man stood up. He was a little below eye-level with Traver – *and he doesn't blink*, Traver realized.

The stranger shut his eyes quickly then opened them again. "You've misinterpreted us completely. Like your organization, we are an enterprise of idealists. If there is a chance of something worth finding, we aim to find it. It's as simple as that."

Traver paused for a moment. Something like respect for his opponent was rising to the surface of his consciousness. The stranger had earned a debate, anyway.

It was Traver's turn. "In history, enterprise by exploration has only ever led to a small number of things. A people will discover a new land, and then promptly fight over it. If there are natives there, the natives will be oppressed. Diseases previously unknown and unaccounted for will be unlocked, leading to mass illness and death. If there are new resources to be found, they just turn into further fuel for war. That's the cycle, don't you see? If that's how it has always gone here on Earth between countries, how do you think it's going to work out any differently when you try to conquer the stars?"

"Do you believe the things you say, Mister Graff?" The man asked quickly, as if he'd either not heard Traver's argument at all, or had simply processed it instantly and moved on.

"Belief is your commodity to trade in, not mine." (*god this is good; I wish I was broadcasting right now*) "I don't believe things. I know them. I don't think you can say the same for your sciences. Your aspirations will always require a certain amount of belief."

"Belief is required to take us to a certain threshold, after which we secure tangible data. For centuries we believed that if we looked hard enough, we would find other life. That belief brought us to Zilly, where we did find it. Would you deny that?"

"You found plant life. That was thirty years ago – everyone knows about that. Why would I deny it?"

"That's more than just a resource. More than just a discovery. It changes the way we perceive ourselves in the universe."

"To what end? Does that perception make a difference to our well-being, to our treatment of one another? It's completely outside of our relevant experience, so I think not!"

The shorter man straightened his composure as if he was offended, somehow adding several centimeters to his height and looking eye-to-eye with Traver. "You talk about the destructive cycles of history. None are more pathetic than the search for meaning, harmony and resolution for ourselves. That search is what leads to war and suffering because nobody can ever agree on which harmony is more harmonious. Looking inward has been tried, Mister Graff; it's been tried for hundreds of thousands of years and in the meantime we've nearly worn out the planet on which our species depends. Perhaps our *relevant experience* is not enough anymore. Perhaps if there is anything that will save us, it's out there. Who is going to reach out to it, if not us? If not now, then when?"

Traver had to acknowledge the man's tenacity. But he also knew this was an argument that would simply never end. "You're not going to change my mind, and I'm clearly not going to change yours. So why are we still talking?"

The stranger smiled. "We're just barking at one another. If we are, as you believe, animals without a right to higher aspirations, then perhaps barking is all we can do. We can communicate but never really confer."

The man reached into his pocket again, this time producing a small card. He held it out in his flat palm, as if it was a peace offering.

Traver eyed the card suspiciously. "I'm not going to change my message. Nothing will make me tell my listeners something I don't myself hold to be true."

"Nobody is asking you to. You simply know how to reach people, and we think we can reach even more through you."

Traver took the card, and then the man was gone.

On the card was written: *YOUR ATTENDANCE IS CORDIALLY REQUESTED AT A SPECIAL CONFERENCE TO BE HELD AT THE AURORA NEW YORK OFFICES, MARCH 16TH AT 8PM.*

He sat down in his broadcasting seat, or rather fell into it.

"Weston," Traver called dreamily after a few moments. The producer reappeared at the studio's doorway.

"Yes Mister Graff? Everything alright?"

Traver didn't take his eyes away from the card. "Call Karl and have him bring the car back for me. I need to take a sick day."

The truth was, Traver felt awful. He usually tried to suppress hints of feeling unwell, so it was a bad sign when he finally became aware of the symptoms. The nausea he'd ignored for weeks finally forced him to take notice. When the bodyguards opened the door and Karl came in to usher his boss back to the aircar, Traver found himself barely able to stand.

"Karl," he said once he'd dragged himself to the parking tower and the aircar had taken flight, "I need you to take me to the doctor."

"Of course, sir. I'm sorry you're not feeling well. Do you need me to call ahead and make sure you have an appointment when we get there?"

Traver clicked his slidescreen shut. He'd just finished sending a message to his doctor's personal number. "No, Karl. I want this to be very quiet, very discreet. Can you help me keep it that way?"

"Of course I can, sir."

The visit to the doctor led to a referral to a specialist, which led to a series of tests. First it was urine samples, and then blood. It wasn't until he was prodded with a long, painful needle that collected a particle of bone from his femur that he grew nervous. Bone tests could only mean one thing that the doctors must suspect.

Two days went by, during which Traver heard nothing. He was not so naive as to believe that "no news was good news," but all the same the nausea seemed to subside and he allowed a little hope to creep into his mind.

He kept his distance from Dana and the children for those days, opting instead to rent a hotel room. His self-imposed exile served two purposes: to prevent contagion from spreading to his family, and to save himself the embarrassment of looking as weak as he felt.

On the third day he received a call from his doctor. Karl picked him up and drove him to the hospital, where he was told the news.

Dana was sitting in the easy chair when Traver came home.

"Mister Graff has arrived in the docking garage" announced the comforting voice of the house A.I. system.

A few moments later, the lift opened and there stood what looked like a ghost – a pale version of Traver with tossed hair and wrinkled shirt. For all Dana knew of her husband, he may as well have walked in covered with blood; that was the extent of disaster signaled by even a hint of Traver in disarray.

She leaped out of the seat and ran to him. "Usually I'd say you don't need to talk about it if you don't want to, but I'm not going to let you have the choice this time. What's going on?" She led him to the couch, onto which he collapsed like a sack of meat and bones.

She sat beside him. For minutes, maybe hours they sat together, Dana waiting patiently for Traver to open up his mind to her, which she knew he would do eventually if only she stayed there with him.

"I saw the doctor today. I've been seeing him since Friday."

Dana hadn't known that. But she remained patient.

"Blood tests came back fine. Piss tests came back fine. Then they ran bone tests. Ran them three times just to be sure."

She knew what he was going to say. Completely unlikely as that thing might be, her intuition told her that it was the truth.

"I'm sick, Dana."

"Eams?"

He nodded.

* * *

The options were laid out for Traver by his doctors. Once he was able to distill the truth from their technical blathering, he found that the options were really only twofold: gradual crumbing of the bones and death within a year, or drugs, followed by slower crumbling of the bones and death within two years. The best treatment he could be offered was the same as was available to most of the public: sickening amounts of oral medication and a few monthly shots. A little physical relief and an extra year of time was all that he could hope for.

"Is that the only treatment?" he asked his primary physician during his briefing, two days after the diagnosis. "I read about something else. There was a more effective process being worked on…" He nearly added "*by Aurora*" but stopped himself.

"Yes, by Aurora," the doctor finished for him. "I'm afraid that's not a treatment that has been made available to the public just yet. It's experimental, as far as I know. You'd be better off sticking to the proven relief that we can provide you."

"A little comfort for an extra year isn't good enough. What can I do to start the process of looking into that experimental treatment?"

"I'm afraid you can't do that. It's out of my hands – and before you ask, it is not even a question of money. Our medical network sponsored by the SASH simply does not support experimental treatments."

* * *

On March 16th, Traver found himself at Aurora's table.

"We would never ask you to change," said Mr. Gladstone from the head of the table. "You should maintain your principles as you've always done. Keep talking to people in the same manner as you do on your show – if, in fact, that's what you continue to believe. But we're inviting you to do so from a platform that is slightly removed."

Traver raised an eyebrow. "And by removed, you mean?"

"Billions of kilometers removed" cut in the other Aurora man, the one with the five-o'clock shadow.

Traver was hardly intimidated by the room full of suited administrators. This was turf on which he was used to fighting. He could usually chew up a roomful of these overdressed twerps and still have room for breakfast. And he'd come to the table this morning intending to do just that. Now, he felt differently. Maybe it was the three weeks of treatment, which left him sick to his stomach and unable to maintain a proper exercise regimen. The doctors had told him he was responding well, that the treatments could be reduced after a few more weeks. That was something to look forward to. At the moment he was feeling reasonably well. But all the same he found himself listening to the men at the table, letting their words affect him. His own passivity came as a surprise that was, surprisingly, not unwelcome.

"How does this benefit your corporation?" Traver asked, grasping for ways to be argumentative.

Mr. Gladstone, who happened to be the Senior Overseer of Aurora Operations in the Eastern United States, continued in his solemn, gravelly voice: "The public has taken an increasingly contentious viewpoint when it comes to our missions and our longterm goals, due in no small part to the work of your organization." Traver wished he could feel flattered. "To combat this, the solution is not to bombard the public with good press. No, that's fighting fire with fire. We need to just pull the curtains back a little – let them see that we're not the bogeymen with clandestine technology behind closed doors."

"But that's what you are, no?" Traver received a few nasty looks from some of the lesser executives. This pleased him. "You do the majority of your work with zero transparency, your funding is completely privatized, and as for longterm goals – well, I study your company for a living and I don't have the first clue what your longterm goals are. My point is, why do you need the public at all?"

"We don't *need* them. But we do *want* them. Having a large number of enemies is never beneficial. Public support is positive. Call it a matter of numbers."

"How am I going to change things for you? Whatever the means of broadcast, my message is going to be the same."

"That's good! People trust you, and when they see you up there, they'll take notice. We'll have created a large scale discussion that's honest – that's transparent. It doesn't matter with whose side the public chooses to sympathize."

Traver paused for a moment. He reached for the glass of water on the table in front of him. Usually, his rule was to never drink the offered water, since it put him in a position of dependency. Now he drank it without thinking.

"You're wanting publicity – any publicity. Even my scorching critiques up there will benefit you in the end. It's all a stunt. That's what you're telling me."

"We're being honest with one another, Mister Graff."

After the meeting, Traver was able to pull aside the ever-average five-o'clock shadow man for a moment, well out of earshot of Gladstone and the others.

In a hushed, shaking voice, Traver murmured: "I think, before we talk any further about my going to space, I need to disclose that I have…I have…."

"Stage Two Eams. Yes, we know." The shadow man was nonchalant.

Traver shouldn't have been surprised by this point.

"That would disqualify me, I think. A liability like that, nobody would want to deal with. The lack of medical access, the risk of contagion. Not to mention, the physical dangers to myself..."

"You're mistaken. There will be significant medical access onboard. What's more, experts seem to agree that an extended experience in zero gravity will successfully postpone some of the worst effects of bone degradation."

Traver's eyes brightened and his head cocked slightly, even before he was aware enough to suppress the visible effects of the excitement he felt.

The man went on, maybe or maybe not having seen Traver's minuscule change of expression. "Doctor Shurovsky assures me that your condition, under the proper treatment, will take several years to advance to a state where it will cause you any physical risks during space flight. She of course will approve you for travel, should you accept."

"Doctor Shurovsky?"

"She is our most prominent Eams researcher. Her treatment is proving much more effective than the conventional ones. We will ensure it is made available to you, if it isn't already."

Traver seemed to be at a loss for words. His mind was churning. *What aren't they telling me,* he thought, though he knew the likely answer was *everything.*

The man took a step closer to Traver, his voice dropping to a whisper. "The Eams is *why* we selected you. Of all the popular anti-expansionary activists we could have spoken with, why do you think we've been hounding you? The Eams is why."

* * *

Every Thursday and Monday, he began to visit Dr. Galina Shurovsky, Aurora doctor, for his injections. The treatments were quite exorbitant in cost and would remain so as long as Traver had not signed any contracts with Aurora, but the money was a small price to pay for a fighting chance against Eams (and became even smaller when he considered the depth of his bank account).

Dr. Shurovsky was a tall, harsh-featured woman who looked angry even while she smiled to greet him. "Mister Graff! You're looking well. Let's take a look at how you're doing, shall we?"

Traver would first be subjected to an hour-long scrutiny under full-body scanners. The doctor and her assistants compiled the scans into three-dimensional models, which they picked apart and studied inch by inch, determining the scale of the damage.

Then they would give Traver a shot of muscle relaxant – specially formulated to leave his lungs unaffected – so he would be temporarily paralyzed but fully aware, and move him into a bleak sterile tank without windows. There a monstrous set of metal spider-like legs (if spiders had twenty-six of them) hung from the roof, each ending in a nozzle and needle. These spider legs were fed via internal tubes from a vial filled with Dr. Shurovsky's special formula, a whitish-clear liquid that made Traver uneasy at the thought of being pumped full of it.

Traver was laid in the center of the tank, attached to breathing tubes. Unable to move, staring upward at the shiny spider that waited only on a minuscule electronic pulse to pounce on him, he knew what it was to be in hell. The promise that it would all be over in an hour only made this hell worse, since another such encounter awaited him at the next appointment.

The doctor watched the monitor screens as they filled the tank with viscous fluid. The rag-doll that was Traver Graff was lifted off the floor, floating gently and inevitably toward the legs in the ceiling.

The legs initialized. They opened up, unfolded, spun and buzzed around him. Scanning his body, each of them focused on part of him to stab.

He found himself screaming, but it was a scream that never made it past his brain. The paralysis was complete. He could only watch, through the thick clear fluid that made him feel like he was drowning, as the metal arms froze in place, all poised like angry wasps just waiting for a reason to move in for a kill.

Somewhere behind a wall, Dr. Shurovsky looked over the scan images and the targets selected by the needles. She made an adjustment or two. Then she pressed a button.

The spider's legs clenched in, with Traver in the middle.

Spiders. He used to catch unsuspecting flies, releasing them into the intricate webs of weaver spiders above the door of his childhood home. He'd always found pleasure in the suffering of lesser species, and could spend hours watching the hunter pounce on the helpless bug, wrap it tightly in its arms with a strangely violent intimacy, then transform it into pulpy, unrecognizable remains.

He was now the fly.

There was no pain at all during the procedure, but that didn't stop his traitorous brain from inferring pain where it should have been. Twenty-six needles pierced his skin, his tissue, and his bone, and then rested there forty-five minutes, soaking his bones in Dr. Shurovsky's formula. The needles held him in place as he floated.

"You performed wonderfully" smiled the doctor when the two hour ordeal would come to an end. Traver couldn't smile back, since the paralysis was still wearing off. He was in a wheelchair with Karl standing behind him, ready to usher him as needed. "Don't eat for the rest of the evening, and apply the antibiotics to the needle entry points every two hours. I will see you next time."

The paralysis would wear off about two hours later. Then Traver curled up in a ball, the pain in his joints sometimes too unbearable to allow him to move. There on the floor he would dry-heave until late at night. Dana sat with him, but there was nothing she could do to make him more comfortable.

Every Monday and Thursday. No matter how much longer his life was to be, this would likely be the rest of it.

It was no decision at all. Traver's free will was just a trick of language. He was always going to accept Aurora's offer.

* * *

First thing on Friday mornings, he dressed, carefully combed his hair, applied foundation to hide his pale face, and had Karl take him to work.

When he told Karen Tiplins, President of the SASH, that he'd verbally agreed to accompany an Aurora remote mission, she responded less than kindly.

"It's a free ride for their propaganda! They want to use us as a channel to get their message out to the world."

"It's not their message. It will be my message – *our* message."

"They'll have you in a controlled environment. They could change the way you think. Put something in your water, show you brainwashing material. Who knows what they can do!"

Traver didn't let out the chuckle he felt building; Karen represented the delusionally paranoid part of the SASH, for which he secretly held a humorous contempt. "I'll be my own man. I've been assured a technical assistant of my own choosing, and a medical team dedicated strictly to me." He hadn't informed his own society about his Eams, so he hoped the mention of a medical team would go unquestioned. It did.

"I won't broadcast it. If they want you, they can have you. But I won't have a part in it."

"Well, broadcasting through Aurora's channels *would* defeat the whole purpose. I have, however, spoken with our syndication partners. They're more than happy with the idea; it means record ratings for them. They've agreed to keep me in my usual time slot, with or without sponsorship from the SASH. Of course they'll remove all the SASH logos and references, if you still feel this way."

Karen acquiesced to allow the broadcast, in the end.

* * *

He chose to tell Dana last. Dana, who had stood by him through thick and thin, sickness and health, until death. This was almost too much for her – the last straw on the proverbial camel.

"How long?"

"Two years. It's the shortest mission they can do. The usual is four years or more."

"Four years or more; for astronauts – for trained people who've sacrificed their whole lives for that, that insanity! You're not trained, and you haven't sacrificed your life. Have you? Will you?"

"Dana. I don't have much more life."

"What about the kids?"

"They can either watch me get worse and worse, turning into a jellyfish who can't even make a fist without crumbling my bones, or they can watch me do that after I get back from space."

"The treatments might work."

"But I'm only getting Galina's formula in the first place because of Aurora. Do you think they'll keep me on these treatments if I refuse the offer? No, I'll be back on those placebo vomit pills. Then I'll be dead in a year, for sure. At least if I stick with her injections – and they'll be treating me during the trip, too – I'll get a few more years."

Dana looked away. For a month she didn't look back at him, nor did she speak to him except when their children required the facade of an intact parental unit.

As for the children, Allie and Damian were not blind to the fact that something had drastically changed in their family dynamic. Children always know. Allie, sixteen and on the verge of womanhood, turned a blind eye as she thought fashionable. It wasn't until Damian, the more sensitive thirteen year old, mustered up the courage to approach his father and ask about his health that Traver realized it might be best not to let them find out about his departure through the media outlets.

One day after school while their mother was absent, he asked them both to sit in the living room, where he spent the better part of ten minutes deciding whether to tell them first about his health or about his approaching venture. For once in his life he didn't know the right words to use for either revelation, so he made idle small talk, asking about their school, their friends, their hobbies. It occurred to him that this was the first time he'd ever tried to actually talk to his children, and it was an experiment he was failing. Why had he waited until now, when the matters at hand were in fact life-changing and galaxy-spanning, to have a simple human-to-human conversation with the two people he had brought into the world? His ruminations brought him to silence as his small talk, an empty art which he had never bothered to perfect, fell flat.

The children did not have the patience for this "talk," which had already gone ten minutes too long. Allie, who had all the sensitivity of her mother, interrupted Traver's silence. "Dad, just tell us what you're trying to tell us. Is this about you being sick, or you going into space?"

Traver should have felt relieved that his daughter had removed his conundrum. He didn't. She had spoken for him, and that made him angry. His mind was filled with an urge to jump forward and grab Allie by the throat. It was a half-second urge, gone before his face had the chance of betraying a hint of rage. Instead he smiled bitterly and nodded.

"Did your mom tell you?"

"No. We're not stupid though. You look like a corpse and you're careful with your food and utensils, like you don't want us catching something. And, you don't talk about anything except Aurora and space anymore – at home just as much as at work."

Damian chimed in. "We were wondering if you were just going to go without ever telling us."

"Or drop dead," finished Allie. "Whichever one happened first."

To maintain his smile required a great deal of effort on Traver's part. He wanted nothing more than to leave the room, ending the conversation. Perhaps this was why he had avoided talking with his children for their lives up until this point: this was no conversation at all. Still, he put on his best face and told them the truth.

Afterward, tears came to Damian's eyes but there was otherwise no reaction. Both children stood up without a word and left the living room. Traver stayed behind, seated in the couch all alone. The rage that simmered in his mind did not explode outwardly this time, but it also did not dissipate. Through the millions of half-whispered angry voices in Traver's head came one thought that was clear as day: he would be leaving nothing behind.

....

The Aurora Manifest, A Monthly Journal, 4/1/2176

We are proud to announce the solidification of plans for our first manned mission to AMA-712.

It has been public knowledge for months that Aurora has been making plans for another long-distance mission, our first in nearly three years. Negotiations with the Pilot's Cooperative have been ongoing for months as they reviewed the details and goals of our mission. As our avid followers will be well aware, any manned missions that we send into space require the approval of the Cooperative board ever since the 2148 Pilots' Strike. Happily the negotiations have ended in resolution and our mission has been provided with a captain and first officer who will transport our research team to the planet.

The destination will come as a surprise to many of our readers; AMA-712, which orbits WOLF 359 some 7 light years away, has not featured in any public speculation since the Pytheas *automated probe was sent to the planet to gather data back in 2158. Behind the scenes at Aurora, the readings that the* Pytheas *brought back have been analyzed for nearly two decades, leading prominent scientist Dr. Abrahim Misleh to call AMA-712 "the most intriguing mystery in the current age of space-travel."*

Dr. Misleh has spent thirty years studying deep space phenomena. His career goes all the way back to the Zilly mission. In the years since he has put his mind to such mysteries as LACY-4 and the Nile meteorite, though his primary focus, according to his own testimony, has remained AMA-712. He will be personally leading the research team on the upcoming mission – his first time in space.

AMA-712, originally labeled "TY-71887" upon its initial discovery in 2143, was renamed a decade ago in honor of the three scientists most responsible for contributing to our knowledge of it: Agerton who discovered it, Misleh who has spent years studying it, and Aguilar who oversaw the Pytheas *mission.*

AMA, which is more than eight times Earth's diameter, is believed to be largely or wholly composed of gas. The precise composition cannot be determined using traditional instruments; the outer gases are too erratic and unpredictable to read, while the inner atmosphere is too thick to allow scientists to detect the makeup of the planet's core. Dr. Misleh and his peers believe the answers to these questions may contribute to our fundamental knowledge about the way planets formed billions of years ago. The primary goal of this mission is to give the scientists a closer look at the planet from orbit, allowing them to collect samples and take readings personally.

Many details about the mission, such as the ship, captain and crew manifest (with the exception of Dr. Misleh), either have not been determined or are not yet cleared for public release. The departure date has been set as sometime later this summer, with a mission time of about two years — six months of travel time each way with a year spent in orbit.

Further updates will be provided as details become available.

....

"And the next year's worth of shows, I will be transmitting from space." It was in early June when Traver made his announcement to the world.

For some reason unbeknownst to the statistics experts at the SASH and unpredicted by the broadcast syndicator, the public erupted at Graff's announcement. Perhaps it was the unlikely pairing of skeptic with space mission, or the excitement at getting a look behind the scenes in one of the unknowable off-world projects about which so many people whispered, but the world responded with disproportionate zeal.

The media hawks descended on his home. Dana could no longer

pretend to ignore what was happening, and she prepared to take their children indefinitely to a more private domicile. Her mother's house on the Pacific Coast was the most likely destination, where she could be out of the media's eye and unaffected by her husband's public antics. Traver could not help but feel grateful when the Aurora Corporation stepped in with its own private security force, a veritable army, protecting his house day and night from the prying eyes and ears of sensationalist broadcasters and making his family's exile unnecessary. His old security guards, so abruptly replaced, were less grateful.

At some point during the frenzied blur of preparation, media reports and bone treatments, the day came for Traver to sign the contract.

The five-o'clock shadow man came to his home, much as he had upon his first visit. With him were two witnesses, neither employees of Aurora nor of SASH.

The shadow man held out his slidescreen, already open with the contract visible, to Traver. Traver held it in one shaking hand as he skimmed through it.

He already knew what it contained. Lawyers Brucker *and* Bruckner had both thoroughly examined the document. As it had been paraphrased and summarized by Chad, it went something like this:

Traver Graff will be accompanying a manned mission to AMA-712.

Aurora will assume full responsibility for Traver's safety during the mission, given his full cooperation and adherence to procedure. Training for proper behavior in a ship environment will be provided as necessary.

Medical staff will be on hand to ensure Traver's continual treatment with Dr. Shurovsky's Eams suppression formula.

The mission will depart in September of 2176, with a return no later than September of 2178.

Compensation will be nonexistent, as Traver Graff is NOT serving as an employee of the Corporation but as a guest. However, Mrs. Graff and the two children will receive substantial remuneration, should Traver suffer delay, injury or death.

Traver is free to engage the crew as he likes, within ethical boundaries. Pilot's Cooperative limitations apply, with regard to the captain and first officer. They must choose to initiate any contact with passengers [as outlined in Cooperative Code].

Traver will broadcast regular hourly segments on a weekly basis, to be transmitted back to Earth and shown to the public. The content of these segments is at the sole discretion of Traver Graff, with ONE exception [see below].

The exception to Traver's freedom of content while broadcasting is as follows: Traver is NOT to reveal his condition of Eams Infection to the world until the jump has been made and the vessel has left the Solar System. After that point, and before orbit has been established around AMA-712, the announcement WILL be made, along with a full report of his condition, his suffering, and his treatment.

Traver and the SASH will own the rights to their broadcast...etc.

The lawyers had taken issue with a few of the points they considered "highly irregular." It was Traver who put their minds at rest, or at least talked them into standing down their protestations.

He saw showmanship at work here, and nothing more. Aurora knew the value of a good story – a moving story, about a celebrity on the last leg of his life, given the chance to see the far reaches of space before he dies, no matter his political stance. It would have people in tears. Traver had no interest in nitpicking Aurora's chosen narrative. He would have one of his own to tell.

He signed the contract.

"Very good" were the only words spoken by the shadow man before he went on his way.

* * *

One July morning found Traver sitting with his children at a delicatessen overlooking the city and the ocean. A million aircars followed their streams and patterns far below, looking more like hive-minded insects than instruments of free thinking humans. Over the ocean the horizon was clear enough to where a towering pier could barely be seen out in the distance – one of the water processing plants that served both as generators and purifiers.

Traver's disappointment at his children's coldness did not stop him from trying to grow closer with them during his last two months on Earth. It was an attempt that met with very little success. For a father who'd never thought about them – while he had provided for, cared for and tolerated them, he'd never been truly *aware* of them as anything more than side characters in his own story – the two had better things to worry about than Traver's ill-timed attempt at bonding. They found the whole situation bewildering, a frenzied blur of adult emotions – *"Dad has Eams and he's going to space so now he wants to get to know us"* – that were just overwhelming enough to be uninteresting to them.

But they weren't monsters. They saw their father's pain and appreciated it to the extent that they could. While unable to fully commit to a newfound bond, they both put on their best acting faces and went along for the ride when it wasn't too inconvenient. As a result they found themselves treated to cake, ice cream and whatever else their hearts desired on any days they were free from school. Neither complained.

"I don't get why you hate space so much." Traver's gaze came back from the ocean to where his son was addressing him over a coffee-cake. "And if you hate it, why are you going?"

Allie, certain that she understood things better than her kid brother, answered for her father. "He *has* to, get it? The companies made a deal. It's a big publicity stunt for both of them, and dad's just caught in the middle."

Traver chuckled a little. He looked back out to the sea. The tower was slowly rising, becoming clearer against the blue sky. In another hour or so it would reach its full height as it suctioned in a full load of water, millions and millions of liters. Then the tower would plummet downward, shooting out the filtered water while concurrently generating enough power to run New York for a whole day. What a beautiful creation of efficiency and cleanliness. Aurora had been behind the research.

But what about the fish? His wondering only lasted a second.

"I did have a choice in the matter. I agreed to it. And I don't hate space. Not yet anyway."

"Of course you do. That's all you ever talked about."

For the first time in his professional career, a hint of doubt whizzed through Traver's mind. In a flashing moment, he wondered whether he'd misplaced his emphasis, whether human ambition for something greater than itself was an antithesis to apathy instead of the escapism he'd accused it of being.

The moment passed quickly.

"Maybe I just want to see firsthand what all the fuss is about."

"Will you bring me back a space rock?"

"If I get the chance to pick up any space rocks, I'll bring you back as many as I can carry."

CHAPTER THREE
ATEN

Captain Louisa Fletcher was to pilot the *Aten* to AMA-712. An upstanding member of the Pilot's Cooperative and a veteran long-distance specialist, she had contracted with Aurora only twice before, on longer missions. This was to be among the shorter flights of her career. A two-year job was an easy paycheck.

Her first officer was Nelson Akachi, an acolyte to the Cooperative trying to log as many travel months as possible in hopes of earning his own captainhood.

Aurora's presence onboard was to be purely scientific. Dr. Abrahim Misleh was the primary researcher, having the greatest passion for the project given his decades of devotion to study of AMA. His staff would be made up of seven other scientists, with a dedicated onboard lab in the ship's aft.

Traver's medical staff was also under Aurora's umbrella, consisting of Dr. Shurovsky's own protégé Dr. Philip Marin and his two assistants. They had a small medical bay set aside near the lab, specialized for the bone injection treatments.

Traver had been allowed one personal assistant and one technician (both thoroughly vetted by the Corporation and the Co-operative). His longtime driver and maybe-even friend, Karl, was approved to accompany his boss and attend to his personal needs. As for a tech, Traver requested Weston Hillquist, his show's producer in New York. Weston however was unable to pass the physical requirements for space travel and instead recommended Lance, a young technician who worked behind the scenes of the SASH broadcasts, silently saving the show day after day. Lance had double-majored at the Aurora Technical Institute, making him both overqualified for his SASH position and a perfect pick for a deep space broadcast.

The total crew count was to be sixteen souls.

The *Aten* was not a research vessel, technically speaking. It had been manufactured for long distance transportation of personnel under S.T.A.R.S. Corporation in the early days of deep space flight. As was proper under the Codes written in the wake of the 2148 Pilots' Strike, the ship was the private property of its Captain, having been signed over to her by the Pilot's Cooperative upon her ascension to the post. As Fletcher's ship, the *Aten* was contracted along with her on whatever journeys she made but refitted according to the mission's purpose.

Traver was familiar with Lance and of course Karl, while Dr. Shurovsky introduced him to the doctors who would be continuing her work. The scientists, however, Traver would not be able to meet until all were onboard. The captain and first officer he might never meet at all if they chose to keep themselves isolated. He read the complete manifest and studied all the documentation he could find on the ship and crew, trying to maintain disinterest in those aspects not directly connected with himself or his well-being. The disinterest was alarmingly feigned. In spite of himself, he was eager to meet the crew and see the ship, and wished he could do so sooner.

The final month of waiting was long and Traver's patience wore thin, but the time finally came.

It was with tears in his eyes that Weston wished Traver "good luck," as the celebrity show host removed the last of his things from his studio at SASH.

"I'll be glued to the screen every week. I won't miss a word."

"I would hope not. I'm going to be transmitting through these servers, same as always. Someone's got to be here monitoring my levels."

"You bet I will, boss. Our next regular show's in two years, yeah? Just walk on into your studio and I'll make sure it'll be like you never left!"

Traver saw the unyielding devotion in the fat man's quivering face and felt powerful. He felt envy, too; how fortunate were his followers who, like Weston, hung on his every word and looked up at him as their teacher – those people had something to believe in, to depend on. Traver didn't have those things. He only had himself.

He smiled at Weston. As a result Weston's face jolted into a tearful grin and he rubbed a chubby arm across his wet eyes. This was too disgusting for Traver, who had to look away. As he walked down the hallway he didn't look back.

* * *

On his last morning at home, Traver sat in the kitchen and ate his breakfast with relative calmness. The children had gone to school, having said their last goodbyes with warmth that was surprising but welcome. They seemed to view his departure as just another business trip, albeit a lengthy one. Traver now tried to view it the same way, for what that was worth.

The quicklift arrived on the floor. Dana walked out. Traver's calmness vanished in a flurry of heartbeats, as he wondered how Dana planned to treat his final day.

At first she seemed to ignore him as she had for nearly three months. She walked to the kitchen control panel and muttered in her order: "the usual." The A.I. knew what this meant – the stoves turned on, the refrigerator whirred and spat out two portions of synthetic egg-whip, while the coffee filters switched themselves out and the water began to drip.

She sat down. There was only one table in the kitchen, so she was forced into proximity of her husband. Of course, she may have chosen to sit elsewhere, regardless of seat availability; but ignoring him from nearby was so much more torturous than ignoring him from afar.

Her food was ready, steaming and savory. The A.I. told her so with a gentle "beep."

For a moment then she lifted her eyes from the table, and looked straight at Traver. He returned the look. It was the first time in months that they had looked at each other for more than a glance. Traver didn't know, nor could he care less, what his eyes said at that moment. But in *her* eyes he read panic, isolation, claustrophobia – the trapped feeling of being inside a nightmare. He didn't understand it. He hadn't even known her eyes to be capable of holding that much potent terror. Had she been nurturing some deadly fear for the whole course of her long silence? If she had been and he had done nothing to assuage it, he would never forgive himself. After all, half of their long cold distance was his doing, as he acted under the assumption that she wanted to be left alone. *But, she wanted me to break her silence. I've done more harm than good.*

She stood up and walked to retrieve her plate. She faced the back wall of the kitchen, her back to her husband. But she didn't turn around. She stood stone-still for a few moments longer than made Traver comfortable.

Then he saw her hand reach up to her face. She was crying.

It was time to break the silence for her. He stood up and walked to her. In the four steps it took to reach her, he started to plan what it was he would say. It would be gentle, it would be self-abashing. He would beg her forgiveness, he would offer her assurances that he would never again leave her side, once he returned…

"You're going to die out there."

He'd barely put his hand on her shoulder. She blurted this out before he'd found his perfectly-arranged bouquet of words. The silence had been broken – violently shattered.

"Why do you say that?" It wasn't anger that he felt. Or maybe it was. Maybe that was even anger coming through in his voice. But didn't he have a right to be angry? He hadn't asked for this. Not for Eams, not for space, not for his wife to berate him. Yes, his voice was trembling.

Dana turned to face him. She'd forgotten all about her perfect breakfast.

"You're not going to come back."

Now Traver wondered what his own eyes were betraying. Far back in the corner of his subconscious that watched and judged his own mind's behavior, he was desperately trying to find a clear view of the situation, but there was none. Was he angry? Or was he afraid? If afraid, what was he afraid of? Death? Certainly, he was. But was he also afraid of space? Was space the same as death? To Dana, to everyone else he was leaving behind, it seemed to be so.

"Yes, I am."

His voice was no longer angry. He made sure of that, regardless of the turmoil within. Dana collapsed into his arms.

It might have been hours they stood there in the kitchen, Dana sobbing quietly and Traver holding her, staring into nothing at all, trying to make sense of the madness that had taken over his life. How had he gotten here? Where was he going?

Even if their embrace didn't quite last hours, Dana's breakfast was cold by the time she got to it.

* * *

It was time. An aircar arrived to pick him up at noon on the dot. Launch was scheduled for 8:00 in the morning on September 17th, 2176, which was four days away.

He had never been to the launch facility. The training center where he'd already learned the basics of spaceship behavior was part of the basement level of the New York Headquarters, where cadets, hopefuls and veterans alike all received some degree of training before moving on to the simulations. These were run out of the massive complex in the New Mexico wasteland that also hosted the launches themselves.

Traver was a guest, not an astronaut, so he had no real need to be run through a simulation. Nonetheless for safety's sake a fully immersive simulation sequence was written into his itinerary. If he was going to react badly to the anti-gravity or the jumps, it would be best to find out before he was outbound.

The flight to New Mexico by private zip jet took forty-three minutes. The SASH had once flown him to a meeting in Los Angeles in better time. *Not impressive at all, so far,* he told himself.

Traver disembarked at the Albuquerque airport, where he was ushered to an airshuttle for the final three hundred kilos. The sight that met his eyes outside the windows was the first to make him feel like a traveler in an alien land. It had been decades since he'd visited an unincorporated city like Albuquerque, which existed outside the shelter of any habitable zone. Some residents could still be seen, going about their business in the cracking asphalt streets far below, their skin parched in the unrelenting dry heat. Traver knew that most of the world looked like this now, treeless and abandoned, but a whole city devastated by the dry-up and deserted during central-ization was a sobering reminder of the state of his own planet. The functioning cities like New York, in which he'd spent the majority of his comfortable life, were rarities likely owing their existence to Aurora's research. For someone who talked so much about the sad state of affairs in the world, Traver had seen and experienced very little of it. Begrudgingly he wondered whether he should rectify that, should he make it back from space.

Due to a miracle of fortunate timing, Traver's approach to the Aurora complex occurred just during the Friday time slot usually reserved for his broadcast. He did not fail to notice.

"Lance. Call Weston."

"What do you want me to ask him?"

"Tell him we're going to broadcast."

"Right now?"

"Right now."

"We're not scheduled to start remotely until next week."

"They're probably filling the time with political ads. Nothing we can't boot."

"Actually, they gave an extra time slot to the Giovanni D'Arco show" (a zealous anti-religion figure. *As if we still need people like him in our happily godless world,* Traver often thought.)

"Oh god, that drooling dinosaur? Even more of a reason to get me on the air."

Lance made the call. A few minutes later Traver was once again available for billions of enthusiastic (and perhaps a few thousand unenthusiastic) viewers. It was his first time broadcasting in months. He hoped the world would remember him.

"You see that? That's the Aurora launch facility. And that's where I'm headed. Yes, this is really happening. Yes, I'm a little nervous. I'm going to outer space in four days. It's not every day I can say that. But none of that is the reason I've decided to begin broadcasting today, breaking my promise to withhold from talking to you until I was in flight. No, I want you to look at *that.*"

He directed Lance to point the cameras out the windows of the speeding shuttle. Out there, the complex was still kilometers away but it lay over the desert like a massive shadow, shining jet black and studded by white towering spacecraft, some of which lay in various docks and bays while others stood out in anticipation a kilometer or more from the facility center.

"I know you've all seen the pictures of this place. But god…it's huge. I'm sure even these images we're capturing don't do it justice, so for a moment try and look at it through my eyes. I'm speeding toward it at a hundred and twenty kilometers per hour but it's barely growing in my sight line. By the time this broadcast ends, we still may not have reached it. That's how massive it is. See those tiny white needles? Those are the ships. One of those must be the *Aten*. Anyway, I'm burning time boasting on behalf of the company that built this place. They aren't paying me for any of this, but they should be. Hell, this would be free tourism advertising if they opened their doors to the public! But that's not why I'm here.

"Look at it. What do you feel?

"Keep looking. Think about the size. Think about how long it took to build. How much money. How many ambitions were contributed, how many dreams fulfilled? And think about what it's here to do. Really. What is it here to do?

"When I look at it, I feel cold. I feel nothing. Because when I ask myself, 'what is this place here for?' the only answer I have is, 'nothing.'

"Did you ever play with builder blocks? I'm not talking about the computer rendered ones – I mean the real, solid plastic builder blocks. Maybe I'm old, but I used to play with them. 'Play' isn't the right word, really – at least I wouldn't have called it that. 'Build' is what I did. I built towers, I built castles, I built mountains – yes, I built some spaceships. I felt so good when I was building them – I felt like I was making a statement about myself, about my power. I knew for a moment what god would have felt like. But when it was finished all that good feeling went away. It was just me and a...a what? A stack of blocks? Something that could be torn down and put back together in a million other shapes with no loss. What I'd made was a testament to human arrogance. And that is what you are looking at here, in the middle of this desert.

"There's nothing wrong with a pride project. I wouldn't give up my years with builder blocks for the world. But what's the point? Are you going to stop there? Look at your impressive but pointless tower and shout *that's enough!? I'm done now!? That's my contribution!? Look upon my works, ye mighty!?*

"The last time I played with builder's blocks, it was with...with my children. They were young – toddlers at most. They had found some flowers growing through the cracks in the sidewalks outside of our apartment – that was when I lived in a ground-level housing unit, and of course before the dry-up had quite finished off the last of the natural-grown plants. The flowers were going to be trampled, so the kids plucked them out, put them in water and brought them in. They got this idea that they wanted to build a little garden. Well, there was no room to plant them outside, and it was getting cold at night, with November coming on. So we decided on a tiny, portable tiered garden. I pulled out my old blocks and together we built it. We matched the colors so each shelf had a theme, and we glued the pieces together so that this would be the final form for these blocks. When it was finished we filled it in with soil, they planted the flowers, and we all took care of it. Now, the vegetation has filled out and grown over the sides, and to this day it's still in my house, by the window in the parlor. It's a relic of the world before the dry-up, the world as it should be. Joy. That's what it brought. That's what I felt when I looked at it. It's what I still feel.

"Look at those towers again. Those are builder's blocks with no flowers inside. This cold creation, this celebration of ourselves, it's a stepping stone at best. When we rejoice at the things we make and the places we can go as if our doing so is the victory, we've led ourselves into a dead end. We'll only feel cold."

"That's Weston calling. We just ran out of time."

But Lance didn't need to tell Traver that. The talking had ended precisely at the cutoff. Mr. Graff was finished now.

There had been no builder's block flower garden. Traver had already been living in a penthouse when his children were toddlers and the plant life in New York had already dried up by that time. But neither his audience nor Traver cared. There was a tear in his eye, which Lance pretended not to notice.

* * *

The simulations promptly shook Traver out of any reverie into which he had fallen. The space jump was not known for being pleasant, and that particular simulation was alarmingly realistic. It was explained to Traver, in layman's terms, that astronauts on any trip requiring a jump lasting longer than two hours were put into stasis, a temporary paralysis that closely resembled a coma. Two hours of jumping was all that the body could stand. Unfortunately, the journey to AMA-712 would only require a jump of one and a half hours – tolerable for the human body and not worth the risks associated with stasis. Traver and his fellow passengers would be awake through the whole thing. The simulation prepared him only by terrifying him. He would have much preferred to be helplessly surprised when the time came for the real thing.

In the jump seat of the simulator, he was securely strapped in until he could no longer move a muscle. Even his face was braced with a cage so that the most minuscule movements would be stifled. Traver had never considered himself claustrophobic, but this utter restraint was maddening. It reminded him of the Eams treatments, but without the needles.

The jump had its own version of the needles, though. It was the combination of a thousand different sensations all happening at once; bright light that was blinding even through the solid walls and clenched eyelids, a thin screaming sound like a transit train running over overstretched piano wire, and worst of all a pulling sensation all across his body. Worse than any needles could be, this felt like a billion tiny but infinitely heavy weights had been attached to every square centimeter of his skin, then shook and pulled in all different directions at the same time.

How the simulator managed to create this sensation, he never thought to ask. But he was certain, somehow, that the real thing had to be even worse.

Aside from the normal vomiting and readjusting, he was fine. Dr. Shurovsky, who had accompanied the company to the desert facility, noted that Traver's bones were up to the task, responding well to the treatment. As long as the injections were maintained regularly, Traver should have no complications.

As long as the injections were maintained regularly. Two days before departure he was subjected to his final earthbound injection sequence, performed by Dr. Marin under Dr. Shurovsky's watchful eye. The treatment was horrible as it always was, and more so than ever Traver was aware of the strange sensation of the doctor's formula swimming all through his body, doing god-knew-what in his blood and bones on its mission to suppress the Eams bacteria. Before agreeing to the contract, he'd had the choice to stop treatments if he'd wanted – to let himself just crumble and die. Now the choice had been taken away. He was trapped. Maybe he'd imagined a freedom upon leaving. Maybe some naive part of his brain (to which he never would have admitted) had looked forward to stepping up and off of Earth as a way of leaving behind the Eams, and the treatments, and death itself. Now he wasn't feeling any of that. He'd be in a small metal box, subject to the same killing bacteria and the same hellish treatments. Space would be the same existence in a different place.

* * *

The morning came. At 0300 Traver was summoned from his room on the north side of the compound, the housing section where engineers and scientists lived during their tenures at the facility.

At 0400 he stepped into his suit. It was pressure-protected and sealed. In a best case scenario, the suit would be entirely unnecessary for the initial takeoff sequence, but it was a precautionary measure should anything happen to the outer shell of the ship upon ignition. There was also a bag near the groin which, as it was explained to him in careful terms, he would be able to relieve himself before, during or after the launch.

A little after 0500 he was ferried across the kilometer of tarmac that lay between the compound and the launchpad. The sun hadn't risen and the cool desert air rushed by Traver's face. A dozen gigantic spotlights lit the launchpad and the ship that towered upon it. He got his first good look at the *Aten*. He'd seen it from the windows before, where it appeared to his untrained eye to resemble any other spacecraft – there were plenty to see in the old pre-censorship movies he'd seen as a child, and plenty more now plastered up and down the space-happy media sites. But to see it up so close was something completely different.

There was something alluring about the design of the *Aten*. Of course it resembled the general shape of hundreds of other ships, all similarly fit to the precise specifications required for long-distance jumps. But something in the curvature of this vessel, the gradual sloping and lack of angular features near the nose, made it seem somehow graceful, exotic even. But that shape, by sublimely defying the viewing mind's attempts at identification, was as unnerving as it was beautiful. To an unprepared and casual onlooker it seemed alien, something beyond humans' capability to design, let alone to construct on such a large scale. For the ship was massive, much larger than Traver's mind's eye had conceived it to be. The size and the shape of it made perfect sense of course, but something about the *Aten* inspired dread for Traver. His stomach churned a little and he felt a cold sweat on his forehead despite the cool morning breeze.

He lost track of the time, but it was about 0600 when he was finally loaded onboard the ship. Indeed, he was loaded rather than entering with his own two feet. The bucket seat in the transport car, into which he was strapped, was brought under the *Aten's* stern bay door. A sort of vertical conveyor belt hooked onto his seat, detaching it from the car and pulling him up into the hull of the vessel.

Up the loading chute he went. It was well lit by a million tiny lights hidden in the walls. He passed compartment after compartment, some labeled for storage and others for maintenance and mechanical access. All the compartment doors were closed and locked, indicating that he must be the final piece of freight to be loaded.

A mechanic waited at the top of the chute, where a round hatch opened into what seemed to be the floor – currently vertical – of a short tubular chamber. Seats were stacked along the wall closest to and parallel with the ground. The mechanic guided Traver's seat to a set of latches on the wall into which it locked effortlessly. Traver lay back, staring upward from his reclined position.

"Better get comfortable. Supposedly we're stuck here for the next three hours" Lance, already strapped in, said from the next seat over. "I guess we didn't qualify for window seats on this plane ride."

"Realistically it may be more like five hours," droned the unpleasant mechanic. "Really, whenever the captain says you're safe to unbuckle. After that, this will be your station during any jump period or major maneuver. Otherwise you won't be spending much time in here."

Traver read jealousy in the mechanic's voice. Here was a man who'd likely dedicated his whole adult life to Aurora's pursuit of the stars, but who was now stranded on Earth and strapping completely unqualified guests into their seats for free tours of space. Life wasn't fair, but Traver had never posited that it should be.

The mechanic locked on the crew's helmets, completed his checks and re-checks, and descended the chute, shutting the door behind him.

The occupants of this chamber were all Traver's own team and his doctors. In a way, this was his own dedicated chamber. In addition to the swell of pride at his own perceived importance, he felt responsible. These five people were leaving the safety of Earth because of him. If anything did happen to them during their two-year mission, unlikely as that was, it would be his fault.

But the eager looks and the "thumbs up" from his traveling companions, from Dr. Marin at the far end of the chamber to Lance beside him, quickly convinced him that they didn't see things in that light. All of them were guests on a once-in-a-lifetime trip, for which they were more than happy to take a risk.

The hour of waiting passed slowly. The chamber was quiet, though the transmitters in their helmets picked up all the chatter from the cockpit and from the control tower. They were also able to speak to one another via intercom, though the anticipation was enough to shake them all into silence.

Captain Fletcher's voice came through the clearest as she performed pre-checks and diagnostics. From what Traver had researched about Louisa Fletcher, she was a reserved pilot but not necessarily an antisocial one. Hearing her voice intrigued him to no end. It added an air of mystique to the two unseen figures at the helm of this ship. He couldn't wait for the launch to be over so he could make their acquaintance, should they choose to appear.

"Twenty minutes. I repeat, twenty minutes until launch" came Fletcher's strong voice over the transmitters. Traver shut his eyes. Part of him was exhausted from the days of simulations and treatments, eager to take these remaining moments to catch some sleep while he was prone in this comfortable jump seat. Despite the exhaustion, his nervous excitement would never let him sleep until long after the ship was becalmed outside of Earth's atmosphere.

Dr. Marin and his two assistants sat calmly, staring straight ahead. Even if they had never been to space, this was just another assignment during which they needed to remain calm under pressure. They were trained for precisely that.

Time slowed even more. Traver looked sidelong at Lance, whose eyes were shut as he sweated under his helmet. Next to Lance, Karl was shaking uncontrollably. Poor Karl – the man had only ever been a driver on Earth, handling wheeled limousines in his younger days and then making the transition to aircars. He didn't know anything different. Everything about this journey would be a shock to him. But hell, it was all a shock to Traver too.

"Ten minutes."

Eternity.

"Five minutes."

Engines roared far beneath them. The chamber shook, beginning with a slow vibration and escalating slowly.

Still, it seemed like eternity.

"Thirty seconds."

In spite of himself, Traver found that he was breathing heavily. His heart was racing at what seemed a dangerous rate. *God forbid I have a heart failure now, and waste all these peoples' time and a shit ton of money*, he thought.

"Five…four…three…two…"

He couldn't hear the final number, if it was uttered at all. The engines, spouting a thin, clean blue flame when seen from the outside, still produced an incredible roar that resounded through the metal hull of the *Aten* like an echo chamber. The shaking intensified until Traver was certain his jump seat would come undone from the clamps that held it to the floor, that he'd be tossed around the room like an errant kernel of popcorn.

Yet the seat held. The straps that braced his arms and head down kept the shaking from affecting his neck or joints. Not that he needed to be strapped back; an immense weight, a g-force he couldn't imagine, pressed him back entirely into the seat until he wasn't certain he could have moved his hand even without straps.

They had told him the rough patch of the launch would last no more than thirty seconds. He couldn't trust himself with any accurate awareness of time now, but it seemed much longer than that.

A voice was coming through the intercom. It might have been Lance's, shouting something about "wishing there were windows," but through all the noise it was impossible to hear with any clarity.

The steadying effect as they broke free of Earth's atmosphere was gradual, so much so that Traver was not conscious of the violence dissipating until it was gone completely. He found himself once again relaxed in his chair, able to move his head and his arms a little (as much as the straps would allow) without discomfort.

The sound of the mighty booster engines continued for some short time. Then a cracking sound resounded through the ship, and Traver caught himself throwing a startled look toward his neighbor.

Lance seemed unconcerned, which put Traver's mind at instant ease. Of course the sound was only the boosters falling away as the *Aten* took on responsibility for its own mobility for the remainder of the journey. Once the crack had passed, the rumbling of those engines grew suddenly silent, replaced by the almost pleasant, soft whir of the *Aten's* own propellant jets.

"I've unfastened your seats. You're free to take off your helmets if you wish and move to your cabins" came Nelson Akachi's deep, gentle voice over the transmitter.

The doors at either end of their chamber shot open, revealing a cylindrical white corridor leading forward and backward. The passengers stood up – or rather pushed themselves up into the gravity-free space of the chamber – as they were released from the jump seats which proceeded to fold back into the walls. Through the corridor leading toward the back of the ship they could see the opening of another identical chamber, from which emerged the eight scientists.

Traver and company moved into the corridor through the door that had opened behind them. Without gravity they drifted, pulling themselves using rungs that hung along the ceiling. From here it didn't take Traver and his team long to find the cabins they would call home for the next two years.

The corridor that ran down the center of the ship's habitable section was made of three conjoined segments – fore, mid and aft – separated by the antechambers used for launches and jumps. The doors to these chambers, which also served as airlocks, were generally open except during launches and, in rare cases, emergencies.

The *Aten*, compared with many long-distance passenger vessels, was fairly large, with a capacity for thirty people if every cabin was filled. In its younger days it had been purposed for making the really long journeys with the largest crews for work on distant space stations, remote planetary landings, and evacuations. For the mission to AMA-712 it had been refitted. The lab in the ship's aft was equipped with complete apparatus for scientific research, while an injection machine for Traver's treatments had been installed in the medical bay just fore of the lab. In the far rear of the ship, adjacent to the back of the lab, was the pod bay. Three of the detachable pods, usually intended for evacuation or quick trips to and from other vessels, were rebuilt to withstand various atmospheric elements and to take data readings. Since these could travel nearer to the planet than would likely be safe for the ship itself, the pods would collect samples from the atmosphere and surface.

Three separate living cabins had been set aside for the passengers. As a result, though most had never experienced confined quarters for any amount of time, they found the *Aten* unexpectedly comfortable and roomy. Traver, Lance and Karl shared a cabin near the center of the ship, attached to the mid corridor just opposite the doctors' quarters. The berths of the scientists were in the aft nearest the lab, while the captain and first officer had rooms up front just behind the cockpit. That was the geography Traver had been able to glean from his research and from his brief conversations with some engineers.

It took only a few hours for the passengers to settle in. The cabins soon became normal as hotel rooms, if hotel rooms had no gravity. The romance of space travel, if it existed at all, did not exist in these windowless quarters, where silence reigned except for the constant drone of the engine and the ship's immense speed could only be felt as the slightest of vibrations.

As for conversation with the others on the ship aside from Traver's bunkmates, there was none to be had. Dr. Marin and his assistants were amiable enough but maintained a nearly inhuman professionalism. They steered toward medical topics whenever conversations occurred, and that only when they crossed into Traver's cabin to perform a checkup every twenty-four hours or a full injection procedure every seventy-two. The scientists in the aft made a ghostly presence on the ship – Lance saw two of them talking earnestly but quietly in the corridor once, while on his way to the privy. When they spotted him, they paused their discussion, looked at him with uncomfortable sidelong stares, and waited until he was gone.

As for the captain, she was nonexistent. Traver's hopes that Fletcher would make an appearance, that he would have an opportunity to speak one-on-one with a veteran pilot, sloped downward and began to plummet after forty-eight hours passed in space and no sighting occurred.

Whether he was a more personable being or whether his office required some measure of social decorum, First Officer Akachi was the first person onboard to make the social rounds. His good natured warmth was a welcome change from the constant isolation that seemed dominated by the cold hum of the engines.

"This is Nelson Akachi, first officer of the *Aten*. May I come in?"

Lance was just in the middle of setting up the makeshift recording studio – a task in zero gravity that was proving more challenging than expected. At the sound of a voice coming through the door's intercom, all three occupants of the room looked at one another, as if to make sure the sound was real and not imagined.

Traver nodded. Karl, unwittingly taking on the servant's role he'd performed on Earth, propelled himself toward the door. For a moment he fumbled with the switches and buttons by the door's latch.

"The blue button lets you talk. Touch the green latch and it'll open the door." Akachi's helpful voice surprised Karl, who seemed to touch the green latch by panicked accident rather than intention. The doors, double-stacked to serve as an airlock, swept open. Akachi made an imposing figure. He was tall, taller than a ship like this seemed to allow for; had gravity been at play here, he would have needed to duck to walk through the cabin door. His skin was jet black, blacker than the Pilot's Cooperative uniform which he wore in its fullness, with the silver Owl, the Cooperative's insignia, pinned just above his heart.

He extended his hand. "It's a pleasure to have you onboard. I have to apologize for keeping so much distance until now, but my duties have kept me busy and this has been my first waking chance to step away from the cockpit. And you, you must be Mister Graff."

Traver nodded and moved to the door. He shook Akachi's hand, finding its grasp to be firm and all-encompassing.

"Thank you. I'm glad to learn that we're not alone on this ship. Now at least we know there's somebody at the wheel." Traver adopted the sardonic persona he'd been yearning to unleash in space but had been unable to due to the lack of an audience.

Akachi grinned widely – if he was caught off guard by Traver's pertness, he deflected it with more of the same warmth and kindness. Traver decided it was a warmth and kindness he wouldn't necessarily trust.

"You're in good hands. Captain Fletcher and the *Aten* have made many journeys together. She regrets that she is unable to introduce herself at this time. Have you met the other passengers?"

"I'm afraid the science team has yet to show interest in making our acquaintance."

"That's too bad. Those academic types like to keep to themselves. I'm on my way to talk with them, I'll be sure and put in a good word for Traver Graff, the great friend of science." Akachi's tone never shifted to reflect the sarcasm that must have been there.

"That would be appreciated" returned Traver. "It's going to be a long two years if we aren't all on friendly terms. Now I'm sorry to rush you off, but we have a broadcast coming up and we should finish setting up for it." The broadcast was still twenty hours away, but Traver felt it was a good enough excuse to dismiss the first officer. With Akachi absent, Traver could once again become the highest-ranking person in the room.

Lance finished setting up the recorders with plenty of time to spare. When it came time to broadcast, a corner of the cabin had been set up to facilitate Traver. A chair, equipped with straps to hold the host from floating away, was clamped to the floor in front of a SASH poster, brought for this exact purpose, which was secured to the wall to serve as a backdrop.

"Testing. One two three. Can you hear us, Weston? Are we coming through?"

Traver glanced impatiently at Lance, who waved a placating hand. "It's going to take a little bit. When we say this is 'live,' we only mean it's as close to 'live' as we can get out here."

About a minute later came Weston's reply: "Louder and clearer than ever. You're on in four minutes, but you'll want to start a little early. Lance should have worked out the math."

Lance nodded. "This is the easy one" he said, carefully looking at the watch he wore. "But once we jump, that's where time is going to get a little weird."

* * *

The first broadcast from space seemed underwhelming to Traver. He spent his time outlining the living conditions, the experience of takeoff, the strange existence of living without gravity. But all of these had been outlined for audiences hundreds of times before, going all the way back to the ancient times of the 1960s; though the experience itself had changed a bit since then, the manner of describing it was the same. Nothing was new under the sun (or apparently beyond it). Traver found himself with little else to say thus far. He had neither disappointment nor disgust, nor enough awe to drive a passionate monologue of any kind. So he did what he could with a sardonicism devoid of feeling, poking at the very fact that, despite two hundred years of technology and unfathomable amounts of money and effort, space travel was very much the same experience as it always had been.

It was a hollow critique and he knew it. But maybe, just maybe his audience would overlook his content this time, distracted by the fact that he was speaking to them from forty million kilometers away.

Halfway through, he turned to Lance, and motioned for him to take the spotlight. Lance appeared confused. So Traver clarified. "I like to think that, while things have gotten stale in the realm of space travel, this SASH broadcast is a bit of a breakthrough, considering the number of people we are reaching and the distance the transmission will be traveling. You can thank Lance Lanka for heading up the I.T. on this venture. He'd like to share some of the details of how we'll be reaching you next week."

There was a gleam of annoyance in Lance's eyes. He'd received no warning about being thrown in the sights of billions of people. He had always preferred operating safely behind the scenes. But here he was, and Mr. Graff had left him no way out. He moved beside Traver, within range of the cameras.

"Alright, like Mister Graff said, I'm Lance, um, Lance Lanka that is, a tech with the SASH for five years now. I've been working on his shows for a while, and I'm very excited at the new format that we're tackling here." Traver nudged him. *Get on with it* was the implied command.

"So, the transmission you're watching right now is pretty basic broadcast technology. It's essentially a glorified radio signal being sent out from the ship's radar, and our satellites are picking it up and taking it home to you. However, that's going to have to change once we make our jump. For those unfamiliar, the jump is when we leave the Solar System and travel an immense distance within a minuscule period of time. Jump technology has been in use for just about forty years and it's what makes this kind of travel possible. Once we make our jump to the star system where AMA-712 is located, an old radio signal would take anywhere from a decade to thirty years to reach Earth. That's a margin that is not really acceptable for our live broadcast format, so…" He paused, waiting for at least a chuckle from his small audience in the room. None came.

"So, we'll be utilizing jump technology once we get that far out. Ships have been sending signals this way since the technology has existed, but this is the first time it'll be used for any sort of public broadcast. Now, propelling a ship, something large that contains a lot of mass, through multiple light-years within a few hours requires a jump drive, with which the *Aten* is equipped. In layman's terms, the drive allows the ship to tear through space, rather than travel across it. That takes a lot of energy and can only be done twice on a journey, once on the way there, and once on the way back again. A small amount of information, however, like a sequence of particles carrying data, can be sent in a similar way while using much less energy. When we're near our destination and transmitting to Earth, each 'piece' of our broadcast will be bundled up in a tiny particle group and then jumped through space. They'll be mapped toward the Solar System, where the satellites will unpack the data and send it via radio signal the rest of the way to Earth. In the end, a transmission from another star system will take a little under two hours to reach your home entertainment centers."

Lance was visibly excited. It didn't really matter to whom he was talking; this was the subject matter that made him happy. He may have even forgotten about the huge audience that was watching and listening to him.

Traver didn't forget about that audience, and he started to worry before Lance had even launched into his passionate description of jumped broadcasts. This was all turning into a veritable celebration of technology, something that should be avoided at all costs if this strange experiment was going to turn out any way besides farcical. Not that there wasn't something beautiful in man's ability to overcome overwhelming distances, but it was a beauty Traver could not publicly admit to.

"Thank you Lance. You clearly understand the details far better than I do. Let's hope that our being here is a step in the right direction, with this technology finally being used for widespread communication instead of being kept for Aurora's private benefit."

Afterwards there was silence between the three passengers. Traver sat by himself in the corner of the cabin. His mind should have been racing as it usually did after a show, but it was still and silent. Because of that he felt nervous. Perhaps he even felt afraid. He'd been confident in his own words before now, confident that he'd be able to produce a powerful message here or anywhere else in the universe. Now he wasn't so sure. If his confidence stood on shakier ground with every increase in distance between himself and Earth, then what would happen after the jump?

But no. He wasn't superstitious. Surely his mental prowess could not be dependent on his proximity to Earth.

A message from Weston came in, reporting that viewership numbers had broken their previous records, as expected. This was not encouraging for Traver, who wished he could have given the world something better.

With nothing to say, no one here to talk to, and naught to do but wait, Traver took to the gym apparatus. In lieu of a proper rec room onboard, the cabins were equipped with these devices. When not in use, it was a sphere about one meter in diameter set in to the wall. It rolled out and unfolded into a series of different configurations that allowed for strength training and cardio exercise, necessary for a body in a gravity-free environment.

Traver spent a half hour working his arms and abdomen, then a half hour on his legs before losing interest. He strapped himself into his bunk and slept soundly, his infected bones sighing with relief in their freedom from the affliction of gravity.

* * *

"Return to the antechambers and secure yourselves. We are approaching our jump point." Fletcher's message broke the growing illusion that she didn't exist, and the passengers responded by leaping to action with the suddenness that might follow an abrupt and unpleasant waking. Nobody could quite tell how much time had passed (Lance's timepiece declared it was a little over eight days since the launch). The initial enthusiasm and sense of discovery had worn away as the passengers fell into a haze, disoriented by the lack of a day/night cycle and hemmed in by a lack of windows. The approach of the jump meant some change, at least.

"This is going to get us approximately six-point-five-two light years closer to our destination, in the time of about an hour and thirty-two minutes." Akachi's voice was cheerful. It reminded Traver of tour buses he'd ridden through the historic, pre-centralization districts of the city in his younger days.

"The remaining point-zero-zero-zero-zero-two-five light year will be what takes the majority of the next six months. We can't jump right up to the planet's system because our margin of error is just wide enough to where it could land us right inside a star. So we'll jump outside the star system and then troll on in with our good old propellant jets." Traver was sure that Akachi relished the opportunity to travel with inexperienced and impressionable passengers.

Fletcher shared none of his social enthusiasm, and cut off his educational session sharply: "We've our clearance from global control and we're jumping on my mark."

Traver rolled his eyes downward to check his jump seat straps, and then checked them again. He didn't need to; Akachi himself had already made the rounds, securing the seats and locking the passengers in, so they wouldn't have been able to leave if they'd wanted to. "You have your piss bags attached? You'll probably need them" he'd said with a wide grin that was in no way mocking.

The gentle whirring of the engines had been replaced by a snapping and crackling all around them. It sounded like the ship had been electrified against an army of giant bees that crashed against the outer shell and exploded like popcorn. Traver had been told the ship's behavior would change in preparation for tearing through space, but he hadn't expected anything so jarring and nightmarish.

"In thirty seconds." Fletcher's voice was calm, maybe even bored. That was some small comfort to Traver at least, for whom the jump was something to wonder at and to fear. If Fletcher was bored, how bad could it really be?

"Three, two, one."

It was bad.

First the popping and cracking around the ship became constant, deafening. It was a metallic roar, like industrial grinders were eating away at every inch of the ship's outer shell.

Then the inside of the ship started glowing. A white-hot light began at the walls and seeped inward. It looked like the ship had sprung a slow leak and was filling with raw, liquid light.

The bodies of the passengers themselves were forgotten as their senses were overwhelmed – that was a mercy, since the pressure in the ship, despite the suits, was nearly too much to bear. They were pressed back into their seats until not a single muscle might have been twitched, if they had thought to try.

Blindness followed. There, behind eyes that were either closed or simply incapable of sight, eternities passed. Infinite space seemed a trivial thing as, for an indefinable period of time, their minds became aware of a reality of ungraspable size, scope and time. Everything happened, and nothing. Nothing could be seen, and everything.

Traver woke up. He hadn't been strictly asleep, but he couldn't remember the exact moment the ship had fallen out of the jump and stillness had resumed. He felt fine, physically. The simulation had been accurate, as far as the stress put on his body. It was that other feeling he hadn't been prepared for; the feeling behind his eyes, somewhere in his consciousness, that he'd slipped out of reality for a moment and looked at it from the outside.

He remembered the science fiction books and films of his youth, when those sorts of things were still widely accepted. He remembered how their versions of space travel sometimes involved a slip out of our dimension and into a parallel reality. Pseudoscience and nonsense, of course. Jumps had been fully explained in terms of the known and quantifiable laws of physics. Nevertheless, that other-worldly feeling was not easy to shake. He wouldn't be mentioning it in his broadcasts.

Even after the jump seats were unlocked, it took all the passengers a long while before they had the will to move. Some time later (*has it been hours? has it been days?)* Akachi's ever-amiable voice shook them and provided a reason to move with purpose.

"Would anyone care to see our sun? It'll be smaller than you are used to seeing. The cockpit will be open."

Traver and his companions stirred and pushed themselves up and into the air. *Thank god for the weightlessness,* he thought, *or I might not be able to move at all.*

The journey up the central corridor was dreamlike. It was not the journey of a few individuals floating across to their rooms. The scientists had emerged from the antechamber nearer the aft, joining the doctors and Traver's crew. Whereas before the various groups had been shy, separate, standoffish, now there was an eagerness that joined them all. Where their eyes met, there was a smiling gleam of expectancy. Before, they had been strangers. Without a word spoken, they were now family. And like a family of hopeful animals joined by instinct they swam through the air together, aiming for the open doors that led into the cockpit, that sanctuary of space travel.

Admission to the cockpit was rare under any circumstances. Even for the scientists who had traveled deep into space before, this might be a chance in a lifetime. And even though it had been Akachi that extended the invitation, the permission must have initiated with the captain herself. Traver came to that conclusion just before he reached the cockpit doors, and he felt a little closer to her.

Akachi stood to greet them, grinning as if his face had been frozen since the last time they all saw him. Behind him sat Fletcher, her back to the newcomers. She relaxed in her chair, feet propped up on the console in front of her, clearly satisfied with her own demonstration of expertise.

Beyond the console, that array of switches, dials and displays that was splayed out before Fletcher, were windows. The windows surrounded the room on front, right and left. Beyond the windows, space. Those who entered the cockpit for the first time could almost convince themselves for a moment that they were floating in it, surrounded on all sides by stars without the protection of the ship's shell.

Sixteen people barely fit inside the small cockpit, but they managed. Traver and some others who entered first were crowded closer to the windows.

What a relief it was to see outside the ship! It provided some sense of freedom from the claustrophobia that had marked his life onboard.

But it was just space. The awe faded from his eyes the longer he stared out into it. It looked the same as space always had, aside from a few rearrangements of stars (which he, no expert in astronomy, could not discern). Blackness, studded with dots of light. He felt a twinge of something new, something that was exactly what he'd hoped he'd feel up here – boredom. This *was* something he'd mention in his next broadcast.

"That's our sun." Akachi pointed to a small dot, far off to the left of the ship and approaching the stern. "I remember my first time seeing it from out here. It's a strange feeling. Earth is a speck you can't even see."

The doctors gawked, the scientists smiled with professional appreciation. Karl was in tears and Lance trembled. Traver thought he might be the only passenger who was unimpressed, and that made him happier than he'd yet been on this voyage.

He turned to look at Fletcher. He couldn't help himself – this was the first time he'd seen her in the flesh, though he had seen pictures of her while researching the crew. She was the only other person in the room not lost in infatuation with their surroundings. This was all normal to her, normal as Traver's own daily walk down the SASH hallway to his recording studio. But it wasn't boredom on Fletcher's face as she stared aimlessly into nothingness. It was peace.

She must be forty-five years old, Traver thought. Grey swept the edges of her hairline above her ears, and she'd made no effort to hide it. *Maybe older. At her age, people lose their purpose, start to doubt themselves. But doubt isn't something she's ever experienced, or ever will.*

She turned her head slightly, effortlessly. Her eyes found his. He wanted for that moment to feel significant, for their shared glance to communicate a mutual sense of importance. Instead he had to look away. He'd never felt eyes laugh at him like hers did.

CHAPTER FOUR
MISLEH

Time passed onboard the *Aten*. It passed both slowly and quickly. With no external reference for days, weeks or months, the passengers had no way to internally judge its passage. Timepieces informed them of the hours and the *Aten* brightened and dimmed its corridor lights based on a twenty-four hour schedule, but all that wasn't enough to compensate for the lack of a natural cycle. Trapped in the variations of endless dim, the passengers could only wait, and wait, and wait.

Extended isolation between cabins would have been unbearable as the months progressed, so inevitably there came to be mingling between the scientists, doctors and guests. It began with the young scientist Dr. Bjornson making a social call at the doctors' cabin and asking if they'd like to share dinner and a conversation. The gathering must have been a success, for it was repeated the following cycle until it became a regular event. Over the passing weeks, Lance grew friendly with Dr. Bjornson (who shared his passion for communications science) until at last Traver's cabin too received an invitation to join a dinner.

The cabins would take turns hosting all fourteen passengers in a ceremony that was at first cramped, hurried and silent, but with time became something of a party. The conversations grew livelier and louder, the close quarters grew more comfortable, and games and songs were not uncommon.

"This is the closest thing I can compare with a college dormitory experience" remarked an eager young scientist named Zhang after a dinner that had become exceptionally rowdy; "Not that I would know. I'm only here at all because my time in academia was spent with face pushed firmly into book." Nods of agreement came from everyone but Traver, who started to think perhaps he was the only person onboard who had spent his younger years thoroughly enjoying himself.

That the scientists were, for the most part, warm and inviting toward Traver came as something of a surprise. The reserved distance maintained by a few of the older members of the team (such as second lead researcher Dr. Friedrich, who was a bit of a curmudgeon) was a result of naturally cold demeanor rather than personal distaste. Traver had expected to find himself something of an unpleasant legend among them, a figure despised by all for being such a publicized thorn in their sides. If he was either of those things, the scientists did not make their antagonism apparent. Though Traver made no immediate friendships (as did Lance and Karl) and he maintained a quiet composure throughout most of the dinner parties, he was never met with an unfriendly eye or a rough tone. His own career as a science-denouncer was hardly commented upon, and if it was, the context was always limited strictly to his Earth-based political views. He wasn't certain whether to feel relieved or disappointed.

Akachi joined the social proceedings from time to time. His presence enlivened the gatherings even more, an unexpected but not unwelcome result of an officer fraternizing with civilians. He was a bottomless well of stories, sometimes holding a captive audience for hours at a time. His years spent in the Nigerian Air Force provided limitless adventures, tragedies and anecdotes. How many of the stories were true and how many were fabricated or had grown with the passing decades, nobody cared. What was certain was that Nelson Akachi was the most interesting person any of the passengers had ever met. A word from him had the ability to arrest the attention of a room full of people like a magnet near shards of iron. Traver knew that his own words could hold the same power, of course, but this was neither the time nor place to use them.

Traver's least favorite moments during the long journey were these, during which he shared space with the first officer. When a dinner was being held in the cabin of the doctors or the scientists, he would find a good moment to excuse himself whenever Akachi appeared to claim all the conversation for himself. But when it was his own cabin's turn to host a dinner and the uniformed African god deigned to make an appearance, Traver could only smile and bear the endless monologuing, disliking Akachi a little more at every perfectly phrased turn of his tall tales.

Somewhere in Traver's brain, a minuscule group of cells glowed bright with the hope that Louisa Fletcher might make an appearance. But she didn't.

Gradually Traver lost interest in the social calls, Akachi or no Akachi. He continued to attend purely as a matter of decorum, but his mind was rarely with his happy-go-lucky companions. The one and only person — aside from the absent captain — who did begin to spark his interest was none other than Dr. Abrahim Misleh himself.

The eminent scientist was a quiet, middle-aged man whose most noticeable features were his short, bent stature and his excess of hair. He would be sighted freshly shaven and trimmed at dinner, only to appear with a disorderly and unshaped beard from his temples to his adam's apple within twenty hours. It was an odd thing to notice, but Traver's observational skills were keen and he intended to keep himself in practice.

Misleh rarely spoke during their gatherings, though he would laugh, sometimes uncontrollably, at even the most benign jokes. His small frame had a way of jiggling when he was excited that was almost adorable.

It may have been his imagination, but Traver thought he sometimes would catch the little man studying him from across the cabin during dinnertime conversations to which both men were bystanders. What it was Misleh found so interesting about him, Traver couldn't guess. But every time he'd try to return the eye contact, the scientist would shift his focus elsewhere.

Traver often wanted to approach Misleh after a dinner had ended, but he could never find the right topic to begin a conversation. What could he talk about with a man who'd dedicated his life to science? He began to hope for a chance encounter in the corridor, where perhaps circumstances would provide the right words to say, but no such encounter occurred. Traver briefly considered making his way to the scientists' cabin near the aft, but he quickly dismissed the idea when he envisioned himself trying to explain a purpose for his uncharacteristic visit.

If he'd been asked, Traver would not have been able to explain his fascination with Dr. Misleh. Perhaps it was the man's childlike demeanor despite his age. Perhaps it was his importance as a singularly noteworthy figure in the scientific community. What is most likely is that Traver found Misleh intriguing because, despite the scientist's animation and constant emotiveness, Traver could not even begin to read him. Misleh was as mysterious as he was amiable.

Their company was first made under Misleh's prompting, when the scientist requested to sit in during one of Traver's injection sequences. Dr. Marin deferred the decision to Traver, who gave his not-unenthusiastic permission to let the senior scientist observe.

Misleh stayed quietly in the corner of the medical bay while Traver was undressed and paralyzed. Once the Eams victim was placed inside the tank with the spider arms, he could see through the clear casing that Dr. Misleh and Dr. Marin had begun to talk.

Misleh appeared excited and awestruck, asking questions that Marin answered rigidly.

After Traver's torment was over he was gently strapped into a chair while the paralysis wore away. Since his mouth was still completely numb and useless, he was unable to stop Misleh before the latter departed back to his own cabin. But Traver had been given the fuel he needed for an introductory conversation.

"I must be quite the fascinating lab rat," Traver said to Misleh five hours later, when they found themselves beside one another in the doctors' cabin while the dinner tubes were being unpacked.

Misleh's eyes opened curiously wide, an effect exaggerated by the lenses of his glasses.

Traver smiled then. "I've only been wondering why you seemed so interested in my treatment. If Eams studies happen to be another specialty of yours, I would love to hear if you have any better solutions."

For a moment longer Misleh stared at him, looking almost perplexed that Traver was capable of speech. Then he too smiled, his round face scrunching.

"No, no no. I am not an expert on Eams. For that, you are already in the best care. Galina is a good friend and we have worked together from time to time. It always interests me to see her latest projects. The compound she has created to treat Eams is a breakthrough science."

"That's good to hear. A second opinion from you, of all people, is encouraging."

The scientist chortled. "I'm glad you think so."

"From all I have read, you have a lot of clout in the scientific community."

Misleh's eyes dropped and the skin beneath his all-encompassing beard turned a shade of red. "Alright. If that's what you've read."

Traver spun himself around to face the scientist straight-on and dropped his voice to a whisper. "So, as someone who has spent your life becoming an expert in your field, what would you say to someone like me, who has spent the past decade poisoning public opinion against people like you?"

A few sets of eyes in the room turned questioningly at the sight of Traver speaking so closely with Misleh, but his words went unheard.

Misleh's smile vanished and he looked up at the taller man before him. Traver was still smiling and his tone had been nothing if not kind. The question had not been a challenge; it was a treaty.

"I would say –" Misleh squinted until his eyes nearly vanished beneath the folds of skin – "I would say that you are only hurting yourself, by keeping your mind closed. Also you are hurting the other people whose minds you shut down. But if we are the ones you have been trying to hurt, I would say that you have not succeeded; public opinion is not what carries our hopes, or we would all work in the media instead of in research."

Traver could not help but grin. The little man's reply had been mathematical, not confrontational in the least.

"This is the sort of dialogue I want to have!" Traver's voice returned to full volume; by now the cabin was full of other voices and nobody bothered to pay attention to his conversation. "No more straw men, no more backstabbing. I want to be told, by someone who would know, where you believe I've been wrong. There is no public to convince out here; it's just us."

Misleh's smile returned, now taking the form of a comfortable, knowing grin. "My work brings me joy, as does talking about it. I'm glad to discuss it with you. Food is another thing that brings me joy, and we seem to be missing dinner. May we eat first?"

So Traver began to spend his time in Abrahim Misleh's company both during dinners and in the interims, the silent spaces of time during which the rest of the passengers kept mostly to themselves.

Traver found his company refreshing. The scientist's passion for their journey was an antidote to Traver's own intentional cynicism. Misleh didn't seem capable of discussing his studies in any sort of calculated manner without getting carried away, his body jiggling as it did with excitement. But Misleh's was not the corporate, greedy enthusiasm Traver had seen before in so many facets of Aurora operations; he was the real deal, a man whose life was given completely to the discoveries of higher meaning. Traver had never encountered a belief so untainted by ulterior motive, so he didn't know how to criticize it.

Several hours before one of Traver's broadcasts (most of which continued to lack any real zest), he found himself moving slowly through the corridor with Misleh. He was being schooled in the restorative environmental benefits that would eventually result from the Egypt meteorite's devastating impact, when a thought occurred to him and he changed the subject.

"Abrahim…" Their relationship had quickly grown to exist on a first-name basis. "Tell me about AMA."

Abrahim did not respond with excitement. He did not jiggle. He blinked a few times and carefully removed his thin glasses from his hairy face.

Traver had no idea what his question had sparked.

"AMA… Now that's a most peculiar specimen. So peculiar that it has been my primary focus for, oh, nearly three decades now. Other studies, they've come and gone, but that one, that most important one, has always been there waiting for me, right where I left it.

"People ask me sometimes, 'why AMA? Why not better places like Remnant Zilly, LACY-4, the Dawn Belt? These are all destinations where we might learn about life. Dead balls of gas, on the other hand, cannot enlighten us. Why waste your time? Abrahim, think about life.' My answer to that? Life, is…"

He paused for a moment, looking aimlessly at the walls of the corridor. Then he planted his glasses back on his face and looked squarely at Traver.

"Life is bullshit. It's intriguing to look at, of course, but it's a fruitless study in the end. You start with us and work backwards, to animals, to fish, to plants, to clumps of cells, but the final question is always 'where did it come from?' Like a brick wall, that question stands at the end of every path. And nobody is happy to have a question without an answer, so we get the silly inventions like aliens, gods, spontaneous generation, just because people needed something to fill in the blanks."

Traver never thought his intellect capable of truly falling in love, yet here he was, madly infatuated with this strange scientist's mind. He'd never seen pure science before. This was not the delusion of popular scientific belief against which he'd ranted for years. Removed from the self-deception and emotional blindness that turned science into a thing of faith, this was not so bad.

Misleh kept going: "Of course, life is only a tiny thing in the universe. It's very selfish to focus oneself completely on the study of life, just because we happen to be in possession of it. That's why I think Zilly, LACY-4, these are not great mysteries or discoveries. We already know the universe is capable of producing life in one place, so why not another?"

Traver felt the urge, or rather the need, to interject as devil's advocate. It was his job, after all. "And AMA-712 *is* a great discovery? How? What could possibly make it different? In my observations, all scientific pursuits eventually end in unanswerable questions, which is why I find it more efficient never to ask the questions in the first place."

Abrahim finally chuckled, producing the familiar jiggle. "Your thought is a tempting one for anyone who's been frustrated one too many times. But the scientific hope lies in the eventuality of perhaps finding a line of study that leads only to answers. If not answers, then at least we can make a discovery of something else the universe is capable of. Something like life, but not life. Then, using life and this other, second discovery, conclusions can start to be drawn about this universe of ours, how she operates, why she does the things she does."

"How will AMA help you?"

"We were very fortunate to find AMA. No other planet is like it. To put it simply, it's very old. Old is an understatement. It's the oldest thing we've found. It goes back in time beyond the known stars, maybe beyond the Milky Way. The gas around the planet is thick, protective. It seems not to have been disturbed, making it an invaluable time capsule."

"I'm not an expert, but a planet can't be older than its star, can it?"

"I have concluded, and its patterns support my hypothesis, that AMA is a migratory planet. That is, it was once orbiting another star entirely, then it drifted away or was swept off by the star system we are approaching now. This may have happened once, twice, more. For longer than our galaxy has held its current shape, the planet has been a wanderer, latching on to any star that passes by. Like a lonely man."

He chuckled again. Traver chuckled too.

Misleh's laughter ended in a long sigh. "We would know so much more already, if the planet's atmosphere were not unreadable. Doctor Eduardo Aguilar and I sent the *Pytheas* probe years ago. That was of course before Eduardo lost interest in our project. From that probe we learned some things – some very interesting things – but not enough. We don't know what the planet is made of and I worry that even if we learn that, we still won't know why it behaves the way it does. AMA is greater than the sum of its parts. I think, somewhere deep inside, it holds magnificent secrets. It will tell us, if we only know how to ask it." His eyes glinted as he looked at Traver, then quickly looked away. "Maybe it will tell us about the early form of the universe, before life, before…all this."

He waved his hand, indicating his general surroundings. Lance, at that very moment drifting unnoticed from the cabin, saw only the tail end of the gesture and mistook it for a signal referring to himself.

"Yes?" he asked.

"Excuse me?" returned Misleh, uncomfortable at being interrupted.

"Were you? Oh…sorry." Lance realized his mistake. "I, uh, Mister Graff, we're nearly ready to start recording. Karl would like to start getting you in makeup."

"Of course." Traver moved to follow Lance. But an idea struck him.

"Doctor, would you be offended if I asked you to repeat the conversation we just had, while being recorded?"

Misleh's eyes again opened unusually wide, appearing comical through his glasses but perhaps deadly. Traver feared that he'd asked a damaging question, one that might forever drive that brilliant mind away from further conversations.

But the scientist's mouth curled into a smile and he started to laugh heartily, jiggling more than ever. "Of course. Most people don't ask me to talk about AMA. I thought everyone had grown sick of hearing about it; many of my peers accuse me of pseudo-science when I discuss the things I believe to be true of the planet. But I am more than happy to talk to your large audience."

The broadcast began half an hour later. They staged the conversation to proceed in a similar course as it had originally taken. Traver couldn't be completely certain, but he thought that Abrahim, without losing his conviction and excitement, repeated everything he'd said with word-for-word accuracy.

Traver had never met a person he admired so much.

* * *

His good mood could only last until the next time the doctors came for him. That routine was inescapable: twice over the course of what would have been called a week on Earth, Traver was harshly reminded of his ailment when he was ushered afterwards into the medical bay for the prescribed injection sequence.

It was worse up here than it had been on Earth, perhaps because it was so easy for Traver to forget, while suspended weightlessly, that his bones were being eaten away by a myriad of hungry bugs impervious to traditional medicine. The more he grew to love the version of himself that emerged in the close quarters of the *Aten*, the more his medical appointments came as a kick in the teeth to remind him of his own fragile mortality.

Just as at the medical facilities on Earth, he was given an injection of muscle relaxant to paralyze him. Dr. Marin and his assistants Ultrecht and Akers would unlock the medical cabinet to retrieve a vial of Dr. Shurovsky's formula, over which they kept an obsessive, protective watchfulness. The vial was plugged into the tank of the automated injection machine. Then Traver was pushed into its waiting spider-arms which proceeded to pounce on him, stabbing him in twenty places at once.

For the most part he became desensitized to the soreness inflicted by the treatment, at least. His body adjusted his tolerance for needles until he barely felt the punctures at all, even once the numbness wore away. The whole process was an awful chore, taking a toll mentally more than physically. Traver exacerbated the mental trauma, endangering his sanity by keeping count of all the treatments he'd had while onboard, counting down the ones that remained before the destination was to be reached. The grand total should be around two hundred and twelve, if travel time estimates were correct. He felt that this count helped him keep track of the passage of time, giving him some context for the length of the journey. The side effect was a near-constant repetition in his head, a small voice drumming away over and over again with the current count: *forty-two treatments down, one hundred seventy to go. forty-two treatments down, one hundred seventy to go. forty-two...* After a while the voice was there when he woke in his bunk, and it was there when he laid back down twelve hours later. It was there when he exercised, it was there while he ate. And still he was caught off guard when, twice a week, the doctors came for him.

All the lapses of sanity, all the pleasant and unpleasant conversations, all the longings, revelations and rivalries came together into an alien breed of *status quo* that was established onboard the *Aten*. The environment came to be accepted as normal by everyone onboard, from the veteran astrophysicists to the glorified chauffeur. Each and every one of them would have been more than content to see that status quo continue for the entirety of the two-year sojourn.

It didn't.

The end of the status quo began four months after the jump when Traver, as per his agreement with the Aurora Corporation, made the announcement to the world that he was dying of Eams.

More accurately, the end began when an unexpected transmission came in from the SASH headquarters, several hours after one of Traver's shows. Since his cabin was set up to send and receive transmissions only during the allotted broadcast times ("borrowing" the communications from the cockpit even on a weekly basis was already stretching security regulations), he found himself summoned unexpectedly to the cockpit by his least favorite first officer.

Traver's second visit to that mystical control room of windows left a much deeper impression than did the first. The vision that met his eyes, upon encountering the universe again, was enough to distract him from his distaste of the grinning Akachi and his equal longing to make contact with Fletcher.

The night sky, star-studded as it was before, had been just that. But whether it was the angle of the ship or the months spent traveling at Mach 75, one star was much closer than it had been. Directly ahead of the ship's trajectory lay a bright dot that was more than a dot. It was bright enough to leave a mark in his vision when his eyes looked away, bright enough to cast a white shimmer through the cockpit and over its occupants. What most struck Traver was how, the longer he looked at it, the more it grew round, three-dimensionally so, until his mind started to grasp the huge spaces that lay between him and the star, between the star and its cousins. Night sky had only ever appeared a speckled, flat canvas to him before, but now he began to grasp a more complex reality.

"Would you like to see your message?" It was Fletcher that asked him, rather than Akachi. That was probably why Traver responded so quickly, snapping his gaze back to his immediate surroundings.

"Yes, please. Thank you for notifying me."

At a tap of Fletcher's (*well-proportioned*, he thought) finger, a monitor on the console flickered to life. Weston appeared on the screen and began to talk earnestly, sweating as he did when things at the station were going less than ideally.

"I was supposed to make this message as professional and non-partisan as I could, but hell, boss. I just want to talk man-to-man, and if I'm being honest, Karen's mad. She's in one of those moods – all this is off the record, so I'm gonna go ahead and say that. She's in one of those moods where she thinks everyone's out to get her and the SASH is about to crash and burn if she doesn't save it."

"He takes a while to get to the point..." Fletcher commented dryly. Traver had warmed to Weston's babbling over the years, but now he felt embarrassed that the captain had to hear it.

"Nobody seems to be happy with the direction the shows are taking. I mean, I think it's still great. But the ratings are declining, the viewership is dropping week to week, and Karen and the board, and the PR people, they all think you're...you're...sending...sending the wrong message." At the last words, Weston's eyes dropped and he spoke in little more than a trembling whisper.

Weston wasted a lot more words, but the point was clear. The SASH didn't like that Traver was publicly tolerating his time in space, let alone appearing to enjoy it. They had been hoping for a barrage of Traver Graff's famous tear-downs, his critiques of modern society that lifted up humanity's fundamental nature even while destroying the credibility of its most deeply-held beliefs. Instead, the world was being treated to a tour of the cosmos, complete with scientific mumbo jumbo and odes to modern achievements.

In other words, Traver was doing the opposite of what his audience wanted him to do.

He remained still for some time after Weston, nearly sobbing, wrapped up his transmission ("they want you to reframe your message. I hope you understand. We all want you to stay on the air").

It wasn't that Traver was surprised. Certainly, the message had come sooner than he expected, but he'd never lost the sense that he was painting space travel in too favorable a light. Nevertheless a pang of anger shot into him, then rested heavily somewhere beneath his consciousness. *I should have received this privately*, was the first thought that formed without his actively shaping it. But there had been no privacy. The captain and first officer had viewed the message first, and then again with Traver – there was no knowing how many times they'd viewed it before they called for him. Louisa Fletcher had had a front-row seat to his humiliation: the famous Traver Graff, media personality, brought low by a squabbling bunch of Secular Alliance bureaucrats.

That was the first thought. Traver's second thought ran much deeper, driven into the undercurrents of his mind by what must have amounted to a lifetime's worth of suppressed hate. This thought said: *They don't give a damn what I think.*

He had never been a man to give himself up to hatred – anger, yes, but never hate. He believed hate made a person small, robbed him of control, and took away whatever moral high ground he might hope to maintain. This time was different; he already felt small, he'd lost all control over his situation, and if anyone had moral high ground now it was SASH. Hatred reversed all that. Hatred felt good.

Perhaps it was the advance of the deadly bacteria that made Traver feel less like himself. Perhaps it was the vast distance between himself and his home planet that made him somehow, in fact, not himself. Whatever the reason, Traver let go of the barriers that had kept the dangerous parts of his mind at bay.

They don't give a damn what I think. His mind repeated it once, twice, a hundred times, faster and faster until the words fired off rapidly and overlapped like a chaos of firecrackers going off in his head.

"Do you need a moment longer?"

Traver turned to find that Akachi was beside him, hand resting firmly on his shoulder.

How long had Traver been frozen there, blinded by the whirlpool behind his eyes? Not long. Akachi, in his show of sympathy, hadn't had time to revert to his face's default position of grinning. Fletcher, for her part, hadn't even bothered to turn and look at Traver.

His wits were not gone. He took a half-second to observe himself, and judged that he'd maintained his composure. His face was not flushed, his hands were not shaking, and his eyes had never shut. That was good. He could still save face in front of these deities of the cockpit before he stormed off to impose his own divine retribution on the world that had wronged him.

"No, but thank you for notifying me. One thing I might add: please don't bother me with further messages like this, unless it's something really important."

"Of course." Akachi's grin, long-delayed, finally found its way to his statuesque face.

Traver nodded curtly, and turned away with a precise rapidity that was quick enough to express confidence but not so rushed as to be insecure.

A moment later he was outside the cockpit. It took all of the willpower still at his disposal to resist looking back one more time, to see whether Fletcher had finally turned her head to look at him. But he knew that didn't matter anyway.

It didn't matter anyway. None of it mattered. What was the point of holding onto those ancient facades of professional dignity now? Where had those facades gotten him, really?

He turned. Akachi was facing the controls now. Fletcher's body faced forward in her seat, but her head was craned over her right shoulder. Her eyes were locked on Traver, full of what looked like pity.

He met her eyes without blinking. His head lowered slightly, but his eye contact was not broken. He felt something, some red-hot invisible substance spilling out from the whirlpool in his head, shooting out of his eyes. Whatever her eyes had begun to say in the instant their gazes met, his eyes had overpowered and silenced them. *I want* – Traver's eyes would have said, if they were organs that could produce speech – *I want to matter.*

Fletcher didn't turn away. Or she couldn't.

Then Akachi shut the doors of the cockpit.

Traver smiled. There was no reason to smile, but reason was no longer driving Traver Graff.

I want to matter.

Somewhere between the appearance of Weston's fat face on the screen and the fall of Akachi's hand on his shoulder, Traver's machine of a brain had clicked and calculated a course of action into existence. The hate-storm that filled his mind still couldn't obstruct that clear constructive process. By the time he asked Akachi to desist from forwarding him any more messages from home, the plan was devised and set in stone even if Traver's conscious self wasn't fully aware of it.

Drifting back toward his cabin, in the few moments of time he would have to himself before returning to the social world of the *Aten's* passengers, he filled himself in on the details of the plan and decided that it was good. It was time to get to work.

"Lance. Do you have a paper and pen?"

"Pardon?"

"Paper and pen, like our grandparents used to write with."

Lance was almost as confused by the calmness and confidence with which Traver made the request as he was by the request itself.

"Um…half a second."

Jumping out of bed (where he'd been happily napping until Traver burst in), Lance hurried to dig through his supplies. It wasn't common practice for something as rudimentary as paper and pens to exist onboard a spacecraft – or anywhere else for that matter – but Lance's experience with technology had taught him the invaluable dependability of old-fashioned ink.

"Here." He handed Traver a pen, one of the ancient pressurized models designed for NASA in the 1900s, and a ream of paper.

"Thanks." Traver snatched it away as he strapped himself into his bunk with all the agility his body could muster. The moment he settled, his right hand started to scratch away on the paper at an inhuman pace.

Lance watched with curiosity for a few moments, but dared not ask what had struck Traver as so important that it had to be immediately written down. He looked at Karl, just now entering the room, with a hapless shrug.

The scratching of pen on paper went on. Karl and Lance were able to sleep, but every time they woke their ears were greeted by that sound, as if a machine had been forgotten and left running. In a way, it had.

Lance and Karl weren't terribly surprised when their boss failed to join the chess tournament in the scientists' cabin. They blamed his absence on exhaustion and his newfound writing project, whatever that might be.

They remained unsurprised twenty-four hours later, when Traver made no appearance at the poetry reading with the doctors. He'd had an injection treatment during that cycle, after all, and was likely exhausted as a result.

Worry started to set in on the third day-cycle after Traver had visited the cockpit. It was his cabin's turn to host the others for what Lance had decided would be "virtual game night." Traver, usually on the forefront of efforts to make the cabin ready for company, never stirred from his bunk, nor did he say a word to anyone.

"Come to think of it, I haven't heard a word from him since he came back from seeing the Captain," Lance whispered to Karl in the safety of the corridor. "Has he said anything to you?"

Karl shook his head to the negative. "He's barely stepped foot out of the cabin; just to use the head and get his treatment, and I've been bringing him his meals. I don't even know if he's slept."

"Well…I'll start setting up some of the old games" (Lance had stashed a drive full of his childhood favorites) "and we'll hope for the best."

As they moved back into their cabin, Lance reaching for his roll-up virtual screen which he kept secured by his luggage, the last thing they expected was to hear a sharp voice come from the direction of Traver's bunk, mixed in with the scratching which had become part of the room's natural ambience.

"Will you be using the cabin later?"

Lance had to look twice to ensure the voice had emanated from Traver. It had.

"It's our turn. Game night. If…if that's still alright?"

"I'd like the cabin to myself, actually."

He never lifted up his eyes from the paper. Lance now noticed that Traver had burned through the entire ream. By now he had turned it over, covering the back sides of the sheets, one by one.

"Oh. Okay. I guess we can ask the scientists…"

"I'm sure the doctors wouldn't be against hosting twice in a row" chipped in Karl.

"Good," was Traver's only response.

Karl was quick to turn to the cabin's door, but Lance lingered. "What about the next time? Will you be alright letting us use the cabin in twenty-four hours?"

Now Traver looked up at them. Those who knew Traver (Lance and Karl counted themselves among those who did) knew that his eye contact was never unplanned, never anything but strategic. A soul found by Traver's eyes became a target, a cog in his mind's gearbox about to be put to some premeditated use. This time was different. His eyes were open fully and there was no motive behind them. There was nothing at all behind them.

"In twenty-four hours, Lance, we'll be recording."

Lance paused a moment and did a bit of mental arithmetic. "But we're not transmitting for another eighty-two hours."

"I know. We will be recording though."

Traver looked back down at his work, his eyes releasing their unfortunate victims. Karl slipped out the door, and Lance followed quietly after discreetly gathering the equipment he would need.

The scientists graciously agreed to host Lance's game night, and he spent the next several hours rigging a makeshift rec room in their cabin.

Nobody stood a chance against Lance at the games several hours later, nor did anyone care that he had stashed several pre-censorship shooter sims; global censorship laws didn't apply out here, and everyone knew it. While he playfully gunned down his fellow passengers in the three-dimensional environment amid the laughter of all, Lance's heart was not in the victory. Something heavy and Traver-shaped was weighing on his mind.

If he had only known the full weight.

CHAPTER FIVE
GRAFF

"Can you set up the session?"

"What, now?" Lance had only just come back to the cabin. He and the others had been at the virtuals for nine hours. Karl had retired halfway into the session, and now Lance was eager to follow suit.

"Now. I'm ready."

Tired though he was, understanding washed over Lance as Traver sat up in the bed, holding the ream of thoroughly-utilized paper. After understanding, he felt relief. Traver had been writing show segments. Of course. Why hadn't Lance come to that conclusion before? His boss hadn't lost his mind or succumbed to a space fever. He was simply being prepared. Obsessively, disproportionately prepared.

"Sure, Mister Graff. I'll have it ready in a few."

The recording equipment was relatively quick to set up when transmission was not imminent, but it still took an hour or more for Lance to fully disassemble the virtual-reality rig, for which he'd cannibalized many of the sensors.

While he worked, he noticed the eerie silence that had taken over the room. The familiar scratching of pen against paper was a thing of the past, and the engine's purr had taken back its place as the only sound. Traver was letting himself drift near the floor now, maintaining a sitting position, his eyes shut in some sort of contemplation.

"Ready to go." Lance's declaration was made more of sighs than of words. He looked at Karl, saw that he was still sound asleep in his bunk, and felt a twinge of envy.

Traver didn't bother with makeup. He didn't need to look in a mirror to know he looked like the pale rider of death minus the horse, but that was precisely the appearance he wanted. Anything else would have been dishonest.

Lance looked on with a frown, either of disapproval or tragic disappointment, as Traver sat in front of the cameras. The once-great man's hair was greasy and stuck up wildly over his left ear. His face was thin and pale, with dark circles below each eye that reached past his cheekbones. As if his body was aware of its appearance, his shoulders sagged unconsciously, making him look even thinner than he already was. His appearance had been like this for months, of course, but it was never so apparent as when he sat under the lights, face free of makeup, for the purpose of being broadcast to Earth. He reminded Lance of the ghostly shells of worn-out celebrities that one often sees posted in the cheap and desperate media outlets. But, Traver was never supposed to be that kind of celebrity. He was never supposed to be worn out.

"Before I start," Traver said, "can you get me a copy of my contract with Aurora?"

It was the very last request Lance had expected, but he obliged. He produced his slidescreen and found the contract (it had been extensively copied and backed-up for legal reasons aplenty) and held it out to Traver.

"Thanks, Lance. Alright. Let's go."

Traver began the hour by reading the clause of his contract stipulating that he should withhold the announcement of his condition until he was outside of the Solar System. "So here I am, fulfilling my end of the contract and telling you all the news." It was a straightforward, no-nonsense revelation that he had Eams and that he was dying. He proceeded to relate the emotional duress that such a discovery entailed, and went into detail about the painful treatments under which he'd been subjected. A lesser speaker would have used this content, knowingly or unknowingly, as a plea for pity – if not for pity, then as a display of strength, to show the world his bravery, all under the guise of offering inspiration for any viewers back on Earth who might themselves be suffering from this or any other condemnatory illness. Not Traver. The power of his words lay in their utter coolness, their lack of sentiment. That he was undergoing an unfathomable amount of physical and mental strain was just a fact of life. That he would die was equally factual.

As he spoke, Traver's confidence grew. He was handling himself with perfection. This calculated approach was the precise sort of thing that had drawn him to the Secularists in the first place; his ideology was not a merciful one, nor was it open-minded or idealistic. His breed of secularism was heartless. Traver could find himself in the throes of mortality and still separate himself from the romanticism usually so interconnected with disease and death.

It was as good a recording as Traver had ever produced, and Lance grudgingly concluded that his boss's writing spree had worked.

The hour finished, and Traver sat back from the recording scanners. Lance smiled and reached for the dials to switch off the system.

"No. We're going again," Traver sharply stopped him.

"We are?"

"Yes. Leave it on. Start a new session."

Confused, Lance moved to the control box and created a new recording. "What should I call the new one, boss?"

"The date of the next broadcast. It'll be January 24th, right?" Traver's mastery of the Earth calendar after months with no reference point was nearly as astounding as the plan which was now becoming clear to Lance.

"Uh, yeah. It'll be the 24th."

"Sir, if I may be so bold; you may want to change your shirt." This was Karl, who had woken up and listened silently from his bed for some indefinite amount of time. "Toss your hair around. Make it look like a week has gone by."

Traver smiled, "Of course. That's why you're here Karl," and proceeded to do as Karl had suggested.

Lance was no longer confused. Just overwhelmed. "Okay. Recording when you're ready."

Traver nodded and embarked upon another hour. His voice, dry and clear as ever regardless of his physical condition, flowed into a rhythmic pattern of ascending and descending timbres, rapidly fluctuating in tone and volume when it came time to make a point, while points followed one another with precision, keeping the beat like a timpani.

Traver no longer talked about his days in space or the phenomena he encountered in his new setting. He returned to his roots, as if he was back in the studio at the SASH building. With his second segment he ranted about the medical industries, their proclivity to taking advantage of those needing medical care, and their bias against the unwealthy. Nipping in the bud any potential accusations of hypocrisy, he launched from there into a tirade against the undeserving wealthy classes. He included himself under this umbrella, closing the segment with a melancholy apology for being able to afford expensive medical treatments – treatments that could likely only extend his comfortable life a little, rather than save it – with riches that came from a lifetime of performance.

"And that's our hour. I think everyone's gonna love that one. It's a good change of pace, going back to what people remember about you." Lance was eager to please and even more eager for Traver to be finished.

"Good. Glad you think so. Karl, how many shirts do I have packed?"

Karl and Lance shared a glance. Karl, at least, knew where this was headed. "Eleven, sir."

"Pick the next one for me. Randomly, but not *too* randomly. Occasional repeats would be believable."

Lance kept his mouth shut while Traver again changed clothes and shuffled his hair. He sat back in front of the cameras and sensors.

"You ready?"

"Yeah." Lance stirred quickly, feigning enthusiasm. The truth was, he was exhausted.

"Here we go." And the hour began.

And after that hour, another. And another.

* * *

During the sixth hour of recording (the one titled "FEB21"), Lance's eyes finally slipped shut despite his best efforts, and he dozed. Karl noticed. Traver noticed, though he didn't miss a beat. Nobody would have been able to tell by watching him, but Traver's confidence was badly affected as he began to dread two things: one, that his sound levels would peak or go quiet without Lance to monitor, or two, that Lance would snore.

The hour ended and Lance never snored. He jumped to attention when Traver shook him awake.

"I'm sorry, Traver – Mister Graff. Did...did I sleep through the hour?"

"Yes. Can you double check the levels please?"

Lance took a glance at the wave readouts, and nodded with relief. "Levels are good. Honestly, your levels have been consistent; I haven't needed to tweak them at all."

"Then how hard would it be for Karl to handle this for a while?"

Lance's face fell and his eyes widened. He wanted to answer the direct question, but he was physically too worn out to stop himself from saying what was on the tip of his tongue: "How many segments are you going to do?"

"All of them."

Lance shut his eyes for a moment, trying to calculate. His eyes nearly stayed shut and lost themselves in dreamworld, but with effort he finished the arithmetic and re-exposed his pupils to the light. "You have five more to go, before we get you to orbit around AMA."

"I have eighty-four to go. That'll get us back home."

Traver smiled gently, seeming either undaunted or simply unaware. Karl and Lance were at a loss for words, but then again it wasn't their words that were important. "Show Karl how to start the recording. Then you can get some rest."

Lance was grateful to hear it, despite his professional reservations against someone monitoring the sessions besides himself.

"Title the file here…and you're recording when this tab lights up. Stop it the same way as you start it, and be sure to press 'save.'" Karl nodded. His own tasks of looking after Traver's toiletry, clothes and general wellbeing were more complicated than this.

* * *

Lance slept, and the recording continued. When Lance later awoke and switched places with Karl, Traver was still going strong. They'd moved to near the end of April's segments, well into the time during which the *Aten* would be orbiting the mysterious planet. Traver's monologues moved on a clear trajectory one to the next, becoming harsher as they went, more scathing against a broadening number of industries, mindsets, classes and faiths. He condemned with increasing amounts of vitriol all the different forms of selfishness, a headline beneath which he came to include all beliefs, pursuits, causes, comforts and efforts that did not directly and without controversy contribute to the tangible betterment of the world. It seemed to Lance and Karl (though they never spoke up to share their mutual feeling) that Traver was slowly working his way to a full-fledged condemnation of humanity. Not that he ran the risk of losing viewers. Yes, he may have been isolating himself from wide swaths of his audience, but even at his most hateful he was a hell of a lot of fun to listen to.

Somehow, more than sixty hour-long segments passed by. Lance and Karl ceased to hear what was said. Though they took turns sleeping and monitoring, they both started to feel themselves part of a claustrophobic and cyclical nightmare where time was kept only by the relentless sound of Traver's tireless voice. Interruptions in the form of intrusion never came; the pilots were silent, and Karl took a moment sometime near the middle of "June" to slip away and alert the other passengers that he and his bunkmates would be occupied for the foreseeable future.

At the end of the sixty-eighth segment of the longest recording session in SASH (or space) history, Traver pushed himself back from the recording seat and did something that brought a gleam of hope into his assistants' infinite underworld. He yawned. Both the other occupants of the cabin were awake to see it, and snapped to full attention.

"How are you feeling?" asked Lance.

"Is there anything you need?" prompted Karl.

Traver looked at them with slight confusion, the first emotion aside from determination which he'd displayed for what seemed like an eternity. "Everything's fine. But isn't it time to transmit to Weston?"

It was. Lance had forgotten all about the concept of time, and they were scheduled to send the segment – that first segment, recorded so many hours before – to Earth for broadcast.

"Should I send them all?"

Traver paused a moment. The thought hadn't crossed his mind. He'd planned as far ahead as committing his performances to the digital medium, but not so far as the timing of transmission. There was a lot to consider in the brief moment he had to answer Lance before he would start to appear hesitant.

There were certain disadvantages to transmitting the bulk of the recordings; nobody – not the SASH, Karen Tiplins, the Aurora people or Gladstone – must have even the slightest suspicion that all the messages were recorded in one sitting. Weston could be trusted to maintain the facade, gradually unveiling broadcasts week after week if instructed to do so, but that of course depended on Weston remaining the *only* producer to receive the transmissions and being able to maintain the subterfuge for the next two years. Traver's reputation for integrity, not to mention the jobs of his staff, were at risk should the word get out that the "weekly" broadcasts were inorganic.

On the other hand, what if something were to happen to Traver, or to the *Aten*? It would be an insurmountable tragedy for the recordings to be lost, should some accident befall him. The best way to ensure their preservation would be to send them on to Earth now, for better or for worse. But then again, if Traver were to drop dead six months into the mission, the event would be reported by the captain and the news would be made public. After that news, the continued weekly broadcasts would prompt some questions about just how dead Traver really might be.

Pride won out in the end. Dead or alive, Traver wanted his words to reach back to Earth. What was the point otherwise?

"We'll send them all in one go, once I have them all done. For now, just send the first."

They sat and waited as the transmission sent, wrapping into the jumpable data package and then shooting off through the light years.

Maybe it was the yawn, or perhaps Traver's moment of hesitation that *had* been noticeable, but Lance felt confident enough to venture a question as they awaited the verification of transmission.

"Aren't you robbing your audience, just a little? They're not going to make it to the part where you see the planet. They won't get to hear about – whatever it is that Misleh ends up finding. Wasn't that sort of the point of all this?"

Traver didn't mind being asked the question, though he was surprised at Lance's naiveté. Then he considered that Lance, unlike himself, had not spent countless hours working up an unhealthy cynicism regarding his current position in the SASH, in Aurora, and in space. The tech was justified in his simplicity and deserved an explanation.

"I'm not here because of the planet. I'm not here because of Misleh. People don't really care about what this mission is going to find, and the people who do care are not the people in my audience. I'm here to spout words that people will enjoy. They don't need to learn about the world outside of themselves, and they certainly don't need to believe what I tell them. They just need to turn off their brains, and listen.

"If Karen wants a cookie-cutter Traver Graff, then that's what she's going to get, and that's all. Me, I want to enjoy the rest of this trip as much as I still can. I'm not here for Aurora, or my audiences, or the Secular movement. I'm here for myself, now."

With his next hour, he attacked the very people who didn't want to learn about the world outside of themselves, people who turned off their brains and listened endlessly to the likes of Traver Graff, thus allowing their own opinions be formed for them by the unsubstantiated words of popular truth-makers.

The final twenty-two hours passed quickly, at least in comparison to the endless hell that came before. There was light at the end of the tunnel now, or a star at the end of a space flight.

As the grand finale approached, Lance and Karl found themselves unwilling or unable to sleep. Their anticipation grew into actual enthusiasm, a sense that they were somehow making history. They knew that Traver must have carefully crafted a mind-blowing ending to all this – here they were with front-row seats, experiencing the final chapter of Traver's Space Sojourn a year and a half before the rest of the world.

Then the finale came.

"Near the beginning of my journey, I was told to resist the urge to tell you all about my experiences out here. Not because those experiences were secret, not because they were dull, but because they didn't reflect the program that you were all intended to hear. You're not supposed to see the expanses of space as I do. You're not supposed to hear about the incredible sciences that bring me here. You're just supposed to hear me – me, whom you have heard time and time again for years – me, who never really has anything new to say. I tear people down. I don't construct, I don't build. I just point my finger at the other people who do try to build, and I say 'they are doing it wrong, so they should stop!'

"And you're all perfectly content with it. Are you going to turn off my program because I stopped talking about space and science after my sixteenth episode out here? Maybe a few viewers did, but those people wouldn't have been part of the regular audience anyway, so who needs them? The fact is, *you* just needed *me*. You needed me so much that you kept listening. You kept listening when I pulled the wool over your eyes, sat down in my little cabin and talked to a microphone for ninety hours straight.

"That's right; you're hearing the words I spoke just a few months after I left Earth. You listened this whole time and you never even noticed or cared. Why did you do that? I didn't have anything to say, because I didn't even know yet where I was going, what was going to happen when I reached the planet, or if I was going to come back at all. But none of that mattered to you. You just wanted to hear my voice droning on and on, tearing things down. Even when I tore you down, you heard but you didn't listen. You laughed knowingly, you smirked smartly, you masturbated to the hatred, because that's what you do. You felt like you were part of something. You were included in an opinion. You could sit back and agree with me, and then feel satisfied that you were right because the person you agreed with was me instead of all those poor goddamn lost souls who were wrong because they dared to disagree with me, and so dared to disagree with you.

"January of 2177 is still not over for me. I don't know what the future of this journey holds. But I am excited for it. Excited to see where this journey ends. More excited than I think I've ever been for anything before. I want to share that with you, but you don't deserve it because it's not what you want to hear. I'm being used by you all, just as much as I'm being used by the Aurora Corporation, by my very own Secular Alliance. None of you care about what I think, about what I have to say – about, god forbid, if I were to change my mind or decide I was wrong about something. I'm just a tool.

"I'm being used by both those corporations, because while they may face each other down as enemies in public, in their hearts they're the same! They don't want the truth. They don't want to know about the things that make the universe spin, the things that make the human heart tick. They just want to control the way you all breathe, and think, and believe. You'll exchange one belief for another if they tell you to, and you won't even realize you did it.

"Yes; if I'm a tool, then imagine what you are. You, my billions of good friends and loyal listeners, are not even pawns; you're the bits of manure used to grow the grass that the cows will eat to then be butchered to feed the pawns.

"But here I am. Tearing you down again. Spreading anger, hatred, all the things that you will eat up, the things they want me to shout at you. Is there a solution to all this? Of course there is.

"In the time I've spent up here so far, brief as it has been, I've met people who are more than pawns. I've met kings and queens. People who don't spend their days letting their truths be formed by empty voices like Traver Graff. They look out. They see what's beyond them and then they do more than look; they grasp for it! These are the truth-seekers, these are the people who don't have belief because belief isn't something they need. The truth of the universe is in front of them, and they alone have what it takes to jump into it.

"I won't admit to having led you astray. There's never been a word I said to you that I don't stand by. But your lesson is over. It's time to shut the books and lift your faces to the daylight. Say goodbye to the SASH and its cherry-picked truths. Say goodbye to Traver Graff.

"Shut off your transmitters, smash your entertainment centers, erase the recordings you've made of me, and delete your compilations and collections.

"Will you listen to what I'm saying? Probably not, because again, you aren't here for what I think, what I want, or what I experience. But maybe, just maybe I will reach some of you. For those of you who do listen and hear, remember *this* as Traver Graff's last message before he goes deep into the unknown reaches of space, to a planet with a key to the origins of existence as we know it: stop living for yourselves. Live for the people you love. Look around you, at the things you can reach, and touch, and feel, and heal. When you look into the stars, don't just see the light, but feel the billions of years it has taken to reach you, and then ask yourself 'why.' Do that, and maybe you can join the truth-seekers. I hope to join them myself, and my first step is to say goodbye to you."

Traver looked anything but healthy as he sat back away from the recording scanners. His voice may have survived the strain of ninety hours, but his body showed all the signs of sleep deprivation and starvation. But a glow, felt rather than seen, was emanating from him. He smiled at Lance and then at Karl, both who, despite having had no specific expectations for the closing message, had not prepared themselves for *that*.

Traver unstrapped himself from the chair. His weak body surrendered to the embrace of the gravity-free room and he floated a little ways back, his eyes shutting as he finally gave in to his inner scream for sleep.

Akachi's voice rung out on the ship's intercom. "Mister Graff, Doctor Marin has been waiting for you. It's past time for your treatment appointment. He didn't want to disturb you, but I'm under the impression that this is fairly important – you may correct me if I'm wrong."

Traver's eyes tightened, then snapped open. He was no longer smiling.

After the treatment, he slept for nearly thirty hours.

Lance, blind to the fact that Traver had requested a halt in transmissions from the SASH, waited impatiently for a message from Weston regarding the Eams announcement episode. Given the chance to join the other passengers for a delayed game of Continent Conquerors (the scientists still embracing the games they'd played as bespectacled youngsters), Lance instead chose to wait by the transmitter, anticipating a message that would never come.

Traver slumbered like a log in the bed across the room. The exhaustion was well deserved and Lance knew it, though he couldn't help but wonder whether he was the only one with an itching curiosity to know how Earth had responded to the news of Traver's ailment. He was sure that when Traver awoke, he'd immediately ask whether they'd received anything.

But he didn't. When Traver finally did wake up, he didn't do or say much of anything. With the exception of the occasional visit to the privy, he kept to himself in his bed, maintaining a stoic silence and staring at nothing in particular.

"I haven't gotten anything from Weston" Lance finally interjected, several hours into Traver's silence.

"I know." And that was all Traver had to say on the matter.

On Traver's instruction, Lance forwarded the entire collection of eighty-nine future episodes to Earth. He protected the data with an encryption that Weston would recognize and be able to unpack. For safety's sake, Lance asked that Traver record a brief segment instructing Weston to maintain the illusion that each episode was being sent live, but Traver refused. For one thing, he had committed to no longer sitting in the recording chair, and insisted that his days of broadcasting from space were now officially over. For another thing, he proposed that Weston was intelligent enough to figure out what was required of him.

Lance was a cautious man, and recorded the instruction segment himself.

And so, forty hours after the conclusion of Traver's final broadcast, his final eighty-nine hours of transmission were packed into a virtual data capsule then sent jumping through light years of space. It was a good one, Traver knew — maybe his best ever. It was the note he wanted to end on, and as he lay strapped into the bed, watching Lance give the "thumbs up" after the transmission, Traver sincerely hoped it *would* be his last.

He thought little about Dana anymore, or about his children. Their memories, along with the SASH, the broadcasts, and Earth itself, belonged to a part of his mind that was being carefully compartmentalized and stowed away. There was a faint awareness — faint and becoming fainter — that the journey would eventually come to an end, that two years would pass quickly and he might again find himself on Earth. Then on Earth those realities of family, job and boredom would all come streaming back to the forefront. It would be a most unfortunate reversal of the progress he had made. But there was still time before that happened: nearly twenty months during which, Traver began to hope with a suicidal eagerness, he might end up dead.

Death was an acceptable outcome of the journey.

* * *

"Your reaction to the treatment is incredible." Dr. Marin had just performed a full-body scan on Traver, as he did monthly for the sake of status updates. During the length of the scan, Traver had been puzzled by the doctor's raised eyebrows and pursed lips, both strangers to the rigid man's usually emotionless face. "Doctor Shurovsky had a few — very few — test subjects respond with this level of success, and those subjects were all younger than you..."

Younger than... Traver stopped before his mind had the chance to react to the implication that he was old. Instead he let himself focus on the fact that he'd missed a birthday somewhere on this timeless trip. Forty-three should not feel very different from forty-two; such was usually the way with each advancing year. But this time, he did feel different. *He* was different.

"...but I've never seen anything like it, myself. One hundred percent of cases I've personally overseen have just descended into worse and worse structural fragmentation, no matter what I did. That's why I had a hard time approaching yours with a positive outlook, if I may be honest."

"That's reassuring." Traver smiled, but the humor was lost somewhere in the air between him and the doctor.

"But that might be changing. Look at the image scans, and you'll see the structural decline hasn't only been arrested, but it's reversing."

Traver fully expected to see another meaningless picture of his own skeleton, uninterpretable by a layman, like all the others he had seen before while in the grip of Eams. He casually turned his head toward the image on the computer. Then his head did a slight double-take and his eyes latched on to what he was seeing. This image was different from the others, and even he could see how. Before, the images of bones had been blurry, obscured by tiny specks and clouds which he'd been told represented weakened areas due to the presence of the bacteria. This time, the skeletal structure appeared clean, sharp, with fewer markings.

"Does this mean the treatments can be lessened?" Even a few less appointments every month would be a relief on Traver's mind and body.

"No. By no means, unfortunately. If anything, this is the time to increase the dosage. But we'll hold it steady, as Doctor Shurovsky prescribed."

Traver shrugged. It had been worth asking, anyway.

Dr. Marin went on: "The truth is, I didn't believe for myself, apart from Doctor Shurovsky's insistence, that recovery was really a possibility. I hadn't seen that play out. Now I'd go so far as to say that I'm a believer."

As Traver shut his eyes and underwent his excruciating-as-always treatment an hour later, he felt a surge of some alien feeling. It wasn't quite hope – he'd felt that before once or twice. It wasn't quite joy. He was no less resolved to accept a reality where he never returned to Earth, but now the possibility occurred to him that he might be destined for more than simply dying in space. Maybe this was belief. A belief in what exactly, he could not have said. Perhaps the nature of belief was to place a trust in something unknown and unexplained.

His body was weak as usual afterward. That much never changed. More and more with each sequence of injections he could imagine that he felt the patented fluid flowing through his veins, swimming into his heart, lungs and brain. This time in particular he felt – or imagined he felt – the soothing, slightly pulsing effect it had on his body. Perhaps only because of what Dr. Marin had said, it felt good. He felt strong.

Upon returning to his quarters, he did not collapse into bed as was his habit. Instead, he surprised the idly-reading Lance by stripping off his shirt and gazing in the cabin's mirror, studying himself while holding his own flat but loose belly. Without gravity, the skin pulled away from what had once a set of solid abdominals, now invisible beneath the drifting sea of flesh.

Attention to his body had fallen far on his list of priorities during the months on the *Aten*. Whatever exercise regimen he'd established onboard hadn't lasted past the jump. Now the effects of a lifetime of self-discipline were nearly undetectable.

He moved to the gym apparatus, folded it to the configuration for crunch/situps, and leaped in. Four hours later, he had changed configurations eight times. Sweat sprayed off of him and formed into droplets in the air, before being sucked away into the air system.

When he finally rested, he waited just a few hours before jumping to bike mode.

Every several hours afterward he returned to the apparatus, even when he felt himself on the verge of collapse. There was lost time to make up for. If he was going to live after all, he would do it as if Eams had never been.

CHAPTER SIX
AKACHI

To say that the passengers of the *Aten* returned to some state of normalcy over the next month of their journey would give their situation too little credit. This became the most serene and joyful time yet. The regularity of social calls between technicians, assistants, scientists and doctors returned and increased. The doors to each cabin were nearly always open to the other passengers. New acquaintances became unlikely friendships. Scientists and doctors shared knowledge, fascinated one another with their ideas and generated new perspectives through their meetings of minds. Lance had never considered himself to be a man of science, but he was able to participate fully in their conversations by virtue of his various skill sets and his degrees from ATI (from where many of the younger scientists had received their doctorates). Karl proved himself to be well-versed in art and literature, rounding off the more philosophical bent of their conversations.

And Traver grew more and more closed off, to everyone but himself. The more he dedicated himself to his exercise regimen – the more he shut off the wants and desires of his past life and looked ahead to whatever mysteries awaited at the end of his journey – the more he began to look at the other occupants of the *Aten* as a troupe of lesser creatures, and became less and less successful at hiding his disdain. Only two of the other souls onboard were what he might consider to be his equals. Of those two, Misleh had reciprocated his approval through the development of their friendship. The other – the captain – remained enigmatic. The fact that Traver had not yet won her over remained a thorn in his side. For him, the journey would not be over until he could somehow communicate with her, convince her of his value and find her vulnerability. She was the last of the *Aten's* mysteries.

First Officer Akachi was not so stingy with his presence, continuing to visit the passengers with more regularity as time went by. Traver avoided him when he could, but there were only so many places where he could hide. Even from across the corridor, Akachi's deep voice would bellow out from a cabin as he laughed, recited and sometimes sang. What was more unfortunate, Dr. Misleh seemed to thoroughly enjoy listening to Akachi; he would stare at the officer with eyes wide and mouth agape during his stories or jiggle with uncontrollable laughter during his jokes. If spending time with Misleh meant spending time with Akachi, Traver knew it was a sacrifice he'd begrudgingly make.

His mind always wandered when Akachi was talking. He'd find his mind's eye occupied with abstract, imagined shapes that danced and exploded, growing large and infinitesimally small at the same time while existing in all the colors of the wheel and more besides. He didn't know where the shapes came from or what they meant, but he saw them – felt them – more and more often, and not only during Akachi's storytimes. They came to him when he drifted off to sleep, when he exercised, or whenever his mind was not otherwise occupied. He never stopped to analyze them or wonder about them, but they made him feel violent.

It was because his mind had drifted that, one cycle after dinner, he was blissfully unaware of Akachi's current tale about the time he'd saved a drunk and lascivious member of the First Norwegian Family from a group of Martian ex-convicts while stationed in the failed city of Graceland – himself off-duty and also drunk. To the chagrin of everyone else in the cabin, Akachi was not able to finish the story before Traver snapped back to reality, looked dazedly at Akachi and said the first thing that came to his mind.

"Why are you here?"

"What?" Akachi was still grinning, though the jollity in the room ground to a halt.

"I was given the impression that our pilots would remain apart from the crew. Both of them. What makes you different from the captain?"

There was neither a hint of rudeness in his voice nor scowl on his face. Traver's inquiry seemed honest enough, if strangely-timed.

Akachi replied in good humor. "The captain and I are different people. She likes the silence, I like the company. None of us are prisoners onboard our ship, are we?"

"But we are forbidden from talking with you, or engaging with you, or entering the cockpit without your instigation. Cooperative Code, we were told. Is it fair to the passengers that your freedom extends to our cabins while ours is limited?"

Akachi straightened up and moved back, his mouth falling open in mirthful disbelief. "If I am not welcome in the cabins, that is something I should know, and I will leave!"

Gasps of "no, of course not" came from the other inhabitants of the room.

Traver kept his eyes trained on the first officer. "I just want our positions to be clear, according to the official Cooperative rules. We, the passengers, know our boundaries. What are yours?"

The brightness that shone from Akachi's dark face never faded, but it was clear that Traver was wearing on his nerves. "I understand what you are asking. The Cooperative protects their pilots, that is all. That is why there are precautions to keep the passengers from interfering with our duties. But there are no requirements to keep us in the cockpit, or apart from our guests."

"Actually –" A timid voice spoke up unexpectedly, and all heads turned to see that Lance was its source – "they do frown on too much familiarity. At least, that's what I remember."

A pause followed, during which Akachi's grin nearly faded.

Traver encouraged Lance to continue: "How do you remember?"

Lance went on. "It was one of the things that kept me back from going on to pilot school, even though I qualified. It was the only reason, really, otherwise I would be an officer by now, probably."

A knowing simper came to Akachi's face. "So you wanted to be a pilot?"

"Yeah. I guess it wasn't very realistic or anything. I used to read all about Sova, and Merrickson was my biggest hero of all. I just wanted to make jumps as far as I could go and see star systems nobody had seen before. But then I studied the Cooperative. It's not all so much of an adventure as I used to think it was."

"You should not have let the Cooperative discourage you. That is what they try to do: overwhelm you with the rules and regulations until you give up. It's how they thin the ranks of their cadets so that only the strong become pilots. But once you are in, look! We have more freedom than they said we would have."

"I don't know about that." Lance spoke with the sad nostalgia that usually accompanies memories of missed opportunities. "I studied the Code. I spoke with Cooperative veterans. I even heard a talk by Admiral Sova. All the emphasis is on isolation. Members aren't allowed to be married; they need to live alone even when they're off duty. I got the impression that anyone who wasn't able to handle that sort of loneliness wasn't going to ever make it to a captain's rank. You're not there yet, Officer."

"No. No, I am not." Even Akachi sounded wistful.

Traver broke in to the silence that followed. "If it's promotion you're hoping for, perhaps you would have better luck following the captain's example, and respecting the segregation."

Now the first officer laughed, but the laughter was subdued unlike his usual boisterousness. "Perhaps I would. Perhaps you are right. Can I help it if I am not like Louisa?"

Traver fumed. *Louisa.* Akachi dared to use her first name?

"Can I help that I do not agree with everything that comes from the Cooperative Code? Our founders believed that isolation should be strengthened instead of relieved, so that a captain all alone in a cockpit for years at a time will not miss the company of other people, and so won't go mad with loneliness. Perhaps this is true. I have never made a solo trip, so maybe I would not know about that."

"I had a different impression," said Lance, his investment in the conversation making him no longer timid. "I thought the isolation was meant as protection. The Pilot's Cooperative was founded in 'forty-eight as a way to monitor all space travel, stop illegal departures and prevent the sort of unethical science experiments that caused the Pilots' Strike. Since the captain and officers need to maintain the rule of law, they need to be completely impartial. A captain without any human ties can't be bought or sold. I guess my interpretation of the Cooperative's place in history was, simply put, that the isolation keeps the pilots honest."

Traver could not help but smile, not at Lance's neurotic excitement but at Akachi's troubled face.

The officer looked at Lance for a long moment then looked down at the floor. He forced the grin back to his face and again looked around the room.

"I think we might both be right, you and I. Maybe there are lots of good reasons for the officers to keep to themselves. But between all of us, what is there to worry about? We are all friends, no? No unethical science experiments going on, that I should know about?" He laughed heartily again, missing the glance, unreciprocated, that Dr. Marin turned toward Misleh.

Traver could only smile. He knew that the passengers would be seeing much less of Nelson Akachi after this conversation.

And he was right. Neither Akachi nor Fletcher was anywhere to be seen for a period of a month or more; he never visited the cabins while she never made any announcements.

The effect of their silence on the passengers was not a good one. Eager expectancy turned into nervous premonition as the journey neared what must be its final approach. While there was no diminishment in the cabin dinners, the gatherings grew quieter with the surge in anticipation. The less the crew conversed and laughed, the more they imagined the green planet as it must soon appear visible from the cockpit. They longed to see AMA but also dreaded it. Even though all were grounded men, many with their roots in hard science, they were not immune to the irrational fears that affect a mind so far away from familiarity. In their thoughts, the technology was fading away, along with the pilots, the corporations, the ship itself. They became a group of wide-eyed humans whizzing through infinite space toward a goal that hadn't fully been defined, but which would surely yield boundless reward in enlightenment or terror.

Or perhaps it wasn't the whole company of passengers that saw things that way. Maybe it was only one.

* * *

It was a "night cycle," when the lights were dimmed and most of the passengers were asleep. The occupants of Traver's cabin were all slumbering soundly when the door's alert sounded.

Karl leaped out of bed, floating toward the ceiling before pushing off to answer the door. Traver also woke up. "Who is it? We're asleep" he chided.

"Captain Fletcher. May I come in?"

Karl froze, drifting sideways through the room like a shaped balloon. Traver froze too, though he hadn't left his bunk. Lance just snored.

"Is this a good time?"

Too many seconds had passed since her initial declaration, and Karl, the first to unfreeze (after bumping the floor with his head), panicked to make up for lost time. "Yes, it's a good time. Right, Mister Graff? I'm coming to the door. Just give us a moment or two, if you please. We don't mean to...we don't want to keep you waiting!"

Traver, meanwhile, dove out of bed for a change of clothes, unwilling to be seen by Louisa in his coverall pajamas. He reached out and gave Lance a quick shake.

Thirty seconds later, the three occupants of the room were fully dressed, the beds were straightened and the lights were on.

Karl opened the door.

Fletcher was in her pilot's uniform. It would not have surprised the passengers if it was the only set of clothes she possessed, self-cleaning and self-ironing. Akachi had at least appeared garbed in variations on "well-dressed" – that's how they knew he was human. Fletcher had yet to prove that she identified with the species.

She looked in for a few silent moments, her eyes surveying them and the room with a distant but steady gaze that might have been distrust. *This is a step down for her*, Traver contemplated. *We're just passengers, not usually worth her time.* Suddenly Traver thought less of her. He saw that in her self-importance, Fletcher was fragile. Unlike Akachi, she could never survive a world that wasn't insulated, that wasn't of her own design.

"This is unexpected, Captain! But you're welcome." Traver initiated the conversation, to prevent the silence from becoming uncomfortable.

"I wanted to find you during a quiet time. It's my understanding that you've all become very fond of sharing spaces, roaming from cabin to cabin."

"Yes, we have. It's been that way for some time. The first officer has joined us occasionally."

"But I'm only hoping to speak with you. Here, or wherever is convenient."

She looked directly at Traver now, as if the others in the room didn't cross her mind (or exist at all). She shut her mouth tightly and widened her eyes slightly with expectation. She would not be the next one to speak.

So Traver said "Karl, Lance, maybe you could step out for a minute or two?"

Lowering their heads respectfully, they both slipped out past the captain, who still neither looked at them nor shifted aside to make their passage through the narrow door any easier. The moment they were outside, Fletcher moved in and shut the door behind her.

Traver started to say something along the lines of "*What's the occasion? I wasn't aware of your making cabin calls before, so I have to assume this is important.*" He only made it as far as "What —" when Fletcher began.

"You have not transmitted in more than a month."

Traver froze, his mouth still shaped to form the beginning of the word "*occasion.*"

It had crossed his mind that the pilots would have some faint awareness of his cessation in broadcasts, but his conclusion had simply been that they wouldn't care. They must have more important things on their minds.

"No. I haven't."

"You have an agreement with the Aurora Corporation, which also contracted me."

"Yes, I do."

Traver was caught. He had a very brief moment to decide whether to tell her the whole truth or to make the self-destructive decision and let her go on believing that he'd simply given up. The fact that he'd played a fast-and-loose game with his contractor – with her contractor too – might not sit well with her. Despite the amount of thought he'd given to the brief moments he'd been able to study her, he still had no idea what kind of person she was, whether she had anything like a sense of humor, or whether she was a stickler to the law's letter. This conversation began to enlighten him as to the likely answers to those questions.

Before he was able to move forward with the lie, he reminded himself that she had likely still been receiving transmissions from Weston. She'd probably been viewing them, and as a result was already aware of the whole truth, including whatever the state of affairs must be at the SASH after Traver's recent round of bombshells.

Fletcher pulled herself into Lance's chair, which was closest to the door, and tossed a seat-strap over her shoulder. Grounding herself in the room while Traver floated by his bunk gave her an even greater sense of authority than the uniform already lent.

"Can you offer an explanation?"

In the moment, Traver didn't feel like a passenger or a guest. He felt like a subordinate officer answering for some failure in the performance of his duty.

"I recorded them all already. My final transmission last month consisted of the entire set of broadcasts I agreed to."

Fletcher nodded slowly to herself, her eyes never leaving Traver's face. *She doesn't blink either*, Traver couldn't help noticing.

"You're a passenger on my ship because you agreed to operate on a weekly basis while onboard."

"I have taken a liberty with the details of the schedule. Not everyone might agree with my decision. But I don't believe I've violated my terms in any way. Weekly broadcasts have been transmitted from space, as my contract required."

Fletcher's response was immediate. "I am not in the habit of giving free rides. What's more, I do not tolerate the presence of useless individuals on my ship. If you have performed the entire duty for which you're here, then tell me: what is your use?"

Coldness crept through Traver's body, starting at the back of his head and moving downward and out. When he felt it in his fingers he had to check to make sure they weren't shaking.

But he had no answer for her.

Again she nodded, this time aiming her eyes away from him and toward the floor, which she appeared to find more interesting.

"It's not my intention to frighten you." *Could she tell I was frightened? Was I?* "I want you to understand your current position."

"You mean, namely, that I don't have one?"

It was a good enough retort to make Fletcher look at him again. It might have been Traver's imagination, but a hint of a smile seemed to flit across her lips and then disappear.

"They told me you'd most likely die onboard, before we even reached our destination." It burned his pride a little, but what else had he expected?

"Who told you that? My society, or your corporation?"

"Aurora is not mine, any more than the Secular Alliance is yours. They had to convince me to let you onboard, just as you needed to be convinced to come. In my case, they used your short life expectancy as a selling point."

"And did it work?"

"Yes."

It wasn't the conversation he'd anticipated having with the captain, but it was honest. Nothing was being held back.

"What do you do, when somebody dies onboard?" It was the next thing that came to mind, and he had to say something.

Her pause was lengthy. She looked back down at the floor. "That depends," she said softly.

He thought to ask for clarification, but saw that she was planning to continue.

"It depends on the person who dies, and how."

The coldness resurged over Traver's aching body.

Fletcher went on: "Aurora wants their employees brought home, and we oblige where we can. But the captain can make a determination as to whether the energy spent in preserving the corpse is worth the trouble. One deciding factor can be the physical condition of the body; has it been burnt, mauled beyond recognition? Then returning it to Earth won't be of any benefit for anyone. A second consideration is as simple as this: did the deceased have loved ones? How many? Are they prominent, influential? Those decisions lie with the captain, but there is always politics involved. Whenever possible, as we do with all Cooperative members like ourselves, we set adrift those who pass – it saves valuable resources. In the ship's aft there is a jettison tube for that purpose."

Traver felt that the answer had somehow been directed at himself. "And what about passengers? Guests who are neither Aurora nor Cooperative?"

Fletcher still didn't look at him. "The decision lies with the captain."

There was no clause in his contract with regard to the fate of his remains, should he not survive long enough to come home alive. He had no reason to particularly care, but he couldn't help finding the idea of being bodily committed to space troubling. The thought had never occurred to him that his physical body might never return to Earth. Somehow he'd always been sure that it would.

It didn't matter now. He had moved the conversation away from its origin point, and that was a shaky win for him. "Thank you for the clarification, on several points."

She unbuckled herself from the seat and drifted toward the door. She reached to open it. "I can't remove you from my ship. But it's no longer my duty to keep you onboard. Consider this a conundrum of your own making."

Traver spoke before she could reach the door handle. "What do you think of me?"

She paused and withdrew her hand from the door. She turned to him, pivoting in the air.

"It's beyond my professional purview to answer that sort of question, Mister Graff."

He'd never heard her say his name before. He liked it.

"Then let me answer it for you. You find me to be a waste of space and a blowhard. I'm a leading figure in an industry that relies on empty shock value in order to retain an audience. I've likely never done anything actually useful or noteworthy my entire life. I'm self-centered and self-aggrandizing. As far as you're concerned, Eams is just evolution's way of eliminating pathetic individuals like myself who would have died at a much younger age if it weren't for the comforts afforded by modern society – comforts that are a result of the very enterprises that I've been rewarded for trying to demolish."

Now a smile actually came across Louisa Fletcher's face. She looked straight at Traver.

"You really do like to talk a lot."

And she opened the door and vanished into the dim corridor.

Hate. That was what filled Traver's head, overflowed through his ears and over his eyes, so that he neither saw nor heard Karl and Lance when they came back into the cabin, bewildered by the captain's sudden visit and curious for an explanation. He was unaware of himself going to the gym apparatus, his muscle memory driving him. He was unaware of the hours that passed, his body mechanically pushing beyond its previous limits. He didn't feel pain, and he was nonreactive to the prompts of his concerned assistants.

The only thing visible in his mind's eye was Fletcher's face as he'd seen it in the moment before she turned away. Light wrinkles beside her eyes – low, center-parted hairline – cheeks a healthy tan complexion, clinging tightly to her face. She wouldn't be considered a great beauty by most standards, but she displayed a handsomeness and craft that made her more irresistible than any charm.

But the smile. Her winning smile, accompanying the words that drove him into the ground, was both breathtaking and infuriating.

At some point, he fell asleep. Lance and Karl gingerly strapped him into his bunk and, relieved, returned to their own slumbers.

When he awoke, Traver had only a very blurred memory of the conversation that had taken place. It had no more effect on his mood than a light nightmare might have had. He went about preparing his breakfast in thoughtful silence and spent some more time on the gym apparatus. Lance and Karl never got answers about the captain's visit. Once Traver had woken and his emotional blockade had fallen away, they didn't dare ask again.

Traver presently left the cabin and began to wander the corridor, hoping that some interesting member of the scientist team would come along and strike up a conversation. He gradually worked his way from the mid section of the ship, through the antechamber and into the aft corridor. There he got the conversation he was looking for, and more.

Among the scientists, excitement was a palpable presence in the air. Unlike Traver and his crew, they'd been painstakingly counting the hours until AMA-712, and their countdown was nearing completion. There'd been no word from the pilots, but no news was good news and they were expecting their first sighting of the planet within a week's time.

"What it must look like from the cockpit..." Misleh mused longingly. He seemed glad to find Traver.

"The planet?"

"Yes. They can probably see it. A tiny green dot now, but growing. Maybe they can even see the circle outlined against the blackness beyond."

"I'm surprised they haven't invited you into the cockpit to see it."

"Eh. I'll see it soon enough. I shouldn't be too impatient."

"I think they should ask you. You're the expert. You're the one who's spent your whole life studying it. Shouldn't you be among the first to see it?"

Misleh's face scrunched inward almost comically, becoming something nearly unrecognizable as a face beneath the untrimmed hair that covered his cheeks. "We might not even be near it yet. If we're only a little behind schedule, then they can't see it from the cockpit and we're excited prematurely. That's very possible."

"You could go ask them." Traver was watching Misleh's expressions very closely. By now he felt he could read them, teddy-bear-like as they were, a little better than before.

Now, Misleh's expression said *If there is a chance of seeing my planet, then with all my heart, yes!* But his voice instead said "No. When the time is right, they will tell me. It's not my place."

"It is exactly your place. I'll go with you. I'll do the talking, if it would put you more at ease."

Misleh's face deadened completely, his eyes looking with some longing toward the front of the corridor – the direction of the mystical cockpit – while his cheeks and mouth fell slack, the loose skin puffing out in the gravity-free environment.

"Come on" Traver said, and reached for the ceiling rungs to pull himself forward through the corridor.

"How are *you* feeling, Traver?" Misleh's question was little more than a loud whisper that carried all the way to where Traver now drifted inside the antechamber.

It caught Traver off guard. He stopped himself and turned around. "Me?"

"Yes, you. We're getting closer to the planet now. Are you anxious at all? Feeling different? Irregular thoughts?"

It was strangely touching; Traver had never heard the scientist inquire about his own health. Nevertheless he was confused. "Doctor Marin has asked me about my health on a regular basis. My answer is always the same: I'm feeling fine."

"Yes. I speak often with Doctor Marin. But I wanted to speak with you. Perhaps if there are symptoms you have not been comfortable discussing with him, you might tell me? Especially now, as we approach AMA."

Traver was not interested in discussing his condition. He'd put it out of his mind for too long, and to address it in-depth with Misleh would remove the spark of excitement from their friendship.

"As I said, I am feeling wonderful. But we *are* approaching AMA, and I think now is as good a time as any to see if the pilots will let you into the cockpit to see it. Follow me!"

Mostly, Traver was itching to approach the cockpit once again with confidence. After the conversation he'd had with Fletcher, he longed to see the look on her face when he reached the open door accompanied by the most important of her passengers, demanding he be allowed inside. He only hoped Misleh would follow him.

He moved through the open door leading through the antechamber, then through the next door into the forward corridor before turning back to see if Misleh had moved with him.

But he would never know whether Misleh planned to follow.

He was hit by a noise and a flash.

The noise hit him before the light did. Instantaneous as a gunshot but a thousand times louder, he felt it rather than heard, as if two hammers were swung down on both ears at once.

Then the flash came from the corridor behind him. Even though he hadn't fully turned around, the brightness was enough to blind him.

He was hurled backwards from the antechamber. His head slammed against a handle-rung in the ceiling.

Within a half-second, the nearer door between corridors had slammed itself shut, cutting Traver off from the source of the chaos in which Misleh had been caught.

His pupils had rapidly constricted in the extreme light, so in the dim corridor he now found himself in what seemed complete darkness. His ears rang incessantly. His body went limp. He drifted by the door, waiting. Waiting for something, anything else to happen. He was incapable of moving anywhere on his own.

Utterly numb to the passage of time, Traver didn't know how long he waited. It was no more than a minute.

Akachi appeared out of the darkness, his voice fading in and out through the buzzing in Traver's ears. "Are you hurt, Mister Graff?" was the sum of the sounds Traver could make out, though the meanings of words themselves were unclear to him.

Traver squinted at the first officer, who finally gave up shouting and instead took the smaller man by his shoulders and spun him around in the air, giving him a cursory look over. The shoulder-length hair on the back of Traver's head, usually so carefully attended-to, had been partly burned away, and the back of his shirt was charred. No matter; Akachi was satisfied that there were no harmful burns or abrasions. "Don't move too quickly. Your senses will recover." Traver didn't understand the meaning of these words either.

Lance and Karl had rushed out of their cabin at the sound. Their confused voices added to the cluster of noises that was building in the corridor's tiny atmosphere. An alarm was sounding through the intercoms of the ship while vaguely electric-sounding pops and buzzes could be heard from behind the closed door.

Then the cabin across the corridor opened and the doctors emerged: Philip Marin in the front, leading the concerned and agitated trio. It only bewildered them more to see that Akachi was not dressed in his normal uniform, but in a protective suit that made him appear even taller and bulkier than his regular stature.

Akachi was the only one to speak coolly and with purpose. Though he didn't raise his voice, its clarity was enough to separate his from the rest and to make him instantly heard. "Take Mister Graff inside his cabin. Doctor Marin, take a look at him and see that he's alright. Everyone else, go back inside and shut the doors. Do not open the doors no matter what you hear, until I come and tell you to."

His command of the situation was such a relief to the fragile and frightened minds around him that they had no choice but to obey right away. Traver, now contracted into the fetal position, was whisked away by Karl and Dr. Marin, and with Lance they vanished into their cabin, shutting the door. The doctors followed suit into their own room.

What none of them saw was Akachi breathing deeply and shaking his limbs, as a sports player shakes to loosen his extremities. Then he reached into a compartment above the antechamber door and produced an oxygen mask equipped with a small tank. The tank he strapped around the back of his neck while he cupped the mask to his face. Over his head he pulled the hooded portion of his suit, and sealed it tightly at the neck. He performed this equipping with near superhuman speed. Then he waited.

He had put on his suit hurriedly, neglecting to enable his suit's transmitter. So when Fletcher's order came, it broadcast over the general intercom. Her voice was shaky, unsure – a different Fletcher than even Akachi had ever seen or heard: "You're clear, Nelson." He opened the door and stepped through into the antechamber. In front of him was the second door, still providing a seal against pressure and oxygen leaks between sections. He waited for the first door to shut behind him. Then Akachi opened the second.

The sight that met the first officer's stern, dark eyes was a blackened corridor that had once been white. The grills in the floor and ceiling, vents for the dispersion of oxygen and pressurization, were quite melted. Molten drops of metal floated in the air, slowly hardening as they cooled, bouncing harmlessly off Akachi's suit by the time he passed them.

The door slammed shut behind him though he couldn't hear it. The corridor was utterly silent – eerie, even for a man with Akachi's nerves. The air had been emptied out of the compartment by Fletcher's controls, rendering sound dead.

It was the doors in the aft to which Akachi looked first. The door leading to the lab was shut. That was good. The one leading to the scientists' cabin was shut. That was better. The door to the medical bay housing the doctors' equipment and Traver's injection gear was blasted, jittering back and forth on its tracks, trying to shut but having no luck.

Something black floated in front of Akachi's face while he approached the doors slowly. He knew it was the diminished and charred remains of a human being. He gritted his teeth. One passenger lost was too many. Perhaps he was not a perfectly selfless pilot, but as an officer he would have been more than willing to give his own life rather than have the fatality count increase to two.

He made his way to the door of the scientists' cabin. It was still shut, having been locked as part of the emergency protocol. Part of the reason Fletcher had kept the power on, running the risk of additional sparks, was to keep that door locked. Should the power be shut off the locks would disengage and the scientists, if still alive, would have the ability to open the door into the suffocating vacuum of the corridor. If they were still alive at all.

Akachi knew he would need to open the door, but feared what he would find inside. The readings on the cockpit consoles had indicated the fire as only being in the aft corridor and medical bay, before the sensors had been destroyed. The readings still declared the passenger cabin was safe, but he didn't know whether to trust those readings.

His hand trembling, he entered the code to override the safety locks, and opened the door. He slipped inside the tiny pressure chamber, shut the first door and waited for the pressure to normalize.

It did. He breathed a huge sigh of relief and opened the second door. The scientists were confused by the ruckus and angry at having been locked in, but they were alive. The room was intact and the occupants were breathing.

Quick as a snake the first officer whipped into the room and shut the door behind him. He unsealed his mask, then seven questioning voices all emerged at once from the silence.

He commanded the chaos by answering their jumbled questions with a question of his own. "Is everyone accounted for?"

"Doctor Misleh. Doctor Misleh is out there. Did you see him? Did anyone see Doctor Misleh?"

Akachi knew now who the charred, miniature leftovers of a corpse belonged to, but there would be no advantage in alarming the survivors. Action was next.

"Please calm yourselves. Breathe deeply! There has been a fire. No cabins were affected, and that is very good. But you need to move out from the aft to the next corridor, because we do not know how well the systems back here withstood the blast."

He succeeded in calming them to the point where they could act in an organized fashion, directing them to put on the safety suits which were stowed in a compartment against the wall.

While they donned the suits, he opened a second compartment to reveal the eight oxygen tanks contained within. Each tank, he knew, was connected via plug into the air duct system of the ship, to maintain a constant pressure in each tank over the passage of time. This connection had not served well for the present circumstances, and each tank was red-hot, the oxygen burning from the inside. If the explosion in the corridor had not relieved the bulk of the pressure, these tanks would have blown already from the heat.

He pushed the door's blue button to activate the intercom and connect with the cockpit. "Captain, you need to turn off the air to the aft cabin." No response. "Captain!" Nothing. The explosion must have knocked out the comms to this part of the ship.

Akachi turned back to the scientists.

"There's no more time. The fire has reached the air system in your room. You each need to take my oxygen tank. One by one I will escort you out, but quickly!"

He took the oxygen tank from his neck and attached it to the oldest of the scientists, Dr. Friedrich. Without much gentleness he pushed the scientist into the chamber between doors, where their bodies were tightly crammed. Taking a deep gulp of air, Akachi held his breath and opened the next door. The chamber was swept clean of pressure and oxygen, and Friedrich would have been suctioned out uncontrollably if Akachi was not holding him tightly. Still holding his breath, he began to navigate through the flickering corridor, scientist in tow.

It took a full minute for Akachi and Friedrich to reach the mid antechamber door, and an additional twenty seconds for Akachi to open the doors and deposit Friedrich to safety.

"Stay here. I'll come back." And Akachi, retrieving the oxygen mask, was gone again.

Six more times he made the breathless trip up the corridor, each time with a scientist in his grasp, each time hoping that the people he rushed to safety would be too distracted to recognize Misleh's remains for what they were – if they did recognize it, he hoped they would be too level-headed to panic.

The aft cabin still had not caught flame by the time Dr. Bjornson, the last scientist, was pulled out, though the air was palpably heating. Akachi left the cabin door open as he pushed away.

Lungs straining, Akachi pushed Bjornson into the antechamber, one door away from his six confused collaborators, then he moved inside the door himself.

Just before he reached for the button to shut the door maybe for the last time, a flame licked out of the scientists' cabin at the far end of the corridor. Bits of beds, books, clothes and other paraphernalia shot out into the corridor, but were not fast enough to escape being engulfed in the inferno that followed after them.

Dr. Bjornson watched in awe at the sight for the millisecond during which he and the officer witnessed the second explosion. Then Akachi shut the door before the blast wave could hit them.

CHAPTER SEVEN
AFT

While the first officer was foregoing oxygen for the sake of the scientists, Traver recovered his senses in his cabin. First he began to recognize the faces around him, and then the words coming out of them. Once he'd accurately processed his surroundings, the memories came back. Then he lurched forward from where Dr. Marin had sat him down. "Abrahim…Abrahim was behind me. Something happened in the corridor!" He stumbled up and pushed his way toward the door, which Lance and Karl dutifully blocked.

"Officer Akachi says we should stay inside." Karl's voice was shaking. "I think an accident might have happened."

"Maybe I can help. Maybe Abrahim needs a hand, and I can help!"

"Not in your condition. You have a mild concussion from the blast wave." Marin joined the others in blocking Traver's way to the door.

As if the doctor's newsflash made him aware of pain, he raised his hand to his head, grimacing as the adrenaline faded and the throbbing headache began. But when his hand brushed the back of his head and discovered the swaths of crispy or missing hair, his old vanity returned. Depression took hold of him faster than he could process the realization, and his body went limp.

"What happened?" he murmured over and over again, as his helpers pushed him back into his bed and strapped him in. They didn't have an answer for him.

The next three hours the passengers spent in silent bewilderment, waiting impatiently for an update. The scientists had been herded by Akachi into the doctors' quarters while the doctors now waited in Traver's.

Fletcher's first move had been to cut off the air and power to the entire aft section of the ship once Akachi had apprised her of the situation. Then she and her first officer spent the next several hours geared in their protective suits and masks, treading through the wreckage of the ship's aft and investigating each burnt out vent, each hot spot where the explosion had been at its most intense. They searched for the source of the explosion. When they'd found it, Akachi took pains to find all the remaining pieces of Dr. Abrahim Misleh, which he wrapped in a thermal blanket until something more permanent could be done with him.

Finally the intercom alerted all the passengers. It was Akachi, his voice more pert than they were used to hearing. "Gather in the fore corridor. All passengers."

Sheepishly the passengers streamed out of their two remaining cabins. Nobody knew fully what to expect. The scientists, having at least seen the aftermath of the disaster, still had no idea what had gone wrong or what it meant. Those in Traver's cabin were even more lost in bewilderment. Traver's feverish mention of a "flash" was not sufficiently descriptive.

"There has been an accident."

Both Akachi and the captain stood at the cockpit's bulkhead door, while the thirteen other occupants of the vessel gathered in front of them. Some were nervously shaking, others were more stoic.

By now all of them knew, or at least suspected through the power of rumor, that Dr. Misleh was gone. That was true despite the fact that none of the scientists, all too panicked and confused during their trip through the disastrous corridor, had spotted the corpse and recognized it for what it was.

As for Traver, he was calm now. He hadn't spoken a word for hours. He'd recovered from the shock of losing his hair, but behind his calm demeanor the moment of the flash was replaying. *He'd pulled ahead of Misleh, then turned, then* boom. *He'd pulled ahead of Misleh, then turned, then* boom. Could he have done something different? Could he have changed the outcome, stopped the explosion? Could he have saved Misleh? No. Of course not. But he could, yes, he could have died himself. He just somehow hadn't.

Fletcher spoke slowly, subdued anger making its way through her smooth and authoritative voice. "A fire originated in the medical bay. Probably the injection machine for the treatment of Eams, overheating or shorting out during a diagnostic routine. A spark got into the vent system and set the air on fire. Everyone on board, not only you passengers who were in the aft at the time, are extremely fortunate to be alive, and that the fire did not spread before it could be caught. Doctor Abrahim Misleh was not so fortunate, as he was caught in the corridor at the time of the blast. It would have been instant and painless."

The murmurs, the increased shaking, the pained faces of those listening made it clear that the instantaneous nature of his death was not a comfort they were hoping for, but she went on.

"His remains are reposed in the aft bay for the present. In twenty hours we will hold a service for him and release him out of the ship.

"For the rest of us, the most pressing issue is the oxygen. The fire did unfortunately reach one of the aft reserve tanks. After everything has been added up, we've lost thirty percent of our air supply for the journey."

Some of the murmurs turned into moans, none of them intelligible.

Traver shut his eyes. He'd stared at Fletcher's stern face for long enough. She had avoided glancing at him.

"I should make clear that we did have a surplus. While we have lost a good deal of our total supply, we still have enough to reach our destination and return, with an orbit around AMA-712 lasting three months. But in the interest of not cutting our supply too close, I will by no means orbit for longer than two."

The scientists shook their heads.

"That said, I personally do not believe the mission's completion to be our best course of action."

Traver's eyes shot wide open.

"A damaged ship should alone be cause to turn back immediately, and the only reason I might consider extending our travel time is because we are so close already to our destination. Of course, Doctor Misleh's tragic demise will seriously undermine the value of the research, according to my understanding."

The scientists all spoke at once, though none managed to make themselves heard. The captain held up her hand.

"If you wish to correct me, you will have a chance to do so before I make a final decision. After the service for Doctor Misleh we will discuss this again. In the meantime, we will all take appraisals of our situation so we can approach the decision with a level-headed sense of responsibility. The lab is intact, and I know you consider yourselves fully capable of performing the research necessary to the mission; but honestly ask yourselves whether, at this juncture, that research would be worth the considerable risk of spending eight more months in space. As for Mister Graff and company, keep in mind that the injection machine was completely destroyed. There can be no more treatments for your condition."

If Traver heard what she said, he didn't show it. He was still staring at her, and for a brief moment she finally returned the gaze.

Then she nodded at Akachi, who was brooding beside her but alert as ever, a true force of reckoning for any passenger who might panic and get out of hand. She turned toward the cockpit and the first officer had the last words: "The damaged part of the ship will remain inaccessible. Distribute yourselves between the two remaining cabins in whatever way you find to be comfortable."

Fletcher opened the cockpit door, and something caught the eyes of the passengers closest to the starboard side of the corridor, Traver among them. From their angle, they could see a bright green dot, lost amid the infinite stars but separate, more prominent. Angelic. AMA.

Traver's thoughts stopped.

Seeing it even as a speck hanging in space was better than all the telescope images in the world. It was separated from their eyes only by a pane of glass a few centimeters thick. Every bizarre theory about the planet, every wishful hope for discovery came to vibrant and fantastical life in the minds of those who saw it for that brief moment (Traver among them).

Then the door shut. The vision disappeared from their eyes, if not from their minds.

The pilots left them on their own to disperse, to discuss and to despair.

They neither dispersed nor discussed. The thirteen souls hung in the hallway, looking like their programming had been shut off; a baker's dozen of empty robots stalled and waiting to be reactivated.

Fletcher's announcement had been maddeningly inconclusive. That the mission would be cut short was certain. But, how short was it being cut? As to whether they would make it to AMA at all, was she leaving that decision to them, or had she already made her own? More importantly, how much danger were they *really* in of something *else* going wrong?

Those were the thoughts madly racing through the minds of all but Traver. Traver was calm. He had seen his light at the end of the dark tunnel. Everything would be alright. He knew that the right decision would be made, that they would continue on until they reached Misleh's magnificently mysterious planet. After that, nothing mattered.

He shut his eyes again.

Those around him finally began to stir. Their stirrings became movement and their mumbles became speech, and they spilled back into their rooms.

"Come on, boss. You feeling alright?" Traver didn't respond to Lance. But he opened his eyes and turned suddenly with a motion that caught his assistants by surprise. In the blink of an eye he had moved past them and vanished into his cabin. Lance and Karl shrugged at one another and followed him. Inside, they found him hard at work on the gym.

Within the hour, Dr. Marin rejoined them from his own cabin, where he'd been holding conference with his assistants as well as the scientists (if indeed a subdued and dreary argument mixed with tears and sobbing could be called "conference").

He found the new company to be equally dreary but almost entirely silent. Traver had not spoken a word, and was still strapped in to the gym apparatus, working up a rainstorm of sweat. Karl and Lance sat by him.

Neither loyal assistant had any personal stake in the journey or the research, and as a result they felt awkward, out of place, and not a little bit lonely. It now became clear to both of them that, whatever camaraderie they'd established with the onboard professionals during the flight, there would be an inevitable point of separation – come the mission's success or failure, the scientists would become too preoccupied for their casual friendships. Turning around and heading home right now was a possible outcome that didn't sound at all bad to Lance and Karl. But in the hierarchy of the ship they were the peasants, so of course the only opinion to which they would have any right would be Traver's.

"How are you holding up, Mister Graff?" asked Marin, after first nodding in greeting to Lance and Karl, then determining that Traver was aware of his presence.

"I'm feeling good. Really good, especially considering the circumstances." Traver's reply was sudden and enthusiastic. So enthusiastic, thought Lance, that it almost didn't feel real.

"What are they talking about on your side of the ship?" He climbed out of the apparatus and folded it up, but did not put his shirt on. His muscles had returned to a shade of their former shape, and his presence in the room was not without intimidation.

"That's partly why I came over here. In addition to checking on you."

"Like I said, I'm fine. You don't have to worry about me, Doctor."

Dr. Marin frowned at him and rubbed his thin hands together unconsciously.

"We don't…we don't know what to do. Abrahim is going to be missed, more than I think we even realize. The scientists are putting a brave face on things, but they're going to have to admit they don't know where to start without him."

Now it was Traver's turn to frown. But it was more than a frown. It frightened Lance.

Marin went on. "But my concern is you. Your health is the reason I'm here. She mentioned it as an afterthought, but I think the captain should be putting much more priority on you at this point. This has quite possibly – and I won't mince words with you – this accident may have put your life at risk."

The moment of silence before Traver spoke was uncomfortably long.

"I'm alright now."

Marin smiled a bitter smile. "You may feel just wonderful, but Eams isn't going to retreat because you've increased your physical exercise, as beneficial as that is."

"You said I was fine now." Traver's response this time was quick. Too quick.

The doctor had to take a moment before he spoke. "The Eams was in remission, yes. Better than I've ever seen. But cure is still not really an option. This is not the time to stop treatments – this is the *worst* time to stop treatments. Ideally we should be pushing back against it now with more regularity than ever, doubling down on the amount of formula in your blood. Since we can't do that, our next best option is to get you back to Earth as soon as we possibly can."

A cold curtain fell over the room, invisible but tangible. It seemed to emanate from the shirtless figure who was now drifting above the others, lean and composed. His surviving long hair flowed around his head and he stared sternly at them like a judging god.

"Is that what you believe?"

Marin was nervous now, and his voice raised in pitch to betray that. "It would be in our – in your best interest. If Eams beats you, Mister Graff, I'll have failed in my job. That's both a personal and a professional concern. You're too valuable to lose, and for you to move closer to the planet without continued injections is just too uncertain a prospect..."

Traver was no longer listening. He'd heard all he needed to hear. Without further acknowledgment he turned back to the machine, unfolded it, and began to pump the weighted levers into the air. He stared emptily into blank space as if Marin had never so much as stepped in to the room.

The doctor sighed and looked helplessly at Lance and Karl. They looked helplessly back. Nor could they say anything to him, not with Traver haunting the cabin. Even if their master wasn't paying attention to them now, he would hear anything they had to say and carefully watch if they were to slip out for a more private conversation later.

When the doctor had finally given up and exited, Traver surprised both his companions by looking at them, then even more by pausing his exercises and speaking to them. He hadn't forgotten about their existence, though that was not entirely comforting.

"Do you agree with me?"

Neither knew how to respond. Lance, always the braver of the two, ventured a few words. "We aren't sure what you're thinking, to be honest." Karl followed this up with a nod and a shrug, meant to say about the same thing.

Traver nodded grimly, as if he expected such naiveté. "To die isn't failure. That's going to happen anyway. To fail would be to turn around before we get to that planet."

Karl nodded; "I'll agree with that," and then he looked at Lance for approval. Lance was silent.

"But I'm not worried," Traver smiled as he went on with his repetitions. "We'll get there. I have a good feeling about where we're headed."

Traver himself paid a visit to the scientists' cabin a few hours later. He was greeted by much of the same despondency he'd heard from Marin. Here in a room full of six scientists and three doctors he was vastly outnumbered, and far less intimidating.

"Forget about me for a moment, and my health. I knew the risks when I signed my contract with Aurora. The next few hours, these hours of decision, should be spent thinking of Abrahim, and what he would want."

"We *are* thinking of Abrahim." Dr. Friedrich was very nearly sobbing. He was the senior scientist and Misleh's secondary – a wealth of knowledge himself when it came to AMA's potential. "But that is the problem. He wrote volumes, bibles worth of literature on the planet: some speculation, some fact. None of us have even come close to that sort of enthusiasm."

"Then we should honor the work he did, by using the tools he gave us to continue his studies." Traver's use of the word "us" was noticed by one or two of the younger scientists, and it bothered them. Nevertheless they were even more bothered by the use of the first-person plural by Friedrich, whose implication of unanimous disinterest was more than a little insulting.

"Maybe Traver is right" chimed in Dr. Bjornson, the youngest of them all. "Maybe we shouldn't be so quick to throw away the research because we lost one member of the team."

Emboldened by his colleague, Dr. Zhang joined the defense: "We do have the credentials to continue the research. Maybe even a shorter orbit would be worthwhile. We could go back with something, instead of nothing."

"Not…not that I'm suggesting we overrule the captain," Bjornson quickly backtracked. "If it's not safe, then nothing is worth risking more lives."

Friedrich held his hand to his forehead, generally feeling over-whelmed. His voice shook now. "Traver, will you step out here with me?" and he motioned to the cabin's door.

Once they were alone in the corridor, Friedrich spoke in a hushed tone, as if relating the greatest of secrets. "You should try to under-stand, Mister Graff, it's not about what Abrahim left us to work with. It's about what he *didn't* leave us. The things he wrote down, many of them are observations anyone with a telescope and a college degree could make, if their mind is good enough. But the rest was in his head. The things he hoped to find out, they were too important to him to write."

"Did he never talk about them?"

"Always. He talked to no end."

"Then you should know what we're looking for."

"He talked *to no end.* Don't you see? Always he was developing new ideas. Always changing his mind, always imagining new things. I don't know the first thing about what was really going on up in his head. There was just too much that came out of it. Brilliant, all of it. But, too much."

"Find out what the planet is made of. That's what I gathered from my conversations with him. It seems simple enough to me."

"Yes. That much is simple. But where's the real value in that if we don't know how to interpret the results? This is what my young peers don't understand. Misleh's mind was operating on a level so far above the average, he was somewhere between brilliance and madness. He wanted to apply the findings to his theorems about the expanding universe – visualize the big bang – trace the chemical reactions that first sparked life. But I don't know how he was going to do any of those things. I could tell you if the atmosphere is mostly helium, I could estimate the planet's age, but I won't be able to change the known scientific landscape, as Abrahim could have done."

"You don't have any way of knowing that until we get there."

"Yes, I do." Friedrich's voice lowered to a shaky whisper, barely audible. "I know because the actual tests he meant to conduct are secret. Parts of his research were never disclosed to us. He worked closely with people at Aurora who don't exist to the rest of the world, and those are people I do not want to answer to without Abrahim. Understand? This is completely over my head, over any of our heads."

Friedrich's fear did not affect Traver. "We just need to see it. Whatever Misleh was hoping to find, it might be impossible to miss."

Now Friedrich tilted his head curiously, quizzicality in the narrowing of his eyes. "Like what? What do *you* think we'll find?"

The truth was that Traver had no idea how to respond in a way that Friedrich would respect. There was no scientific answer he could give. But then again, he wasn't interested in cheapening the subject with technical jargon. Misleh certainly wouldn't have.

"If you look at a human being under a microscope, you'll see a construct of carbon, a billion bouncing cells. You can study that, but you'll never know the person. To do that you need to take a step away, see the entirety of the thing. Then you can have a conversation and learn about it.

"Abrahim didn't have any idea what he was going to find on AMA, but he believed in it. That goes beyond science. Maybe the planet will be greater than the sum of its parts. Forget about the atmospheric makeup and step back. Maybe it'll speak to us."

Friedrich's mouth fell agape. His surprise was not one of awe, nor was it appreciation. People like him had never been part of Traver's target audience.

"Mister Graff...Doctor Abrahim Misleh was imaginative, and perhaps he did put an exaggerated faith into the object of his life's study. But even he didn't think we were going to find god."

* * *

Long after Friedrich returned to the doctors' cabin, Traver remained in the corridor. Again he was unaware of the passage of time. Again he was blind and deaf to anything around him. The only thing apparent to his mind's eye was Friedrich's thin ivory face, gawking, slightly smiling as if speaking cutely to a monkey in a zoo. *Poor, dumb Traver Graff*, the face seemed to say. "Even Abrahim didn't think we were going to find god."

How does he know?

How did he know?

Karl put a hand on Traver's shoulder, which brought the latter back to the present. "You should get some sleep. I wish you could see yourself right now."

Traver's exhaustion conquered over his pride.

The bunk was welcome after the recent events, which were more taxing on his body than he'd realized. His singed hair was not the only casualty of the explosion. His back and left side were covered in bruises from where the shock wave had thrown him into the corridor wall, and minor burns covered his right arm. If he could have seen himself, he would have seen a pale creature with dark, sunken eyes under which the skin had turned a shade of blue. He didn't know the last time he had slept, and even less when he'd last eaten. The rigorous hours he'd spent pushing his body to its physical limits had done more harm than good.

He locked himself into the bed and began to drift into sleep.

The hatred he had built up over the last twenty-four hours fell away, and so did his defenses. In their place, an overwhelming sadness splashed over him, then started to slowly cover him. He caught the glint of a tear in the air, drifting away from his eye.

"Is it my fault?"

"What?" Lance looked at him with gentle surprise.

"My treatment machine caused the explosion. If I wasn't onboard, Doctor Misleh would still be alive."

Lance got up. This version of Traver, vulnerable now, was a pleasant change from the intimidating one. Lance hadn't had the luxury of feeling confidence for some time, but here it was. "Is it your fault that you're sick?"

A pause, then: "no."

"Is it your fault that the *Aten* is an older ship, with slow auto failsafes that didn't lock down the air systems in time?"

Traver hadn't thought about that. "No."

"Anything can cause a spark. It could have just as easily been the lab equipment, or one of the gym machines. There's no way anybody could have predicted what happened, and there's nothing anyone could have done."

Traver was silent. But he hadn't fallen asleep.

Lance waited a moment before he said what he knew had to be said. If there was any time to say it, it was now.

"You know sir...you know we're going home, right?"

Traver was silent.

"I was talking to the others just now. Everyone thinks it's the best thing to do. It seems to be what the captain wants. And I know it's best for you. Frankly I've been a little worried about you. I don't think you could handle another eighteen months, even if you did have your treatments."

Traver was silent.

"I know you're not happy about it. I know it kind of throws the whole broadcast schedule into a weird light. The segments we sent to Weston might not have the exact effect you wanted them to have, if you come back halfway through. I get it. I know that makes you angry."

It hadn't. But it did.

But Traver was silent.

"We'll figure something out. We'll hide you from the public eye if we need to. There's a solution, I know. My point is, this isn't the end."

Lance stopped when he saw Traver's eyelids fall shut. He smiled to himself. He'd succeeded in talking Traver to sleep. Maybe he'd also succeeded in helping his boss come to terms with the unfortunate turn of events – even if it took several more of these conversations at times when Traver was vulnerable, Lance was more than happy to put forth the effort. Mostly, he was happy that, if the current tide stayed consistent, he would be going home.

But Traver hadn't fallen asleep.

Several hours passed. The silence in the cabin deadened into the lifeless quiet that takes over when a room is drained of human consciousness. The sense of deadness was nearly enough proof for Traver, but a snore from Lance convinced him that his bunkmates were asleep.

Out of the bunk he crept, gently letting himself drift to the door. It opened silently enough, and then shut behind him.

In the corridor he took a left – away from the locked-down aft and the other cabin – and pulled himself forward, through the fore antechamber and toward the sanctuary of the ship.

Somewhere inside Traver, his screaming had stopped. The endless torment, the circles of questions, the fears, the doubts, the hatred – all were silent. He moved with a singularity of purpose. He'd no notion what that purpose was, because thought was no longer driving him.

He reached the door. He buzzed the intercom and waited.

He'd never approached this door before while it was closed. A key reader, activated by keychips belonging only to the pilots, was the only apparent means to enter. Shut, it was impenetrable, a solid smooth gate with no gaps or ridges to indicate where or how it slid open. There could be no breaking in to the cockpit. Only three blemishes lay in the otherwise sleek surface: at waist level, two small dents and a scratch, the only evidence of what must have been a fearful bludgeoning. The history of the ship was colorful, and at one time, someone unlucky had tried to break into Fletcher's stronghold.

"Can I help you?" Akachi's voice through the intercom was terse already, and even more so now that the passenger was breaking sacred policy.

"I want to see Doctor Misleh."

The pause that followed was lengthy. He knew the pilots were discussing his request. Discussing him.

"The lab is not currently accessible. That part of the ship is inhabitable."

"I'm more than happy to wear a suit." Traver's voice was trembling. But he felt nothing.

Another pause. This one was briefer.

"I'm sorry. You will have the opportunity to pay your respects with the rest of the crew. The service is scheduled for seven hours from now." Akachi again.

"But we won't get to see him, will we?" His voice cracked. Tears welled in his eyes. But he felt nothing.

"I'm going to be painfully blunt with you, my friend. Seeing what is left of the good doctor will not put your mind in any state of peace. It's better that you and the rest of the passengers remember him as he was in life."

A tearful choke escaped from Traver. (Escaped? No – that would imply that it was not intended.)

"You'll need to return to your cabin now."

"I was the last person he spoke to. Did you know that? I was with him. I saw him just before...just before the flash of light hit him..." His words sputtered and trickled into gibberish. A hurricane of tear droplets circled from his eyes and around his head, trailing off toward the air vent.

Silence followed from the cockpit.

Traver's breath heaved, then gradually steadied. His next words were more measured. "I was thinking about what happened, and I think it's my fault. Without my being onboard, the treatment machine wouldn't have sparked the oxygen fire. My assistant tried to tell me I wasn't responsible – Lance really is a good friend – but he's wrong. It is my fault. I've been nothing but a thorn in your side this whole time, and now I've doomed the mission."

He paused for a moment, feeling nothing. Then he resumed: "I shouldn't even be here. I shouldn't have agreed to come up here. Even if I thought I was doing it for the right reasons, it was only to satisfy my ego. I wanted to feel good about myself before I died. But this isn't worth it. I want to go home."

A hint of surprise was then evident in the first officer's voice. "It is likely that we *are* going home."

There was a camera outside the cockpit door, by which the pilots were able to carefully monitor Traver's actions. But there was no way to observe the minuscule hardening of his face at that moment. The way his eyes deadened and his cheeks drew in – that, they could not see. So they didn't know anything but what his body language expressed: a breakdown of emotions so easily predicted at a time like this.

"I know. I've known for a while, but I fought it. I was angry. I was feeling too guilty to acknowledge it. But I don't want to be angry anymore. I don't want to cause any more stress onboard. Nobody deserves that now."

Fletcher's voice: "Your candor is appreciated. Unfortunately, now is no time for it."

"Just a minute with Misleh. It's the peace of mind I need."

"Mister Graff…"

"I'm…losing touch…my mind has been racing, I'm losing track of time. Doctor Marin says I'm going to be dead before I get home. I don't want to die like this! I don't want to die in space! I just want to say I'm sorry. I'm sorry to you, I'm sorry to…to Abrahim."

And he broke down again in tears.

A minute went by. Two minutes. Three. All was silent, except for the whir of the engine, continuing pleasantly as if the ship had not nearly exploded.

Traver's sobbing ran its course, then faded away. He drifted outside the cockpit door, occasionally reaching out a hand to prevent himself from floating away down the corridor but otherwise unmoving. His eyes were shut.

As in the sightless vision behind relaxed eyelids that so often precedes sleep, Traver saw infinity. But it was more vivid now, even more real than the sensation that had overwhelmed his mind during the jump. His eyes searched back and forth, scrutinizing the darkness, studying the nothingness that lay behind everything. Shapes began to take form; the colorful, dancing shapes that had become so familiar to his subconscious sight. He wanted to be closer to that nothingness full of shapes, but an infinity still lay between him and it.

Then, Akachi's voice. "Step back from the cockpit door, please."

Traver looked up, wiped his face in his sleeve, and backed away.

The door opened.

Akachi was dressed in his protective suit. Under one arm was rolled another just like it, and in his hand was one of the small oxygen tanks.

"You need to put this on."

Traver was a little clumsy putting it on, just as he'd been clumsy putting it on during the "emergency procedures" simulation back on Earth. But his instructors had assured him that an emergency was unlikely enough that a little clumsiness was not to cause worry. If only he'd practiced a little more. Now Akachi held back and watched as Traver struggled in the gravity-free corridor, pushing his left arm into the right sleeve and twisting the torso tightly around his waist. Akachi never helped, and Traver even thought once or twice he may have smirked.

Finally, within a few minutes he was fully garbed. Akachi now moved forward to attach the oxygen tank to the back of his neck. "The air ducts in the aft are still punctured. Oxygen leaks right out of the ship. I can't find the leak yet, or else we would have re-oxygenated the section already." The intercoms inside the suits, now activated, allowed Traver to hear Akachi. "We want to have it habitable again in time for Misleh's service, so that all the passengers can watch him be set adrift. I should be spending this time looking for that leak, and fixing it."

If Traver still had internal monologue, it would have noted that Akachi had had nearly fifteen hours without interruption and still had not fixed the leak. A few minutes here, spent giving Traver peace of mind, wouldn't seriously interfere with the repair efforts. Akachi was being petty.

But Traver didn't have an internal monologue. His mind was as silent as the airless rear corridor of the *Aten*.

Akachi keyed open the door. First they stepped inside the antechamber between doors. The first door shut, locking out the habitable atmosphere behind them. The next door opened and exposed them to the damaged aft. Traver drifted through and the door snapped on his heels. He expected to hear a clang or at least a whoosh, but there was nothing.

It was dark inside; the power had been cut off back here. Akachi tapped the light affixed to the hood of his suit and it blazed to life. He motioned for Traver to do the same.

It was the first Traver had seen of the corridor since the moment of the explosion. Though the debris had been cleaned up (Akachi would have answered the internal monologue by saying that clearing the rubble, inspecting the interior and preventing further damage – not to mention gathering the human remains – had been priority over finding the leak), the sight was still surprising. The explosion had made the corridor all but unrecognizable. Even with the larger chunks of wreckage removed, it was like the ship itself was a charred corpse, two small humans having stepped inside its empty torso.

The two suit lights swung back and forth, pivoting with their heads. Akachi, who was in front, did not miss Traver's light training steadily on the broken door of the medical bay, now frozen halfway open.

"There is not much left in there. That room was wrecked worst of all."

As they passed the door, Traver swung his light inside, and stopped following Akachi. He could see what was left of the spider-like injection machine, mangled and blackened. The legs had all bent sharply upwards and some had come disconnected completely; the spider was dead.

Traver noted that this bay had not been cleaned as had the corridor. There was so much equipment, so much storage for medical supplies that it would have been impossible for Akachi to pick the room clean in the time that he had. The bulkier items would likely stay where they were, displaced until the ship returned to Earth.

"Come on. Let's keep moving."

"I just want to see."

"I'm not giving you a tour. You asked to see Doctor Misleh, and that's where we're going."

Traver stared into the ruined medical bay as if hypnotized. "It can't be fixed?"

Now Akachi made no attempt to hide his smirk. For the first time since the explosion, that wide grin returned to his face. "I would wish you the best of luck to try!"

Then Traver pulled himself inside the door. Akachi's grin disappeared.

"What are you doing? I said you can't go in there."

Traver didn't stop. He kept his face and his light pointed straight ahead, illuminating the melted monstrosity.

"I don't want to have to take you back up front by force..." The first officer moved with surprisingly accurate fluidity, turning around and shooting inside the door. His heavy hand fell on Traver's shoulder.

Now Traver turned sharply, his light hitting Akachi squarely in the eyes. "God damn you!" Akachi fell back a little. He'd seen Traver emotionally broken, but never enraged. "God damn you! I'm dying! I'm dying and this machine was the only thing that might – *might* save me. Now I'm six months from any real medical treatment, and I'm going to spend that whole time in agony while my bones turn into powder. Do you know how that feels? Can you imagine it?"

Akachi had turned his eyes away from the light. There was no face for him to see, only a bright light above blackness from which the shouting came. But Traver could see his face; all traces of Akachi's grin were gone, and his eyes were wide with surprise.

"If you think it will help, then look at your machine. Look!"

He stayed solidly in place while Traver turned away, his anger seeming to subside as quickly as it had risen.

For a few moments Traver wandered around the machine, gawking at the utter destruction it had wreaked upon itself with a single misplaced spark.

Akachi was watching him closely. But no matter.

The storage drawers built into the wall were still intact. Bent and blackened, but intact. They'd never been locked. Only the Eams treatment formula itself, priceless and patented, was kept behind a second lock in the secure medicine cabinet. But for all the other items the security of the room's main door, accessible only to the doctors and the pilots, had been considered enough.

Traver reached for one of the drawers. It stuck at first, but with a jerk it opened.

"What are you looking for?"

"Some of my medicine. Maybe it will at least relieve the pain."

"Talk to Doctor Marin about that. Do not go ingesting medicines by yourself, even if it is just for the pain."

"I will talk to him."

Traver's hand found what it was looking for, and dropped it into the pocket on the hip of the suit. It was not a vial of medicine.

"Alright."

He gave Akachi a bitter nod and stepped out of the room. The first officer sighed, then led the way farther toward the back of the ship.

Very rarely had Traver been back this far. He had frequented the scientists' quarters in recent months, but he'd never had cause to go where the corridor narrowed and led to the laboratory.

The fire had had less impact back here; the waving spotlights revealed the walls to be very near their original whiteness, brushed over with a thin layer of soot.

Akachi's keychip was unable to open the door; that would have required electricity where there was none. Instead he pulled back the key reader to reveal a mechanical number pad. He entered a code then reached for a small lever hidden behind the button mounts, manually unlatching it. He laid a strong hand against the door and slid it open. They floated inside.

The lab was pristine as it had been for the length of the journey, untouched by flame and, for the most part, by people. Even the scientists had spent little time in here without the presence of any specimens to collect, test or observe. Akachi moved past vats, tubes, monitors, hoses. The room was dark but the sheen of the glass and the clean white metallic walls served as better reflection for the headlamps, and the whole space glowed faintly. In the very back of the room was a small door opening to a final compartment: the pod bay at the true aft of the ship. Akachi leading, they entered.

Set into the wall of this compartment were seven ports. Three, Traver knew, were directly attached to small research pods large enough to transport a cubic meter worth of specimens. Three of the others must be evacuation vessels (a meaningless comfort more than anything – evacuation into a small pod with no jump capability would be a death sentence out here). The final port, in the middle of all the others, was an access hatch opening to the outside of the ship. Mounted against this port was a casket-sized black tube. Traver had never seen it but his conversation with Fletcher had told him what it was. Every ship had one.

"He is ready to go. When everyone is here, we will turn on the power and open the port. Off he will go into his final resting place."

Traver just stared at the cylindrical device. "I want to see him."

Akachi gave not even a nod of response. He pulled a lever on the side of the casket that unlocked it from the port in the wall. It pulled away, drifting half a meter off the floor.

"Do you know what you will see? This is not like looking at a body, peacefully resting."

Traver nodded. Akachi pulled another release lever, and the top of the casket slid open, half the circumference of the cylinder sliding parallel along its length. Then he reached inside and unfolded the thermal blanket in which was wrapped the remains.

The sight did not shock Traver. He was far beyond the capacity to be shocked, now. But the dry, burnt husks of something that was once bone and meat were nonetheless not what he had expected to see.

His face showed no feeling, nor reaction of any kind. Traver's look at the remains only lasted a moment and then he looked back at Akachi.

"Are you happy now?" asked the officer.

Traver nodded, so slightly as to be nearly imperceptible.

Akachi, wearing a version of his customary grin that now looked exasperated and tired, shook his head and began to slide the top of the tube shut once more. As he did so, he threw one last glance at the broken leftovers of the scientist. "We won't open it again for everyone to look at. This is the last time we will see him."

It was the last time Akachi would, indeed.

Traver's hand slipped in and out of the suit pocket. Akachi never saw the hypodermic needle that it held.

When Traver pushed the needle into Akachi's neck, the first officer reacted with the speed of a snake. Without a word he shot round, his arm whipping into Traver and throwing him clear across the chamber where the smaller man was pummeled against the opposite wall.

Akachi grabbed at the syringe that stuck out of his neck. It had easily pierced the protective suit (which was a safeguard against contamination and loss of pressure, but was not one of the heavy duty spacewalk suits). It was bobbing with every motion and pulsing slightly with every beat of his heart. He pulled it out. Whatever was inside had already been injected into his veins, and it was too late. He could feel his body weakening almost instantaneously. By the time he realized what was happening, his hand had gone lax and released the needle, which drifted away into the darkness but not before Akachi saw, by the light of his headlamp, the small label that read "*muscle relaxant.*"

Whenever Traver had undergone treatment, the paralyzing had been done under circumstances in which the patient was immobile. As such, it was very difficult for him to know for certain how long the drug took to reach full effect. The whole process felt like nothing at all; one moment he would be lying on a stretcher, and some indefinite number of moments later he would be lying on the same stretcher but without the ability to move.

Watching Akachi now, Traver learned just how quickly the drug took full effect. Within a matter of thirty seconds, the impregnable tower of speed and strength that had been Nelson Akachi transformed into a soft and pliable shell. Whether by the movement of the ship or by some last, imperceptible contraction of his muscles, his body folded into a fetal position and he drifted forward slowly toward Traver. His eyes stared listlessly at the man who'd tricked him, and Traver knew how much anger and confusion must be hiding in that still-present mind, behind eyes unable to express it.

While Traver was surprised at how fast Akachi had been incapacitated, he knew well how long the paralysis would last. It should be long enough.

The tubular casket had not slid shut all the way. Akachi had jarred it slightly when he pushed Traver away, disturbing the Misleh charcoals which now began to float up into the space above the open lid.

Traver pushed himself forward. This took more effort than he'd been anticipating, and he moved slower than he wanted to. He had fallen hard against the wall. His body, already battered from the explosion, absorbed a significant shock and his head was ringing. Nonetheless he succeeded in propelling himself toward the center of the room, headlong into the oncoming first officer.

The task of stowing Akachi in the casket was no easy one. The box was made to facilitate a man at full size, but Akachi was something greater than that. He pushed the limits of what such a container was able to hold. Traver grew exhausted dragging the paralyzed man through the room's space and painstakingly holding each limb into the cylindrical device. There were no straps within to hold a body, since the whole point of this casket was to shoot the occupant out through the port and into the final resting place in the darkness beyond. When Traver managed to put Akachi's torso fully into the tube, the legs began to drift upwards and the whole process needed to be repeated.

Finally Akachi lay prone, fully within the horizontal container. Traver, breath heaving, stared down at him through the murky droplets of condensation and sweat that had built up on the inside of his visor. Akachi looked back.

He was helpless now, this decorated military man, explorer, captain-in-training – the man with innumerable stories (of which only half needed to be true for his life to have been more colorful than most people can even hope for) – this man who had alone saved the lives of seven scientists in the wake of the accident. Traver had beaten him with a needle. He looked into the elongated capsule, studying the figure of the man he'd despised since the first time he'd seen his grinning face. Grinning no more.

He slid the cover of the casket shut. Akachi's idly staring face disappeared.

If someone else, some third party had been present in the room to ask Traver what he was planning or how he had decided it was time to eliminate the first officer, Traver would not have been able to respond at all. He had no plan. The wheels inside his head were still. A new, strange set of instincts were driving him forward toward the only thing that mattered.

So he found his momentum stymied when he pushed the casket back up against the port, locked it into place and tried to empty the contents into space. To do so required a passkey to be entered into a control panel mounted into the wall between the bay room and the lab. Even if Traver had somehow known the passkey, there was no way to enter it since the control panel required electricity to operate, and this part of the ship was still dark. Of course, there was probably a workaround for cases where a crew member needed to access the exterior of the ship during an outage, but knowledge of such a process would have been limited to the woman in the cockpit and the man currently paralyzed inside the casket. Neither could be asked.

Akachi would need to wait.

Traver set about cleaning up the bits of Misleh that still floated around the room. Most were near the size of baseballs, though some were smaller and some larger. One chunk, what must have once been his wide, jiggly torso, was the size of a large cooked turkey. All these pieces Traver caught and wrapped back into the thermal blanket (which had accompanied the remains when they drifted out of the casket). The bundle, all wrapped and filled with parts, was no bigger than he could carry under one arm. Traver looked for a place to stash it, and opted for one of the pods docked to the aft, accessible via a port in the rear wall. The latch mechanism for the pod's port was simple enough for a layman to operate, so Traver opened it and carefully stowed the late scientist inside.

Satisfied that the room looked the way it had when he'd first entered, he made his way out through the lab and back up the corridor, using his flashlight to cut through the darkness.

A new problem arose when he reached the antechamber door at

the far end of the blackened corridor. The door was shut, of course. He tapped his gloved finger against the automated button, but it was dark and unresponsive, like the rest of the hallway. His finger searched for the manual latch and found it. He pulled on it, and felt a satisfying click. But nothing happened.

Traver realized that he was breathing heavily. Exertion had caused panting before, but now this was something closer to panic. His calmness was slipping out of his grasp.

Again he tried the button, and again the latch. The door must have been securely locked down due to precautionary measures, and he didn't know how to unlock it. Akachi surely knew, not that he would be in any condition to explain.

But perhaps there was a key. Traver nodded affirmatively to no one but himself, and stiffly reigned in his rapid breaths. He turned back down the hallway.

He didn't like the thought of reopening the casket. It spoiled the sense of finality with which he'd watched Akachi's face disappear beneath the lid, presumably for the last time. But it had to be done.

Sliding the top open, he found Akachi as he'd left him. His eyes were still open, aimlessly staring.

How long has it been? Traver's thoughts were slowly articulating themselves again, departing from the more dependable shape of instinct. As that happened, he realized he was quickly losing track of the time. *How much longer until he can move again?*

Frantically, he started to pat his hands up and down Akachi's body, searching for keys, tools, anything that might help him escape from the dead aft.

He found Akachi's keychip. It would likely not help him at all, not with the power out. But he took it anyway. He found Akachi's belt carrying various instruments and tools, most of which Traver didn't recognize or understand. He'd never been very mechanically inclined, after all. He took the belt from around Akachi's waist, careful not to upset the man's repose. Then he found the gun.

That the officers might be armed was not a possibility that had ever crossed his mind at all. The reality of weapons was not something that would occur to most people. Aside from old, mostly banned fiction with a propensity for glorifying violence, guns had fallen far out of the public's imagination. Public safety enforcers on Earth possessed them, but since harsh bans lay over media coverage of police-related events, few people knew how often officers used their weapons, or what the outcome looked like when they did.

That is to say, Traver had never seen a gun before. From where it had been cleverly hidden beneath Akachi's belt, his hand removed it gingerly. It was small enough to fit within the palm of a larger man (like Akachi), and ivory white in color. He was careful not to jerk or shake it, since he didn't know what it would take to set it off, or what damage would ensue. He wanted to strap it into the belt around the outside of his suit, but panicked at the thought of a deadly weapon pointing somewhere near the vicinity of his groin, suit or no suit.

His frenzied thought process nearly got the best of him. Try as he might to calm himself, his breath was again coming in rapid bursts and his hand was shaking. Then he remembered the jostling the gun must have received when Akachi had first reacted to the injection. It had not gone off then. Indeed, would the first officer have carried something unstable and highly destructive inside a ship whose structural integrity was paramount to the survival of sixteen souls? Perhaps the gun was trustworthy after all. Perhaps it was only a stun gun, or was incapable of damaging inorganic materials. Anything was possible.

Traver had only a very faint knowledge of how to use the weapon, but that could wait. This was no time or place to practice or test it. He slipped it beneath the belt that he'd taken from Akachi, and inhaled sharply. When nothing happened – no accidental discharge, no blast of pain against his thigh – he breathed out slowly. His calmness returned, and his confidence. He was wearing a weapon. That gave him power.

But if Akachi had the means to open the hallway door, Traver had not found it. Continuing to panic would be pointless however, and detrimental to the oxygen supply he had left. How much time had passed, anyway?

Instinct was taking over once again, and his thoughts, those that could be defined in processes and words, again faded into the backdrop of his mind.

The next minutes, or hours, or perhaps days, were spent exploring the laboratory, the medical bay, and the scientists' quarters. It was the lab that especially interested Traver. Not only was it the only area of the ship to which he'd never been privy, but it was here that the mysteries of AMA-712 would soon be unraveled. Many of the contraptions, the tubes, the vials, the vats were unknown to him, but he understood their significance. He felt compelled to refrain from touching anything. It was all too sacred. The silence within was almost reverential, broken only by the sound of the engine as it vibrated through his suit, soft but sacrilegious. Even his flashlight profaned the instruments by illuminating them. He switched it off. Time continued to pass uncounted. Time ceased to matter. Traver drifted in the dark lab, trying to absorb the mystical power of the place. Had he once considered the cockpit to be the sanctuary of the ship? If he had, he'd been wrong. This was the holy place. He envied the scientists who had the knowledge to perform the observations here. Perhaps they could teach him how too, and he could join them. He could make them teach him. After all, their sacred order was in need of a new high priest.

Traver went back into the docking room and opened the pod containing the old high priest, the one who'd been blown apart. Unrolling the blanket, he dug through the pieces until he found the one he was looking for.

Misleh's head was still vaguely spherical. Careful study of the front surface revealed the recognizable basics of a human face, though his already flat features had been made significantly more flat. The front lenses of the thin-frame glasses he'd worn were embedded in what had once been eyes.

Traver stared into those eyes, blank and charcoaled as they were, for a long moment.

"Thank you," he said to the head. And he smiled.

Misleh's skinless, ashen teeth smiled back.

Then Traver suddenly could not breathe. He inhaled several times fruitlessly but his lungs burned. Stars danced in front of his eyes. His oxygen tank had finally run out.

To panic would have been to die, but Traver was beyond panicking now. His instinct made him calm as he held his breath and pushed himself back over to the casket. He slid it open.

There was Akachi again. This time, Traver did not see him as the man he was, or as a man at all. He saw the oxygen tank still strapped to the back of his neck. He saw that the tank's gauge still read "39%." Either Akachi's paralysis had required little breathing, or he had been prudent in his usage of oxygen, in the knowledge that he would need it when the paralysis wore off. Both were probably true. But now, Traver needed the oxygen.

Unhurriedly – because hurry would have expended more effort than he had air for – Traver switched off the tank's outlet and unscrewed the hose from Akachi's suit. He disconnected his own tank and plugged in the hose from the new one without bothering to unmount the empty tank from where it sat on his neck.

He switched on Akachi's tank, and once again breathed deeply. He could feel the relief spread through every artery in his body and he relaxed. After his initial deep breath or two, he focused on keeping his movements slow and his breaths minimal to make this remaining oxygen last as long as it could, for whatever that would be worth. Then he went about removing the old tank from his neck and replacing it with Akachi's.

Akachi.

He turned his attention back to the man in the box. The eyes were still open, but they were no longer looking at anything. They no longer seemed to be living at all. It would have been hard to judge whether Akachi's skin, dark as obsidian, had turned pale, but in the light of his headlamp Traver thought it had lost some of its luster.

Never had it occurred to Traver that he was setting out to kill Akachi. That is, he had aimed to eliminate the threat he posed, but the thought had never taken the shape of removing a life.

Had he been confronted with the need to commit murder directly, it is unlikely he could have gone through with it. But to paralyze Akachi and send him, hidden in a tube, out into space with the push of a button would have given Traver a comfortable feeling of distance from the action. As things had gone, he'd removed the man's life support as a byproduct of self-preservation, too focused to see that the action of saving his own life would end another.

It had. Akachi was dead.

Had Traver seen that the interior of the pod was equipped with several oxygen tanks, more easily accessible and fuller than the one he'd used to replace his own, the one he'd removed from the man in the box? It's possible that he had, now that he thought about it.

Traver stared at the body. Those dead eyes were still aimed in his general direction, unseeing now. The man's two hundred fifty pounds of pure muscle were weightless and stiff inside the open tube.

It had been remarkably easy, yes, and carried out in such a way as to comfort whatever conscience Traver had left. But looking down at the body, Traver did not let his mind hide behind the circumstances, or skirt around his responsibility by dwelling on the indirect nature of the deed. He was Traver Graff; never in his life had he needed to justify his actions. Never had he tainted himself with regret. Now was no time to start weakening his resolve by avoiding the truth.

He'd murdered Nelson Akachi, and that was that.

The diminished head of the scientist was waiting for him, drifting near the room's wall where Traver had left it. After sliding the lid of the casket shut once again, he retrieved that severed relic and, respectfully, placed it back into the pod along with the rest of Dr. Misleh.

Only two things were possible now. Traver would run out of oxygen again, burning through the tanks in all of the pods until he finally expired in darkness, or somebody would walk through the forward door. Either way, he would be ready.

CHAPTER EIGHT
FLETCHER

Captain Fletcher opened the door to the aft section exactly five hours after Akachi had left to accompany Traver to see the remains. She had thought nothing of his initial failure to return. The too-amiable subordinate officer had likely found himself sharing stories with the passengers in a well-intentioned effort to comfort them. She rather hoped that he was busy on the outside of the ship, working to repair the air leak, but her monitors showed no signs of any human presence on the outer hull. When several hours passed, she made an attempt to contact him through his suit's intercom and received no reply.

Her suspicion instantly fell on Traver, the hapless and loud-mouthed fool who had until recently maintained a maddening state of composure. How he could have gotten the best of Akachi was beyond her ability to guess, but not beyond her capacity to believe. Her co-pilot was too soft and trusting by far.

Very rarely did both pilots leave the cockpit unattended. It was only to be done as a last resort per the Code, but now she had no choice. She locked all the controls before donning her full suit – the protective one meant for space walks – and strapping on her own sidearm. She'd seen cabin fever and space sickness take hold of passengers before, and was aware of the dangers such ailing individuals could pose to a working crew. If she had to put Traver down, she would do it.

It was not without caution that she exited the cockpit. Her readings of the ship's internal cameras had told her that neither Traver nor Akachi were anywhere to be seen in the powered sections of the corridor, but she knew there was no such thing as being too careful.

When she opened the door to the aft corridor, she found it empty and silent. "Officer Akachi. Mister Graff. Are you still back here?" She transmitted the words via intercom to be heard by the other suits, the airless aft being devoid of sound. She received no response.

She checked behind her, ensuring that the door shut all the way before proceeding into the darkness. Nobody would slip out behind her, at least.

She searched the rooms: the antechamber, the scientists' cabin, the medical bay. All were as she expected them to be, but there were no signs of the men she was after.

Lastly, she checked the lab. This had been their destination so she harbored a strong expectation of finding them in here.

The room was undisturbed. Fletcher did not know the names or purposes of most of the devices in here, but she did have a photographic memory that retained the image of the lab from her final pre-trip walkthrough. Nothing had been moved or altered.

But the pod bay compartment was where her premonitions lay strongest. Even though she found it empty, there was something not right. She checked the access port to see whether Akachi had used it to exit to the outer hull; the casket-like jettison tube lay in its place against the port, blocking access to the exterior. Akachi's being outside the ship was ruled out.

The circular gate to each pod was latched shut, but that did not mean all the pods were still at their docks. The inside and outside of each pod were equipped with camera monitors that could be viewed from the cockpit and the aft's control panel; however without power the feeds were inactive, so there was no way to know whether any were missing.

So she unlatched the first port. It opened into the research pod interior, as it should.

She opened the second. Another research pod. Enough room for a man to sit inside, albeit uncomfortably, surrounded by measuring instruments and specimen containers. Undisturbed.

She opened the third. This one had not been refitted as a lab tool. It was larger inside; an evacuation pod able to carry up to five people, tightly crammed. Nothing suspicious here.

By this time Fletcher's mind was already exploring the rest of the ship, trying to determine where else her quarry might have gone since the pods were proving a dead end.

But the fourth pod port was literally a dead end – there was nothing there. The pod was gone. The port opened on an outer protective gate, just a centimeter of freezing steel separating Fletcher from outer space.

So that was it. Traver had taken the pod. He'd escaped the ship, desperate to reach AMA for whatever mad reason.

It was possible to unlatch it manually of course, for evacuations during outages. But since the power cut-off command had been given from the cockpit, the pod's backup electricity would be disabled, which meant Traver could not have turned it on. As such, he'd have no navigation, no propulsion. Traver would be drifting in a small steel coffin until he ran out of oxygen or died of dehydration. Good riddance, then.

She was satisfied in part, but not so satisfied she did not open the casket to see whether the pieces of corpse had been removed or disturbed. After all, she had made her promise to the crew, told them there would be a few moments of respect dedicated to those remains before jettisoning them – that was, if the remains were still there. She slid open the lid to see.

That was how Captain Fletcher discovered the body of Nelson Akachi.

Rapidly she moved back up towards the forward corridor, no time having been wasted after checking the body for vitals and finding none. Messages would need to be sent back to Earth, the ship's repairs would need to be performed alone, and worst of all, she'd need to find a way to communicate to the passengers in a way that would not make them panic. Akachi had been good at that sort of thing.

With practiced speed she swam up the corridor, pushing herself from wall to wall, accelerating her movement with an even rhythm. Upon reaching the door she slipped her hand into the corner on her right, the seam where wall met wall. She pushed slightly and a small hidden panel folded upward. Within was a tiny set of numbers, spring-loaded and mechanical. Faster than eyes could have caught, if there were eyes watching (and there were), she entered a fourteen-digit code and some old spring mechanism inside the door sprung free. She slid it open with her hands and stepped forward into the antechamber.

Movements in the corridor were soundless. Fletcher's peripheral vision was blocked by the suit's helmet and, as she believed her quarry had launched into space, she had no reason to glance behind her. That's how it happened that she was closely followed up to the door. It wasn't until she was in the antechamber, when she turned around to place both hands on the aft door to slide it shut manually, that she saw Akachi's gun pointed at her, centimeters away from her face. Traver was the one holding it.

She was too late to shut him out of the antechamber. He was mostly inside, and with the gun already drawn. Her own gun was tucked securely into her belt, inaccessible for a speedy pull. Traver had the jump on her and she froze in place. There was nothing else she could do except maintain composure.

Traver held her in an intense, focused gaze and began to say something.

His mouth opened inside his suit but no sound came out.

"You're not connected. I can't hear you," she said. Traver tried again, yelling emphatically with no audible results.

"Your intercom went idle. You need to re-broadcast."

Traver's face displayed confusion, but his hand holding the gun remained steady.

"It's a button on the right side of your suit. Hold it down."

He raised his left hand, meaning to pass the gun over from his right, but then he thought better. Even a split-second without control of the weapon would be too much. Instead, he reached his left arm around to feel for the button.

As Traver activated the transmitter, Fletcher looked back at his face. "What were you trying to say?" Her voice was dry and unaffected, her eyes without expression. So were Traver's.

"Open the doors and let me into the cockpit with you."

She didn't move.

"I don't want to shoot you, Captain, but if I must, it'll be everyone on board – not just you – who'll die as a result. There's nobody else to pilot the ship, since Akachi is dead."

She sighed and looked at him flatly, as if he was boring her. He was, a little. "I'm aware of the first officer's status. My death in addition to his would be an inconvenience, but hardly a fatal one. There are others onboard who can pilot the *Aten*."

Traver was taken aback and his movement reflected that exactly. His head bobbed backwards with surprise, his movement exaggerated by his weightlessness.

Before he had a chance to respond, Fletcher went on.

"However, we'd all be happier if that was not necessary. Your actions are based on the premise – correct me if I've read you inaccurately – that we were nearing a decision to turn around and go home."

Traver's eyes blazed. "We can't go home."

At this, Fletcher smiled. It was only the second time, to Traver's knowledge, she had ever done that, but now its shape was not at all what he'd imagined it to be. There was something sadistic about it. "You're very sure about my flight plan, over which I maintained sole control and which I've kept confidential."

Traver was completely still. His face was stone and his arm that held the weapon stayed rigidly in place.

Her smile disappeared as quickly as it came. "I was ordered to carry the scientists to AMA-712, and I intend to do so regardless of personal qualms on the part of a few passengers."

Traver's head began to tilt slightly to the side. The hardened glass machine of instinct and control that had been driving his mind nearly shattered. This was unexpected.

"And what about…" Traver could barely make himself say anything. When he did, it was in a halting murmur. "And what about me? My condition, without the equipment for treatment?"

Fletcher moved forward until the front of her helmet pressed against the gun in Traver's hand. "Not a factor in my decision. You continue to have the freedom to live or die, affecting neither my assignment nor the scientific mission."

Traver's eyes locked onto hers and froze there. He searched, probed for something dishonest, some trick hidden deep in her steady gaze. Always he'd been able to read a lie. Now he saw none.

She moved back a little, closer to the forward door. "And if you die along the way, all the better. That was the hope."

If before he'd been unable to detect a lie, he now saw unbearable integrity. About this last hope, anyway, she was telling the truth.

She moved aside slightly, obligingly, leaving room for him to enter the antechamber between doors. Without a word – he had no words that would make any sense at the moment – he slipped in. The gun, the impact of which he was still completely unaware, remained steadily aimed at the captain's face, but she seemed not to notice.

She slammed the rear door shut. A pressure valve released and the tiny room filled with air, then the fore door opened again. Traver was again in the habitable part of the ship. The hell in which he'd spent the last countless hours, in which he'd nearly faced death and in which he'd left Akachi, was behind him.

He was relieved to find the mid and forward corridors empty of other passengers. Any witnesses to the sight of him holding Fletcher at gunpoint would complicate things; at best, his friends would be surprised and might cause a ruckus – at worst they might try to interfere.

Before they moved too far up the corridor he seized Fletcher's gun from her belt and stashed it against his suit. "Go," he said. "Open the cockpit door."

With her usual practiced agility she glided forward, through the next antechamber and into the forward corridor. He followed slower and with less grace. Using both hands to propel himself forward it was impossible to keep the gun pointed, and in a few moments the captain was ten meters ahead of him, within reach of the cockpit doors.

There was nothing to stop her from entering the cockpit and shutting the doors behind her. Traver didn't want to say what he said next, but what other choice did he have? Her hand with the keychip was on the cockpit keypad now.

"Wait for me, Captain. If you're planning on shutting me out, I'll start shooting the other passengers."

His own words surprised him, but he neither regretted them nor mentally retracted them.

Fletcher turned her head to look at him. Even she seemed surprised to hear his threat. She didn't seem concerned, though. The cockpit door slid open in front of her, and Traver, moving quickly but clumsily toward her, suddenly stopped.

At first he couldn't believe his eyes, but several blinks did not change the vision that lay in front of him, through the fore windows of the cockpit.

In the negligible time that had passed since the last time he'd seen through the cockpit windows, AMA had grown to a giant luminescent sphere hanging in the vast space between the ship and the stars. Perhaps it was Traver's own unsteady state, the blood pumping through his brain and his breath coming in nervous spurts, but the planet seemed to pulse. Green light brightened and faded, brightened and faded with a rhythm that was not quite perfect enough to seem clocklike. The surface textures could almost be seen now, and it appeared to undulate and writhe, not with the ordered patterns of a disturbed ocean but randomly, chaotically.

"You go ahead and do that, then." Captain Fletcher's voice.

Traver forced himself to look at her again. He was still waiting in the corridor, and Fletcher was between him and the living round giant that awaited him.

Then he realized how distressed he was. Her words, her calmness had a strange effect on him. He had gone so far as to threaten the lives of his friends, his fellow passengers; why was she so composed?

She raised a corner of her mouth. It was less a smile than a challenge.

In the next moment, something deep inside Traver screamed out. This was the only chance he would have at taking the *Aten* to its destination, and he could feel that failure was imminent. In the same moment, before Traver had even time to raise the gun, Fletcher pulled herself around and behind the door. It slid shut.

The green planet was gone from sight. But before it vanished, had it pulsed once more, brighter than before? Traver thought it had.

"I will shoot them. Captain. Can you hear me? I will shoot them!" He didn't know whether he sounded threatening or pathetic, nor did he care. He was no longer aiming for the dramatic. His days of flair were over, and now the words he spoke were simple truth.

First he tried the door to the cockpit. It was impenetrable as it always was.

He moved back into the mid corridor. It was only when he tried the door to his own room and found it inaccessible that a cold feeling spread over him, and he realized why it was that the corridor had been empty when he and the captain had first entered.

Fletcher had locked all the doors. Locked everyone into their cabins. And she must have done so before she even knew what she would find in the aft.

Then Traver knew he'd underestimated Captain Fletcher. Of course he had. How had he really expected to beat her with no more than a gun he didn't know how to use and a few threats?

The doors to the aft opened: both of them.

Traver whirled around to see, and all at once he saw the lights turn on in the aft corridor, lighting up the blackened walls. Fletcher was powering up the rear of the ship.

The oxygen must be draining out of the corridor, and Traver only had time to decide he'd been very wise to keep his suit on when he saw the lab door open. It was thirty meters to the back of the ship but he saw the inside of the lab as clearly as if he was there. He could see the next door open to the pod bay compartment in the aft, and he knew what was coming next.

He spun round, looking for something to grab hold of. The door handle of his cabin was the only thing within reach. His hand found it.

An audible whoosh. Akachi's casket was shot out the aft port. Then, silence.

Traver felt the immense pull, the vacuum of space reaching up from the newly-opened hole in the rear of the ship, grabbing not just his legs as he held on to the door, but his entire body.

Pain tore through him. He let go of the gun, and it shot out of his hand. With both hands he held on, but he didn't know why he bothered; it was only a matter of time before his strength gave out. This was the end. Fletcher had killed him.

Then, the miracle.

At first Traver didn't notice the lights going out. He certainly didn't notice the whir of the engines becoming silent; it was impossible to hear anything at all.

Within a few moments of his surroundings going dark, Traver knew that the blackness was more than his own eyesight giving out as his arm numbed, trying not to weaken its hold on the door handle. Then the handle slid and the door opened.

The cabin doors would not stay locked in case of a total power loss, and that is exactly what was occurring now. Suddenly the doors were able to be opened. The passengers in each cabin, panicking by now to have found themselves locked in, were straining at their respective doors when the engine died. They would have been better off leaving those doors shut.

Traver didn't know who or what was slipping out of the door, vacuumed over and past him in the darkness. There were two of them at first, heavy and fleshy. The first glanced him but the second hit hard against his face, finally dislodging him from the door.

The next moments were complete chaos. He tumbled, crashed into walls, against doorways, against other similarly tumbling bodies, trying to grab onto anything, anyone. Once his hand found someone's arm and he held tight, but then the other man, whoever it might be, hit the corridor wall above the antechamber door and the hold was broken. The fall into darkness continued, and Traver expected to emerge into outer space at any moment.

The distance was covered in approximately three seconds. It seemed to take hours.

Traver impacted the rear wall of the aft pod bay, then slid toward the empty port where the casket had been docked. He felt the freezing cold of the space beyond even through the suit, but instead of slipping through the hole like a golf ball he felt a human body blocking the way. Someone, whoever it was, had braced himself at the port. No; there were two people here, holding onto one another and preventing one another – or anyone else – from being sucked through. The strain must be enormous. By now, the flailing bodies of half a dozen others had formed a heap against the port. Traver was pinned beneath the pile, against the two struggling forms who were holding them all back from the void. But how much longer could any of them last? There was no oxygen, no pressure, and the temperature was now that of the ship's exterior.

Twelve seconds had passed since the blackout. Still the ship was dark and silent.

Traver felt the men beneath him slipping. Cold hands reached from the pile, trying to hold onto the men who were plugging the hole. Then he felt something shift. Something gave way, and then there was only one man beneath him.

A human form slipped past Traver from the pile of bodies. Headfirst it seemed to dive through the port. Traver, by instinct, grabbed hold of its torso. Those above grabbed hold of its legs and it hung there, head hanging into space.

Fifteen seconds. Consciousness can't last any longer than that, not in space.

The lights came back on. The port slammed shut.

As air and warmth poured into the chamber, only Traver seemed to be aware of anything at all. He at least had been protected by a suit, and hadn't been deprived of oxygen.

The first thing he noticed was the body he'd clung on to. The head had indeed hung clear out into space. Whether or not he'd been dead before or after the port had shut and severed his neck, nobody would ever know.

It was Karl.

Then Traver looked around. All the people around him were squirming, gasping in agony. Their skin was pale and all were varying degrees of bloated, the skin around their eyes puffy and blue.

Instinctively he counted them all. Eight. No, nine, including himself. Ten, counting Karl's headless body. Blood was gushing out of it and pooling in airborne balloons, but nobody noticed or minded.

There were three missing. Three must have been sucked into

space.

He hadn't had a chance to identify the survivors – even he was too dazed to see more than pale, unrecognizably expanded faces – when Fletcher appeared.

"Get moving up into the forward corridor. Move, damn you! Oxygen's still leaking out of the ship back here and I've got to shut it off before we lose a whole tank's worth. Are you listening to me?"

Most of them seemed unable to hear her. They were in a daze, probably unaware they'd even survived. So Fletcher did what must have been in every officer's training for unlikely scenarios, and began to carry them out, one-by-one.

Traver pushed away Karl's torso, which had painted his suit with its blood, and started to help. He grabbed one of the scientists by the armpits to pull him. Laboriously he transported the man through the antechamber. He knew Fletcher had seen him, watched him pull the scientist to safety, but she'd not expressed anything at the sight of him, despite having tried to kill him just sixty seconds prior.

Traver did not go back through to the aft. Instead he made a beeline for his own cabin. Fletcher could clean up her own mess. Opening the port was her doing, after all. Karl's blood was on her hands.

Karl's blood, in precise terms, was on his own hands. Traver first set himself to removing his suit and the mask, which was smeared so thick with red that he could barely see. Then he checked his belt. Yes, the captain's gun was still there. He knew he would need it again.

He glanced in the mirror. Something else looked back at him. Something that looked like Traver Graff. He jumped back, startled.

But no, it was only him. He'd lost himself for a moment and recovered quickly. That was what he looked like. He was Traver, after all.

He looked for a moment longer at the reflected image of himself. He realized what was so strange: he was looking at the image of a dead man, or a man who should be dead. He'd been gifted more time. Whatever had caused the power loss had not only saved his life; it had given him the chance he needed to bring the ship to its destination. He must use that gifted time wisely.

When he returned into the corridor, he found the nine survivors plus Captain Fletcher gathered together just outside of the doctors' cabin. The captain had shut the doors to the rear corridor, presumably cutting off the power and oxygen supply once again before too much could leak away.

A few had recovered enough to hold themselves steady, among them Dr. Marin. As for Lance, he had severe freeze burns on his neck and arms; it must have been he who'd held fast in the port, keeping the others from falling into space. His legs were not moving, and he was sobbing as he ran his hands up and down his lifeless thighs. Dr. Marin, sluggish and damaged though he was, looked at each of the other survivors, applying gels to the worst of the freeze burns. The bloatedness, Traver heard Marin advising, would subside slowly, though it would be painful in the meantime.

Dr. Marin worked all alone. Two of the casualties had been his two assistants.

Fletcher was helping with the doctor's work, now that she'd succeeded in moving everyone within the habitable area. From where she crouched beside Dr. Bjornson she looked at Traver as he emerged. Their eyes locked. Fletcher's were no longer deadened or lifeless. The spark in her gaze was full of determination – or hatred. Whichever it was, it made her look alive. Traver thought it made her look beautiful.

She sprang at him. Before she could reach him he had whipped out the gun and pointed it at her. She stopped. She would not be able to get to him before he pulled the trigger, and from her perspective Traver appeared both overwhelmed and surprised at himself. A bad combination.

"Haven't enough people died already?" Traver said coldly.

A few gasps came from the other passengers, but the reactions were slow and subdued.

"Yes, it is enough death," hissed Fletcher. "You don't need to kill me. I told you already, we're going forward with the mission."

"You also told me to go ahead and shoot the other passengers, right before you tried to jettison me. On neither instance did you mean what you said, did you?"

Fletcher looked around at the others in the corridor. Those who were conscious were staring at Traver in wide-eyed surprise, but none displayed any inclination to attack him. Nor were any strong enough to stand a chance at overpowering him. For now, she was on her own.

"I said what I needed to say. Right now, you should trust me when I say I will fly you to the planet, if that's where you want to go. You just need to put down the gun."

"I don't need you to fly me anywhere. You said there was another passenger able to pilot the ship. Who is it?" Traver demanded.

A pause. Traver closely watched the captain's eyes. "He's dead," she said. "Went out the port."

"You're lying again." Traver read her eyes like a book. "If finding an alternate pilot means shooting you, then I won't hesitate to do it."

Nobody spoke. Fletcher held his gaze without blinking. Finally Traver turned his head slightly, never letting his eyes leave Fletcher's face.

"Lance, it's you, isn't it? Can you pilot this ship?"

Fletcher let out a small breath, betraying her disappointment. Traver knew he was right.

A weak voice spoke up from behind him. "What? Me?"

"Are you able to get the *Aten* to the planet? The captain seemed to think you can."

Lance, tears still melting from his swollen eyes, was edging himself up, slowly regaining the use of his legs. "I...not very well. I passed the tests on simulators but I never completed my certification." The young technician's daze had not worn off, and the soft matter-of-factness in his voice sounded as if he wasn't completely aware of what was happening.

"I think you're smart enough to figure it out. Are you up for flying us the rest of the way?"

Lance began to reply when Fletcher interjected: "It'll be more than flying the ship. Hitting the correct orbit trajectory, calculating the correct speed and altitude – all have to be completely accurate or the ship may break apart."

Traver ignored her, though never looking away from her. "Can you do it?"

Lance nodded weakly, flinching as he did. "I think so. I could try." He still didn't feel fully present or cognizant. He didn't seem to see the gun in Traver's hand through the slits of his swollen eyelids.

"No, you can't," cried Fletcher. "The only sure way of arriving safely at our destination is with me piloting."

"Captain," Traver said quietly, almost under his breath. "If you had succeeded in dumping me out into space, you would have turned around for Earth, yes?"

No answer.

"You didn't succeed, because the power went out. What caused the power to go out?"

It took a moment, then Fletcher found the words with which to respond. "It was an energy burst from the planet's surface. Picked up the reading just before it hit us."

Traver smiled, not cruelly but joyfully. "Then, Captain, I think the planet wants us there. Regardless who sits in the pilot's seat, we will make it into orbit. Besides, with Akachi gone, we'll need you to mend the leak in the aft; the lab will need to be fully operational when we reach the planet."

His words had a strange effect on the gathered passengers. It seemed his voice increased in volume and his body in stature. The gun was still held to Fletcher's head, but the more comprehending of the other passengers wondered whether he needed a gun at all. Even Fletcher seemed to lose the will to gainsay him, though that may simply have been the result of exhaustion.

"Let Lance and me into the cockpit. You'll give us complete control of the ship."

Perhaps the captain preferred not to antagonize him, but she also didn't move a muscle to oblige him.

"We need control of the ship, Captain. Your assignment was to get us to AMA, and this is how you do that."

Lance's consciousness started to trickle back to him, though his thoughts were still coming slowly and without much clarity. He had enough wits to subdue the terror he was feeling. It was a terror unaccompanied by surprise — somehow Traver's behavior over the past weeks had predicted this. Still, with every word Traver said, he sounded less and less like good old Mr. Graff, and more and more like...something else.

"Let me do what he wants, Captain," Lance softly pleaded.

Around them several of the scientists were recovering, finding their balance. All eyes rested on Fletcher. Dr. Friedrich moved closest to Traver.

"He's really going to kill somebody," muttered Friedrich in a shaky tone. Traver heard him and the edge of his mouth quivered. He didn't like Dr. Friedrich one bit.

Fletcher's face hardened, her jaw set in resolution. "Yes, he is. He's going to end up killing all of us if he has his way and takes the ship. I'd rather take my chances with him right now." Whatever was in the air that gave Traver the power of persuasion, she was fighting against it.

Traver's dead eyes looked into hers. The pause that followed was punctuation rather than hesitation.

Fletcher started to move forward again.

Traver still had no idea what the gun would do, or if it would work at all. He had to assume the forefinger was meant to rest on the trigger; in that position he had managed to keep Fletcher subdued before.

He began to move his arm.

The captain flinched but realized with horror – too late – that Traver no longer intended her as his next victim.

Traver swung his arm around faster than eye could see. Trusting in his instinct, hoping that his experiment would work, he pulled the trigger.

Dr. Friedrich's head fell in on itself. There was no puncture, no blood except that which spewed out of his ears. The gun hadn't shot a bullet, instead sending a highly-charged bundle of particles through the air, smashing into his face and shattering it from the inside out. He was dead instantly. His body flew weightlessly through the air in a limp, spinning dance.

At this, the other passengers stood and, weak as they were, moved toward the center of the confrontation. Cries of "let him in," "don't make him shoot me," "I don't want to die right now" mixed together, all aimed toward the captain and increasing in panicked anger.

"I'll kill more! I'll kill more!" Traver was wide-eyed and snarling, the gun pointed now at young Dr. Bjornson.

Why aren't they attacking him? Fletcher wondered. Together they could surround and overpower him, maybe before he would have a chance to fire again. But no; they were pleading with her, begging her to let the madman take the ship, to take them all to a destination that would most likely result in their deaths anyway.

If there was a time to save her ship, it had already passed or perhaps it was yet to come. In any case, it was not this moment. This was a moment for calculated retreat. She hated herself for it. She wished Akachi were still here. He would know what to do in the moment, as he always did.

She went to the cockpit door and opened it.

The green glow, somehow pleasant contrasted with the sterile dullness of the ship, spilled in through the windows and washed over the onlookers. Traver was again greeted with the sight of that wonderful gas planet. The longer he looked at it, the more his cares faded away. Why should he be worried? It was calling to him. It wanted him. Its will would be done.

His gun was trained on Lance as he moved forward into the cockpit, but his eyes never left the windows ahead. That is how Fletcher was able to catch Lance's eye as he passed and move her lips in words she hoped he could understand.

Stunned as Lance still was, he nodded.

Then Traver disappeared with his assistant into the cockpit, and they shut the doors.

Now there was nothing between Traver and AMA-712. Nothing but a little glass and a few million quickly-traversed kilometers.

He couldn't take his eyes away from it. He couldn't even blink, until his eyes dried and began to itch.

"Lance, how long until we get there?"

Lance had barely sat down at the console. It was a set of controls that would have overwhelmed him on a good day, which this was not. He had trouble even seeing the smaller details through his swollen eyes.

"I will tell you as soon as I know, boss. It's going to take me a little while." He struggled even to touch the dials, his breath hissing with pain as he did so.

Traver sighed. "Then we'll get there when we get there. As long as we're going in the right direction."

Lance turned to look at Traver; he was surprised to see a sweetness and familiarity in Traver's expression.

"Thank you, Lance," he said in a voice utterly unlike the growl he'd used out in the corridor.

Lance looked away. It was best for him to just worry about the controls. One thing at a time.

Traver smiled and looked back at the planet. Then he shut his eyes. For the first time in – weeks? months? – he truly relaxed. He was confident, more sure of his chosen path than he'd ever been of anything else before.

One way or another, Traver had always gotten what he wanted. He prided himself on that quality, but it never felt quite right, quite *good* before. This time was different. This time, he knew that he had earned it.

CHAPTER NINE
AURORA

From the personal medical journal of Dr. Edith Fraunen, Global Department of Health. [Unpublished]

My own independent research into the Eams infection nearing completion. Will shortly compile a fully detailed presentation for the board. Uncertain how my hypothesis will be received due to unaffiliated nature of work and unusual conclusion.

- *Nearly twenty varied patients have been studied at diverse stages of infection. I have isolated the bacteria in controlled environment and observed exhaustively.*
- *Claim that bacteria originated from rotting Egyptian fruit trees: RULED OUT.*
- *Claim that bacteria originated as alien microbe from meteorite: RULED OUT.*
- *Claim that bacteria first grew in poorly maintained food factories: RULED OUT.*

Am ready to stake my professional career on the following hypothesis:

- *Eams is originally microbe produced naturally by the human immune system.*

- *Eams microbes are all imprinted with DNA of individual patients. Calcium destruction and consumption was written in by DNA upon release into patient's system. Microbes are self-replicating, hence the contagion.*

- *Abnormal overabundance of calcium would seem to be the root cause, though source of calcium cannot be traced or found in infected subjects. Original patients would need to be studied to find initial condition that caused the immune system to develop Eams, but all original patients are long deceased. First responding medical team under Shurovsky should have been more thorough.*

Will continue work, though research has already been exhaustive.

Report with complete notes will be finished within weeks.

I hope to challenge popular assumptions about Eams.

Contents of journal made available to the medical board of Aurora Corporation with the cooperation of the DOH.

[Dr. Fraunen date of death: 3/16/2176]

....

A nondescript suited man arrived through the front doors of the SASH building and strode to the giant marble desk that was home to four female receptionists (perfect-bodied mascots who were politically clueless, but were at least trained with all the right answers to the usual questions). Weston could see the desk through the glass walls of his own producer's office on the third floor, and while he had no specific reason to give this innocuous and unmemorable newcomer his attention, his intuition told him to be unsettled.

He had no idea what the man in the suit was asking the women at the desk, but it seemed both important and time-sensitive as the stranger kept his face aimed directly at the prettiest of these greeters, moving slowly closer to her as his mouth moved rapidly and his body betrayed a certain amount of impatience. Then, as if possessing a preternatural magnetic awareness, the man stopped talking and, removing his hands from the polished stone desk top, stood straight. He looked upward and pivoted his head around steadily. His gaze passed right by the many other offices visible from the lobby, settling finally on Weston. The sweating producer looked away, lowering his head to his own desk, and proceeded to look busy. When he looked back up not ten seconds later, the man had vanished.

But that was only the beginning.

Weston had been ill at ease for some time, ever since the Grand Slam of broadcasts had landed on his desk. That particular day, nearly two months prior, had begun like any other Monday; Weston Hillquist, the personified transmitter betwixt the heaven-bound broadcaster and his billions of eager worshipers, licked salty grease off his chubby fingers as he walked into his office, pausing only to wipe a smudge and a crumb off the chrome door handle.

To receive messages from trillions of kilometers away was routine now; he didn't understand the scientific process as well as some others, but the result was the same as any other recording session. Once a week, he would find an hour-long broadcast in a specially encrypted inbound message. He'd view the recording for quality purposes (there were very few checks and balances on Mr. Graff's content, with even Karen Tiplins checking in only periodically), then forward it on to Editing. There it would be packaged up with titles and uploaded to the SASH's network. Still sold as "live transmitting," there was no longer anything live about it, but the whole process was impressive enough to atone for a bit of mislabeling.

Today there should be no message; *Traver Talk* had aired three days prior – and what a smashing, devastatingly successful broadcast it had been! Weston knew about the Eams of course, since he had read Traver's contract, but the audience's outcry of grief after the announcement episode (as well as the ratings hike) was a pleasant reminder that Traver was still very much loved by his public.

In any case, Weston was at work now as a fixture of his office rather than as a producer. His pants took the brunt of grease from his fingers since he'd failed to secure a napkin after downing his faux-chicken wings. Satisfied they were clean enough (his touchboard was far from pristine already) he proceeded to peruse his network and inbox.

There *was* a message from the *Aten*. That was unexpected. Weston's attention was arrested. Distracted, he wiped his greasy mouth on the arm of his sleeve.

The transmission was huge: *ninety hours* huge.

It must be a mistake. A glitch. Somehow the transmission must have replicated itself. They'd been extremely fortunate to not suffer any errors so far, but there was a first time for everything.

He skimmed the files, quickly finding that this mother lode of messages was anything but an accident. The intention behind it became startlingly clear to Weston, who started to panic even before he'd found the explanatory video featuring Lance carefully explaining the situation. That one was just an insult added to injury.

Weston's panic led him out of his office and to the building elevator. He tapped repeatedly on the "34" button (where Karen Tiplins' lair was located). By the time the lift began to move, he was second guessing himself. By the time it reached the thirty-fourth floor, he was hating himself for being the overreacting, pathetic weakling that he was. Here he'd been faced with a challenge, a task that lay outside of his carefully-defined career box, and his first reaction was to run sobbing to his boss's boss for guidance? Did he need an authority figure so badly?

No, he really didn't. He *was* capable of being his own man, acting on his own volition. Choosing to enable Traver's untruth, standing alone against the SASH, Aurora and the world, might just give Weston the boost of self-worth that he'd always known he lacked.

Still in the elevator, he nodded and smiled at the executives who milled about on the thirty-fourth floor. Their expectation was that he'd exit the elevator. He didn't. Instead he definitively pressed "3," the doors closed and he raced back down toward his office.

It was nearly all he could do to make the eighty-nine "later" episodes disappear, encrypting them for future retrieval while ensuring their invisibility to other techs. But he did it. Traver's faith in him had been well-placed.

As he sat back in his seat, reeling in the post-adrenaline drop, he began to really appreciate what Mr. Graff had done. There was no way to know why he'd done it, but for the sake of his people back on Earth, a complete set of broadcasts meant certainty and security. There'd be no necessity of awkward explanations to the public concerning lost transmissions, no risk of late broadcasts. Most importantly to Weston, Traver's new messages (given the bits and pieces he'd skimmed of them) would be pure conversation between the man and his audience, without the distractions of space travel's gimmicks and glamours. That was good. Traver would finally reconnect with the core audience, and maybe Karen would finally get off Weston's ass about the quality of the broadcasts.

Weston had slept well that first night.

The weeks passed by and the subterfuge went on. Weston maintained the illusion that each segment was being received and transmitted mere hours before broadcast, and the world responded favorably. Audiences grew by 4% and the *New York Now* heralded the new episodes, reporting: "*Graff's magnificent return to form comes after a shiny but shaky set of segments. It was fun to watch his discoveries during his initial time in space, but that fun was a guilty pleasure that came at the cost of any real depth. Watching Graff ogle his surroundings never felt quite right. The truth is, nobody listens to Graff to hear his thoughts on the marvels of the universe. Thankfully, these recent episodes, scathing and sometimes hard to swallow, have reminded people back home what it really means to listen to Traver Graff.*"

The smashing announcement of Traver's health affliction had already boosted the ratings. Suddenly he was no longer a god, an unreachable figure speaking from a pulpit. He was an everyman. He was dying, just as everyone else was dying. Eams hadn't chosen to spare him, and why should it? In the eyes of a disease, all men are equal.

There was preemptive mourning among his fans. Articles were written about his life, praises were heaped on him, his words were commemorated. Thousands of people gathered together on one particular night for a candlelight vigil. There, a multitude of minds gathered together – not in prayer, because that would have contradicted Traver's brand of secularism – in thought and desire for the well-being and long life of that great man.

And the ratings went up.

Weston had opportunities aplenty to get ahead, to view the future segments in their entirety. For whatever reason – whether he didn't want to spoil the ending for himself, preferred not to devote ninety hours at once, or simply didn't wish to split from the comfortable one-broadcast-at-a-time routine that gave him the feeling of normalcy – he never watched ahead. He saw nothing of Traver's future episodes prior to their air dates, aside from the snippets he'd skimmed at first (and those were negligible).

What he did was send weekly reports back to the *Aten*, notifying Mr. Graff of the success, of the reviews, of the mass sympathies he'd garnered for himself with his Eams. But he never received a reply. After that bulky transmission he'd received one morning in January, all was silent from space.

While the SASH board, the stockholders, and Karen Tiplins found themselves increasingly pleased, Weston began to feel ill at ease.

Then, a little more than a month later, came the message that started the storm.

Weston's first thought was that it might be a prank. Somehow, somebody had gotten through the security walls and hacked into the network, sending what *appeared* to be a transmission from the *Aten*. Of course it couldn't be a *real* message from the *Aten*, since this seemed to be sent from the cockpit. The video, once Weston had unpacked and viewed it, showed the inside of a cockpit and lacked any other context. It seemed to be a feed from an onboard monitoring camera, mounted in the rear corner of the room, lensed wide enough to capture the whole area. Having never seen the inside of a cockpit, Weston felt he was safe to assume at first that the myriad of lights and switches converging over a dark and starlit blanket populated by a gigantic green orb was nothing more than a faked image, some hacker's idea of what a cockpit might look like.

Damn, he thought, *now I've opened it and it's probably too late to stop it from unleashing a network-wide spyware.* He was trying to imagine how he'd explain such a tragedy to his superiors when it occurred to him that he might just be watching something genuine. He decided to look closer before following through on his initial impulse to shut down the video, delete it and unplug his computer system.

Sure enough, there were two figures seated in front of the consoles. Their faces were pointed away from the camera so he couldn't make them out.

Only after watching this strangely unmoving image for minutes or more, Weston realized that there was also a sound feed. There was very little to be heard, which was why he hadn't initially noticed it. What he must have mistaken for white noise or transmission static was the soft buzz of an engine. But the occupants of the cockpit were completely silent, and still unmoving.

Just when Weston felt a combination of impatience and suspicion coming over him, the figure seated on the right turned his head, ever-so-slightly, over his shoulder. His head turned just enough for Weston to see his profile, and to recognize Lance.

Then for a split second the other figure, on the left, whipped his head around too.

Then the recording was done, after nearly eight minutes.

Had it been an accident? Had a brief stream of monitor data

slipped into an unplanned transmission? Probably not; the number of things that would need to go wrong, in just the right ways, was too high. The simplest explanation was that somebody, for some reason, had sent it intentionally.

He watched the recording again, this time looking more closely. The problem was, he didn't fully understand what he was looking at. To his mind, there was no difference between normal cockpit behavior and abnormal.

Except, there was. Traver was the other one at the controls.

He watched it for a third time. Now he kept his eyes on Lance. The turn of the technician's head wasn't quite natural, Weston thought. It was too abrupt, too intentional. It may have been Weston's imagination, but Lance's eyes seemed to dart toward the camera for a millisecond, as if he meant to look at the implement that was recording him. Traver's head-turn was even more abrupt, making him appear as if he'd been suddenly and unpleasantly surprised by something Lance had done.

The fourth time he watched, Weston noticed Traver's hair. It was burnt. And as for Lance, his face was bloated and unhealthy.

Weston froze in his seat, his palms sweating. He was overwhelmed by the sense that something had gone horrifically wrong.

He was at a loss for action, though he was not so incapacitated that he was unable to make another run to the company cafeteria for more chicken and donuts. Armed with the physical consolation that food could provide, he viewed the mysterious video seventeen more times, each time paying close attention to a different section of the cockpit, hoping to find more clues as to the reason for the transmission. He found none – none, that is, but Lance's twitchy head movement and Traver's angry turn, both of which struck him as odder and odder with each repeated viewing.

For some time he sat unmoving, soaking his cheap office chair with more and more sweat.

Already Weston had felt alone. He was the sole guardian of Traver's multiple broadcasts and, with Karen and her board sitting back to watch the money roll in, also the only person at SASH who was actively involved in Traver's ongoing transmissions at all. It had been Traver, not Karen who had hired him, so Weston's loyalties to the SASH were not strong enough to convince him that the organization would have his back should there be any sort of trouble. Whatever this new, strange transmission was, it was his own to contend with. After all, it had been sent to him personally.

The next morning, Weston (who had not left the building since initially viewing the message, and hadn't slept a wink either) followed what seemed to him the best course of action. He attached the video to a digital message from his private address, and sent it on to the Aurora Corporation. Not knowing to whom to send it, he addressed it to the Public Relations Department on their directory, hoping it would find its way to the proper eyes. Frantic and feverish as his thought process had become, he held onto enough mental acuity to judge that Aurora was the better choice to analyze the video than the collective clown act upstairs at the SASH.

It was three days – three long, unbearable days during which Weston, despite his best efforts to forget about the transmission, felt the weight of responsibility growing heavier – before the Aurora man with the five-o'clock shadow came to the front desk of the SASH headquarters.

Upon seeing the man and subsequently losing sight of him (but not before sharing a moment of eye contact with the terrifying visitor), Weston gave in to the full-fledged panic attack that he'd been holding at bay.

When SASH security, accompanying the shadow man and several other representatives of the Aurora Corporation (along with a protesting Karen Tiplins) entered Weston's office, they found him curled up on the floor beside a pile of chicken-and-donut chunk vomit, laughing quietly to himself as tears streamed from his eyes. "Mister Graff is driving the ship," he repeated to himself in staggered utterances between shaky bursts of laughter.

Since it was not Weston's well-being they were interested in, the men from Aurora – there were six of them now – streamed into his office, leaving him on the floor as they surrounded his computer. In a matter of seconds they had proceeded beyond his passwords and found the original video which was to cause so much turmoil.

Of course they had watched it already, but apparently the secondhand transmission wasn't enough. Gathered in Weston's office (which was starting to gather an acidic stench), the shadow man and his assistants viewed the seven minutes and fourteen seconds of Traver and Lance doing nothing in the cockpit.

Then more people arrived from Aurora. And more still. Airvans, black except for the blue circular Aurora symbol, filled the alley behind the SASH building. This prompted a hoard of reporters and curious bystanders to congregate in the street at the front of the building, inquiring as to the purpose of the invasion. And while the SASH spokespeople did their best to explain away the incident (which they didn't understand themselves) as a scheduled satellite system overhaul and transmitter update, the Aurora employees flooded in through the back doors and onto every floor of the building, effectively halting all SASH business.

Karen called the lawyers Chad Brucker and Ariel Bruckner, who in turn called their contacts at Aurora to demand, in legal terms, that the trespassing parties should leave SASH premises immediately. Aurora's lawyers, who owned significantly larger homes than did Brucker or Bruckner, replied with a signed warrant from the Department of Space-Transit Safety (a division of global government), granting *carte blanche* to Aurora for all actions involving the investigations pertaining to a possible hijacking.

That was the first time the word "hijacking" was officially used to describe what may or may not have happened onboard the *Aten*.

* * *

"I don't understand. What exactly is the security risk? If Traver Graff is in some sort of danger, why is this the first I'm hearing about it?" Karen Tiplins was hysterical.

"Your last question is a question for Mister Hillquist," said Mr. Gladstone from Aurora, who had ushered Karen into her own conference room and now sat calmly across the table from her. "It will be one of many questions he's asked once he is able to speak coherently."

"Did Weston know something? What? What is it that he knew?" She rubbed her hands together, pulling at the fingers of both nervously.

"Once again, we don't know yet. Your best course of action at the present is to remain patient and cooperate with us. We will require access to all your files and transmissions dating back to the *Aten's* launch. We hope this all comes to nothing, but we can't take the risk that something has gone wrong out there. We'll know more once Mister Hillquist is feeling better so we can ask him some questions."

* * *

At that moment, Weston was not feeling at all better, but he was being asked a barrage of questions under circumstances that were not at all conducive to any sort of recovery. He had not been allowed to leave his office, so his shirt was still covered in brownish-green reminders of his physical aversion to extreme nervousness. But the shadow man heeded neither the sight nor smell, nor did he seem to notice Weston's uncontrollable shaking and halting speech. The man's demeanor was unremarkable and calm, totally unlike the madhouse that now occupied the rest of the building.

"When were you first made aware that Traver Graff had altered his broadcasting arrangement?"

"A couple weeks – a month actually. A little more than a month. But, but he didn't alter – technically he fulfilled his contract. I – I checked."

"And that was when he sent you all the transmissions, start to finish?"

"Y-yes."

"Did you watch all of the broadcasts?"

"All – all ninety hours?"

"Yes."

"No."

"Wasn't that your job?"

"I didn't think…"

"So if you didn't watch them, did you harbor any doubts about Traver Graff's intentions, motivations or mental health?"

"His what? No…why would I?"

"What about his physical health?"

"Well, he…he has Eams. He told everyone about – about that." Weston stifled a sniffle. He was still far from calm, but now his senses had returned to full functionality. "But somehow that announcement was in his contract. When did you people know he had Eams?"

The shadow man seemed not to hear the question, and went on. "Have you made any attempt to contact Traver Graff or your technical assistant, Lance Lanka?"

"Only with reports on the success of the broadcasts. But that was before I got this video. I haven't sent anything since then."

The shadow man looked at, or rather *through* Weston for a few silent moments. His gaze was neither piercing nor particularly thoughtful – indeed it was so indifferent that Weston, in his continued panic, felt that he was being idly watched by a higher being who, by blinking, might wipe him out of existence.

The man looked away without blinking (for which Weston released a tiny sigh of relief). "It's going to be necessary that you send them further messages. Perhaps one, perhaps more."

"I've sent multiple reports over the last couple weeks. He's just not responding."

"Find a reason to make him respond, but without allowing him to suspect that you know he is in command of the ship. We need to elicit details. Where is the captain? What is the status of the ship, the crew and the mission?"

"Haven't you tried to contact him?"

"Our messages have been directed toward the captain, most of them encoded for only Fletcher to be able to read. Anything we address to Traver would betray our suspicions that something is amiss. You're the only one who would be contacting him under normal circumstances."

Weston raised his hand to wipe the sweat away from his forehead. He saw that the hand was shaking. "But sir, I don't know what will make him answer. He's always been stubborn, and if he sets his mind to radio silence, it's going to be impossible to break through to him."

The shadow man smiled cheerlessly. "See? You know him better than we do, which is the only reason you're still here. If you can't think of a way to elicit a response, then think harder."

* * *

Upstairs Mr. Gladstone's interview with Karen Tiplins continued with a very different tone than that of Weston's.

"The cockpit video allowed us to confirm what we'd known for several days prior: something went wrong onboard the ship. Captain Fletcher had notified us of an explosion that took place…"

"An explosion?" Karen Tiplins took another opportunity to panic. "Was anyone hurt?"

"One of the scientists was unfortunately killed," Mr. Gladstone continued with comfortable warmth. "But no other serious injuries were reported. Your employee was fine, last we heard."

"Oh, Traver's not an employee. He's technically a sub-contractor, with provisions written in for…"

Gladstone interrupted: "Several days later we received a red-code from the captain; that is, she alerted us that there was cause for distress on the *Aten*, but she never followed up with an explanation. Since then, communications have ceased and we can't elicit any response." His voice lowered to a whisper. "To be completely frank, we believe that a second explosion may have injured or killed the captain and impaired the primary transmitters. Graff and Lanka have likely taken it upon themselves to bring the ship safely to its destination, and are thence in the process of turning around for home." He ended with a reassuring nod.

Karen Tiplins thought for a moment, her tiny hands still pulling at each other unconsciously. "We may continue broadcasting his segments, then?"

"Since all parties are still bound by the contracts, it is recommended that you do so."

She noticed the frenetic motion of her own hands and made a concerted effort to place them both calmly on the table. "Well then. I guess it's a blessing in disguise that he did them all at once, after all. Do you know what would happen to our public image if the show dropped off now?"

* * *

Dana Graff was alone at home. The children had been taken on a boating excursion by their private physical education coach. She was glad to have them out of the house, really. At their age, she never quite knew what to do with them, love them though she did. And recently they had been talking too often about their father, who was not Dana's preferred topic of conversation, to say the least.

She had avoided seeing or hearing any of his segments since he'd left on his fantastical journey of escapism. Damian and Allie, both who had religiously watched the broadcasts at their friends' house, asked her why she so adamantly avoided them. She lied and said "it would make me sad to see your dad, knowing that he decided to spend the last years of his life out there just so all the world could see him in space, instead of home with us." But in her heart of hearts she didn't know why she refused to participate in Traver's viewership. She longed every evening to hear his voice or see his face. She *wanted* to tune in to the SASH sponsored station and see the man who had vanished so far away from her life, but every time she nearly gave into the temptation, a stronger, unarticulated part of her took control and stopped her. That's how things went for months and months.

She was appreciative of having time to herself these days, and found herself quite happy whenever she was home alone with a glass of wine and a book. She was nearly forty, and the vast majority of her time on Earth had been spent *with* people: with friends, with crowds, with boyfriends, then with Traver, with children. After all that, now it was time for quiet. That's why she wasn't *angry* with Traver. Not anymore. He had done her a favor by allowing her the time for herself in their five-story home. For that reason she didn't really want him to come back. Maybe that was why she refused to see or hear him on the broadcasts. She hated herself a little for it, but she would not have been wholly upset if he were to die out there after all.

The doorbell rang.

She muttered a few unsavories under her breath as she made her way to the quicklift and down to the first story. She had shut off the A.I. and sent the servants home on paid leave, but the downside of enhanced privacy was an increase in duties such as door-answering. She didn't get many visitors now that Traver was gone, so hearing the door was not a common occurrence.

Waiting for her were four strangers, each wearing an Aurora emblem.

"Missus Graff?" asked the man who seemed to be in charge.

"Yes. Can I help you?"

"Come with us right away. Please."

Dana was left little choice, and she soon found herself separated from her precious privacy and sitting in her husband's old studio on the first floor of the SASH building. She'd visited him here dozens of times. All the faces that solemnly awaited her presence were strangers to her, except for that belonging to Weston.

"Hi Dana. Sorry about all this."

"Hi Weston. If I knew what 'all this' was I'd be more inclined to accept your apology."

"Sit down," commanded Mr. Gladstone, obligingly providing her with a seat in front of a recording device. "Please."

Dana sat in silence. The faces that watched her seemed hungry, waiting for her inevitable questions that would allow them to unleash their flurry of explanations. But she offered no questions, instead forcing them to make the first move.

And Gladstone did. He knew Dana was no Karen Tiplins, so he got right to the point.

"Your husband Traver is in control of the vessel *Aten*. We do not yet know how or why, and he is not responding to our communications."

Dana looked at him blankly for a moment.

"My husband...took over a ship?"

The men exchanged glances. Then Gladstone nodded. "To the best of our limited knowledge, that is what appears to be the case."

"But...he's supposed to be recording his show. What happened? Did he get bored?"

Another silence filled the room as all its occupants searched for the right words to say. Nobody had known what to anticipate from Dana, but flippancy was the last thing they would have expected.

Gladstone raised his eyebrows. "You know Weston? Yes? Good. He asked that we bring you in here today, and he'll explain why." Thus passing the baton – or rather shoving it abruptly – to Weston, Gladstone and the others vacated the room, their footsteps deadened by the sound-suppressing walls of the studio.

Weston looked down at the table. He seemed uncomfortable, Dana thought. She'd always liked the poor, fat producer, even if she did pity him for his undying love and loyalty for her husband. Toward herself and her children Traver had never been emotionally abusive or manipulative, but she did not think the same applied to his studio staff. So for Weston's sake she made the first move of the new conversation.

"Do they want me to try and call Traver?"

"Yes." He answered quickly, looking up at her. If he'd had a tail, it would have wagged.

"Do they think he'll respond to me?"

"Honestly, Dana, it was my idea. It's me who thinks he'll respond to you."

"What am I supposed to say to him? 'I love you honey, come home to me! Don't do anything stupid and get yourself killed. Don't let your kids grow up fatherless!'" Her intonation of a hapless maiden was enough to bring a smile to Weston's face.

But then he let out a sigh. "No. I don't think that will work. You have to pretend...it has to seem like you don't know anything's wrong with him. It has to be something that you would say to him even if he was still doing his normal thing up there and not taking over control of the spaceship."

Dana paused for a long moment to consider. Then she shook her head slowly. "I would never be so desperate I'd come down here on my own just to call him. Even if the house burned down, even if the kids were kidnapped. He would know it too; as long as he's out there, I don't want to think about him and I certainly don't want to talk to him. I'm sorry Weston, but I don't think I can help you."

Weston leaned forward and his voice, cracked though it was, hushed. "It's not *me*, though. It's *them*."

To his chagrin, Dana laughed. "I don't really care who it is that needs to talk to Traver. If it's me doing the talking, my husband is going to think something is wrong. It's not going to work, and it's as simple as that."

Gladstone stepped back into the room. *Of course they were listening to us*, went Weston's frantic thought, upset but hardly surprised. The executive, maintaining a grim silence, pulled at the back of Dana's chair and she stood. With a wave of his hand, Gladstone showed Dana to the door. As she stepped across the threshold, that hand fell on her shoulder and stopped her in her tracks. Gladstone towered over her. "We trust you are aware that your family's best interests lie in your total discretion."

For a moment she went wide-eyed, her lips tightening. But then her face relaxed and she smiled. "You should know that talking about my husband's affairs with the media is the last thing I want to do, even without you threatening me or my children." She turned away from Gladstone, gave a final, sad and somewhat apologetic glance to Weston, and then disappeared down the hallway.

Weston knew that Gladstone's eyes had fixated on his own, but he had no interest in allowing eye contact to occur. He was defeated and trapped. With Dana's exit, he began to sense with increasing discomfort that, while others were allowed to come and go about their business, he was a prisoner of Aurora until this whole ordeal was somehow resolved.

"She was the best option I could think of," Weston moaned.

"We have another." It was not the response Weston was expecting, but he knew better than to let himself feel relieved just yet.

"They should be here soon," and Gladstone sat down across from Weston, in the seat Dana had occupied.

Neither man said anything, and Gladstone's gaze drifted from Weston to the recording sensors, and then off into nothingness. As Weston found himself calming in the silence, his own eyes wandered back to Gladstone's face. The suited man was afraid – terrified. Maybe more than he himself was. There was no tremble, no nervous tic to betray that terror; Weston knew from the cold, perfect stillness with which Gladstone was composed as he stared blankly into nothingness, waiting.

About an hour later, the sounds of footsteps approached down the hallway. Gladstone stood, all signs of his dread falling away, and finally broke the silence. "Not a word to her. She doesn't know the situation, nor will she." Then he opened the door. The Aurora attendants now ushered in a young woman unfamiliar to Weston. She was delicate and pretty though she carried herself with a slouch, her eyes cast down and her face flushed.

"Lucy Kurowski?" said Gladstone. Her timid nod was the only response.

Weston nearly jumped out of his skin. Her name brought back flashbacks of a certain hellish scandal that had assaulted Traver and his team a year prior.

"You've been told what we need you to do?"

Again she nodded, then spoke in a faint, uncertain voice: "They told me, but it's the middle of the night and I'm confused. I don't know why you need me at all. This doesn't really make sense."

"Just say what they told you to say, and then you'll be able to go home. It won't be difficult. Come on." Gladstone ushered her in to the studio, where she appeared dazed by the many cameras and sensors that surrounded her.

A wave of enlightened recognition passed over her face as she looked at the wall behind her, where SOCIAL HUMANITIES was written in big silver letters. "This is Traver, Traver Graff's show. It's where he records. I recognize it now!" Nobody offered any response. Technicians (under Aurora's employ, not SASH's) checked and double-checked the equipment in silence.

"You dragged her into this?" Weston cried once Gladstone had stepped out of Lucy's earshot. Weston's outrage at the reappearance of Traver's scandalous fling, who'd caused so much public grief, lent him a moment of fearlessness in the face of his captors. Gladstone's silence did not deter him. "But how did you find her? Her identity wasn't revealed to the public!"

At this, Gladstone turned to him with what might have almost been called a snarl. "*We* found out about her in the first place," he rasped.

It took a moment for Weston to absorb this information, for his brain to knock the pieces into place. When it did, *did you blackmail Mister Graff?* is what he would have said. But despite his lessened fearfulness he was not yet foolhardy, so he kept his suspicions to himself.

Ten minutes later the recording session had been prepped. Weston sat outside the studio along with Gladstone and several others. Lucy, surrounded by recorders and monitors, nodded meekly toward Weston to indicate that she was ready.

Now Gladstone growled: "The lines are secure? The transmission won't be accessible by anyone else in the building?"

"No…" Weston started to reply, before he was cut off by the Aurora security guard to whom Gladstone's question had been addressed; "We've secured all the data streams. You have complete control."

Gladstone nodded, satisfied. He stood, going toward the door of the studio. "Ready?" he asked Weston. The producer nodded nervously.

Just then another figure appeared in the room. No door had opened so he must have been already there for some undefined period of time, but somehow Weston hadn't noticed the shadow man's presence until now. Weston shuddered a little.

The man strode to the studio door, getting there before Gladstone, who obligingly stood back and waited. He looked in at Lucy, and said: "Say nothing that might bring him back." And he stepped away.

Lucy looked as confused and terrified as ever as Gladstone looked toward her and nodded. In a trembling voice she began.

In no uncertain terms, she stated for the recording that she had found herself pregnant shortly after breaking off her affair with Traver, that she had kept the child (a boy named "Oleander"), and that she had tried to make a go of it on her own (at first with the help of her subsequent benefactor/lover, who had eventually left her to fend for herself). "Now," she said, her feeble voice breaking even more, "I'm finally coming to you for help. Your lawyers and your company will just turn me away. Actually I only convinced them to let me message you by threatening to tell the media about the baby." Then she broke down into sobs, before closing with a heartfelt demand for a yearly pension to be bequeathed to her and her lovechild.

Weston fumed. None of this, of course, was true. He knew it wasn't true, since he'd had his nose deep in the SASH Public Relations investigation to ensure all traces of the Lucy scandal were wiped clean. There had been no pregnancy and Lucy was still attached to her new benefactor, a successful dog trainer named Robby Rothwell. To present the affair business as being unfinished – even for the sake of getting Traver's attention – seemed unfair to Traver, to Lucy, to Weston himself.

"Again. Need to do it again." The shadow man stood up, shaking his head.

"What's the matter?" inquired Gladstone, trying not to sound nervous.

"It's scripted and it sounds like it."

Lucy looked up hopefully when the door opened and she made as if to stand, but then she collapsed, sulking in her chair as the word was given to her that the recording needed to be made a second time.

Again she said her piece. Again the shadow man shook his head and she was made to repeat it. Soon Weston became aware that the tears falling down her face were real tears of exhaustion and terror. Each recording became more emotionally genuine and Weston knew why; they were torturing the poor girl. As they began the fourth recording, then the fifth, Weston's distaste for Lucy turned into pity, and his anger directed itself only toward the men from Aurora who were standing close beside him, directing his every action and watching his every move.

"It's too close to the heart for my liking," muttered the shadow man during the sixth take, while Lucy choked on her own sobs. "We can't take the risk that he'll respond by coming home."

"You needed him to respond. This is how we get him to respond." Gladstone responded with admirable composure, though Weston could still see his terror, indicative of stakes higher than the mere loss of a job.

"Well, under no circumstances can he turn around now. That has to be understood."

Gladstone nodded.

During the seventh recording (it was nearly five o'clock in the morning and most of the eyes in the room – with the exception of the shadow man's – were bloodshot), Weston, too exhausted to be afraid anymore, dared to ask the question that had been on his mind since the first time Lucy made her fabricated declaration: "Even if Mister Graff does respond to this, how is it going to help you?" He received a blank stare from Gladstone, then pressed the issue. "You want to know the status of the crew, and what happened to the captain, but he's not going to say any of those things in response to Lucy having a baby. Why don't you just ask him directly?"

"Who do you think sent the first video?"

"Lance."

"Who is the only one in that cockpit who knows how to pack and transmit a recorded message?"

"Lance."

"And we're giving him a chance to respond. It's *his* message we're waiting for. Not Traver's."

Weston thought he was beginning to understand, but was too angry and tired to be certain. Lucy's monologuing had devolved into little more than meaningless babble, and he was surprised when the shadow man nodded after the eighth go. Gladstone stood and ushered the young woman, now really crying with her whole body trembling, out of the studio. He whispered something to her before she could go on through the hallway. Whatever he said to her, it evoked an even more intense shaking and unevenness in her troubled breathing. Two of the Aurora guards escorted her out and she vanished from Weston's line of vision.

"Send it" was the only command that Weston now received. Nodding, he did as he was told. Using the same transmission process as for each previous message to Traver, he sent Lucy's dramatic plea on to the *Aten*.

"And now we wait." Gladstone was showing signs of exhaustion, as were most of the other techs and guards who accompanied him.

The shadow man was no longer present, though Weston couldn't be sure when he'd departed.

Weston himself couldn't remember the last time he'd been home, and he didn't think now was a good time to ask if he might retire. But he had slept in his producer's chair before when the situation demanded it. Surely Gladstone wouldn't deny him that much.

He didn't realize he'd fallen asleep when he was abruptly woken. The clock, to which his eyes first darted, read *12:06*. It was after noon and he'd slept for more than six hours. He did not regret it except for the fact that he'd been surrounded by Aurora men for the entirety of that time.

It was one of the guards who was shaking him now. A soft *beep* was coming from the computer. Weston knew that beep instantly – it was the beep he'd eagerly awaited all through the previous weeks when he'd heard nothing from Traver after the broadcast barrage. A shiver, a thrill went through his body as he finished the job of jolting himself awake. All his anger and dread, for the moment, dissipated. If this meant they were to finally hear something, anything new from Traver himself, so long silent, then perhaps all these tribulations had been worthwhile.

No words were spoken in the room. Instead there was a silent hustle and bustle as Weston began the unpacking process for the transmitted data and the Aurora techs set up their own equipment to make multiple copies of whatever message had arrived.

Gladstone waited breathlessly, and the shadow man reappeared.

The data finished unpacking, and Weston played the transmission. It was Traver:

"Weston, this message is for Lucy Kurowski. Lucy, you could have come to me before. I'm so very, very sorry…I can't adequately express my apologies for what I've unwittingly put you through. Though, if you'd come to me before, I could have helped you. That you did not was your own decision. For *that* I'm not responsible.

"That being said, it's a relief to me that, at least according to my interpretation of your message, you're not asking for me to be a father. As you know, my fatherhood is accounted for, and there was never room for an addition to the family I already have.

"I won't be back to meet Oleander, since I will likely not be coming back at all, but I'm more than happy to send a yearly allowance that will last his first eighteen years. If Weston would please be so kind as to show this transmission to Chad Brucker, my lawyer, this will have to serve as my authorization for him to set aside a reasonable yearly sum, which you are free to negotiate.

"Thank you for your honesty with me."

That was all.

Traver appeared seated in the cockpit, recorded by the devices generally utilized by the captain for official communications. If Lance was also present, he was beyond the view of the camera. Otherwise the cockpit was empty. A significant greenish glow supplemented the white console lights in illuminating Traver's face.

Traver himself looked haggard beyond what Weston had seen in even the latter broadcasts. He wore a thin and patchy beard, grown to an ugly length. His hair had continued uncut and untended, and his frame had shrunk to a thin skeleton of what it had been.

"Open up the encrypted metadata." Gladstone was impatient. Weston would have all the time in the world to study Traver's unhealthy face, but now time was pressing.

It didn't take long for Weston to detect irregularities in the code of the metadata. "I think this is what you're looking for" he said with some measure of professional pride. He pointed out a series of seemingly irrelevant words, scattered so as to not affect the data stream, and it was less than five minutes before he and the Aurora techs had assembled Lance's message:

KARL MISLEH AKERS ULTRECHT PARKER DEAD FROM ACCIDENTS
AKACHI FRIEDRICH DEAD BY TRAVER
WITH GUN TOOK SHIP

CAPTAIN ALIVE LOCKED OUT
GOING TO PLANET DESPITE FLETCHER
HELP

Nobody read it aloud. Each person in the room internalized it, studying each word multiple times, but didn't breathe a word.

Weston could nearly hear his own heart beating and feel the ripples it sent through the frozen room. Only then did the silence make him wonder: *where is everyone?* The SASH building should be abuzz right now with afternoon meetings and press releases, but this day had been completely silent, the studio undisturbed.

The shadow man broke the silence in a voice louder than the one he normally output. "Copy it down. Copy all of it and then wipe it off their servers." He was presumably speaking to his own men, who like ants set about doing what he'd ordered. Within seventy seconds no trace was left of the transmission, sent or received, on the SASH drives or servers, and the men had packed it all safely into a briefcase which was then rushed out the door.

The shadow man himself followed suit without so much as a glance at Weston.

Gladstone was left behind. Weston feared he remained alone to tie up the final loose end: himself. But the incoming messages and the adrenaline that followed (added to the sleep he'd finally gotten) had erased the helplessness that Weston had felt, and he stood up to bravely face whatever condemnation he was sure Gladstone was about to declare.

But Gladstone continued in a businesslike manner: "It should go without saying that transmissions from the *Aten* will no longer be retrievable by this facility. The Aurora Corporation will deal with all such messages going forward. Our technicians have already made the necessary adjustments."

"And what am I supposed to do now?"

Gladstone seemed taken aback by Weston's fortitude. He answered coldly as ever: "Keep broadcasting every week, of course. You have his material. The rest of this, I trust time *will* help you forget. Have a pleasant afternoon."

But before Gladstone could go, Weston did the unthinkable. He raced forward, cutting Gladstone off from the hallway. The taller man seemed confused by this and stopped in his tracks, allowing Weston to close in on him, bringing his face within breathing distance of his own.

"I'm just going to let this go? No, I don't think so, Mister Gladstone. If it weren't for me you still wouldn't have any idea what was going on out there. There are any number of things I could have done with Lance's first recording – I didn't have to send it to you people. But I did because I wanted what was best for Traver, because he's my friend, and I still want what's best for him. There's no way I'm going to forget about all this."

Gladstone reached into his pocket, a gesture that first gave Weston a fright until he saw the handkerchief that was produced. With it, Gladstone wiped his face of the tiny droplets of spit that had flown out of Weston's mouth during the tirade.

Visibly struggling to maintain his composure (though never stepping back to distance himself from the producer), Gladstone folded the handkerchief, put it back in his pocket, and responded in a calm voice. "You probably noticed that this facility was empty today. We cleared it early this morning to ensure our work would not be bothered by your peers. Tomorrow morning, its work will continue as normal. You, however, will not."

With that, he stepped past Weston, letting his shoulder bump against him as he passed.

Weston watched him go, and the momentary bravery he'd felt now faded away, overtaken by a cold sweat and the threat of another breakdown.

* * *

All that night, despite being once again in the comfort of his own apartment, Weston could not sleep. He feared every bump in the hallway, every whistle of the air system, and even dreaded every moment of prolonged silence. In each instance his mind saw the approach of the skilled assassin he was certain Aurora had sent for him. Staying in his apartment, he knew he was a sitting duck. But what good would it do to leave? Aurora was certain to hire an assassin capable of finding his quarry regardless of where the victim might flee.

But the morning came, and Weston wasn't dead.

Driven by the need for familiar routine after the nightmare of the last two days, Weston went to work at his usually scheduled time. He fumbled his way through the morning commute, stepped clumsily off the airbus at the station, and made his way to the side employee entrance of the grey SASH building. All was done by muscle memory since his mind was some six and a half light years away. He didn't fully become aware of his present surroundings until his keychip, after three swipes, failed to open the employee door.

He made the long walk around the building, up to the big front doors, but his heart sank a little more with every step. That Gladstone's threat had been for his job rather than his life hadn't occurred to him at any point during the long night, but was not much comfort now.

He first walked past the front desk and attempted to open the glass door leading to the elevators. Again his chip failed him. So he made his way back to the desk to ask one of the four clueless receptionists to call Karen Tiplins and tell her Weston Hillquist needed access.

As one of the receptionists made the call, Weston glanced up through the glass walls toward his own office. He saw technicians, four or five of them, hard at work disassembling his computer system.

So that was that, then.

Even before the receptionist tensely put down the interphone, caution radiating from her face, Weston knew to move toward the door.

Sure enough, security guards – the same stonefaced men who had been contracted to watch over Traver – caught up with him, giving him a speed boost of which he would not have been capable on his own.

Without a word of recognition or apology (Weston had seen both men every day for years prior, and once bought them lunch while Traver was doing a special double-feature), they pushed him through the front doors.

Weston was left out in the cold.

CHAPTER TEN
CALLIE

To my loving brother, Fyodor Shurovsky,

My heart was broken to receive your letter. Knowing now the way you feel, knowing how horribly this news is affecting you and your children, I utterly regret having kept my announcement from you. It was my hope to spare your feelings for as long as possible, but now I see how selfish that was, and how it was my own feelings I was sparing.

So I will tell you plainly now, that I have been infected by Eams. That should answer your first question. I will never know where I acquired the bacteria, for my dealings with all my patients were under sterile conditions. Perhaps it had nothing at all to do with my work. That is what I suspect. It could have been a glass of unfiltered water, or a fork that hadn't been cleaned all the way. The odds are nearly miraculous. It is almost as if Eams chose me.

Your second question is an easy one to answer, because I happen to be the expert who knows these things. It is likely that I have less than one year left. I hope your family is prepared to see a lot of me in the upcoming months, because I plan to take a step back away from my work and spend more time with my treasures. While it is tempting to only absorb myself deeper in my work, I believe that my devotion to scientific research over my whole life has robbed me of much of my humanity. Maybe in my last year I can regain some of it.

Your third question is the most complicated to answer. You ask two things, really. The first is whether I have treatments to extend my own life. To that I answer: only slightly. My injections have an effect which has been much exaggerated by my corporation's publicity. At most they will give me a few more months of life, but I will suffer greatly. No, I will not use the treatments, though they were my own development.

In answer to the second part of this question: is there a cure? Yes, and also no. For a long time I have known about something that would eradicate Eams completely from the human body. In some ways I knew about this cure before I knew about Eams, but that is a very long and complicated story.

Why did I not use this cure on others? For the same reason I will not use it on myself. It is too unpredictable. The benefits may not be enough to justify using something we have not been able to fully study. It is not really even a cure, speaking technically, since it pre-existed Eams. It is more an enemy of Eams. That's all I can really say about it, since this subject is not public knowledge.

I'm sorry if that is not the answer you were looking for. I know how hard it must be for you to explain to the children that they are going to lose an aunt. But maybe it will help them to know that I don't feel sad. For my part I have accepted my fate. It seems a beautiful irony that the universe should bestow Eams upon me, of all people. It seems like justice.

I'm afraid I've grown long-winded. This has been enough talk about myself. It would be my pleasure to see you and your family sometime soon. Perhaps Easter? I can hire a zip jet and be in Moscow whenever you will have me. I'll bake my famous minty candies, which I hope the children will remember. They seemed to take a liking to them last time I was there.

With love,
Galina

The weeks that followed his expulsion from the SASH were the worst of Weston's life.

He lived alone. The long hours of producer work had for years prevented him from ever feeling the pangs that usually accompany a lack of human companionship. With no office to go to and no bustling production schedule to maintain, he felt the emptiness crash over him like a cold and hollow wave.

To find new employment or to change his circumstances at all never occurred to him. The money he had put away would allow him to live comfortably enough. It was sufficient to pay rent on his eightieth floor, plushly-furnished Brooklyn apartment and to eat three full meals a day, at least for a while. But it wasn't enough to travel anywhere, to relocate, or (and this was the most devastating) to purchase himself a personal computer system. Programming, transmitting, creating, recording – those had all been his passions, but his work computer was his only computer, and that was something he no longer had.

Some people, finding themselves robbed of their livelihood and ability to pursue their passions, take the opportunity to reboot, to plot a new course, find and overcome new obstacles. Weston was not one of those people. He sank deeper into his couch every day, watching comedies and ordering pastas and cinnamon rolls. Within three weeks, it occurred to him that his savings would last only about two more months of living at his current rate. His response to this realization was to consciously forgo a pricey cheesecake-stuffed pastry desert for three whole nights in a row, before resuming as usual on the fourth.

His fear of the Aurora Corporation dissipated quickly after a week with no assassins arriving for him. But a kernel of frustration remained over the fact that he was cut off from Traver. That, perhaps, was the worst thing of all. On a weekly basis, as a matter of sacred tradition, he turned to the SASH network for the *Traver Talk* segment, and he watched and listened to the words he knew had been recorded months ago. Some of the snippets he had already seen as he'd perused the files upon first receiving them, and some of the sections were new to him. But each show cured his loneliness for a period of sixty minutes during which he was once again Traver's valued, trustworthy producer.

Five weeks into his exile from society, Weston received an incoming call.

Nobody had messaged or called him since before his termination, and he was almost unsure as to what the notification noise coming from his slidescreen might represent. He remembered quickly then laboriously shifted his increased heft from his couch in order to answer.

On his slidescreen appeared a woman in her mid thirties, with dark features and a sharp, arresting voice. Instantly he thought he recognized her but couldn't immediately place her face.

"Hi, Mister Hillquist, I hope I'm catching you at a good time. If you have a moment, I'd love it if you could answer a few questions for me."

"I'm not really interested, sorry." But he didn't cancel the call. He was too curious, not to mention refreshed at the possibility of speaking with a fellow human being.

"What if I told you that I'm with *Debunker Daily?*"

It clicked for Weston. He knew how he recognized her. *Debunker* was a small, digital publication that often clashed with SASH. Ideologically, the goals of both seemed the same, but *Debunker* often accused SASH of unsubstantiated, emotional drivel. Not that anyone paid any attention to the *Debunker*. Weston and others attributed *Debunker's* bitterness to envy over SASH's significant and unparalleled success.

"You're Callie Vargas."

"The very same. And you were recently let go from the Alliance, unless I'm mistaken."

He tried not to betray humiliation in his face, choosing instead to huff and puff clumsily. "How…how do you know that?"

"I asked your former co-workers. It's not a secret, Weston."

"Oh."

"Would you be willing to chat about what happened? Maybe, say, tomorrow over lunch?"

"For the *Debunker*? No. This isn't worth a story."

"The story isn't about you. It's about the Aurora Corporation. You fellows over at the Alliance are no strangers to digging your claws into that cow. Now it's our turn to dip our toes in the water – hot water."

Weston could feel his eyes widening and his brow furrowing, but couldn't seem to do anything to stop either.

"No. I can't help you."

Before she would have had time to hear the punctuation mark at the end of his statement, he ended the call.

The apartment was silent again.

Late that night, long past the time when he would have been asleep had he still worked a job that required him to be awake in the morning, he called her back.

The call took a moment to be answered. He waited, knowing that any journalistic soul worth her salt would hardly be asleep at the ripe and productive hour of one-thirty.

Of course she wasn't asleep.

"If you're calling about the lunch meeting tomorrow, I've already booked another interview so I'm afraid we'll need to reschedule."

"Okay. For when?"

* * *

The following evening Weston met with Callie Vargas at a corner table of the *Downed Eagle*. Weston was completely unfamiliar with such places; this was one of very few old-fashioned bars still in operation in this part of the city, with beer taps, booths and live music. He fidgeted uncomfortably.

"Relax. These places grow on you. Graff loves it here. He and I would sit right over there." She pointed at the bar.

Weston thought it hard to believe that Traver Graff was the type to frequent a dingy, lowlife hole-in-the-wall that served *beer*, but then again he hadn't thought Traver the type to mutiny onboard a spaceship. Life was full of surprises.

"So, Miss Vargas...Missus Vargas?"

"Callie."

"Callie. Tell me about your story."

"You'll have to speak up."

Weston leaned in. Despite the loudness of the place, he was cautious about being overheard. He hadn't in fact been able to sleep since her first call, his fear of assassins having been reignited at the mention of Aurora.

"The story you're doing. What is it going to be, exactly?"

"I already told you. It's about Aurora."

Weston looked back and forth nervously. There was nobody spying on them – not that he could see.

"You know what I mean. What's your...you know..."

"Angle?"

"Yeah. I guess. What's your angle? You *Debunker* people are always saying you won't run with a story until it's rock solid."

"Better than you people, who run with a new idea just because Graff or D'Arco or one of your other leaders of sheep get excited about something new. Don't get me wrong, I love Graff, as a person. But as a public figure, he's a bad, bad idea."

"You still haven't answered my question."

"You're a grump! Come on, we're not on a tight schedule. Enjoy the drink, man! You may have lost your job – a good job – okay a great job – but it's not the end of the world."

It was closer to the end of the world than she realized. Weston thought he should wait to correct her. But he couldn't.

"It's worse than just losing my job..."

A notebook and pen appeared on the table within a half-second. Callie's eyes focused though her relaxed smile never faded. "Yeah? What could be worse than losing a job at the SASH, the biggest social justice hub in North America? You were personal producer to Graff, for god's sake."

Weston tried to answer, but ended up supporting his forehead in his hand, shaking his head back and forth slowly.

"Drink some beer."

"I don't like beer."

"Then you're shit out of luck because that's all they serve here. What else happened the night you were fired?"

Again Weston went silent.

"Your headquarters were shut down completely for the entire day. That hasn't happened before, *ever*. I checked. Nobody I talked to seemed to know any reason for the shutdown, but what they all did agree on was that Aurora personnel had arrived on the premises the previous evening for, I quote: 'transmission equipment installation.' Convince me that it's a coincidence."

Weston thought for a moment, his head still in his hand but no longer shaking. "It was a big installation. A major overhaul. They needed to clear the building." He didn't know how good or bad of a liar he was.

"Nope. No hardware was touched. Nothing changed. I got access to work orders, invoices, and equipment inventories. Not a thing was altered that day. Not officially."

Now Weston looked up at the woman seated across from him. Though her voice had intensified and grown sharper, her casual smile hadn't left her face. She may as well have been jokingly commenting on his over-gentrified choice of clothing, if her countenance was to be believed. Weston began to feel more comfortable around her.

"You must have talked to a lot of people over there. I don't even know who would be the person to ask for work order history, and I've worked there for almost a decade."

"I know how to find things." Her eyes joined her mouth in smiling.

"I could tell you what happened that day. But I just don't want to tell you *here*."

"Fair enough. Too many people. Too much noise. I get it. I'd much rather go somewhere private, quiet, away from crowds. Someplace where, if we were to be followed by Aurora agents, they could nab you quick without anybody noticing, before you get a chance to finish telling me your story. If that's what you want – getting yourself nabbed or killed before I can get the scoop from you – then this place, with all these people around us, isn't at all ideal for this conversation." She raised her eyebrows at him, then chugged her drink. Her pen and notebook remained on the table.

A long sigh from Weston followed. "Okay. Okay. Where to start? I got...I got a broadcast from Traver. Only, it wasn't just *one* broadcast."

So Weston went on, and the hours did too.

* * *

Upon leaving the bar and embarking upon the subway, Weston's trustful feelings, having been encouraged by Callie's never-ending smile, faded away by degrees. By the time he reached his apartment, he fully regretted having shared even a little bit of information – let alone the vast bulk of it – with Ms. Vargas. It wasn't Aurora he feared now (although he realized he'd reasons aplenty to do so), but the dissemination of the information itself. No good could ever come from spreading a story to the public for the sake of a sensation. His own experiences with Aurora, awful as they had been, should not have been allowed to spread any farther than himself.

If he had one consolation, it was that he had resisted the impulse to betray Traver's supposed violent hijackery. For one thing, that was the only part of the story he himself didn't fully believe – there were too many question marks surrounding the precise sequence of events that had occurred on the *Aten*, and until those events were clarified, Traver was innocent in Weston's mind. For another thing, he would not be able to bear a media outlet sullying Traver's reputation with a story that would surely be exaggerated, and would almost certainly lead to a slew of tabloids demonizing Traver as some sort of monster.

With those small comforts in mind Weston was able to sleep that night – until four in the morning anyway, when he again received a call, audio only this time, from Callie.

"I didn't think I would hear from you again so soon" Weston muttered, only half-awake. "Did you forget to ask me something?"

"Weston." There was no mirth in her voice, though Weston was sure she was still somehow managing to smile on the other end. "Did Graff's original transmission with all the broadcasts stay encrypted?"

"Uh, yes. Well, they made me make copies of it all when the truth finally came out at headquarters, but my original copies stayed where I originally hid them."

"Do you remember how to access them?"

"I can't access anything. I'm locked out."

"Yes. I remember that part. Supposing you were given access to the system. Could you find the encrypted data and unlock them?"

"Of course I could. But every step of the process would usually need me to put in my passwords and credentials..."

"Don't worry about passwords and credentials. Can you meet me?"

"What. Now?"

"No. A year from last Tuesday. Yes, now."

"Okay." He began to put himself through the struggle of donning his pants. "Where?"

"Thirty-two-twenty-nine Sable Valley Drive. Did you jot that down?"

"Got it. I'll be there soon."

Sable Valley Drive, it turned out, was not within the city or even its outlying communities. Neither the airbuses nor the subway routes extended out to what amounted to a suburb of an industrial zone.

Weston could usually depend on normal public transit to get everywhere he needed to go, and hiring a skycab (as he now had to do) was well out of his comfort zone and price range. But the driver, a friendly Chinese man named Lao, got him there efficiently in just over two hours.

When the skycab left the travel lane twenty meters above the ground and descended, Weston could see that below them still ran old asphalt roads, crumbling with age. The cab fare increased now for, as Lao informed him, "wheels' wear and tear."

The rest of the ride was bumpy – asphalt roads were no longer maintained, particularly in rural areas of dwindling population, of which this was no exception. The road wound its way past courts and cul-de-sacs, the driver blazing past old rusty stop signs at intersections that might never see two concurrently crossing cars ever again. The homes were large and spread far apart, but where once must have been well-kept lawns and lush trees were only dead weeds and rotting wooden skeletons. The artificial irrigation and atmosphere control systems that fed the city didn't reach this far, and the land was slowly being left to die.

One thing that was a refreshing change was the sky. Aside from a few towering plants and factories, some near and some far, the sky was wide open. In the city, where Weston had spent the entirety of his life, one hardly ever saw the sky. He reflected that there must have been a time when all of mankind could have looked up and contemplated the vast plains of the sky and been awed at the very prospect of exploring it. The thought seemed peaceful.

Lao pulled the cab in front of a dilapidated two-story brick house. Weston looked at it doubtfully for a long moment during which Lao watched him expectantly.

"Is this no right place?" Lao asked to speed the disembarkment process.

"It must be," replied Weston. "Never been here before. Just, I was told to meet somebody here. I don't usually come out this way." Lao nodded understandably, but curtly. Weston's justification was immaterial to the driver, but then again it was meant more for himself anyway.

He paid his fare and stepped out. The cab sped away over the cracked road, and Weston turned toward the house.

A couple of old style automobiles, of which Weston had rarely seen many outside of museums, sat in the driveway. So there was somebody home, at least. He pushed open the creaking picket gate (made of real wood, which was impressive even if it was rotten) and made his way up to the dust-covered patio. He lifted up his fist to knock on the door, but he couldn't do it. Now came the flood of second thoughts and self-doubts. He turned around several times, looking back at the road and contemplating how long it would take him to walk to the nearest truck or train station, versus how long it would take for another cab to arrive should he call one. But neither escape seemed worthwhile, not when he'd already come this far. Yes, he could call the day a waste of time and money, then return to his lonely apartment and go on living in silence until his savings ran completely dry, and then what? Perhaps his current predicament was not a comfortable one, but it was better than the stagnant alternative.

Gingerly, he knocked on the door.

The house creaked in unison with the approaching footsteps, and then the door itself scraped open.

Callie was smiling. "You took a cab from home, didn't you?"

"Um…"

"No wonder it took you so long. Airbus, train, then cab – that's the fastest way. You'll get it."

He followed her inside. The house's well-lit interior bore little resemblance to the shambles outside; clean white walls, smooth rustic floors and sleek modern furniture lent the place a homey if disjointed appeal. The smell of frying food wafted from the kitchen.

Weston had barely begun to wonder whether anyone else was here when a man's voice, soft and slow, called out from an unseen room down the hallway: "is it him?"

"Who else would it be?" replied Callie.

"Tell him he can have some breakfast."

She turned to Weston. "You can have some breakfast."

"Oh. Great. Thanks." Weston never refused gifted food, even in a stranger's home.

"But have him hurry. I would rather this didn't take too long."

Quickly as he could, Weston piled egg and bacon synthetics onto his plate, then Callie rushed him down a hall and into a bedroom that had been converted into an office. It was dimly-lit compared to the windowed kitchen, and once his eyes adjusted Weston saw that the room was more than just a personal office. Transmissions equipment, servers and drives lined the walls or were stacked haphazardly on the floor. Three separate but fully-functioning computer systems sat on desks (and one on the floor). Silhouetted against the dim blue light of one of the desk systems was a gigantic hunched form. It did not move as Weston and Callie stepped into the room.

"Laffy, this is Weston."

Slowly the hunched form lifted its neck and turned, revealing a head that was disproportionately small compared to the bulky creature beneath it. Weston saw a squat face with its chin too close to its forehead.

Laffy's bug eyes studied Weston for a moment, blinking twice too often, and then the head turned back to the monitor like a branch swaying in the wind. "Hey Weston" came the soft, high voice that Weston couldn't believe was produced by so large a person.

Callie stepped fully into the room. "Weston, Laffy is a communications whiz and an old friend of mine."

"Used to work at Aurora" came Laffy's voice before Callie could continue.

"What did you do at Aurora?" asked Weston.

"Communications stuff." The giant shoulders shrugged.

"He's my main source for inside information on the Corporation."

"For your story?" Weston still sounded skeptical.

"For my story."

The big man butted in with obvious impatience, despite the slowness of his articulation. "I'd like to get this over with quickly. I don't want to keep this link open too long. Not that anyone will be looking, probably. Just don't want to take any chances."

"What link?" Weston began to suspect what he was being roped into.

Callie stepped closer to him. "I asked you if you could access Traver's entire set of broadcasts if we got you in to your old system."

"Yes? I mean, yes. I could."

"Well, here you go."

With surprising quickness, the hunched giant rolled his chair back from the computer and stood up. His hunch never straightened but he still towered a full half meter over Weston. "Feel free to have a seat."

Weston inched closer to the computer. Sure enough, it was connected to the SASH media network. Everything contained in the servers in the headquarters facility would be fully accessible to him here. It took a moment before he could fully believe what he was seeing.

"This – this is everything. I mean, all our media is stored right here. Why do you even need the files I hid and encrypted, when you can access the main storage? Those broadcasts have been sitting on these servers for weeks, ever since my boss found out they existed."

Laffy swung his head around and down to look at Callie. She nodded a slight nod that was meant to be imperceptible. As if he'd just been given approval, Laffy turned the unsteady gaze of his large eyes back on Weston.

"Those files require passwords to access. Administrative

passwords."

"Yes, but that didn't stop you from getting in to the system. You obviously needed a password and a lot more to do that."

The giant shook his head sadly. "It wasn't hard to open a link into your servers, but the protections on specific media projects are much more complicated to break through. It's possible…" – Callie threw him a sharp look – "but would probably take too long. Probably not actually possible."

Weston scratched his head. He was nervous again, not because he feared for his life as he had under Gladstone, but because he didn't know precisely what he ought to be fearing should he refuse his new friends' requests.

"Why, though? You haven't told me why you want the broadcasts."

Again Laffy looked at Callie. It was her turn to respond.

"I'm not going to broadcast them myself, if that's what you're afraid of. Just being able to prove their existence should be enough. They'll be the evidence I need to back up my story."

"And what is the story?"

Callie sighed, clenching her eyes shut for a moment. "I'm not done putting it all together yet."

"But you know what it's about, or else you wouldn't be looking for something so specific as Traver's broadcasts."

Now Callie almost sounded angry. "I don't go into a story knowing what it's going to be. The story grows out of the evidence, not the other way around. Who do you think I am? Graff?"

"Like I said," the giant was trying to shout, but his voice couldn't help its soft, friendly sound, "I don't want to leave this link open for too long. So Westing –"

"Weston."

"–Weston, could you please find those files? Quickly?"

The ex-producer took a step back, toward the open door of the office. He felt a strange comfort when neither of the others made a move to intercept.

"Wait." Callie's coolness seemed to have mostly returned. "You're absolutely correct; you have no reason to give up your files without knowing what I'm doing with them. So, I'll show you."

Laffy looked at her questioningly. If possible, his eyes grew even wider. "Show him what? I don't want to stay connected to the servers much longer."

"Alright then, shut down the link. You are able to open it later, right?"

"Yeah."

"There's no deadline on this. For now, let's share the *Pytheas* file with Weston. Weston can keep a secret, can't he?"

Weston looked at her through squinted eyes, not knowing how else to respond.

"Of course you can," Callie answered for herself. "All the shenanigans with Aurora and poor not-really-pregnant Lucy, and you haven't breathed a word to anyone."

Weston was mostly immune to surprises at this point, and his nerves could not be set anymore on edge than they already were. He simply stepped forward again and demanded: "show me."

Laffy sat back down in the chair that struggled beneath him, and moved his large fingers across the keyboards with alarming and unreal speed. Not a minute later, he moved wordlessly out of the seat and made room for Weston. A file appeared on the monitor.

"These are Aurora documents" Weston observed, once again truly surprised.

"Yes they are."

"But they're classified."

"Read it."

And Weston did.

....

Internal Memo – Aurora Corporation, 2157

Spoke with the rep from Cooperative. Pilots will not condone the project to TY-71887 as currently planned due to code sanctions. Aguilar and Misleh wish to proceed regardless. I spoke with Shurovsky and she agrees. We will work around sanctions. Consider project Pytheas *greenlit.*

Please fit a Mollusk-class probe for launch within month. Standard A.I. install for self-piloting and sustained orbit of one solar year.

Probe is to be fit with full array of metering devices: mission's primary goal is to detect vibrations from the planet in hopes of replicating Zilly situation.

Pilot's Cooperative involvement will be nonexistent for 'unmanned' craft. Media dissemination is approved.

Secondary notes: refit hull of the Pytheas *for comatose occupant. Volunteer test subject is to be transported to and from planet while in stasis and given over to Drs. Aguilar and Misleh for study. Occupant is not to be mentioned in briefings or press releases.*

....

Weston read over the document twice. He didn't pretend to understand why it was so important to Callie and her mountainous companion, but he did find several points very confusing.

"What do they mean by the 'Zilly situation?'"

Callie bounced as she took a lively step backward. "Laffy is your man to answer that question."

Weston tilted his head questioningly at Laffy, and the large man began to speak in his soft, plodding way.

"So, everyone knows what happened with Zilly: they found some plants, they sent a space station, then the planet fell apart and the astronaut and the *Virgil* vanished into space. But I was a whiz kid working at Aurora back then. The S.T.A.R.S. company was already using our transmission technology so I was part of the communication team.

"Before we lost contact with the *Virgil*, pulses and vibrations were picked up by the station's computer and *interpreted* somehow. The onboard A.I. had read the tremors as communications and responded. It even communicated to Eve, the astronaut, that the planet was the origin of the command codes.

"We tried to figure it out for years afterwards, but none of us could make head or tail of those pulses from the planet. The A.I. was just so adaptable, it was able to find some sort of pattern and assume it was being contacted."

Weston scratched his head. "Okay. It makes sense to me why that's something they would want to study more. It's too bad that planet didn't last long enough for more research." He sat back in the chair, still staring at the screen. "But...but what's this about the 'occupant' onboard the *Pytheas?* That was just a computerized probe, right? The *Aten* was supposed to be the first manned mission to AMA. That was the whole thing, the whole selling point. Mister Graff and all them – they were supposed to be the first people to have gone there."

Laffy shrugged. He seemed to have used up all his allotted words for the time being.

Weston didn't wait for a response. "Why keep it all such a secret? Aurora was transparent about everything else. Why is the *Pytheas'* real mission not common knowledge?"

"Now you're asking the kind of question I like to hear." Callie bounced forward again and her relaxed smile returned, but Weston no longer found it comforting.

"I didn't know all that other stuff about Zilly either. I mean, everyone knows that the space station got lost when the planet blew up, but the vibration thing; that's weird."

"It's all true though," voiced Laffy. "It was high-classified non-disclosure for everyone who knew about it."

"Why are you talking about it now?"

Laffy again shrugged, an action akin to a mountain rising. "I don't work for them anymore."

Weston paused for a moment, breathing heavily. Then he turned around in the chair and faced Callie. "You haven't really answered my question though. What story are you trying to put together with all this?"

Callie looked at Weston as if he'd just asked the color of the sky, her eyes growing wide above her astonished smile. "Aren't you wondering what they're really doing out there, right now?"

Weston had to check himself before he responded. He reminded himself that, as far as he knew, Callie still was not aware of Traver's supposed mutiny. If she had known about that, then her story would likely be very different.

Weston stood up as quickly as he could pull himself out of the seat, as if he was disgusted by the illicit contents of the computer. "I don't care what they're studying. For all I know they could be going to find out what the planet smells like. Does it really matter?"

"I should think it would matter to you, since your boss is onboard the ship. The story isn't that Aurora is studying vibrations. The story is that Aurora isn't being forthright with any of us."

"That's just your guess! You could be wrong. That probe might have gotten all the vibration information it needed, and now Misleh's bunch is going to find something completely different."

"Then, explain Graff's broadcasts," snapped Callie.

Silence fell. Laffy observed them both like a full-grown man watching two babies fighting.

Weston, unsure where Callie was going with this, ventured: "What about Traver's broadcasts?"

"It's a ploy. It's a cover for something. Aurora wants to distract the public with weekly shows that aren't really weekly at all. They chose a very visible, public figure for some reason. And now there's all this new back and forth with Graff, who's what – riding in the cockpit now?"

Weston saw an opportunity to inquire just how much Callie really knew. "You should know all about it. You're the ones hacking into everyone's systems."

Laffy now felt obliged to clarify: "I only can get access to the Aurora documents from the archives. And company mailboxes, which is how we knew about what happened the night before you got fired."

The mystique of these new acquaintances was quickly falling into shambles. These two didn't know nearly as much as Weston had thought. They were playing guessing games.

Weston looked squarely at Callie, feeling empowered by his perception of her weakness. "So you're a sensationalist after all."

She bit her lip, frustrated. "Sensationalist? How?"

"All you know for sure is two things. One: Aurora does secret things sometimes. Two: Traver already recorded all his broadcasts. I think you're really only worried about number two, because you want to hurt his reputation."

"Hurt his... Graff's a friend – a good friend."

"Or at the very least you want to ride his wave a little, pick up some of that sweet popularity of his. In any case, your story's wrong, because I know some other things that you don't know."

It was hunger that blazed in Callie's eyes. "What do you know?"

"I'll tell you one of the things I know." Weston was feeling in control now, and enjoying it. "Nobody else had any control over Traver getting all his shows done at once. That was his own decision. So that whole thing is completely separate from any Aurora story you're doing."

"You're not seeing the big picture, Weston."

"I don't see that there is a big picture."

"After everything Aurora did to you, I'd think you'd be more than happy to help hurt their image."

"Yeah, I am. You're right. I'd love to help with your story. But Traver isn't part of that story. He wanted to broadcast the way he did, and I'm not going to be helping you change the way people hear him. Say what you want about the Corporation, but those shows belong to Traver."

The giant leaned down, a mighty tree bending in the wind, and whispered something to Callie. She became suddenly calm. "Alright. We understand," she said.

"You do?"

"Yes."

"Then. Good."

"I think you'll change your mind. We also know a lot more than we've told you. There's some more recent communications we've picked up: emails and chatter from just after the night you helped them contact Graff. Much of it pertains to him."

Weston gulped down the urge to ask to see more. He had seen all he really needed to see, and nothing would change his mind.

"Nothing will change my mind. Thank you for breakfast." The food was cold now, and still sitting on the plate which he'd left on the desk beside the computer. For the first time in his life, he'd forgotten to eat.

Five minutes later, Weston was whistling a tune to himself, beginning the long, lonely walk down the decrepit street toward the nearest train station.

* * *

Poor Weston. The universe had no plans to allow him to remain in any sort of peaceful state. Not twenty-four hours after reaching his apartment in the evening, his slidescreen received a newsflash from the "space and science" section of *New York Now* (it was a subscription he'd picked up immediately following Traver's departure).

The headline read: *PILOT'S COOPERATIVE TO LAUNCH INQUIRY INTO DISAPPEARANCE OF VETERAN MEMBER.*

Just like that, the walls of secrecy which had stood between Weston's world and the blissfully ignorant public were shattered. The guarding of clandestine information, it turned out, was not possible in the modern world, not even for a mighty corporation like Aurora.

The Pilot's Cooperative had no interest in maintaining mystique when it came to the well-being of its members. They kept tabs on the whereabouts of all their active pilots, and all inquiries were matters of public record. Hence the very public news that one Captain Louisa Fletcher had fallen off the radar and out of contact.

Weston knew that the inquiry would likely take months, that it might result in a battle over information between the Cooperative and the Corporation before any resolution was found. But the outcome didn't matter right now. Right now, the world was going to find out that all was not right with the *Aten*. The moment that media outlets began to connect the dots – and they'd likely already connected them as soon as the Cooperative's news broke – Traver's broadcasts would be called into question. SASH would be forced to issue a statement, admit either deceit or ignorance, then release all the shows at once or cut them off altogether.

Even from his seclusion Weston was aware of the outcry that followed. Every audience member who had faithfully listened to Traver, every critic that had been interested in disparaging the Aurora Corp or SASH or both, demanded answers. What had happened to Traver? How was he still broadcasting when his captain had vanished? Had the Cooperative tried to contact her through Traver, who was *clearly* still reachable?

Weston imagined the media storm that must be invading the SASH headquarters right now. He was glad not to be there. Let Karen and her cronies answer the bottomless pit of questions. Weston was disconnected now, enjoying his freedom to remain passive. Even if he wanted to, there was nothing he could do despite his having been right smack at the center of the drama. He was aware of the part he had played, but that time felt like a dream now. The only action he was interested in taking was to watch the drama unfold from the safety and comfort of his couch.

A week passed, during which Weston grew a little fatter and a little more depressed.

On Friday evening, he made himself comfortable and prepared

for the only thing that still gave him any sense of community or place. The SASH network flashed its logos as Weston had designed it to do years before, and then the show began.

But instead of Traver's pale face looking down at him from space, Weston saw Karen Tiplins' thin features glaring out from the SASH recording studio.

She was saying something, though Weston was so dazed by the shock of what he knew must be happening that it took him a moment to begin processing the words coming out of her mouth:

"We think it's fitting we use this time slot to say goodbye, for now, to *Traver Talk*. I say 'for now,' because there are a lot of questions out there, questions to which we do not know the answers. The *Aten*, Traver's ship, went out of contact last week. We have not received any new transmissions from Mister Graff or from anyone onboard. The status of the ship is a mystery, and we will leave that mystery to the more capable hands of the people at Aurora who deal with this sort of thing on a regular basis. We hold out hope that contact will be re-established, that Traver will once again send us something. But if the ship was lost, as we are told ships often are, then at least Traver's message, and the message of the Secular Alliance, was vindicated."

Weston didn't hear much more. At some point, Karen cut out and a rerun of Traver's very first show began to play. Weston didn't hear that either. He was too busy pondering the reality of what had just happened.

Of course SASH had done the only thing that they could, for the sake of its reputation. To admit the broadcasts pre-existed their publication would be to admit falsification, not to mention gross negligence and insensitivity for continuing to broadcast while Traver's fate was in doubt. It made more sense for SASH to cut its losses and move forward quickly, distancing itself from the whole affair. The end of *Traver Talk* would be a harsh blow but not insurmountable.

None of that mattered to Weston, though he rationalized it all quickly enough. The only thing that mattered was Traver. Whether he was alive or dead, victim or mutineer were details over which Weston had no control. The producer had been responsible for one thing: transmitting Traver's message to the world. With seventy-nine episodes remaining, the message had been cut off. Weston had failed and the world would never know what Traver Graff had to tell them in the end.

He began to type a message to Callie Vargas on his slidescreen: *"I'll meet with you again."*

The message was barely sent when he heard a knock on his door. It was by now late at night, near one in the morning after a restless and altogether futile attempt at sleep. Weston knew who stood at the door before he got as far as standing to open it.

"Did you just send this message now? Great minds think alike, but I beat you to it by a little." Callie studied the inside of his apartment, nodding her approval as she slipped in uninvited.

Nor was she alone. Behind her stood three people whom Weston had never seen before. Weston stared at them, stammering.

When Callie had proceeded into the living room she turned around. "Oh, may they come in too?"

"Who are they?"

"Weston, this is Drew Mausberg, Lisa Zweicker and Ellen Gandy. Friends of mine. Why don't you all make yourselves at home?"

The trio followed Callie obligingly with little more than curt nods at Weston, who could only look back and forth helplessly.

"I couldn't convince Laffy to come out tonight. He doesn't move out of the house except when he really needs to, so it looks like this is the whole party."

Weston quickly shut the door behind the last of the newcomers and tried his best to be courteous. "Okay. Um, I'm Weston. Are you all hackers too?" The vitality had drained out of his face and voice so the best he could muster was a dull monotone.

"Ha ha, no," Callie answered for them. "But they're helping me with the research, and with some of the funding that goes into that.

Like you, they each have a good reason to want to peel some layers away from the space programs and find out what's underneath."

Drew was an older-middle-aged man with curly grey hair and a face that looked sad despite any number of polite smiles. Lisa was an ancient woman who could hardly stay on her feet without falling over, and Ellen was a young, heavyset woman of probably no more than twenty.

"I honestly don't care about what's going on with the space programs. I told you that." Weston's monotone served him well, communicating a complete disinterest in anything that was being said.

"Tell him about yourselves. Drew, you go first."

Drew tightened his lips as if remembering a painful memory. "You remember the Zilly mission?"

"Everyone remembers the Zilly mission. Why is it all you people seem to care about is the goddamn Zilly mission? That was thirty years ago."

"Eve Abaddon was my fiancé." Drew spoke in a hushed tone as if in eulogy.

"The astronaut?"

"They've never released any details about the final fate of her station. Only that it was lost. I never found out what happened to her."

Weston thought he saw a tear forming in the curly-headed man's eye, and he felt a twinge of empathetic sadness.

"Lisa?" Callie prompted.

The old woman took a moment to gather her words, and when she did manage to speak her head twitched unhealthily. "My son, Teddy Zweicker, was declared missing in twenty-one-fifty-nine when his ship disappeared in the Dawn Belt. It made headlines. But, he came to visit me two months *after* the news broke. We'd already had the funeral and everything, so I couldn't believe it when he walked in the front door. I was so happy to see him, but Teddy, he was nervous and, and strange. He couldn't remember many things. When we were talking, he'd go in and out of forgetting who I was. He spent the night but the next morning he was gone, and I never saw him again. What do you think the media people called me when I told them about it? Crazy. They called me crazy."

The old woman's head continued to twitch and her lips still moved but no sound came out. Callie moved on. "Finally, Ellen. Tell Weston about your dad."

Ellen perked up and spoke with a confidence that Weston found impressive given her young age. "Callie said you read the file about the *Pytheas*? So, you read about how they had a volunteer onboard that nobody knew about. That was my dad, David Gandy. Really, we weren't supposed to know. All he told us before was that he was going on a long business trip for work. He did that all the time – he worked for Aurora as a researcher. But anyway the night before he left he came in and told us to 'watch for him in the sky.' I remember, that was exactly what he said. Well he never came back from his business trip. A couple years later I connected the dots; it was the same date as the *Pytheas* departed. My dad was onboard. The *Pytheas* came back, but where's my dad?"

Silence held reign over the room for a few moments.

Weston needed to turn away from the guests. He was overwhelmed by emotions: pity, sorrow, exhaustion. Dread was strongest of all.

"They've been trying to get answers for years, and they're not the only ones" resumed Callie. "For a while it was enough that the Pilots' Cooperative was overseeing all the space missions. But that's not going to cut it anymore, if Aurora is finding ways around the sanctions and doing things it shouldn't."

Weston motioned to his kitchen stools, offering them up to the guests. All looked at the seats but none sat, so Weston lowered himself down onto one of them. "I guess you're here because you want the broadcast data from me."

"Yes," Callie was hawklike in her quick reply. "The sooner I can put together a complete story, the sooner we can bring the fight to Aurora's doors and these people can get their answers."

"If I get you the broadcast data, I want two promises from you."

"Yes, name them."

"I want all the information you've hacked, or retrieved in different ways, that's about Traver."

As he spoke, Callie held out her hand towards Drew, who handed her a sheaf of papers. She in turn handed it to Weston at the very moment he completed his demand.

"There they are: everything with Graff's name that we've pulled out of Aurora's recent communications. Printed on good old paper, just to be safe."

Weston took the stack of documents in his hand, carefully as if it was a sacred text. "Are you planning on using these for your story too?" he asked.

"There are pieces of it that I'm including, yes. I'd make the whole thing public if I could, but then I'd run into a legal issue or two."

"What's the second thing you want?" Drew was less patient than Callie, and his red eyes indicated that he, unlike her, was not used to being awake at this hour.

"I want your promise that you'll run all of Traver's episodes. SASH isn't going to do it, so somebody has to."

Callie reached out a hand and placed it gently on Weston's shoulder. The touch surprised him. Then Callie sat beside him. "That's the idea, Weston. I said before that Graff is a good friend of mine. I feel the same way you do about his message not reaching the audience he intended."

Feelings continued to rush into Weston's chest as if they rode on the blood to his heart, and he found himself nearly choking up. It took him a moment before he could say anything.

"Traver hired me, you know. He picked me out from about a dozen techs who had been working on the show when the position opened up. SASH wanted to hire from the outside, but Traver asked that I do the job. So I work for Traver. SASH may have fired me, but I'm still *his* producer."

"And they cut off his broadcasts," Callie was rubbing him on the back now.

"I know why they did. And I wish it didn't need to happen this way. I just think it's my job to get them on the air, one way or another."

Callie smiled. This smile was not part of a facade; it was a smile of anticipation as, in an matter of moments, she understood she was going to achieve her dream of becoming a known contender in the game of public opinion – and all at the expense of a poor, fat ex-producer whose only fault was being too loyal to Traver Graff.

....

Transcript of video documentary [unaired]:
"The Cairo Chaos," compiled by Carolina Vargas in 2166

Vargas: It's only my third day back in Cairo after the time I spent here three years ago, and already I can feel how different a city it's become in that short time. First the food shortage then the meteorite strike, then the devastating outbreak of Eams, have all contributed to making the culture here one of agitation and fear. Gone is the rich culture that I found in the early days of the famine, and in its place is a shyness, an aversion to outsiders, an overall sense of...despair.

But yesterday I was fortunate enough to find a man who was willing to talk to me. Amon Gamal was here during all three consecutive crises, and he lived to tell the tale. Here's my interview with Mister Gamal, who sheds a new and strange light on what really happened in Cairo.

Gamal: Hello.

Vargas: Hello, Mister Gamal! Thank you so much for taking the time to speak with me today.

Gamal: *Yes. Of course.*

Vargas: *Tell us about the year of the famine. How did that affect you, personally or at a cultural level? Obviously the whole event was a horrible crisis, but did anything stand out as being particularly odd, or out of place?*

Gamal: *I remember…I remember it was all bad. Very bad. My mother, she died of the hunger, before the help came. And one of my grandchildren, very small, very thin, nearly died also. We thank god, when the corporation arrive with the food, with the supplies, with the tools to fix the factories.*

Vargas: *And the doctors too. Don't forget about the medical aid they sent.*

Gamal: *I do not forget. No. But the doctors…it was very strange. Very strange. They give us medicine. Medicine for headache, for stomach pain. But they call for the healthiest, men and women, no children, and they give them…uh…*

Vargas: *Injection shots?*

Gamal: *Yes. Shots. They give shots. My son, he get a shot. He was healthy, strong. He asked: why? Why does he need shot? They didn't answer. They only said "he needs to have this shot." Every day, they give him shot.*

Vargas: *But it wasn't only your son.*

Gamal: *No, not only Kareem. It was maybe a hundred. Maybe more. But a hundred, yes. They give them the shots, and they fix the food, and they leave. Then everything was good for almost a year.*

Vargas: *Tell us about the meteorite.*

Gamal: *Before the doctors leave, they talk a lot about the meteor. When they feed us, they talk about the meteor. When they give the shots, they talk about the meteor. We didn't ask why. But it did seem strange that they wanted us safe from the famine, safe from disease, but the meteor? They did not care so much. Let it kick up the dust and choke the city for weeks. [he shrugs] When it finally came down from the sky, the air was very bad. We all breathed* in much dust, and some died but not too many. It was far away from the city. It could have been much worse.

Vargas: Finally – and this is the topic that I'm sure is hardest for you to talk about, Amon – will you talk about the infection? Eams?

Gamal: My son...my son was one of the first to notice that his bones... his bones were hurting him. He would try to hoist buckets of water on his back, then he would fall to the ground, terrible, terrible pain. There were doctors here, but they did not know what was wrong. More people had their bones hurting, and then the bones were breaking. In twelve months Kareem could not walk, or even hold a candle. Then he tried to eat and his teeth broke. No doctors knew how to help, and he... [here Gamal breaks down in tears]

Vargas: Eventually the doctors came, right?

Gamal: Too late, yes. The same doctors came again, the Aurora ones. They wanted to know where the bone-eating came from. They did a lot of tests and they gave some more, some different shots. They learned how to control the sickness, to make it less pain. But, it was too late, of course.

[Footage never publicly released. Stored in the *Debunker Daily* archives.]

....

A week after *Traver Talk* had been abruptly canceled, in the early hours of a Saturday morning, a posting by a little-known media outlet called *Debunker Daily* began to receive an unprecedented number of views. By the mid afternoon, all the major American news outlets and stations had linked or referenced it. In the evening, lawsuits had been threatened to remove the posting but it was too late – the remaining eighty hours of Traver's broadcasts had been stored, copied, downloaded and saved onto millions of drives and servers across the globe. The news was out and there was no reversing it.

Members of SASH, from Karen Tiplins to the receptionists to the janitors, began to receive death threats and hate messages. Bomb threats were made against their headquarters as a mob holding signs reading *TELL US THE TRUTH ABOUT TRAVER* marched for hours around the building. On Monday the SASH headquarters were shut down. For security reasons nobody was allowed to come into work.

The Aurora Corporation was silent.

Karen Tiplins gave an ill-fated press release during which she claimed: "we are trying our best to find the hackers responsible for stealing this data from our servers, and to bring them to justice." Perhaps she hadn't realized it, but admitting that SASH had ever possessed the data at all was to admit guilt in the eyes of the public. Two days later she stepped down as president of the SASH.

Weston had been among the first to find the posted broadcasts. He had, after all, been waiting impatiently for them. It was a moment he'd anticipated for god-only-knew how long, since this would be his first time seeing them in full. He began to let them play through.

Hour after hour went by and Traver's voice droned on from his seat in his cabin on the *Aten* – Traver, looking more and more tired, his hair growing more disheveled, his shirt changing periodically, but nothing else in the cabin around him shifting. *Anybody could have seen these were all recorded at once, if they'd just paid attention,* Weston let himself think once, early on. *Why is there so much fuss about his goddamn schedule choices?*

But to his frustration, Weston couldn't bring himself to focus on Traver's words; his mind was trapped within the pages of those Aurora communications he'd been given by Callie, thanks to the hard work of Laffy.

He'd read them through a dozen times. Two dozen, maybe. The vast majority of what they contained was not news to him, simply documenting the events of the night during which he'd been Aurora's prisoner in the SASH studio.

It was a final communication that continued to trouble him. It had been sent mere hours after Traver's message to Lucy had come in. Weston didn't know what it meant, but it confirmed a deeply held fear, buried so deep he hadn't even known he'd feared it.

With the words of the document repeating themselves in front of his mind's eye, blocking out the impassioned diatribe that was unfolding in front of him, Weston sat in a daze through the first twenty-one of Traver's episodes. Then there was a knock at the door.

Two public safety officials stood outside the apartment. One held a stun-stick, the other a set of restraints.

"Mister Hillquist? There's been an inquiry into your involvement in a data theft."

* * *

Weston spent the night in a holding cell, answering questions directed at him by an enforcer of the Data Security Department. Weston's encryption and subsequent decryption had been discovered and identified. The folks at the Debunker responsible for making the information public had claimed innocence in the theft of data, pointing to Weston as their source. "We were ignorant," went their official statement, "that he was no longer an employee of SASH, or that he had secured the data illegally." Weston offered a counter-accusation by directing the officers to 3229 Sable Valley Drive, but when they arrived at the remote neighborhood they found only an empty house with no signs of transmitters, computers, or an old Aurora employee named Laffy.

* * *

If Weston had been still at home for the next sixty hours, he would have eventually come to the end of Traver's broadcasts and seen the penultimate recording: a tacked-on interview by Callie Vargas where she laid the claim, in no uncertain terms, that SASH and Aurora had been lying about Traver, trying to cover up and hide his final, passionate message that was sure to be too controversial for their liking. "Censorship – that's what's happening. What ever happened to Traver Graff being able to say whatever he liked, whenever he wanted? For my part, I have no such reservations, and as a personal friend of Traver's, I am honored to be the one to ultimately present his final message to the world." Then the final message played.

That was it. There was no Aurora story, no digging into the old *Virgil* and *Pytheas* missions, no conspiracies about space vibrations. But Callie Vargas was a rich woman now.

* * *

"Shut off your transmitters, smash your entertainment centers, erase the recordings you've made of me, and delete your compilations and collections.

"Will you listen to what I'm saying? Probably not, because again, you aren't here for what I think, what I want, or what I experience. But maybe, just maybe I will reach some of you. For those of you who do listen and hear, remember that this is Traver Graff's last message before he goes deep into the unknown reaches of space, to a planet with a key to the origins of existence as we know it: Stop living for yourselves. Live for the people you love. Look around you, at the things you can reach, and touch, and feel, and heal. When you look into the stars, don't just see the light, but feel the billions of years it has taken to reach you, and then ask yourself 'why.' Do that, and maybe you can join the truth-seekers. I hope to join them myself, and my first step is to say goodbye to you."

Traver's final message reached its mark. There were riots. Transmission stations were set aflame. Aurora opened the doors of its facilities to its members and their families seeking personal protection. Employees who were found in uniform in unfriendly urban areas were beaten, and some were killed. Traver Graff became more than a household name; he became something of a god. Vigils that had been held for his recovering health were now repeated with greater frequency and with higher attendance, but now the crowds didn't just hope for his well-being; they shared poems about him, gazed at pictures of him, silently asked for his advice. People screamed at the night sky, demanding that the universe relent and send back the man who had imparted so much wisdom and then vanished into darkness.

* * *

Weston had access to the news and major media outlets from his cell where he'd been locked to await a long-distant and never quite scheduled trial. Two weeks after his incarceration he stumbled across a piece of news that he found very interesting – though oddly enough considering the climate, it had hardly made a splash in the public storm. Aurora announced that a second mission had indeed been commissioned by the Pilot's Cooperative as a part of the ongoing relationship between the two establishments. It was a search-and-rescue mission meant to retrieve Captain Fletcher (and secondarily any other survivors of the *Aten*) should she still be alive to retrieve. Captain James Merrickson piloted the *Iris*, his instructions being to reach *Aten* as soon as possible.

Since Weston had been recently invested in news like this, he had enough awareness to know that Merrickson, by reputation, had a penchant for daring space-jumps that, while life-threatening and borderline illegal, gave him a good chance of closing the margin and reaching the *Aten* in a fraction of the time it had taken Fletcher. That was good.

But Weston's mind was not at ease. He waited, he paced, he forgot to eat his meals, his pounds fell off like skin from a shedding snake, and all the time he contemplated that strange final message from one Aurora official to another. The papers given to him by Callie still sat in his untended apartment but the words had been perfectly preserved in his mind's eye:

URGENT. Pilots' Cooperative involvement inevitable.

Best case scenario is zero interference. Subject is moving mission forward independently at present despite Fletcher's plan to abort. His self-motivated arrival at AMA-712 is ideal.

IF Cooperative intercepts mission, SUBJECT MUST NOT BE

TAMPERED WITH. Subject must reach AMA-712 prior to retrieval. IMMEDIATELY make offer to JM. Ensure project is uninterrupted. If retrieved, Subject Graff is to be brought back undamaged.

Weston's subconscious fear was now given realization; onboard the *Aten*, Traver might not have been a guest at all.

CHAPTER ELEVEN
ORBIT

D*ear Dad,*
    I'm writing just moments after hearing the news. I've only landed three hours ago and have barely torn myself away from the bullshit, the paperwork and the post-trips and the clean-swabs. Aten *took a hit from a rock the size of a pea that split a rivet seam, so the Corporation's insurance agents are going to need to do an inspection and I'm going to need to give them an interview. Honestly I don't know when I'm going to be able to rest. I can't remember the last time I slept.*

They told me Mom passed last month. I try to think what I was doing at the moment but I can't, because I have no way to reference the time. Time is different the farther I go, and I went far.

You seemed upset in your message. Of course you seemed upset. But don't be upset with me for not responding sooner; they can't pass us personal messages while we are on missions. And don't be angry with the Cooperative for the code that I agreed to. You knew what it entailed when I gave them my life. I'm not my own person anymore.

I do wish I could have seen her one more time. The last few missions were longer than the normal, so I don't see how I would have made it home any time in the last eight years, but it would have been lovely none-theless. When is her funeral? I can't promise that I will be able to attend, but perhaps I can try if you give me the date.

Can you make it to New Mexico? I'm in Aurora housing until the next job. I'll probably be off-world again as soon as the ship is cleared. I don't know how long that will take but would love to see you. If you can travel here then it's a sure thing. We can have dinner. If needed I can send travel money.

Love you Dad. I'm sorry about Mom.

-Louisa

....

"We're here."

The words came through strong and clear, the first time the intercom had made any sound since Traver's takeover.

A strange excitement as well as unexpected relief swept over the remaining doctor and five scientists. Once the initial shock upon Friedrich's and the others' deaths had abated, the survivors had begun to entertain the fear that Traver had died shortly after entering the cockpit, perhaps murdering Lance as well. The prospect that the ship might be pilotless was somehow worse than being in the hands of a madman.

"We're here," Traver repeated. And yes, there was palpable excite-ment. Arrival at the planet meant a resumption of the mission as it had been planned. It meant the scientists going back to work. It meant discovery. Explosions and murders be damned; things might finally be getting back on track. For these traumatized researchers, most of whom had rarely in their life stepped foot outside a lab, the only familiarity that remained was the work itself.

Louisa Fletcher was neither excited nor relieved. But she was stirred. Patiently she had waited for an opportunity to take back her ship, and now that waiting might be nearer an end, for better or for worse.

Yes, she had waited, but not idly. The first hours after Traver had shut himself inside her control room she had spent in the vent system beneath the cockpit. It was pitch dark, and the heat hellish. She crouched like a tiger ready for the pounce, one hand on the hatch that separated her from the illicit occupant of her pilot's seat, the other holding a knife.

The hatch remained locked.

"Unlock the hatch" she had whispered, or rather breathed, to Lance as he'd reluctantly followed his master. She thought he had heard, that he had comprehended the message. Any moment the hatch might unlock (as it could not be accessed from the outside without the command from the console).

Five, six, seven hours she'd waited. Her muscles never relaxed as she readied herself to spring. Sweat pooled in droplets from her neck, from her face, and free of gravity drifted slowly away until the tiny chamber was filled with fine, hot mist. The only sound, beside the echoing roar of the air system and the engine's constant whir, was that of the drops of sweat sizzling as they splashed against the hot metal walls of the vent.

But the unlock command never came. Lance had not heard, or he'd been too damaged and dazed to understand.

Any other attempts at breaking in to retake control of the cockpit would be pointless, and none knew that better than she did. The main door, once manually locked from within (a detail Traver had not overlooked), could not be opened from the rear, even with a captain's keychip.

The third and final opening in or out of the cockpit was a port in the wall that opened into space, and that port would also be inaccessible from the outside.

Fletcher was at last forced to surrender her vigil in the vent, though she returned at intervals to see whether Lance had discovered the back door. He never did. Still, he was no fool and, as the only sane person currently in the cockpit, he was the best chance she had of taking back the ship. She would wait.

The second thing she did was proceed through the ship, covering up each of the ship's monitoring cameras. Each room contained two and they were inset into the corridor walls at intervals, but Fletcher innately knew the location of each and every one. Traver might have control of the ship, but she saw to it that he'd have no way of keeping track of her movements.

Traver's weeks-long lack of correspondence with his passengers was hardly surprising; the cockpit was completely self-sustaining, supplied with food and other necessaries that could last a year or more if carefully rationed. There was nothing Traver would need from the rear compartments of the ship, and no reason for him to contact the others. Should he decide to wax eloquent before an audience, Lance would surely serve, willing or not.

Fletcher expected she would continue to hear nothing from Traver until the ship reached the planet. She counted the hours, estimating the time until they should reach AMA. When they did, Traver would no longer have a need to stay in the cockpit. She didn't know what he planned on doing, or whether he planned at all, but she supposed he would need to emerge eventually. Then she would make her move.

While being forced to wait, Fletcher carried on with routine as if nothing was amiss, as if her duties placed her here in the passenger cabins. She undertook the medical care of the remaining passengers (including that of Dr. Marin, who had caught a case of pneumonia after being exposed to space). She went about ensuring that the two cabins previously belonging to the doctors and to Traver's staff were suitable and comfortable for the survivors. Her own quarters, just behind the cockpit, she transformed into a temporary medical cabin for the more severely injured. If she ever slept herself (none of the others ever observed her to do so) it must have been in the corridor. Akachi's cabin she left undisturbed.

Fletcher was acutely aware that the antechamber doors, the only things separating the livable section of the ship from the airless and deadly aft section, were fully controllable from the cockpit for their opening and closing. She had tried using that to her advantage to dispose of Traver, and she knew full well that he was capable of something similar. Such a large section of the ship being unlivable was too great a risk, so she made it her next project to find and repair the hull leaks which had resulted from the initial explosion. Even though an extended absence in the aft meant leaving the cabins un-protected and the cockpit door unsupervised, she itched to see her old ship whole again. So she donned her suit and once again entered the cold segment of the ship that had seen so much recent death.

It didn't take too long before she found the two leaks. Both were hairline fractures in the hull surrounding the medical bay, one above and one below the charred injection apparatus. That damned spider machine; she did not need reminding that it had caused the explosion in the first place, but seeing it again forced Fletcher to acknowledge that somehow or other, every catastrophe traced back to Traver. Hate was too kind a word for what Fletcher felt for him. Hate was reserved for those whom she respected.

She sealed both spots from the inside, a temporary but effective fix. A proper mending would require heavy machining from the outside as well, but Fletcher preferred not to exit the ship while the controls of all entries and exits were at the mercy of the current pilot.

With the survivors situated more or less comfortably in the forward cabins, there was no need to spend the extra oxygen and make the aft fully operational. It could once again hold air if needed, and that would suffice.

"We're here." It was the third time those words had been repeated over the course of an hour. This was neither the shaking, bothered voice of latter-day Traver nor the pompous and confident voice of his broadcasts. The words were delivered with an eerie calm. Peace-fulness.

Then: "I wish you could see what we're seeing."

Dr. Zhang, the scientist with whom Dr. Marin was sharing a ration, turned to his companion, a faint smile on his face. "It must be beautiful."

Marin, who had once prided himself on his trimness but now sported a long brown beard that made him look tired, did not share the expression of wonder. "'*We're,*' he said. So Lance is still with him." Zhang nodded, his mind elsewhere.

Captain Fletcher did not stir from where she drifted near the cockpit door. After the first announcement, she watched the scientists scurry from one cabin to another across the corridor, and was unsurprised that they did not approach her. They were all prone to be distracted and excitable, but she was neither.

Soon the scientists had all congregated into the cabin that had been Traver's. They talked in earnest, rediscovering a fervor that hadn't been felt onboard in months. Possibilities were discussed and processes reviewed. Would AMA be helium-based? Why had its makeup been undetectable using standard methods? If there were new elements involved, how might that factor in to lab work? If the atmosphere could be penetrated safely by a pod, could the core planet structure be determined?

Marin did not join the scientists. He did not share in their passion, and may have been the only person onboard who was filled with a deep sense of dread. The journey since Traver's coup had been uncertain, full of questions without answers. With their arrival at the planet came that sense of certainty that had been lacking in the interim: they'd made it to their destination under the very worst of circumstances, and now home had never been so far away.

He instead went to Fletcher. Her eyes were shut when he joined her in the corridor, but her tenseness was only one of the reasons he knew she was not asleep.

A thousand questions burned in his mind, but he decided it best not to interrupt whatever concentration Fletcher was in the midst of. He waited by her for a long moment. The babble of the scientists from the cabin faded away. Anticipation seemed to take hold of everyone, the unchanging hum of the engine adding to the suspense as Traver's next words were expected.

It was Fletcher who broke the silence, softly, not opening her eyes. "We're in orbit."

"How do you know?" Marin knew it was a pointless question. It was by now common knowledge that Fletcher was one with her ship, that she knew every change in course, every acceleration and slow-down by feel alone. As he'd expected, she did not answer.

"We're in orbit around the planet," Traver's verification over the intercom was timely. "A full rotation will take us about seven hours. I am turning the power back on to the lab, and after our first full orbit you should be ready to begin the work of collecting samples from the planet. Whatever Doctor Misleh would have done, do it."

As if driven all by one mind, the five scientists poured out of the cabin and made their way toward the mid antechamber door. Finding it locked, they turned like a frantic herd and made their way to Fletcher in the forward corridor. Her eyes were open now, her face unreadable. "Are we able to use the lab?" Zhang asked eagerly. The others followed suit in their enthusiasm: "You fixed the leaks, right?" "The pods should still be in working condition." "Do you know if the beakers and drums are intact?"

Dr. Marin looked from Fletcher to the scientists, shocked at the attitude of the latter and surprised at the lack of reaction from the former, but said nothing.

Quietly, looking straight ahead at no particular one of the scientists, Fletcher pushed herself through their midst and down the corridor. Floating to the back of the mid section she reached to the keypad beside the aft door, her fingers moving across the numbers faster than human eyes could follow. A light turned green.

"The aft hull is air sealed again," she said coldly. "Now it's unlocked, so you can go in and out as you please."

"What are you doing?" Marin was visibly disturbed. "He might be lying about turning everything back on; if there's not oxygen or pressure, we're all going to die when you open that door!"

Fletcher moved closer to the scared doctor and hissed: "He won't lie about that. This is what he wants. For now, we play along."

She backed away. Without so much as a moment's hesitation, Dr. Zhang slammed his fist against the greenlit button and the door slid open. He raced forward through the antechamber to the next door, also unlocked, and opened it.

If for a split moment the scientists doubted their decision, half expecting to be greeted by a dark, airless vacuum, their doubt was put swiftly to rest. The aft was alive with light and the sound of engines humming and air rushing in and out of the vents. Except for the burn marks on the walls, likely unremovable until the ship was next brought into dock for major reconditioning, there was nothing to remind the scientists of the horrors that had recently visited here.

"Yes, of course. We play along. That's the best course of action," said the nervous Marin to Fletcher when they were once again the sole occupants of the mid corridor. She looked at him, a hint of annoyance in the curl of her lips. Then she made to move away, toward her cabin-turned-medical-bay.

"But..." The doctor stopped her and she halted in the doorway, her annoyance no longer subtle.

"Whatever you're planning – I know you're planning something – to get the best of Mister Graff...I need you not to hurt him." Her eyes narrowed. He retreated a little: "*Too* badly, anyway. I mean, I'm his only remaining doctor. I was charged with his well-being, and that's still my only reason for being here."

"Your reason for being here, Doctor, is that unlike your traveling companions, you survived your patient's violent hijacking."

"Yes. Yes. But." He paused, choosing his words carefully. "Mister Graff's mental health is just as much my charge as is his physical well-being. I've been hired to that end by the same corporation that contracted you to pilot this ship. I have to find any opportunity I can to lend my expertise to the effort of his recovery."

The curl vanished from Fletcher's lips. She tilted her head back slightly, as if preparing a rebuke. But she said nothing, instead turning and shutting herself in to her cabin.

By the time seven hours had passed and the first orbit was presumably complete, the scientists had prepared, checked and double-checked all their equipment. They'd practiced exhaustively for this moment prior to departure, and dreamed of it for the past six months, their dreams not interrupted even by the mayhem along the way. Zhang, to whom leadership had fallen after Misleh and Friedrich, oversaw the work, seeing to it that each individual beaker, tube and drum – of which there were hundreds – was ensured against leakage and contamination. But not one of the scientists begrudged the tedious work. They had been let loose to play in their own natural environment, from which they'd been cut off for far too long.

* * *

"It's time," Traver announced. "We've gone all around the planet, and I've seen all of it. Launch the pods, and start your testing now. Report back to me with your findings."

Lance didn't know whether Traver would understand the findings once they were reported to him, but he knew by now not to argue. What had begun as psychological imprisonment had become physical torture as Traver became more and more comfortable in his role as captor. The first time he'd struck Lance was after discovering a transmission being sent: a segment of video taken from the cockpit monitoring system and forwarded to Weston. Traver's first instinct had been to smash the cameras (which he did), and then to continue his smashing against Lance's already damaged face.

Lance dared not try anything so blatant from that moment onward. He had to trust his cry for help, subtle as it had been, had reached Weston, or anyone on Earth for that matter. He knew, of course, that one simple action from him would unlock the cockpit door, or the hatch in the floor. Or hell, he could open the external port and flush himself, with Traver, into space. But Lance's self-preservation instinct was too strong still, and he had no more interest in dying from exposure to outer space (something he'd come far too close to doing already) than he did in being beaten by Traver. Even if Lance were to open the door to Fletcher, was there any guarantee Traver couldn't outsmart her again as he'd done once before?

Traver did not become any easier to endure as they neared the planet. His monologues and diatribes became more incessant. He demanded Lance's full attention, sometimes waking his assistant from sleep to listen to some newly-realized wisdom regarding man's relationship with technology or technology's relationship with the stars. Lance was forced to slip into five-minute naps whenever he could, waking out of fear even on the occasions when Traver did not shake him awake. As for sleep, it seemed Traver no longer needed it. Here was yet another reason Lance never made any attempt to wrest control; Traver was always watching.

No words could express Lance's gratitude when Lucy's video arrived. Before the recording was fully unpacked and playable he had started to work out how he might respond effectively. He feared, of course, that Traver would smell a ruse and shut the whole thing down. But as the message began to play through, he was pleasantly surprised at Traver's reaction. The supposed impregnator did not take his eyes away from Lucy's face. His stern face melted, his jaw relaxed slightly, and Lance thought that he was actually *moved* by it.

"Can I reply to this?" Traver asked a few silent moments after Lucy's face had vanished.

"Yes, of course" replied Lance, careful not to seem too eager. But his concern was unnecessary, as Traver seemed wholly concerned with his response. It contained exactly as much tenderness as Lance expected from the crazed murderer beside him, but Traver seemed painfully insistent on getting the message just right. About a dozen were recorded before Traver, watching it back several times, finally approved it to be sent. During the process Lance had no trouble encoding a message undetected by Traver. It was sent and, for a moment, hope was restored.

Traver fell silent afterward. Either Lucy's testimony had deeply affected him, or his attention had finally been consumed wholly by the spectacle of the planet.

The planet. Its magnificence couldn't be denied. It had appeared a bright shade of green from afar, but as it grew into something that had a globular shape and a defined surface, the colors became indescribable. Despite his best attempts at cynicism, Lance found himself awed as each time he looked away or even shut his eyes, he would look again and find something new in the way the planet shimmered, winked, and transformed to shades of blues, greens and yellows he hadn't known existed. Perhaps that awe was partially responsible for Lance's reluctance to take any action that could directly lead to Traver's downfall. Whatever the rational arguments against it, the planet did seem to be calling out, beckoning. It was hard to resist.

In the silence that fell after Traver's message for Lucy, Lance's hope turned to despair. This happened for several reasons: for one, the reality sunk home that, no matter what action might be taken by Aurora, no rescue could come soon enough to realistically make any difference in the face of further impending disaster. For another, there was a part of Lance's mind – no, his soul – that found oppression in the possibility of *being* rescued, and thus of never reaching AMA-712.

He would not previously have anticipated it but Lance now missed Traver's obnoxiousness, which would have given him a not-entirely-unwelcome interruption from his own divided and gloomy thoughts.

That gloom faded as the *Aten* neared the planet. Neither man minded the silence of the other, or largely noticed his existence. The planet was all. Slowly it filled the cockpit window, and as it did so the consistency of its surface became more and more undefinable. The eye wandered as it gazed, following swirls, colors that shifted and changed, and bright spots that appeared and faded in what might have been seconds or hours. The flow of time seemed to stop dead in its tracks, and though the *Aten* continued its approach at a constant rate, it seemed to do so outside of any count of hours. Clouds appeared in the inner atmosphere of the planet, some fleeting and spotted, some blanketing large swaths of the thicker gas below. Hints of definition became visible through the atmosphere, darker shapes like continents that did not maintain their form for more than a few hours at a time before shifting, reforming and combining like living Rorschach blots.

The core must be spinning at an incredible rate, thought Lance in a rare moment of articulate thought, *for the gas structures of the planet surface to shift so quickly and drastically. But, that's something the scientists probably already know.*

To ease the ship into orbit was beyond Lance's limited piloting skills, yet he never felt the slightest pang of anxiety. The nearer the surface came, the more he felt at peace. The *Aten* itself alerted him when the ship was within orbiting elevation, approximately nine hundred kilometers up from what passed for a surface on that gassy soup. Lance followed the guidelines determined by the computer and steered the ship outward from its direct trajectory.

There had been a time, no doubt, when pilots were required to make last-minute calculations based on gravitational pull, speed of approach and trajectory angle, during which a minor misalignment might have resulted in expulsion from orbit or catastrophic slip into descent. No doubt Fletcher herself was capable of such calculations, and they were still necessary from time to time even in this day and age, when a computer might still fail. But by some great fortune the *Aten's* computerized course proved true. With no further effort by Lance, the ship eased into orbit.

Lance slowly awoke to the presence of Traver beside him. It took him a moment to recognize it as a fellow human, and a further moment to identify him. At last it struck him that the sounds coming from the mouth of that being were words, and that the words were being directed through the intercom to the other crew members onboard the ship. As if a dream had ended, Lance's stark reality flooded back to him with clarity, and he wondered how he'd let it slip away. Not for the last time.

"Activate the lab, Lance."

It felt strange to have Traver's words directed at himself after what had felt like eons in a timeless vacuum, but Lance gathered his thoughts quickly. "The aft may still have an air leak. I don't know if it'll hold, and we don't have much oxygen to waste."

"The leak is fixed."

"How do you know?"

"She would have fixed it by now."

Lance looked doubtfully at Traver, but the firm, all-knowing look on the broadcaster's face dispelled all question. Yes, Fletcher had sealed the aft, because Traver said she had.

Power was turned back on in the rear sections of the ship, and oxygen flow was opened up. The readings showed that the pressure was holding. It should now only be a matter of time before the scientists began their long-awaited work. *And why not?* thought Lance, *we're here now, so there's no reason for them not to do what they came here for.*

Lance's attention became absorbed by the spectacle of Traver himself, who now hungrily studied every visible part of the rotating planet's surface with an increased enthusiasm his assistant had not thought possible. Equally as fascinating as the changing surface of the planet was the fascination with which Traver observed it. He did not blink, turn his head, or avert his eyes, not even when Lance called out to him that the ship had completed its first orbit. Traver only responded to him in a soft whisper: "Tell them to start."

Reluctant to have his own voice heard over the intercom but dreading what might happen should he disobey, Lance instead chose to appeal to the one part of Traver he was sure was intact: his ego.

"I think the honor should be yours, boss."

Traver tore his eyes from the gleaming planet, looked at Lance and smiled. Then he made the announcement, initiating the operation for which the *Aten* and its ill-fated crew had been sent.

* * *

The next month passed slowly.

The work of the scientists was not something that could be done quickly. A year had been allotted for the research, and even that for what amounted to a cursory examination. Without Misleh, Friedrich or a definite timeline, the men under Zhang did as much as they knew to do, as quickly as they could.

Pods were sent at twelve hour intervals, gathering samples of the atmospheric gases and taking readings for pressure and temperature.

The gases that were returned to the laboratory for observation yielded informative results. Helium, hydrogen and other trace elements were found. The atmosphere was non-toxic and moderate in temperature. If not for the pressure and utter lack of oxygen, it would have been nearly habitable. The scientists grew more enthusiastic with each new batch of gas that was retrieved.

As time went on the pods were sent deeper, penetrating the lowest regions of the atmosphere. About three hundred meters above the surface (which did appear to be a smooth plane, despite being constructed of gases and liquids), the pressure readings became too high for the pods to continue safely.

"That the pressure is so high above the surface is incredible," mused Dr. Zhang regretfully. "Our pods can withstand the Mariana Trench, but not the gases above the surface of this planet. Whatever substance lies below, we may never be able to reach it."

It was deduced among the scientists that some truly fascinating discoveries must lie in the swirling surface beneath the atmosphere. But the ship was already short one pod thanks to Traver's impromptu jettisoning of Misleh's remains. As Zhang surmised and Fletcher insisted, to send remaining pods into crushing pressure, certain to be irretrievable, was not an investment worth making.

Traver disagreed.

Zhang had tasked Dr. Bjornson with the unforgiving task of approaching the cockpit door and giving twenty-four hour reports to Traver via intercom. Fletcher was always present at these reports, making Bjornson's task no less stressful by pushing him to antagonize Traver with a less-than-satisfactory status. She hoped to draw him out of the cockpit by impressing upon him the inefficacy of the scientists' efforts. Her hopes were never rewarded. Though each report resembled the last, with Bjornson's enthusiasm forcefully suppressed as he emphasized the disappointing results of the cycle's collections, Traver's responses never amounted to more than a serene "thank you."

That changed on the twenty-eighth day of orbit (rotation ninety-five), when Traver again took it upon himself to make an announcement to the entire ship.

"The pod will survive the trip. Send it to the surface."

The scientists were eager to accept Traver's message as all the permission they needed to proceed, but Fletcher disallowed it. She ordered Bjornson to carry another message to Traver, politely informing him that the pod's journey would not be possible, that the pressure would smash the metal pod into a football-sized nugget before it ever reached the surface.

For five minutes or more, Traver didn't respond. Fletcher's hopes rose. Her hand tightened around her knife as she waited beside the door.

When the response came, it was just as calm as ever. "I'll handle it. The pod has been sent." Fletcher's grip grew impossibly tight, then she flung her arm holding the knife into the wall, bending the blade in her anger and leaving a gash in the metal by the door.

Bjornson flew away from her, frightened as a rabbit. But Fletcher's outburst was short-lived. She exhaled and disappeared down the corridor. Bjornson, eager to rejoin his peers, hurried to inform them that either a pod had just been lost forever, or they would soon be receiving a sample of AMA's fundamental ingredients.

Both the cameras and sensors for Pod P-02 fed into the control panel just outside the aft bay, where Zhang, Bjornson and the others watched anxiously. Their controls did nothing, as the cockpit had overridden their ability to remotely drive the motors. All they could do was watch and wait.

The descent yielded little visual excitement; the external camera lost sight of all but foggy gas halfway through the atmosphere, while the interior camera revealed only the inner tank. The pressure readings increased and the elevation readings dropped. Four hundred meters, three hundred fifty, three hundred. It dropped beneath the elevation which had previously been the horizon of closest approach. Pressure readings reached a critical point.

Dr. Marin joined the scientists, and a few moments later even Fletcher came to see.

A red alert appeared on the sensor, warning that the pod would not hold out any longer. Elevation reached fifty meters.

The external camera crackled and cut out. Then the internal camera followed suit.

All watching held their breath.

Thirty seconds went by, while the pressure warning remained critical.

Fletcher turned away in disgust, but spun back a half second later. The light turned green, the pressure indicator returning to normal.

"Did it make it? Is it still there?" Zhang asked, despite having the very same information before him as Fletcher had. She said nothing in reply, her eyes fixing instead on the monitor screen which still flickered.

The sharp voice of Traver intruded from the intercom, shaking the watchers out of their suspenseful vigil. "The pod is safely beneath the surface of the planet, and I still have control."

The internal camera monitor flickered back on and all the scientists let out a collective sigh of relief. The pod's interior looked to be intact. The sensor data reappeared on the control panel; elevation hit negative ten meters and continued dropping, settling near negative thirty.

The external video feed never returned; the recorder must have been crushed by the atmospheric pressure. Yet from where the pod drifted just below the surface, the readings remained normal. The inner camera feed showed liquid being pumped into the pod's internal collection tanks, a process that continued for two hours until Traver chose to signal the pod and call it home.

Again the crew watched the readings nervously as the pressure turned critical, staying there throughout the ascent. Miraculously it made its way back through the lower atmosphere, reaching three hundred meters of elevation where pressure was no longer so intense. An hour later Pod P-02 docked to the *Aten*.

Fletcher opened the port a moment after the pod was locked in. She examined it for damage, which she found to be extensive. The smooth outer hull had been wrinkled beyond recognition, looking as though the metal had been superheated to a liquid state and then shot through with turbulent ripples. How it had survived the return trip while lacking the aerodynamic surface required for a smooth takeoff, she had no idea.

The specimen contents of the inner tank were emptied, channeling through the wall-mounted pipes and dumping into the large drums at the aft end of the lab. None of the scientists had any idea what the contents would be, apart from the little they had been able to see from the camera feed.

They heard hisses and splashes from within the drums. Zhang waited closest, everyone else gathered around him staring longingly at this historical storage drum. The final pressurized push could be heard from within, the final liquid drips resounding.

"Gentlemen," Dr. Zhang announced, turning to the others. "While it is regrettable that our leader Abrahim could not be with us, this is the moment we uncover the mystery – at least, the first layer of mystery – of AMA-712. Whatever has transpired on the journey, this is the reason we are here."

None of his companions stopped to listen to what Zhang had to say. They all rushed forward, turning on the pumps and filters that would begin the process of separating the contents of the drum based on density, shifting the materials to the glass beakers and vials where they would finally become observable.

The beakers filled with a dark green liquid, thick and viscous. As it was pumped into its new storage place it swirled and separated itself into two floating bubbles, one black and one bright, reflective green. The edges of each bubble, despite the thickness of the fluid, took the form of a mist that thinned into nothingness.

The flasks in turned filled with a gas, barely visible except for a slight greenish tint which betrayed its presence.

The men of science took a few moments to assign themselves tasks and to establish a process, then they began their long-awaited work.

* * *

"We need to send a message to Earth!" came Bjornson's shaking, excited voice when he made his next report five hours early. "To Aurora. To the science teams, to the journalists, to our families…"

"Why? What did you find?" Traver responded impatiently. His pride was hurt that the first instinct of the scientists was to tell their employers what they'd found instead of telling him. Hadn't he been the one and only person responsible for carrying the mission forward, allowing the research to happen at all?

"It's a new gas. A whole new element," Bjornson went on as if un-interrupted, "incredibly reactive, and without a freezing point that we've been able to find yet."

"*Maybe* a new element" came Zhang's steadier but no less excited voice.

"Maybe…there are lots more tests we need to run. We should

send this home because, whatever it is, it could possibly be a whole new entry on the periodic table."

Traver frowned while he continued to stare at the planet below. What was the point of this journey if *"freezing point"* and *"periodic table"* remained the focus? Such a superficial examination was the equivalent of trying to make a new friend by cutting off that friend's thumb to memorize his fingerprint. The swelling, swimming surface below held greater mysteries than molecular construction. Whatever Misleh had been aiming to do, it was surely not this.

Misleh. If only he were here; *he could tell us what to do.*

A light whisper from Lance reminded Traver that the junior scientist was still awaiting a response. Ten minutes had gone by without Traver's answer (but what was ten minutes in the greater scheme of things?)

"I will pass along what you've told me" said Traver. It was a fair enough response, he thought. What more could they want from him?

"Um." Bjornson lost none of his excitement despite his timidity. "We appreciate your offer but it's too complicated a message to pass along. There's a dialogue that needs to open up between our team and the oversight committee back at headquarters. To do that we need to send them scans of the molecular structure with thorough observational notes detailing proton counts, chemical reactions, temperature fluctuations…"

"I understand!" The volume of Traver's shout was enough to startle the listeners on the other side of the intercom, let alone poor Lance.

But he caught himself mid-outburst. Traver had not lost his temper since the matter of Lance's video transmission, and he would not let it happen now. He had always prided himself on his restrained expressions of anger – now, with the defining moments of his life so close, was no time to turn into an animal.

He shut his eyes and breathed slowly in and out. Two more minutes passed.

"I know that trusting me is not the first instinct for any of you. But do you also think that I'm oblivious?"

"I'm sorry, I don't know…" The confusion was genuine in Bjornson's voice.

"You can't expect me to believe that something so trivial as what you've just told me is really worth writing home about. You've only barely begun the work. We're just getting started. If I open the cockpit door for you, and then the captain – yes, Louisa, I know you're listening to me – takes that moment to push me out once and for all, then you'll never make the discoveries you've come here to make. Don't waste this opportunity, Doctor."

"But…" Bjornson's excitement had faded and his confusion had amplified; "A new element. If this isn't something to send home, then, what is? What else are you expecting us to find?"

Traver could feel Lance's questioning gaze: probably anticipating another outburst. *No. Patience for now.*

"No messages will be sent until we're done here." Tersely, he cut off the intercom, terminating what was left of the conversation.

Lance was still looking at him; Traver could sense it. It was a helpless, questioning look, one that the assistant had turned on him many times since they'd taken the pilot seats. Traver had never returned it. He had to appear confident, strong without question. Even a quick look thrown at Lance while the latter was afraid and in need of answers was too much a display of Traver's own humanity. Humanity was something he needed to let go.

This moment was different. Perhaps it was because he'd begun to doubt himself, ever so slightly. Perhaps he felt an acute sense of smallness, helplessness in the face of the monumental mysteries he seemed unable to comprehend. No, it was neither of those reasons; the truth was that he could not help feeling human again, and it was because of Lucy's news.

He now turned his head and returned the look. Lance's eyes darted sideways for a moment, blinked, then returned. It took a moment, but they warmed to the exchange.

Traver looked at Lance and realized that he'd been wrong; Lance's gaze was not confused or questioning; it was completely terrified. At that, Traver felt a twinge of guilt, and then an overwhelming sense of loneliness. He had isolated his only living companion on a journey neither of them fully understood. Lance had tried to reach out to Earth for help, but perhaps that was because Traver had never even attempted to communicate what he was feeling. Lance clearly did not feel what Traver felt, that much was clear, yet the assistant had not done anything to truly sabotage or endanger the continuing journey, despite having the power to do so. For that, Traver was, yes, grateful.

"I haven't lost my mind, Lance."

"What?"

"It's what Fletcher thinks. If it wasn't what the scientists thought, then it is now. You're afraid because you think so too."

Lance said nothing, but a familiarity began to sparkle in his eyes. Just talking to the poor young man was restoring his confidence. That was good.

"I'm still me. Still the same Traver Graff whose show you worked on for...two years?"

"Four years."

"Right. And to be honest I didn't remember your face, or your name. Same with all the techs. Weston's was the only name I needed to remember. I've never been a very good boss. Just like I've never been a very good father."

Lance's fear dissipated even more. There was something like sympathy as he looked into his master's eyes, which had produced a set of tears.

Then Traver turned back to look at the planet.

"It's calling, Lance. I've been able to feel it for months now. It's calling; I'm just not close enough to hear what it's saying."

The sympathy, the emotional bond to which Lance was nearly ready to contribute, vanished. He joined Traver in turning to look at the ball of gas and green liquid below. "What *what's* saying?"

"The planet. AMA. It's not just protons and periodic elements. It's alive. It's trying to talk to us but we can't hear. I'm the only one trying to listen, but so far nothing is clear. I need more time."

Lance turned back to look at Traver. Several tears were now streaming over the man's face; whatever emotion was there, it certainly wasn't fake. Lance grew braver: "When it talks, what does it sound like?"

Instant excitement appeared on Traver's face, and he opened his mouth to respond. Then he paused, mouth agape and eyes shining green with the planet's light. "It…" he stuttered after a moment passed, "It's as if my whole body is suddenly awake. A billion tiny points, from my feet through my chest to my arms and head, are lighting up and telling me to pay attention. All of me – not just my ears, or my mind – is hearing something. Receiving something. I try to respond, but I don't know what to say."

Lance had no inclination to respond. Even if he had, he would not have known what to say either.

Despite his very best attempts to appear dispassionate regarding the scientists, Traver remained intensely curious for Bjornson's next report.

The report didn't come.

No communication of any kind came to the cockpit for ten, then twenty, then thirty hours. Seven times Traver reached out over the intercom, demanding a status update in a voice that was strategically disinterested (despite his feeling anything but disinterest). Silence was the only answer he received.

The ship's interior monitors yielded nothing, as they had done from the beginning – Fletcher had not missed a single one. This left Traver, and Lance with him, blind to the ship that lay behind them. An uncomfortable sensation came over Traver. He began to feel just how vulnerable he was, after all. Cockpit or no cockpit, controls or no controls, he was trapped in here. Just as he'd taken for granted

Lance's extent of power over their continued command, he realized he'd also overlooked just how much he depended on the rest of the crew. Even Louisa. A single decision on their part – on her part – and he could be cut off, blinded and deafened to their actions.

A sudden paranoid thought struck him. As if to test it, he initiated a controlled launch for one of the inactive pods.

Nothing happened. *ERROR: DISCONNECT* was the message he received from the console. The captain had somehow rerouted control of the lab pods.

At that, Traver's paranoia grew. If Fletcher had the power to rewire controls out from the cockpit, it might only be a matter of time until the ship itself would no longer respond to Traver's commands. At such an eventuality, what good would it do him to have ownership over the cockpit? This was nothing more than a cold, isolated room full of lights and switches. It could be his tomb.

"Do you think something might have happened to them?" asked Lance. The thought had not occurred to Traver, because such unselfish thoughts rarely could.

"To the scientists?"

"To them, to the captain. I don't know, but it's strange to hear nothing from them."

Traver was glad to hear that Lance shared his perplexion at the crew's silence. It reminded him that he wasn't alone in his endeavor after all; Lance was right there with him.

There was no way to know for certain, of course. Traver was blind to the rest of the ship. He could ask "is there anything wrong" a thousand times and never receive a reply. The only way to know whether something had befallen the scientists would be to exit the cockpit and see.

"Or it's her next ruse," Traver murmured. "She thinks she can force me out of the cockpit by a process of alienation. Eventually, she hopes I'll grow so desperate for a status update, for any kind of response, that I'll simply walk out, leaving the door wide open behind me."

"Maybe." Lance cursorily checked the sensors and gauges, trying to make himself focus. But all the readings were unremarkable, so his mind once again escaped into that constant state of mild panic which had become normal. "Would you send me? I can see whether anything has gone wrong."

"No," snapped Traver. "An open door is all she needs." But that wasn't his real reason. He knew they could manage to slip Lance through the door quickly, before Fletcher would be able to react. But he didn't want Lance to go because he knew he wouldn't come back.

Neither Lance nor Traver said anything more for some time. The *Aten* cycled around AMA twice more and they waited for something to happen, for someone to reach out to the cockpit. Traver kept his eyes painfully focused, rarely blinking, to see whether any pods flew by the cockpit on their way down to the planet, but there were none. All was silent except for the smooth, constant rev of the engines and the maddeningly regular beeps of the console.

No, there was another sound. A new noise coming from the back of the cockpit.

It was several hours before either Traver or Lance acknowledged the sound as existing in more than their imaginations. Lance was the first, turning his chair tellingly toward the door and tilting his head in question. Traver's lips tightened and he nodded slightly. Together they stood and moved toward the apparent source of the sound.

It was a soft, resounding vibration that seemed to be emanating through all the walls and ceiling, but its loudest point seemed to be on the other side of the door.

"They're cutting their way in," Traver realized.

Lance said nothing. He just stared at the door, his eyes growing wide.

"But the door can't be cut through. Can it?" Traver turned to Lance, the confidence gone from his voice.

"No. At least, not with any tools we have onboard. Not in an efficient amount of time."

"If they cut long enough, could they get through the door?" Traver put one hand on the metal as if to bolster its strength.

"If it's tantalum alloy, like they usually use for these doors, it could take weeks. No, more than weeks, because it'll eat through saw blades like butter."

"What about a torch?"

"That might be faster, but torches aren't supposed to be onboard, because of the fuel supplies and the flammability. Anyway, it sounds like a saw. A torch we wouldn't be able to hear. Listen."

But they could hear nothing at all. The sound had stopped.

"Did they give up already?" Lance asked, failing to hide the disappointment in his voice.

"No. She wouldn't stop. Something else is happening."

In silence they waited, dreading the continued stillness nearly as much as the possibility of the noise's resumption. Traver returned to the pilot seat to continue his watchful vigil over the planet while Lance stayed by the door. Lance found it a relief to be free, if only by a distance of two meters, from Traver and from the controls. The greater freedom, he found, was from the haunting vision of that ever-shifting green globe that lay beyond the window. Just staring back at the door, that hard, tangible surface, cleared his mind from a fog he hadn't noticed before.

"There!" Traver's exclamation shook Lance from his temporary relief. Lance followed the line of Traver's pointing finger, toward the planet. He saw nothing but the familiar alien horizon.

"What? I don't see anything?"

"It's a man!"

Traver's pointing hand followed an even trajectory downward and sideways, but still Lance saw nothing.

"Where are you pointing? I don't see anything."

Traver slowly lowered his hand and withdrew it. "He's gone, now."

"What do you mean, it was a man?" Perhaps it was because of his proximity to the contagious confidence of Traver, but Lance refused to allow himself to believe his companion was hallucinating.

Traver wasn't. While his eyes were peeled, taking in the vastness of the planet surface while also surveying its minute details, he'd spotted a small silhouette, darting away nearly faster than an eye could catch. It had fallen to the port side of the ship and quickly drifted away, momentum helping it keep up with the ship before it vanished.

Traver did not answer Lance's question. He had too many questions of his own, with little hope for answers.

Instead, he stared out into the abyss for a long moment, then lost his temper again.

He slammed his fist onto the intercom button, screaming into the voice reader: "Why won't you tell me what is going on back there? I am in control of the ship! You've cut off my communications but the real control is mine! I just saw one of the crew jettisoned out. Yet you're keeping me in the dark, knowing how dangerous that is! If I retaliate by taking an action that results in deaths, I hold you responsible! Talk to me! Talk to me, Louisa!"

His voice cracked and broke down, quieting by the last word. Traver's whole body shook, and sweat drifted in quivering pools around his head.

Instead of receiving an answer, he was once again greeted by the droning, buzzing sound. But now it was not coming from the door; it was coming from below Traver's feet.

"Now what is she doing?" He jumped up, startled, his eyes darting across the floor.

"The service hatch. She must be cutting into that now."

"I didn't know this was a service hatch. Can she open it?"

"Not unless you let her in." Lance felt a twinge of guilt. How many times had he had the opportunity to open it without Traver's knowing? But then he remembered that opening the hatch would have only been effective with Fletcher underneath, immediately available to push through; if he'd opened it without her there, it would have relocked within seconds and then he would have had Traver's wrath to contend with. His guilt vanished.

"But can she cut through? Is it alloy like the door?"

Lance was no expert in metallurgy and his knowledge of ship-building as a craft was only cursory. Nonetheless a single look at the shiny grooved floor was enough to tell him that this was not the same material as the door.

"She can probably cut through it."

Traver raised his arms behind his head then lowered them again, attempting to stem his threatening loss of temper. "Then why didn't she do it before? She's had months to try and get in here; why not try cutting through the hatch in the first place?"

That thought was a new one for Lance. But it only took him a moment to know the reason. The terrifying reason. "It's an air vent. If a spark were to catch fire down there..."

The distraught expression vanished from Traver's face. It was replaced by the relaxed confidence of sudden moral superiority. He looked directly at Lance. "She's risking the whole ship?"

Lance could only nod.

"She is putting nine – eight – lives in direct danger, just to get to me."

Lance nodded, this time adding in a shrug. "I can only guess."

Traver had already turned away from him. He grabbed hold of the pilot's seat and pulled himself down until he was on hands and knees, his face just centimeters away from the floor. Traver could feel the reverberations of the saw coming through. It was a more palpable vibration than that which had come through the door, and Traver knew by the feeling and the sound that it was only a matter of minutes before Fletcher burst through the floor, ending his reign once and for all.

Or the ship would explode, incinerating them all in a matter of seconds.

With that thought Traver fueled his rage and he screamed through the floor: "Eight souls onboard, and you're prepared to sacrifice them all to take back control of your ship? You're willing to give your own life, but for what? Is it that important that we go home? Has Earth been that good to us?"

Traver pushed himself back up and into the seat. He seemed exhausted. He grit his teeth and shut his eyes. Lance saw that tears had once again appeared on his face; he felt obliged to offer some small amount of comfort, but could think of nothing to say.

Through his tightened teeth Traver muttered "They've given up on looking. The scientists aren't even trying anymore."

Then he said something that Lance, until the moment he died, would never be able to stop hearing play through in his mind's ear: "It is going to be very angry with us if we stop looking."

Lance knew his boss has come unhinged. He'd had no doubts about that since Traver had pulled the trigger on Dr. Friedrich. But the time spent alone with Traver in the cockpit had forced him to hope that Traver was onto something, that this mad pursuit of knowledge was the right course of action. It was a mission so important that it might sometimes demand actions that seemed inhuman or even mad.

Lance had fallen to a combined malady of Stockholm Syndrome and space fever, the loss of good judgment sometimes displayed by astronauts who give in to the overwhelming sensation of their surroundings. But now upon hearing Traver, shaking with terror, display signs that indisputably pointed toward some far more extreme delusion, something snapped inside Lance and he freed himself of at least one of his two maladies.

* * *

One meter below their feet, Fletcher crouched in the darkness of the vent, her only light the orange glow of melting steel and scattering sparks. The sparks lodged themselves in her face near her unprotected eyes, extinguished quickly by the sweat that drenched her. She knew that any one of those sparks could catch on the air, and then she would be dead in a moment, followed shortly by everyone else onboard. It was a knowledge that was disconnected from her resolve. Things had gone too far, and the most recent incident with the scientist had alerted her to just how far she had let them go.

Only four scientists now remained, after the unexpected suicide by self-jettisoning carried out by Dr. Bjornson. Upon receiving Traver's final, hope-destroying message, all the researchers had begun to feel overwhelmed but none reacted as badly as he. He had gone straight to the flasks of planet gas and begun to study them closely. After several hours of examining the strange substance he'd become sullen and moody, refusing to converse with his companions or even write down what he observed. When Fletcher had given the order to stay clear of the cockpit door and to cease all sample collections and communications with Traver, Bjornson seemed not to hear. He stared listlessly at the churning sample of AMA, his peers unsuccessful in their attempts to pull him away. When at last his four companions had all gathered to discuss a plan of action, trying to decide how to possibly satisfy the wholly unscientific demands of their captor, Bjornson had wandered off without a word, dumping himself out of the jettison port. It was his lifeless body Traver had seen from the cockpit, and his death that had been Fletcher's last straw.

Death for all of them was a certainty unless she forced her way back into the cockpit. If the spark were to catch, then at least the end would come on her own terms.

Little by little the steel gave way. Louisa Fletcher had never prayed, but whispered words came now unwittingly to her lips. *Let me break through. Let me break through.*

CHAPTER TWELVE
BLOOD

"Boss, *what's* going to be angry?"

"AMA. It wants to talk with us. We can't leave before we let it. We can't stop the work. It doesn't matter who's in the cockpit, or how many of us are left to see this through. It brought me here to talk to it, Lance."

Lance stared into Traver's eyes, and Traver stared back. There was not a single spark of performance, or of sardonic humor or even insanity in those deep blue eyes. There was only earnestness, unyielding passion. Belief.

There was nothing Lance could say that would make sense. Nothing made sense. This might be an extended nightmare episode where reality had crumbled and given way to an acceptable level of utter nonsense. Perhaps some nightmares should be allowed to run their course, uninterrupted.

"We need to be closer." Traver latched himself in to his pilot's seat before Lance fully understood what was happening. He took the ship's controls in his hands, hands which had never before directly piloted the ship, and pushed them forward.

"What are you doing, Mister Graff?"

The computer initiated an alert prompt. Buttons flashed and alarms beeped as the console warned: *ORBIT TERMINATED. VERIFY DIRECTION?* Traver entered the verification command. With the mental practice developed over many countless hours spent watching Lance pilot the ship, Traver plunged the nose of the ship downward, toward the planet.

"Traver!"

The cockpit windows filled with green, the star-studded blackness disappearing beyond the peripherals. Lance was thrown upward out of his seat, hitting his head on the cockpit's ceiling.

He was a little dazed, but not too badly to know it was now time to terminate the nightmare at any cost. He did not need to do the mental calculations to know that the ship would become trapped by gravity within less than two minutes. Even if he would be able to quickly push himself back down into his seat and buckle himself in, Traver, whose chair was within arm's reach, would very likely beat him into a helpless pulp if he tried to take control of the ship. Even if Lance *could* maintain control despite Traver, he had no idea whether he could succeed in righting the ship and returning her to orbit. He'd been able to guide the *Aten* on a direct, constant course, but he feared he'd fail at fighting this sort of momentum and gravity without tearing the ship apart from the stress.

The *Aten* descended, gaining speed. Twenty seconds had been lost already.

Fletcher. Was she still below? There was no way of knowing whether she had been able to continue cutting; the ship was now rattling and the engines roaring, both drowning out the relatively soft buzz of the saw. She had probably been thrown back by the sudden change of course.

Ten more seconds wasted.

Lance could afford no more time to think. His arm shot upward, smashing his palm into the ceiling to propel himself back downward.

269

As he descended, his body flailed, instinct helping him to take the only action that now made any sense; he kicked Traver in the head.

The man reeled back, his neck strained and twitching as his body, still latched into the seat, was unable to follow the momentum of the kick. In the seconds it took Traver to recover, Lance grabbed hold of the strap of his own seat with his right hand, knowing it would take too long to strap himself in fully. He had only one hand free. Floor hatch, or flight control? Instinct again answered the question for him. He used his hand to grab the control from which Traver's grip had just relaxed, and jerked it back.

It wasn't a proper maneuver, but it bought some time. The ship lurched. Lance was thrown downward now, his right arm hitting the back of his seat and bending backwards. He heard the crack of his elbow and knew it had snapped clean, but the adrenaline prevented him from feeling a thing.

It took him a long moment to push himself up from the floor to which he'd been centrifugally attached, using the only arm that was of any use. But for that moment, with the side of his face pressed firmly to the hatch, he heard the saw.

Traver had the advantage of time, but he squandered some of it by indulging in his rage, landing a kick against Lance's ribs. *That should keep him down*, he was convinced. Then he turned back to the controls and, with a jerk just as abrupt as Lance's, shoved the control back forward.

Again the ship dove forward. Louder than the engines, louder than the rattle of atmospheric interference was the sound of heavy cracks and metallic groans. Lance heard those sounds as he was once again levitated above the floor. He knew the ship could not handle another such turn. For it to hold together, the *Aten* needed to be handled with finesse of which neither Lance nor Traver was capable.

Lance grabbed the seat strap again, this time with his left hand, before he was out of reach. Firmly he wrapped it around his limp right hand. The pain rushed through his arm now, shooting from elbow to fingertips all at once. He clenched his teeth as he anchored himself. He knew he must remain within reach of the controls. It would only take another minute or so for the planet's gravity to imprison the *Aten*, and Fletcher would never cut through in time.

Traver was intent, his knuckles locked over the elevation control stick. Lance did not feel or hear his own scream of pain as he used what power was left in his right wrist to rotate himself, angling his body so that his left arm could once again reach the console.

His hand touched the controls. He entered a command quickly, sloppily. *COMMAND NOT RECOGNIZED,* the console responded. Lance took a deep breath and steadied his hand.

Traver turned, his attention pulled away from the spectacular vision of yellow-green oceans in front of him. He let go of the control, his hand forming into a fist.

Lance once again entered the command.

Traver's fist landed against Lance's face. It was a hard blow, and the assistant went immediately limp.

Below, there had been a barely audible clicking sound. The hatch was unlocked. Now it shot open. Fletcher's kicking leg followed, then the rest of her body. Her eyes, set in a grimy face spotted with burn marks, were ready for the kill as they locked onto Traver.

Traver's hand went toward the gun still attached to his belt.

Fletcher did not pause to right herself, instead swinging her legs around, smashing her boot into the side of Traver's head as he turned toward her with the weapon.

His neck was lurched sideways, impacted at the same angle as before. He slumped in his seat.

* * *

Traver's vision returned slowly, as did the feeling in his lower extremities. Opening his eyes, he first saw only a black and green blur, but he didn't know where the cockpit ended and the planet began. For a moment he was hopeful; if the planet still filled the view through the window, then it was too late for Fletcher or Lance to disrupt their descent. They would find themselves in AMA's embrace.

But the green was receding, the blackness of space taking its place.

The controls. He had to get back to the controls. If he could only redirect the ship back toward its destination, Fletcher would eventually run out of time to correct course.

He tried to move. His body did not respond quickly. Looking around, his eyes adjusted and focused; he saw that he was no longer in the pilot seat. His strap had been unbuckled and he'd been pushed adrift. Lance still hung lifelessly in the air, tethered to his chair, while Fletcher sat tensely in the pilot seat. The gun floated off in the far corner of the room.

Traver looked at both hands. They were free, as were his feet. Of course, Fletcher had had no time to do anything more than quickly push him out of the chair and then do everything she could to regain control. It was clear that she had succeeded in that much, but she'd perhaps not taken into account that Traver would return to consciousness so soon.

His arms moved sluggishly; not since his rugby days in college had he suffered an injury that affected his consciousness.

But just as quickly as he rediscovered the motor skills to move his arms, he inched himself closer to Fletcher's seat. She seemed not to see or hear him. She was leaned over the controls, intent on the task before her. The ship underwent no lurch. The rattle reduced by degrees as a long, slow groan sounded through the ship's skeleton before the regular sounds of the engine returned.

Then Traver was behind Fletcher. He prepared himself, judging his own strength and weighing it against the power of which he knew Fletcher was capable. It was his only option.

His right arm pulled back, gathering momentum to land a blow against Fletcher's temple. Before his arm could shoot forward, she turned. Her face was calm; she'd been waiting for him. Traver's arm had already been triggered, and his reactions were too slow to stop the movement. His fist plunged forward through the air.

His eyes locked with Fletcher's. For a moment he saw her quiet resolve shining through her dark brown eyes. There was a light behind those eyes, burning hotter than the sparks which had crisped her hardy skin. He'd seen that light before, but only now did he know what it meant: she was stronger than he was. She was more determined. He wouldn't beat her.

His arm extended. Fletcher's arm swung upward to intercept. In her hand was the metal saw, its blade spinning silently.

The speed of her arm's upswing did not halt or even slow as it passed through Traver's. The blade carved through his flesh and bone like he was made of air.

His eyes left Fletcher's face. He looked instead at the forward part of his arm. Slowly it drifted away from him, but as he watched he could not accept why it was he could no longer clench his fist. He still felt each finger, each tendon. In his mind he still possessed full control over his arm, so why was it that his eyes showed him a widening, blood-filled gap between his elbow and forearm?

The blood.

The moment Traver's arm had been severed, Fletcher knew she had finally beaten him. But in the balloon of blood that grew around the place of violence she saw something that arrested her attention.

It wouldn't take long for Traver to bleed out. Already he was turning pale. The look on his face as he stared wide-eyed at his new stump nearly brought a smile to the captain's face. To hell with him. Let him bleed to death. But…that blood.

As it sprayed from arm and arm, the droplets that formed in the air seemed to separate. As if the red drops were sponges being squeezed by an unseen hand, they produced a second substance that oozed out in tiny specks and collected together. The specks were white, and as they collected in the air they grew into bunches nearly the same size as the blood droplets, but they were dry and wispy and looked like snow. Red and white speckled the whole inside of the cockpit; it was perversely beautiful.

The moment passed and Fletcher was forced to ignore the anomaly that was pumping out of Traver's arteries. She turned around and entered the command that opened the cockpit doors, concurrently activating the intercom. "This is Captain Fletcher. The *Aten* is once again under my control and returning to orbit. Doctor Marin, please report to the cockpit immediately for a medical emergency."

By a medical emergency, she had meant Lance's worrisome state; he still drifted lifelessly, his own broken arm wrapped in the seatbelt.

Dr. Marin rushed in a few moments later, dazed from the ship's jostling. He saw the spray of blood and that Traver was its source. Tearing a bandage free from his belt, he frantically wrapped it tightly around the end of what had been Traver's elbow.

"Don't worry about him. Attend to Lance," Fletcher ordered dispassionately.

Marin replied without looking at her, his hands still busy with the tourniquet. "That would be a breach of duty, Captain. Putting aside my professional responsibility to Mister Graff, his life is the one in more immediate danger. It would be a crime to ignore him."

Fletcher knew that to press the issue would be to demand the doctor become privy to murder by neglect. Regardless, she *would* have forced the issue if it had not been for the blood. It shimmered in the air, red and white, unnoticed by the frantic doctor. It distracted her as she wondered, just for a split second, what had *really* been happening inside Traver. Perhaps he could be allowed to live, if only so he could be pulled apart and examined.

Marin rushed Traver out of the cockpit once the blood flow had been mostly stemmed. The one-armed man was still dazed, staring with wide-eyed stupefaction at his injury. Between that and the sedatives of which the doctor was certain to pump him full, Fletcher knew she had nothing to fear from the mutineer. Not for a good while, anyway.

It only took two minutes for the ship to return to orbit. Fletcher checked and rechecked the trajectory, and it was good.

She shut the hatch below, not wishing to waste any more oxygen than was needed. She saw the deep groove she had made in its underside. She would not have made the cut in time. Even if she had succeeded in getting through in time to stop Traver, the cockpit would have been compromised by unfixable exposure to the vent system. She owed everything to Lance.

Gently she unwrapped his wrist from the strangling seat strap. It had been wrapped so tight as to cut off all circulation for nearly four minutes. His hand would likely never recover, but Fletcher hoped that would be the least of the damage.

She brought him into her cabin, where Marin was already hard at work sealing the ends of Traver's severed blood vessels. Traver's eyes were rolling in his sockets but otherwise he was motionless. Fletcher tapped the doctor on the shoulder after she laid the unconscious assistant down. "Do what you can. His arm is broken, and I'm concerned for his neck too." Marin nodded; though his priorities were clearly biased, he harbored no desire to see any further suffering inflicted on anyone, and would do everything in his power to stop or foreshorten it.

Before she left the room, Fletcher took a precaution that even she knew was likely redundant. Against the half-hearted protestations of the doctor, she secured Traver's legs and remaining arm to the bed, using the surgical restraints she'd salvaged from the medical bay. If his consciousness were to return, he'd be helpless to move.

Then she ordered Dr. Marin to do something that provoked his whole-hearted protestations.

"But Captain," he said, "he's too short on blood as it is. Already he would be needing a transfusion, if the blood bags in the medical bay were still any good, which I'm sure they aren't."

"Just do it. One vial's not going to be the thing that kills him."

"I just don't understand what you could want with his blood. It seems completely unnecessary and dangerous to take a sample now, of all times." He was argumentative for how nervous he was. Too argumentative, Fletcher thought. And too nervous.

"It's an order, Doctor."

Countermanding Fletcher was a pointless endeavor. After all, here was a woman who had cut off a man's arm without blinking, then considered the action not harsh enough. Marin siphoned a vial of blood from Traver, sealed it and reluctantly (*too* reluctantly) handed it to the captain.

She held it up to the light. The blood inside seemed normal enough. No white crystals separated themselves from the thick red fluid. But then again, it hadn't been exposed to air, as had the droplets in the cockpit. Perhaps the blood cells remained fused with the anomalies – whatever the anomalies were – as long as the blood was sealed. Why Marin hadn't mentioned the abnormality, which he must surely have seen by now on the outside of Traver's wound, Fletcher could only begin to guess.

She made her way to the aft of the ship, carrying the vial with her. She found the lab reasonably free of disarray despite the abrupt movements the ship had undergone. The scientists seemed surprised, and pleasantly so, to see that Fletcher had emerged victorious, but none were in any mood to celebrate. In fact, they said very few words at all, remaining utterly focused on their work. Bjornson's suicide must have been weighing heavily on them.

"Do you have time to test this blood?" Fletcher asked, showing the vial to Dr. Zhang.

"Why?" Zhang's tone sounded suspicious, or even defensive. The captain assumed that too many conflicting and disheartening commands had made the scientists wary of further requests.

"This is Traver's blood. If you just take a look at it, I think you might find something strange."

Zhang seemed intrigued, at least. He nodded and took the vial from her. "What exactly am I looking for?"

"I can't tell you because I don't know. Just tell me if there's anything out of the ordinary."

When Fletcher was able to return to the cockpit and finally spend a moment there without urgency, she noted that little had actually been altered during her time away.

The recent mess of blood had all settled in an airbrush pattern on the walls and ceiling. She shut the door behind her and set herself to cleaning, but not before entering her personal credentials at the console to unlock the encrypted messages she knew she must have received. There were dozens of them, and she was not surprised. She scrubbed the floor as she let the messages play through, listening to those that contained voice recordings while setting the computer to read aloud the textual transmissions.

As expected, the vast majority of the messages from the past months were status requests from Aurora and the Cooperative. The requests grew more and more insistent and alarmed as time had passed with no response from the *Aten*.

The messages transitioned to a series of notifications, with Gladstone appearing first to offer an explanation of the actions they had taken to reach Traver, and then a promise that help was on its way. Messages from the Cooperative corroborated the assurance that Merrickson had left port in the *Iris* with orders to reach AMA as quickly as possible.

Fletcher was not relieved at that news. On the contrary, it enraged her. A rescue mission was likely to receive much of the credit for any survivors making it back home. The financial costs incurred by Aurora for the rescue mission – Merrickson as a contracted pilot did not come cheap – would be a black mark on her own record for having required a rescue in the first place. Of course, she did not require a rescue, having taken back the ship on her own – but who was to say what story would be told?

Upon hearing the last of the transmissions, Fletcher's anger fueled the energy with which she scrubbed the last of the blood off the wall. She had begun to calculate travel times, devising a plan by which she could leave AMA's system before Merrickson arrived, when a final message, disconnected from the others, arrived.

It was a textual message, coded with Aurora as the source, but she did not recognize the sign-code of the sender. The priority level was set to *IMMEDIATE,* an encryption only available to the highest of Aurora's executives.

The computer would not audibly read such a high clearance message, so Fletcher, having scrubbed up the last of the blood, sat back in the pilot's seat to read it herself:

Cap Fletcher. Primary mission update: ensure arrival at planet, followed by safe return of subject GRAFF. Damage is not to be inflicted on him, in body or mind. Preserve him during orbit and bring him back for mission completion. LOSS OF GRAFF IS MISSION FAILURE.

It was hard for Fletcher to believe what she had read. She read it through a second time, sure that she had not misunderstood the very simple commands of the text. If it was anger that she had felt before, now uncontrollable hate poured behind her eyes, filling her head like boiling blood.

She shut down the message commands. She would not respond to Aurora, that much she knew. Let them think the ship was still Traver's. Let them think whatever they wanted to think. She was not an employee of Aurora; she was a contractor and she owed them nothing. If she wished to return without Traver, she would do just that.

She would do just that.

* * *

Marin finished tying off Traver's arm, cauterizing and sterilizing the ends. Traver was fully tranquilized and attached to life support, so there was nothing more for the doctor to do now. He turned his attention to Lance.

The assistant had a severe concussion in addition to the broken arm and fractured rib, but otherwise he was intact. It took him several hours to regain consciousness, during which Marin was able to cover his whole right side in a spray foam cast.

When he did wake, Lance tried to turn his head with no success. All he could see was the ceiling of the cabin and part of the doctor's head looking down at him.

"Where's Mister Graff? Where's Captain Fletcher?"

"Graff is here. The Captain's in the cockpit."

Lance relaxed. His eyes, one of which was black and blue and oozing thick blood, shut again. Before he could again let himself sleep, there was one more thing he wanted to know.

"Is Mister Graff alive?"

"Yes. He is going to be fine."

It was not the answer Lance had expected, but it was, as it should not have been, a relief. He slept for the next twelve hours.

* * *

The captain had no intention of softening the blow that would accompany her command that the studies were to be cut short as they left AMA for good. She had no second thoughts about the action, nor would it do any good to show signs of weakness. Still, cold commander though she was, she was not insensitive to the plight of the scientists as they approached the cockpit at her orders. The poor souls had been forced to run a gauntlet, and the emotional strain on their lot had been worse than that of anyone else onboard, sans perhaps Lance. What small satisfaction they had gotten in being able to see and study AMA under Traver's short command, she was about to take away from them. She hoped, for their sake, that perhaps they would have found something worthwhile in the time they'd had, because that time was over now.

The morose crew of silent surviving researchers, the ones she was expecting, did not arrive. In their place were four excited professionals who seemed to think they'd been summoned to give a lengthy account of their revitalized work. Fletcher opened the door and was barely able to greet them before Zhang and the three others all began talking at once.

She waited with a visage of patience, understanding few of the technical phrases which were being tossed around. At last she interrupted, startling the oblivious children out of their rhapsody of excitement. "It is not necessary to report your findings to me. My duty is to transport you, and unlike Graff, *I* have no interest in involving myself in your science."

She started to go on with her dire announcement, but Dr. Zhang interrupted her in turn. "But you were interested in the tests of Mister Graff's blood sample."

Now Fletcher paused. In spite of herself, she *was* interested. "Does your report pertain to those tests as well?"

"They pertain to one another. They are connected. Come and see."

Fletcher could afford to delay the cease-command for a few hours. Even she was not above the temptation of curiosity.

"The abnormality in the blood was very easy to find," Zhang explained vigorously as they all entered the lab. "Isolating a few of the alien particles was less easy, but I managed to do it without disturbing the others. The rest of the sample has still not separated. See?" He pointed to the vial. The blood was red, with no immediate visual evidence of anything amiss.

"But these —" he ushered Fletcher to a separate vial, in which sat a tiny dusting of what looked like snow — "these are the ones I extracted."

"And what are they?"

"Calcium crystals. Completely organic, though most of them contain foreign DNA, not Traver's. So, most likely lab-grown. But there is a small percentage..."

"Lab-grown?" Fletcher cut in. She cared little for the finer points of Zhang's explanation.

"Yes. But as I was about to say, a small percentage shares his DNA as if it was produced by him. A very small percentage. For the most part, yes, it appears to have been made in a lab. Once a structure has been established for a crystal like this – a sort of blueprint – then it would be easy to replicate."

"For what reason?" A thought – an ugly, insidious suspicion – wriggled its way into Fletcher's mind and planted itself there.

"Reasons, I can't say," replied the scientist, whose relative unconcern was frustrating. "But you haven't yet asked what it is these crystals do."

"What do they do?" Fletcher asked, too impatient to care that she had no control over the conversation.

"Well, the ones that I have isolated, they do nothing. As soon as they're separated from the blood, they seem to become inactive. But *with* the blood. Here. Watch." He placed the vial of blood under a microscope, the view of which was displayed on a monitor that Fletcher could see.

The red blood cells were brought into focus, floating and bumping into one another. Fletcher looked closer. More than half of the red cells were host to small hitchhikers: spiked white discs, looking more like saw blades than snowflakes at this magnification, latched onto the blood at a ratio of never more than one per cell.

"Alright, I see them," agreed Fletcher, wishing the demonstration could be done away with in favor of a straightforward statement.

"If we isolate one of the cells and follow it with the microscope," he casually set the machine to do so while he talked, "we can watch its behavior over a period of time."

The captain's eyes narrowed as she carefully watched for some strange movement, some unexpected behavior that would clarify the purpose of the crystals. But there was nothing to see; the chosen crystal was hard as a rock, moving only in tandem with the red blood cell it was riding.

"I don't see it. Tell me what I'm supposed to be seeing."

"Nothing. There is no physical behavior that is obvious to the naked eye."

Fletcher's breath hissed out in frustration.

"But!" Here Zhang produced a wide smile full of teeth, "We switch on the radio spectrometer in the microscope, and this is what we see."

The image on the monitor darkened to a dull grey-black. "Is this another instance where I'm not going to be able to see anything?" she muttered, no longer hiding her annoyance.

"No," said Zhang. "Look, there." He rested his finger against the screen. Right where his finger had pressed, a tiny white light pulsed, barely able to be seen against the murky field of vision. Fletcher's first thought was that Zhang's finger had somehow affected the screen, but when he withdrew his hand the pulse continued.

The small, blinking white blur pulsed at random intervals, sometimes multiple times within a second, then less than once in four, and then faster than human eyes could count.

"I see it. I don't know what it is."

Zhang switched the device back to microscopic view. "It's a slight energy emission. Each one of these crystals is sending tiny signals. And the most fascinating thing is, of the many thousands of crystals in this blood sample, they are all transmitting with the same patterns!" Zhang nearly shook with excitement.

Fletcher still failed to recognize why these facts were particularly interesting. "Tell me what it all means. What impact does this have on our assignment and on Traver?"

Now Dr. La Salle, Zhang's immediate senior, moved up quickly, being so bold as to touch Fletcher on the shoulder and usher her to the other side of the lab. "While Doctor Zhang was studying the blood, I observed the gas from the planet. When we finally compared notes, we found something really thrilling." Fletcher surrendered herself to the scientists' narrative, which was certain to continue as planned despite her pleas for triteness.

"These gas molecules are generally very active, responding to various forms of energy input, so it didn't surprise me at first when they began to charge themselves and shoot off electrical pulses. You'll have to see for yourself."

He pointed to a clear glass vat, full of the drifting greenish gas. "And this," added Zhang with a smile, "you'll be able to see with your unaided eyes."

Fletcher saw. The green gas flickered at intervals, turning from a dull matte color to a bright near-white. The regularity of the flicker changed, displaying patterns similar to those of the blood crystals.

"Is this related to the blood pulses?" Fletcher queried, finally connecting the pieces in front of her.

Ls Salle replied, "The electrical pulses in the gas didn't begin until you brought the vial of blood into the lab."

"And when we noticed that," Zhang carried on, "we compared the pulse patterns. The calcium crystals will produce a certain set of radio emissions, and that set will be repeated by the electricity in the gas after a delay of point two six seconds."

"They're communicating?" Fletcher would have been happier to have simply been told as much, but in making her own realization she did come to appreciate the narrative the scientists had created for her.

Zhang, La Salle and the others all froze in place, staring at Fletcher as if she had spoken sacred words. Then, "yes," whispered Zhang.

The following silence lasted a moment before Fletcher interrupted it, keen to carry out her original intention despite her increasing interest in the discoveries. "Do you have all you need to continue this work from home?"

Again they all stared at her, but this time with bewilderment. La Salle gave voice to it: "From home? You mean Earth?"

"Yes. Gather whatever else you will need over the next twenty-four hours. After that time, we will be leaving the AMA system behind. Thank you for your continued efforts."

She smiled curtly, nodded, and departed the lab. The four scientists looked after her, unmoving and unspeaking, the smiles gone from their faces.

"Doctor Marin," Fletcher called, opening the door to her cabin-turned-medical bay. "If you can step away from the patients for a moment, I need you to let me into the medical bay storage."

Marin looked up nervously from where he was studiously reading near Traver's limp body. "Why do you need me to do that?"

"Only doctors had access to that medical storage. You are the remaining doctor."

"I know that. But why do you need to get in?"

"I need to know if any of Traver's medicine survived the explosion."

"His Eams formula?"

Fletcher nodded.

Marin looked back at Traver. "He's gone without treatment for months now. He looks pretty bad, but giving him a shot of the formula now isn't going to do much if the bacteria has been growing this whole time."

"It's not for him."

Marin wiped his forehead. Fletcher noticed that he was sweating, though the air systems were maintaining a comfortable cool.

"*If* any of the formula survived, it would still be a breach of medical ethics for me to allow it to be used for anything besides its intended purpose…"

"Doctor." Her eyes lit up with a spark that frightened the doctor more than medical ethics hearings ever could. (*Not that the ethics is what concerns him*, Fletcher thought.)

A few minutes later she opened the door leading into the blackened medical bay. Marin moved in gingerly past the melted spider machine. "I haven't been in here since it blew up. Are you sure it's safe?"

"Your injection machine caused the spark. It's dead now, so I think the room is safer than it ever was."

The doctor went to the locked cabinet that housed Dr. Shurovsky's priceless concoction. He touched his keychip against the keypad, which was once bright and clean but was now dull, the screen smashed and burnt. "The screen is dead. I can't open it."

"There's a mechanical keypad behind." Quickly she crouched down beside him and, with a sharp tool produced from the belt she wore, pried back the broken keypad. As it fell away it revealed an older, spring-loaded set of numbered buttons. "You'll know the code, I have no doubt." Rolling his eyes with frustrated reluctance, Marin tapped out a number on the pad. Something clicked within and the door sprang open.

Several dozens of reinforced vials, each marked conspicuously with the Aurora symbol of which Fletcher was growing weary, lay on the shelves within. There were no signs of damage.

"Here they are" murmured the doctor.

"Good," growled Fletcher. "I only need one." She reached forward.

"What for?" Marin shut the door before her hand could reach it. The lock clicked. Fletcher was surprised, and she swung her head around to look at him. The doctor was clenching his teeth, his lips quivering as he fought against the fear he was doubtless feeling.

"That's not your business" she replied.

"It is my business." Now his voice was shaking. "As I said before, I'm personally responsible for the containment of this medicine. Whatever it is to be used for, I need to know."

Fletcher said nothing for a moment. She weighed the benefits of telling Marin the truth. There was no harm, she decided. His reaction might even be telling.

"I want the scientists to test it."

Marin's composure fell even further. "Test it for what?" His voice was so weak it was nearly a whisper.

"Anything that may have been put into Traver's blood, that should not have been there."

The doctor inhaled slowly, then breathed out. His quiver steadied. For a minute, perhaps two or five minutes, he stared at the captain and she stared back.

"Pointless to look. You won't find anything."

"That's not going to work for me."

Marin shut his eyes. Every muscle in his face became tense. This was no longer hesitation; he was preparing for something, and Fletcher's suspicion skyrocketed. But he acted before she had time to prepare a reaction.

The doctor's arm shot forward and seized the pry-tool out of Fletcher's hand. She tried to tighten her fist around it, but it was too late. Marin retracted his arm, folding his elbow back quickly in one uninterrupted motion. His fist, holding the sharp object, rammed itself into the right side of his neck.

Fletcher grabbed his arm and pulled it back. As she did, he twisted his fist so that his withdrawing arm only tore the wound and made it worse. Blood pumped out of the man's neck in liters, and he choked.

The captain reacted quickly now that she knew what Marin's plan was. Her eyes darted around the room, seeing nothing that would be of any use to her. Knowing that Marin, instantly weakened, was not threatening to her, she tore the buttons from her uniform and pulled her arms out. Whipping the loose garment around, she wrapped it quickly around the doctor's torn neck. Her face, arms and undershirt were covered in a solid coating of fresh blood. Weakly Marin tried to argue, tried to raise his arms, but he'd already lost too much blood to do either. His face was ivory white.

Without a word the captain straddled him, pulling the uniform tight and pulling it tighter. Still, the blood spurted out, soaking through the fabric and not stopping there.

She was losing the battle. "Help! In the medical bay!" she screamed at the top of her lungs. But she knew the doors in the corridor were shut. Nobody would hear her.

She removed her right hand from the unbloodied side of the neck and it joined her left hand in squeezing the area directly above the wound.

The blood drops did not stop forming, disseminating in the air around the struggling pair.

Marin's lips moved, but no sound came out. Then his eyes, which had remained staring up at his would-be savior, rolled up into their sockets.

* * *

For the next hour Fletcher braced herself above his body, trying to hold in the last drops of blood, trying to push air and life back into his lungs. When she finally gave up, she let herself fall back, drifting away from the corpse. Her eyes, already blurred by blood, lost their focus. She stared aimlessly, seeing nothing and thinking nothing. This was the ninth member of her crew to meet his end. The causes didn't matter; whether the crew had died by their own hands, by Traver's, or by explosion, this was the ninth time the captain had failed.

CHAPTER THIRTEEN
AMA

Traver woke up.

"Lance. Are you alright Lance?"

Lance rolled his head over until he was able to see Traver's bed. They looked at one another for a moment, then Lance rolled back again, preferring to stare at the ceiling.

"Am I missing an arm?" Traver's speech was sluggish and slurred, effects of the medication which still heavily inundated his system.

Lance waited a moment, then replied "Yes."

"Oh. I remember now. I thought that would have hurt more."

During the silence that followed, Lance hoped someone would come into the room and distract Traver, or at least provide him with someone else to talk to. Nobody came.

"We're still near the planet. She hasn't started for home yet. That's good."

"Why is it good?" Lance asked, too flustered to play the silent game, yet also too curious.

"I told you before, it wants to talk to me."

"How did you know we are still in orbit?"

"I can feel it. I told you that before, too."

Perhaps it was his own concussion mixing his thoughts, but Lance, not for the first time, suspected there might be something affecting Traver beyond his surface level insanity.

"What made you decide to stop me from finishing the mission, Lance?"

His words sent guilt shooting through Lance like a spear, and the assistant went cold for a moment.

"I'm sorry. Maybe I shouldn't have done that," Lance said. Then he realized what he'd said. The coldness vanished as his heart, beating faster, pumped fresh blood into his head. "No. That's not what I meant to say. I did what I had to do. You already killed nearly half the crew, and you were ready to kill the rest of us. I saved our lives. I will not apologize." Why had he apologized in the first place? Did Traver's words really hold so much power? *I need to get out of here,* Lance thought; *it's dangerous just to be in the same room with him.*

He unclipped himself from the bed and tried to push himself up and out. His head instantly throbbed and his foam-coated right arm threw off his balance. Instead of steadying himself upright, he spun clumsily for a moment until his leg struck the edge of the bed, bringing him to an abrupt halt. He allowed himself a moment of drifting to recover, his head swimming, then he pulled himself back down to the bed.

"Can you promise me something?" Traver went on as if there had been no interruption.

"What?" Lance asked before his better judgment could advise him not to respond.

"If I need to broadcast to Earth one more time, will you help me do it?"

At first Lance wasn't sure he had heard Traver correctly. He wondered if he might still be unconscious and dreaming, or if perhaps Traver was the unconscious one and sleep talking.

"I am going to need to record one last show," Traver continued when Lance did not reply. "It's very important that it reach Earth."

"Why should I?" Lance almost shouted, disregarding the pain in his head so that he could turn sharply toward Traver. "Damn your broadcasts, damn your speeches, and damn your audience."

Traver did not retort, and for several minutes he gave no reply at all. In that time Lance's anger simmered and faded into the same exhausted bitterness that had defined his existence since he first found himself recovering alongside his monstrous companion.

When Traver did say something, it was not the sort of hateful invective Lance had come to expect from him – quite the opposite. "Did I ever apologize to you?"

"For what?" Lance snapped his quick response before becoming incredulous.

"I hit you. Several times, I think."

"Yeah." Lance scratched under his bruised eye. "That was one of the things you did."

"Well, I'm sorry for it. If I've lost your respect, if I've lost your –" he paused for a moment and stared at his stump of an arm – "If I've lost your friendship, then I can't say I blame you."

Traver's left arm pulled curiously at the strap that held him to his bed, as if making sure it was secure. A wistful smile came to his face. "I wish I hadn't needed to hurt you; to hurt anyone. Getting us here, it was something I had to do. But now it might finally be time for me to finish the mission alone. I think we'll be parting ways soon."

Lance's heart leaped in his chest, then landed with a thud. The thought of parting from Traver was both wonderful and devastating. But he managed a coughed chuckle. "How is that going to happen? Are you planning on throwing the rest of us off the ship next?"

"No. I'll be the one leaving the ship." The sincerity in Traver's voice was unnerving.

* * *

Fletcher entered the cabin shortly thereafter, shutting the door behind her. The sight of her gave Lance a start, and even Traver's eyes widened. Dry blood crusted her shirt. Her hair, usually tied back neatly, was unkempt and also matted with red-black coagulation. Her eyes were dull, the skin beneath them sagging and pale. She looked old, older than Traver or Lance had ever imagined her. But as she moved into the room she carried herself with all the poise and authority they'd come to expect. She steadied herself in front of the beds and placed her hands behind her back, scrutinizing the two incapacitated patients. Neither of them said a word.

"I've turned off the monitors in this room," Fletcher grimly informed them after her observation had become uncomfortable. "If upon our return to Earth the monitoring feed is checked, it will look like this room suffered a malfunction. It's not uncommon. Anything that happens in here during this time will go unseen and unheard by anyone who sees fit to review the ship's logs."

Lance looked frightened. Traver continued staring back at the captain, his expression unchanging.

Fletcher went on addressing Traver. "So, while we are unmonitored, I am not opposed to the idea of removing the doctor's patch work on your arm, letting the veins open up again and watching you bleed out. If Lance would like to be spared the sight of the blood, I would consider letting him leave the room while I override the system controls and vent out the oxygen. Alternatively, I could adjust the temperature settings until your eyes ice over and your blood freezes inside you. It could also look like a malfunction."

Fletcher's eyes had lit up again, burning with the ferocity of a hungry animal, but the rest of her expression remained composed. Lance couldn't bring himself to look away or even to blink, and his teeth were chattering with fear despite not himself being the target of the captain's wrath.

Traver coolly looked at her. A smile might have even flickered across his lips, but that may have been a mirage in the lens of rage through which Fletcher was watching him.

"To put it bluntly, Mister Graff, you are no longer welcome

onboard my vessel. The *Aten* will not be returning with you on it, whether you are alive or dead. That is my decision, and here my decision is law. We are leaving orbit in twelve hours, by which point you will already be gone. Take that time to consider your position, or to pray, or to sob – how exactly you spend the time is not something I give a damn about. Am I understood?"

Now Traver did smile. It was not a spiteful grin but a kind, understanding lifting of the cheeks that brought an imperceptible grimace to Fletcher's face.

He had never found the captain's spirit to be so vitally irresistible as it was now. The hate in her eyes, the spite in her words, the blood covering her informal clothing; this was the Fletcher he always knew was there, behind the rigid woman who had spent most of her time hiding in the cockpit. If only his arms were free – *arm*, that was – he could kiss her. But no, things had not worked out that way. Perhaps in a different time, in a different life, in a different universe.

"I understand," Traver said slowly after forcing Fletcher to wait patiently for a reply. "I am confused by one thing, though. You mentioned freezing the room, suffocating me and ripping open my arm, all of which have left me wondering: how *are* you going to kill me?"

The twitch in Fletcher's eye was enough to tell Traver that she had never enacted anything like an execution before. She had thought plenty about his demise but still had not committed to a means.

"I will tell you my decision when it's time." She turned away from them and opened the door.

"Let me go on my own terms, Captain." Traver's voice boomed through the cabin and down the corridor. Lance hadn't heard his voice this strong since the last set of broadcasts.

Fletcher turned back from the corridor and shut the door again.

"You don't have terms. You don't have rights. You don't have that choice."

"But I do have a suggestion."

Fletcher tried not to look like she was listening, but she was.

"Put me in one of the pods and send me down to the planet."

In a brief moment, Fletcher remembered the battered pod, the crushing pressure and jarring vibrations it had endured. There would be suffering. That was good.

"I can't spare the pod."

"Send the damaged one then."

Fletcher searched for a reason to deny Traver this final wish, but she couldn't find one.

She looked at Traver, then at Lance. Her nostrils flared, then she turned again, and was gone. The door shut and once again Lance was alone with Traver.

Traver's smile widened to a grin. He looked at Lance, his eyes bright and beaming with happiness. More than happiness: joy, it seemed. Then he started to laugh.

* * *

The hours passed quickly for everyone. Fletcher spent several of them in the medical bay, cleaning the blood that she had not had time to scrub upon first removing the body. Marin's remains she would store onboard for return to his employers at Aurora, a requirement in any cases involving a semblance of foul play. The first thing she had done upon his death was to display the scene to the four scientists (for whom there seemed to be no end of mental trauma), describe the event and name them as witnesses to her testimony.

Once the blood was cleared away, she took the metal saw (also recently cleaned of blood and bone fragments) and began to cut open the medical cabinet. The material cut slowly, reinforced as it was nearly as strongly as the cockpit door. It would take time, but time was a commodity she now had. With or without Marin, she would retrieve those vials. Before they reached Earth she would have her answers. Aurora would be held responsible if anything unusual was to be found in the formula.

For the scientists, the passage of time was far too rapid. Zhang engaged Fletcher (once she was cleaned and sporting a fresh uniform) in a halfhearted plea for a little more time, for some more samples from the planet or at least from the atmosphere. Fletcher denied every plea and ordered the scientists to secure their equipment then vacate the lab.

She went to get Traver.

He did not argue as she disconnected the bed from the floor and pushed him, still tied down by the legs, waist and arm, through the corridor. It had been months since he'd last been in the aft section of the ship, and he looked with interest at the walls that he'd last seen dark and covered in burns. He smiled when she opened the lab door.

Nobody noticed – there were no scientists in the room – that in the moment Traver was pushed into the lab, the sample of AMA's planetary gas began to flicker faster and brighter, more intense by a hundred times than before. Traver's eyes shut. He seemed to be waiting, or listening for something.

"This is more than you deserve," Fletcher tried to interrupt whatever peace Traver was experiencing.

"I know it is. I can't argue that I've earned any mercy from you or anyone else. But this is the only way we get answers to our questions."

Fletcher immediately thought of her own questions, the blood and the vials. Hurriedly she dismissed the thought – Traver must of course be talking about his own feverish quandary. *His answer is going to be hot, crushing death. Let him be satisfied with that.*

"Where's Lance? I need to talk to Lance." Traver's peace was gone and urgency took its place.

"Lance does not want to talk to you. Your last request is being fulfilled already; don't ask for too much."

Just then Traver turned his head and looked back at the lab's door. He smiled. Someone there caught the edge of Fletcher's eye and she turned to look. There was Lance, grimacing and holding his forehead with his good hand.

"I didn't give you authorization to be here." Fletcher commanded.

"This section is to be vacant for the pod's detachment."

Lance's eyes fell. His shoulders rolled in a little shrug, but he didn't leave.

"Can I help you?" Fletcher demanded, her patience being ground away.

Meekly, Lance mumbled "I'm just going to be useless baggage now. He's the only reason I'm here."

"He was almost a reason for you to cease being here, too. What are you trying to say? We don't have time for this."

"Oh, I know. I don't mean to waste a minute if it means starting later for home. But still, I think I won't be able to live with myself if I don't do my job while I still can."

"And what's your job?" Fletcher had stopped looking at Lance and resumed pushing Traver toward the pod bay.

"If Mister Graff needs a transmission sent back to Earth, I need to make sure it gets there."

Fletcher neither stopped nor hesitated. "I don't give a damn what he says or doesn't say. Do whatever you want."

"Will I have access to the pod camera?"

"If it still works. The monitor feed is here." She nodded sideways at the screens with which the scientists had watched the pod descents. "You can figure out the rest."

Lance raised his eyes. "Thank you, Captain." His voice was louder now, and shaky with excitement. He had told himself that the reason for obliging Traver's final request was for the novelty of the thing. If Traver's audience had eaten up his last messages (as he was certain they must have), how hungry would they be for a death note such as this? Lance would be hailed as a hero for faithfully transmitting the man's words right up until the end. Perhaps that was all true. Certainly there was some selfishness in Lance's motivation. Yet at the same time, he knew he would have done it even if he had nothing to gain. He would have done it just for Traver.

"Thank you, Lance." Traver was still smiling as he looked at Lance from the floating bed. Lance directed his eyes to him from where they had focused on Fletcher. His heart melted as he watched Traver's hopeful eyes disappear behind the next door, into the bay.

"Until the pod is away, please vacate this section." It was Fletcher's last word on the matter, and impossible not to obey. Lance went back into the corridor and then realized the pain had left his head and entered his heart. He was going to miss Traver.

* * *

Five minutes later Fletcher joined him outside the lab.

"He's gone."

* * *

Lance's heaviness vanished, his pain receding. He hurried to the cabin that had been Traver's, quickly assembling the equipment that had been gathering figurative dust since the mega-broadcast of months prior.

As he hurried back through the aft toward the lab, he saw Fletcher still standing there, waiting for him. "Am I clear to go into the lab?" he asked, panting with the unexpected exertion.

"I am going to join you in watching his transmission. If he mentions recent events or conversations, the broadcast will not be sent. It will need to look like he launched to the planet on his own volition."

Lance furrowed his eyebrows, but nodded his understanding. Together they went into the lab.

It took Lance only a few moments to set up the recorder box and to route it into the monitor.

He switched it on.

Traver appeared in the jittery, unstable image. He was sitting tightly but firmly inside the collection tank of the pod, which was meant to double as a mini-cockpit for manned flights. The whole pod, as Lance knew, was no more than two meters long. It was painful to see Traver so diminished as to be crammed in so small a space, outfitted with jump seat and harness though it was.

"Does he have any control?"

"No," Fletcher was fast to reply. "It's still set for unmanned flights. I have control and I've sent him on a direct path to the planet."

"Why can't I hear him?"

Lance began to panic. He could see Traver clearly enough but there was no sound; neither static nor the roar of the pod's little engine could be heard.

"Why can't I hear him? I need there to be sound. I need to be able to hear him!"

"The sound sensor cancels out engine noises. It's meant to detect and isolate anything noteworthy. You'll hear him when he talks."

Lance breathed nervously and nodded. He hoped Fletcher was correct. His mind would never rest if he failed to fully capture this last moment.

He switched on the recorder.

The minutes passed and Traver said nothing. He stared straight ahead through his tiny little porthole window, the green glow on his face growing in intensity. Lance wished that the pod's forward camera was operational so that he could capture the accompanying visual of the approaching planet, but he would make do with the image he had. He just hoped Traver would say something soon. Much longer and he would hit the atmosphere, and then there was no telling how long the camera, the pod and Traver would last.

Lance's heart thumped so loudly he could hear it. Fletcher's eyes were glued to the screen with uncharacteristic interest.

The pressure reading began its slow climb out of the green "safe" zone. Traver's face started to jitter visibly as the pod showed its first signs of atmospheric entry.

Fletcher looked at the time. The pod was nearly ten minutes out from the *Aten*. Another ten and it would be in the high pressure blackout zone. "Is he going to say anything? Or will he show us some charity in the end, and keep his mouth shut?"

Lance didn't know how to reply. He was about to say something defending his boss' choices of timing as being necessary to his creative process, but then Traver spoke.

"I have somewhat lost track of time, so I don't know whether you will be receiving this message before or after the broadcast of my other last segment. In the end, I suppose it doesn't matter. The meaning of my words won't change with the order in which they're received. Regardless, it should be obvious by now that it was not my last segment after all."

And so he went on without stopping.

The readings hit their critical point and Traver was shaken uncontrollably, and still he talked.

The monitors blacked out, the readings vanished. Lance could again hear his heart beating, unaware even that Fletcher was waiting beside him. Then the feed came back, the pod again having survived entry.

And still Traver was talking.

As the pod dove deep within the surface of the planet, far past the depth it had reached before, Lance might have felt that twinge of heartache again. He might have felt a sense of loss or even grief that Traver was about to be gone forever. But in fact he felt none of those things – he was far too confused by the words Traver was saying. They were not what Lance had expected. They were not like anything Traver had said before, via broadcast or privately to Lance in the mad darkness of the cockpit.

When the transmission had been recorded for seventeen minutes, it cut out again abruptly. The monitors went black and the sensors read nothing. Traver's audience of two knew that the signals would not come back again. He was deep inside the planet, beyond their reach forever.

The lab was silent for time that Lance couldn't count. He was surprised by what he felt; as the sound of his heartbeat finally subsided, he found he felt nothing at all.

"Will you send *that*?" The edges of Fletcher's lips actually displayed a bemused smile that she may or may not have intended.

"That's what he wanted to say. It's what he wanted to send." Lance no longer felt the weight of necessity to fulfill Traver's last wish, or any of his wishes for that matter. He felt free, and he even welcomed the feelings of physical pain that returned into his arm and head. Those were at least feelings that belonged completely to himself.

Fletcher shrugged. "Why not? Maybe that's what the Church of Traver wants to hear. But if it's not, who are we to make the call? Send it." Her mood was light, and her slight smile never disappeared as she shut off the pod instruments and left the lab. "Be secured in your cabin in ten minutes. The *Aten* will be leaving orbit at that time."

Lance finished processing and packing the transmission data, then sent it. *That* was the moment when he felt the weight truly lifted off his shoulders. His job was done. He could go home now.

But before he left the lab, something caught his eye. Inside one of the research vats, a green gas was still flickering madly, flashing with a rapidity that was impossible to track and a brightness that hurt the eyes. Once the technician saw it, he could not turn his eyes away.

"Two minutes. Two minutes until we leave orbit. Secure yourselves in your cabins," rang out Fletcher's voice over the intercom, a welcome restoration of some normality.

Lance didn't know what the flashing gas was; that sort of thing was not for him to worry about. Surely the scientists knew all about it. He hurried out of the lab and into his cabin.

....

"I have somewhat lost track of time, so I don't know whether you will be receiving this message before or after the broadcast of my other *last segment. In the end, I suppose it doesn't matter. The meaning of my words won't change with the order in which they're received. Regardless, it should be obvious by now that it was not my last segment after all.*

"I knew that my time here – my time in space, that is – was leading me somewhere, somewhere important. I just didn't know then what direction I was going. A lot has happened since I sent those transmissions. A lot has changed. Here, I'm at what is very likely the end of the journey, and no doubt the most important part. In case you are wondering about the nature of this unfamiliar visual, I am inside one of the research pods that has been sent from the Aten to study AMA-712. We reached the planet's orbit nearly two months ago and now I am descending through the atmosphere to the planet itself. I would say I'm going to be the first person to set foot on AMA, but the planet is made of gas and liquid so the best way I can put it is to say I'll be the first to dive inside. Whatever comes next, I'm ready.

"On second thought, I believe it to be true that the broadcast I sent before was *my last message to you*. For my own part, I have said all I need to say. I'm here now as a conduit, or maybe translator *is the better word for it. That is what I truly believe my purpose has been from the very beginning. From before the very beginning. Maybe it was determined before I was born that I would use my words, that I would become a purveyor of ideas, thoughts, principles, beliefs, until my words were ready to be used for something infinitely more important.*

"I was the only one who could hear AMA. The last thing I intend is to come across as entitled or somehow 'chosen,' but it's the truth. She's been trying to reach out to me for months. I was frustrated because I didn't understand, I didn't know why I was hearing – feeling *these messages. The proximity; the proximity was everything. The closer I got to AMA, the stronger her voice became. Even right now, I can feel...*

"God, I want to shut off this damn camera and just sit here and listen. But I can't be selfish, can I? This kind of communication can only come once in a – well, as far as we know, it's the only time it's ever happened. I'd like to waste it on myself. It's tempting. But really I'm just the messenger. 'Hello AMA. I am mankind.' Ha ha ha. It's not so simplistic...

"Actually, it is so simplistic. My mere existence here as a being that

AMA can feel and hear is the simplest statement of all. Hello AMA. I am Mankind. That's all there is to say.

"She wants to know more. To answer her I only need to be. She can read me like an open book. I can feel her reading me.

"This ride is pretty unbearable. I knew it was going to be rough, but this… I don't know if it looks painful, but it is getting pretty hot in here, and I'm – ha ha – I think I've shattered my elbow. My good elbow. I only have one now. See? I lost a hand.

"Maybe the worst is over. It's calmer now. Hot. Very hot. I don't think I'm in the atmosphere anymore. I know I'm not. I've made it. Ha. I know I've made it. Hello AMA.

"Should I tell her about Earth? About you all? I don't even need to try. I just think it, and she knows. My knowledge of history is pretty good. That's, that's a good thing. All of our past sins, all of our ambitions for improvement, all of our wasted time: there it is.

"I feel…god…she's taking a lot. She's taking everything. She doesn't just want to know me. She wants me.

"No, she wants all of us. Now that she knows about us, she wants us. I don't know how to describe…

"Hunger.

"Thirst.

"It hurts. God, it hurts. It's so hot, and I'm…I feel the pain but I don't feel it. She's taking it as fast as I can feel it. She's taking it. Taking me.

"No…

"Anger.

"It shouldn't have been me. I shouldn't have come. It shouldn't have been me.

"I did. I did. I did what I had to do to get here.

"Dana. Damian. Allison. Lucy. Weston. Lance. Akachi. Karl. Friedrich. Louisa. A hundred others. I hurt them. I hurt them. I hurt them. I hurt them. I hurt them. I HURT THEM. I HURT THEM. I HURT THEM. I HURT THEM. I HURT THEM.

"It was me. Just me. They're not all like me.

"Don't be angry with all of us. I'm not mankind. I'm not mankind. I'M NOT MANKIND.

"Are you angry with me?"

"Yes, I am."

CHAPTER FOURTEEN
IRIS

Fletcher reached for her control lever. It felt good in her hand. She squeezed it while waiting the final thirty seconds before she could leave that damn green planet far behind.

The ship's computer issued her an alert. A signal was being detected.

Probably another message from Aurora, she thought, looking down at her console without much concern. Then her forehead wrinkled, her jaw tightened and every muscle in her body seized. Her heart skipped several beats, but she didn't notice. "It's goddamn impossible," slipped the words quietly out of her trembling mouth.

The computer alerted again. An incoming transmission.

She stared at the screen. She had been so close. This message she would need to answer. There would be no excuse for non-response, not now. But what would she say?

She turned her head sharply upward and looked out the window. She couldn't see him. Not yet. But she knew he was out there, likely just on the other side of the planet. Merrickson and the *Iris* had arrived.

Sweat beaded on her forehead. How was it possible that the rescue mission had gotten here so quickly? Merrickson was fast, but *that* fast? It was unbelievable. It meant losses for Fletcher – loss of credit, loss of respect – but most importantly loss of her chance to open Dr. Shurovsky's vials and have them tested. Every movement onboard the *Aten* would be monitored and investigated; cutting open the medicine cabinet would be out of the question.

A minute passed by her projected time of departure. What would she tell the crew? What would she tell Merrickson had happened to Traver?

It was the thought of being ushered all the way back to Earth, held by the hand like a helpless and lost child, that made her decision. She would not be escorted, not now or ever. Let consequences be what they may; she would return the *Aten* home by herself.

Her hand pulled downward and she was pushed back into her seat. The ship rattled and those awful metallic groans could be heard from the midsection, but within a few moments they were free of AMA-712.

Another alert from the computer. Merrickson was an insistent bastard.

No, this alert was different. It took Fletcher two seconds too many to realize this alert was not a message at all.

She looked at the readings. Energy spikes on the planet surface. A powerful surge directly beneath the ship.

She remembered back to the energy swell months before that, from a far greater distance, had knocked out the ship's power for long enough to save Traver from her first attempt at jettisoning him. These readings were the same, only now the ship was dangerously close to the planet.

She sat forward and craned her neck. Far down, through the misty green atmosphere, she thought she could see the sparkling flashes of a billion bright points flickering within the surface of the planet. They got brighter as she watched.

This was no time to watch the light show. She took the risk of further strain to the hull and pulled the ship's nose abruptly perpendicular to the planet's surface, increasing speed as she did so. The g-force glued her to the chair and the shaking felt bad enough to rip each bolt right out of its socket.

The ship held together. But the readings continued to increase. Something was brewing on the planet, and when it released all hell might break loose.

Full speed ahead. Fletcher grit her teeth and stared into the blackness in front of her. Welcome blackness. Blackness that was her home.

Another alert. This one *was* a communication. No time for that.

Fletcher considered making the jump here and now, considered only for a moment; the crew were not properly secured for a jump. There would be broken necks and jumbled brains. What's more she had not yet finished the calculations; she might go too wide and land somewhere beyond Pluto, without the food or oxygen to last the rest of the trip.

These thoughts went through her mind in a flash. A flash was all the time she had.

The energy readings went wild. The alerts all went off at once. Something bright flashed in front of her eyes, obstructing that welcoming darkness.

Then everything was dark. Silence had complete reign. No alerts could be heard, nor even the sound of the ship's engine. The only light came from the stars.

Fletcher waited. The power would come back. It had to. It had come back last time.

One minute, her internal count reached. Then *two*.

System failure meant no oxygen. She wouldn't be able to wait forever.

Three minutes.

She dashed to the corner where her suit was stowed. In the dark she unrolled it and put it on, working from instinct and muscle memory. Now she needed to be careful how much she breathed; it would not be long before the room's oxygen was gone.

She pulled on the breathing mask and manually opened the cockpit door. Her suit was equipped with a light which she switched on. She made her way toward the cabins, hoping that all the others would already have begun putting on their suits. It would need to be done quickly; oxygen and heat were both vacating at an alarming rate.

In the back of her mind Fletcher knew that, if the power had not come back yet, it likely never would. The backup and the backup's backup should both have fired off by now, but the darkness and silence continued. She could not let the anger and frustration sink in now; there were crew members to save.

She went into Lance's cabin first, knowing he would have the most trouble with his suit, arm broken as it was.

He was already shivering by the time she reached him, breathing heavily from the combination of fear and cold. "Breathe slowly" she commanded, but try as he might Lance only panted faster and harder.

Fletcher slipped one of the cabin's oxygen masks over his face, then helped him with his suit. *Please let the scientists have already done the same*, she prayed to the darkness. If they had not, it might be too late already.

Time was lost again trying to force Lance's arm cast into the suit. It would not go. Already she watched ice crystals form on Lance's bare fingers; he needed to be suited, and now.

She gave him no warning before hurling his arm against the wall, cracking the hard foam enough to get her fingers inside, prying it open. She knew Lance was screaming in agony, his arm certainly re-broken and perhaps shattered, but she was too focused to pay attention. The cast was torn away, his arm forced into the suit and the seams sealed. She left him drifting in the dark cabin, holding his arm and shrieking inside the suit, as she darted to the next cabin.

It was too late. It must have been the utter confusion as they struggled in the darkness that caused each of them to fail in putting on both suit and mask in time. La Salle was wearing his mask but the rest of his body was frozen, arms wrapped around himself in a frail attempt to produce warmth, while Zhang wore neither mask nor suit. His hands were affixed to the suit leg of one of the others, whom it appeared Zhang had been trying to help.

All were lifeless. The cabin was a frozen tomb without gravity.

* * *

It wasn't very long before the *Iris* appeared visible from the cockpit window, first a tiny speck of light rounding the planet's horizon and then a shape with a metallic glint. Fletcher was there to see it. She had nowhere else to go, nothing else to do but wait and watch. Lance sat beside her, his sobs interrupted only by the occasional sharp gasp of pain. Fletcher heard none of it, because the suits' transmitters were powered by the ship's intercom system, and that system was dead.

In silence they waited. Where Lance should have had hope and Fletcher dread, neither held on to any emotion at all. If the approaching ship, the promise of rescue and life were to prove an illusion, neither captain nor technician would have cared.

It was not an illusion. A heavy clunk reverberated through the ship, felt rather than heard, and the *Iris,* old but sleek Envoy-class ship with more distance logged than any other ship in history, docked with the aft port of the much larger *Aten.* The tall form of Captain James Merrickson came aboard first, his jet-black suit and blue light emerging through the port to be greeted only by darkness. From beneath his visor, grey eyes searched every square foot of the bay and then the lab, looking for bodies, for survivors, for any sign of the ship's inhabitants. A green flicker caught his eye, the only bright spot in the blackness, but it interested him not at all.

Accompanied by his own first officer, Merrickson moved forward from the aft, searching each room as he went. He noted the burnt medical bay with its wrecked machinery and partially-sliced medicine chest. The rear living quarters he found empty, as he did the mid larboard cabin, which was populated only by bits of what looked like medical foam. At last he found the bodies of the scientists. Wordlessly he motioned to them, at which point his officer moved in, scanning the room and recording images on a small handheld box.

Merrickson at first thought the occupants of the cockpit were dead too. Perhaps he was more right than wrong. Fletcher and Lance were physically alive, but that was all that could be said for their vitality.

The rescuers rushed the two survivors back through the port and onto the *Iris*. There, a doctor was ready and waiting in the medical bay. Neither Fletcher nor Lance protested – they didn't say anything at all – as their suits were cut off and they were stripped and checked for injuries, oxygen saturation and vital signs. Aside from Lance's bruised head and shattered arm (which was quickly placed back in a new foam cast), both were physically fine.

At last the doctor left them alone. The first officer gave them blankets and supplementary oxygen – Lance used both, huddling under the blanket while taking long, deep breaths of air from the tank, while Fletcher stared and touched neither.

After the doctor retired to his cabin and the first officer vanished into the cockpit, Merrickson joined them in the medical bay. He saluted Fletcher in the manner of the Pilot's Cooperative. She returned the salute. No words were spoken, as nobody ventured to initiate a conversation, so they all waited together in quietude.

No other crew members were seen or heard. The engine was not running – the *Iris* had joined the *Aten* in a slow drift barely within the pull of AMA's gravity – so the silence onboard was nearly complete. This did not seem to bother Merrickson, whose composure was regal and disciplined as he waited and watched, displaying not a tic of impatience. His uniform was perfection, crisp and freshly-pressed, decorated with the Cooperative Owl pin in addition to some twice as many patches and medals than Fletcher had worn. His hair was a blend of blond and grey, his face clean as if he'd shaved just minutes prior. He could not have been much older than Captain Fletcher.

None of this was a revelation to Fletcher, who knew Merrickson both through his striking reputation and by having met him several times. They had even flown together two decades ago, before either had achieved captainhood. But she held no particular liking for him. Despite the utter neutrality of his gaze (which lighted upon one of his rescuees, then the other), she saw something disdainful in his grey eyes, something that might even have been aggression.

She would remain silent as long as she could. Let him believe she was traumatized, lost for words. The longer Merrickson kept his pontificating mouth shut, the more bearable this humiliating stage of her journey would be.

After a quarter of an hour, the first officer appeared at the door. "Captain." Merrickson turned, some whispered words were shared, and then he followed his officer out of the room.

In his absence, Lance looked to Fletcher two or three times, but only for the sake of a momentary, comforting shared glance. There was nothing more to say.

When Merrickson returned, something had changed in his demeanor. His face remained unmoving, his posture as rigid as before, but an undefinable chill swept through the room when he entered. Fletcher nearly considered reaching for the blanket.

"Captain," he began slowly, his voice soft and dark yet not lacking in authority, "I had intended not to hassle you with an interrogation. There will be questions enough for you on Earth. There is one thing of which I must be certain, however, before we can proceed." The weight of his voice and the dispassion with which he perfectly enunciated each sound was both soothing and nightmarish.

Lance squirmed a little and looked at Fletcher, fearing some new misfortune. She kept her eyes leveled at her senior as she replied tersely: "I'm happy to give a full account of events, Captain."

Merrickson reacted with his very first emotion that they had seen: a small turn of the head and lowering of the eyebrows – disgust, or impatience. "A full account, no. I'd have nothing to do with that. I only need your confirmation on the number of fatalities, so that I can be certain my rescue is as effective as it can be."

A heavy swallow and a clearing of the throat was enough for Fletcher to betray her unwillingness to discuss the deaths of her crew, but she carried on with professionalism. "Two survivors accounted for: Lance Lanka, Louisa Fletcher. Fourteen deceased."

"Will you give a sworn statement?"

"I will."

"You will testify that you witnessed, or were given undeniable proof, of the deaths of each of those fourteen souls?"

Fletcher was silent.

"You can confirm there is no room for doubt?"

The *Aten's* captain's face was unmoving as a stern marble bust – Lance worried she was in danger of shattering. "No room for doubt, sir." Her lie was as good as any.

But Merrickson narrowed his eyes while exhaling for an unnaturally long time. "There is one thing I need explained to me. Come, please. Just you, Captain."

Fletcher, her face pale, stood and went with Merrickson. Lance threw her a helpless gaze that was not returned, then he was left alone.

Nearly twenty minutes passed, but time was a blur for Lance. His mind raced but did so sluggishly, and none of his thoughts were clear. He didn't know whether the fear he was experiencing was justified, seeing as he had just been rescued, but he also didn't know whether he would have been happier dead. Dead like Mr. Graff.

Fletcher came back. If her face had been pale before, it was now paper white. She was unaccompanied.

"Are we leaving?" was all that Lance, brave enough to speak when it was only the two of them in the room, could think to ask.

The only response he received was a look. In that look, gone was the unspoken bond of survivors that had, for however brief a time, existed between them. In its place was an expression of pure hatred that Fletcher did not even bother trying to hide. Lance had to look away.

* * *

Even after all she had seen and suffered, Fletcher still held some ability to be shocked when, upon entering the *Iris'* cockpit, Merrickson had shown her a communications screen on which was displayed Traver's face as it had been recorded just a few hours before. The strange message, bewildering and a little haunting, was played again in full for Fletcher, who'd had no intention of ever seeing it again.

"Did this already broadcast on Earth?" she asked once it had played through.

"I don't know," Merrickson growled. "It doesn't matter who else has seen it. Now, *I've* seen it, and to me it does not constitute proof of death."

"No. Not proof," Fletcher agreed, hollowly.

"So, we must recall that pod. Retrieving its contents will give us a definite answer, at which point we will be free to initiate our return voyage."

"He *is* dead!" Fletcher's voice escaped from her control and lashed out before she could catch it. Her senior captain looked at her patiently and waited for her composure to return, which it did quickly. She went on calmly: "Respectfully, Captain, the man was a menace. My report will clarify that position."

"No doubt you are right. But your concerns are not my concerns. If the man had fed poison to a crowd of children, still his return to Earth would be my charge. And if I can't retrieve him alive, then I will retrieve him dead if possible. Do you understand?"

Fletcher tried to understand. Something wasn't making sense. This was not at all the usual protocol for a rescue mission. Why was Traver such a point of interest? Why not the thirteen *good* men who had died on the mission? Where was the insistence on proof for *their* deaths?

"I can't understand, James. I can't see how Traver Graff is of any concern to you. To be honest, I would be relieved to spend at least the next six months' flight without hearing his name, or thinking about him again."

Merrickson turned around, switching off the display that had still held on the image of Traver's face, the point where the transmission had stopped. He sighed, though it was a sigh devoid of sympathy or humility.

"This man is my concern because I am being paid." He turned back around to see the disbelief on his fellow captain's face. "Whatever is left of your friend Mister Graff I intend to bring back to the Corporation, at which point I will collect a reward. It would have been one thing if he was simply gone without a trace. You could have told me whatever you liked about how he died. I would not have received my full remuneration but I would have believed you. However, *this* recording; the metadata shows it was made less than four hours ago. That changes things."

* * *

And so Fletcher returned to wait in the silent hell of the medical bay, with only herself to blame for allowing Traver's transmission to be sent at all. If not for that damned message, they might already have left AMA far behind. For Merrickson to delay their return journey to search for Traver was to add insult to the irreversible injury already suffered by the rest of Fletcher's crew. Where was the justice for them?

Justice. Part of Fletcher began to hope that, impossibly, Traver might still be alive. Not so that he could be rescued – she hoped he would be dying slowly in unbearable heat, or in the throes of dehydration. Otherwise his end had been too easy. More than he deserved, indeed.

Merrickson's officer passed by in full protective suit, moving aftwards to the connection of the two ships. Fletcher and Lance heard sounds of the ports opening and shutting. A few minutes later the lights throughout the *Iris* pulsed, dimming in unison. "Is this ship losing power too?" asked Lance, trembling.

"No," said Fletcher with certainty. "They're running power to my ship. I'll be damned if I know why."

Lance hushed his voice and moved closer to Fletcher. "Then what happened to your ship, exactly, and why didn't the same thing happen to the *Iris?*"

Fletcher turned her bitter face to look at him. "The planet had an energy flare. My ship was the one directly over top of it. That's been our luck from the beginning of this godforsaken job."

When Merrickson again appeared at the door to the bay, it was for Lance that he came. "You are Mister Lanka, the technician?"

"I...I am. Um, sir."

"Put on a suit and follow me back onboard the *Aten.*"

Lance looked helplessly at Fletcher, who offered him not even a glance in consolation. "Why? Why are we going back to the *Aten?*"

"Because you now are a crew member of the *Iris,* and you'll follow my orders."

"Stop," called Fletcher, suddenly moving. "He is still to follow my orders, since the *Aten* is an operational vessel until declared otherwise. He's my crew and he'll do nothing at your request unless I allow him."

Lance drifted between them, looking back and forth and shivering all the while.

Merrickson's lips formed something like a patronizing smile. "Cooperative Code seventy-one, section two: a stranded vessel of uncertain operability, upon joining with an operational rescue vessel, forfeits all subordinate crew and passengers to the captain of the rescuing ship until such time as both ships are declared operational."

Fletcher did not respond, which Lance took to mean he was to accompany Merrickson after all.

* * *

The aft of the *Aten* was still dark, with the exception of the control panel between the pod bay and the lab. The first officer was working there, typing in various commands and running what appeared to be diagnostics. "My ship is currently providing the power for this system," Merrickson explained through his suit's intercom as he emerged from the port behind Lance. "It's charged for several hours' worth of operation. It will now be capable of reestablishing control over the remote pod and recalling it. There's also enough power to seal the pod bay with heat and air for an hour if the pod does return. Do you think you would be capable of overseeing that procedure?"

The officer stepped aside, and Lance looked over the controls once again. He'd recently watched Fletcher use them a little, and their operation seemed simple enough.

"I could. But the signal was lost hours ago. He – the pod I mean – went out of control range when the transmission dropped out."

Merrickson was unaffected by Lance's doubt. "If the signal were to reach the pod and the connection be restored, the system would detect it and give you access to the controls. From there, you could successfully recall it to the dock? It's a simple command."

"Yes. Yes I can. Like you say, it's simple." Lance, in his eagerness to please, barely noticed the first officer had already disappeared back into the port to the *Iris*. "I just don't think the signal could ever reach the pod. By now it could be halfway through the planet."

"He won't be halfway through the planet. The moment at which connection was lost, the pod's computer would have shut the engine off due to lack of command prompts. He'll drift, but like a bad egg the pod will float above the denser regions of the planet's insides."

"So you think we can get the signal back?" Lance had thought he was free of the scourge of hopefulness at the possibility of Traver's being alive, but he'd been wrong.

"The signal is not yours to worry about. Secure the pod. You have my full confidence that when we return, you'll have done your part and we'll have Graff back with us."

"When you return?"

"Godspeed, Mister Lanka." With snakelike speed Merrickson turned and slunk back through the port before Lance fully realized what was happening.

"Captain?"

The port slammed shut and Lance was left in darkness, illuminated only by the control panel and his own suit's light.

"Captain!" He screamed, but nobody responded. The intercom had been cut off.

A heavy thud resounded through the hull and the ship shook. Lance knew the ships had separated. He would have panicked if he'd had the energy, but he'd been drained by the barrage of events he'd endured in the last twenty-four hours. What's more, his head and arm ached fiercely.

He was alone in the lab, his only company onboard being the five corpses that he was certain he'd soon be joining. It should have terrified him. Instead he found the certainty of death – the only certainty he'd had in a long time – to be suddenly comforting.

* * *

"We must not waste any more time." Merrickson moved quickly into the *Iris'* medical bay, hurrying while never sacrificing his composure. "Captain Fletcher, the plan is going to require your cooperation. Please, join me again in the cockpit."

"I'll respectfully decline your invitation."

"You will?" It was more a nonchalant statement than a question.

"I have not relinquished command of the *Aten*, so I still hold my own sovereignty. Your orders, your plans, do not concern me."

"You are correct, Captain. But your only surviving crew member is currently the sole occupant of the *Aten*. He has a single tank of oxygen, enough for us to go about retrieving whatever remains of Graff. If that oxygen runs out while you delay – well, then you have sacrificed your last passenger, for your pride."

Fletcher sprang up, facing Merrickson at a distance of a few centimeters. "How dare you threaten me with the lives of my crew?" she hissed.

Merrickson made no attempt to back away from her. Instead he leaned in closer. "*What* crew?" Then he turned away.

Fletcher hung motionless as a pillar in the medical bay until, several minutes later, Merrickson's voice crackled over the intercom. "There is no time to lose, Captain. One life and perhaps two are depending on us."

"Aurora will know you used coercion," Fletcher stated, her voice holding onto whatever authority it still possessed as she finally passed the bulkhead doors into Merrickson's cockpit.

"Aurora has given me immunity." Merrickson never even looked up from his controls.

Fletcher was not unmoved. "My full report to the Cooperative will leave out no details. You'll be stripped of your Pilot's pins and disgraced for failing to carry out a mission in a humanitarian fashion."

"The Pilot's Cooperative has wanted to strip me of my pin for years. But they can't, because Aurora won't let them."

"Aurora is required to defer to the Cooperative on those kinds of decisions."

"And when it's convenient, they do. But Aurora keeps the authority that really matters. And Aurora values me."

"Because of LACY-4?" Fletcher spit the words at him, hoping to elicit anger, bitterness, or any reaction at all.

She knew little about LACY-4, Merrickson's first claim to fame, except that his discoveries there were noteworthy enough to maintain top-clearance secrecy for over twenty years. To this day he was the only explorer to have reached that planet, which was still the most distant point ever to be visited by man or machine. One of the few known details about the story was that Merrickson had made the journey there as a young man accompanied by his wife, but had come back alone.

"Because of LACY-4, among other things." Merrickson had

calmly turned to her, affected but by no means emotional. "The Corporation, like any major entity, makes judgments based on wealth, be it wealth in finances, knowledge or public opinion. Where there is discovery, wealth is accumulated. Where there is effectiveness, wealth is preserved. And where there is discretion, additional wealth is guaranteed. Discovery, effectiveness and discretion are three qualities in which I excel over any other captain in the fleet. And you, Captain, are decreasing my effectiveness with your delay. Will you work with me now, or not?"

With no choice, Fletcher did.

At Merrickson's request, she gave him her passkeys that unlocked access to the *Aten's* systems, specifically control over the pods. Without losing a moment, Merrickson established a signal that replicated the one sent from inside the *Aten's* lab under Lance's watchfulness; every two seconds it pulsed, seeking the lost pod.

"We're well out of range," Fletcher murmured.

"Range is not the issue, as you well know." Merrickson again kept his eyes lowered to the controls as he shifted the *Iris* into orbit and moved away from the *Aten*. "The signal range is well over a million kilometers. It could reach through the diameter of this planet twenty times over. What the signal lacks is strength to pierce through the upper surface."

* * *

The two ships, each sending out an identical recall signal, began to diverge from one another's paths, the *Iris* orbiting determinedly in one direction while *Aten* drifted aimlessly in the other.

An hour passed. Fletcher often held her breath unconsciously, in the hopes that Lance was doing the same. His oxygen tank would not last more than three hours, and she had little faith that he'd be resourceful enough to find another in the darkened, dead-filled ship.

The *Aten* had been able to achieve a six-hour orbit, but that was a meandering orbit established by Lance. The *Iris* was much faster and under the hands of a master. Merrickson reached the polar opposite side of the planet before an hour and a half had passed. AMA-712 now lay between the two signals, being deeply penetrated by their combined strength and coverage.

In the *Iris,* the computer produced a solitary alert.

Something had met the signal, and had responded. Somewhere down there, the pod was still working. But Merrickson had guessed that much already.

The signal only came the once and then went silent.

* * *

The two captains together stared down at the mesmerizing waves on the planet. Fletcher had never looked at it before – *really* looked. For the brief time she'd been in command of the *Aten* in orbit she'd been occupied with other things. Now she was nothing but a helpless observer, a position which would have been disheartening except for the smooth, comforting roll of greens into one another that was continually taking place eight hundred kilometers beneath the ship but looked as if it was centimeters from her eyes, or inside her own head. Were her eyes even open? The static but swirling colorful non-colors of the planet were paradoxical enough to be a dream. Alternatively this could be death. Did dreams come after death? Would the bright and dull green serenity go on forever? That would be alright.

* * *

The alert came again. And again thirty seconds later.

"There it is." Merrickson's spoken words reminded Fletcher where she was, what was at stake. Her focus shifted to the console.

The alert repeated at shorter and shorter intervals.

"It heard us, and it wants to come home." Merrickson's intensity and the sweat on his forehead betrayed just how seriously he treated the performance of his duties, no matter how stubbornly apathetic his words and appearance. Fletcher hated how much she respected him.

The signal alert became a steady tone and the console began to display sensor data and readings associated with Pod P-02.

"The signal locked?" asked Fletcher with a sense of awe. She was interested in spite of herself.

"Pod is locked to our signal...and to the *Aten's*. Readings are good, but she's had a hell of a ride."

Indeed, the sensors showed the pod to have suffered near-catastrophic pressures and temperatures. Its current position was more bearable if not more temperate; the location was triangulated to a point nearly eleven hundred kilometers beneath the surface. The temperature there was near the maximum of the pod hull's endurance while the pressure was sitting in a mid-to-high zone but well below danger. The pod seemed to be holding its depth, proving that Merrickson's assessment had been correct and the pod, without propulsion, had bobbed on the surface of the high-pressure zones in the planet.

"The *Aten* is closer in position. The pod will respond to her. Let's hope your technician has maintained his focus. If all goes well, he will be receiving a visitor shortly."

Terror of Traver resurfaced in Fletcher, and her mind sought desperately for other ways to kill the possibility of the monster returning alive. "It still needs to ascend through the upper atmosphere. It will never survive another beating like that." She spoke as if trying to argue into creation a reality where her words predicted the future.

"If this were a new pod, perhaps not. But in a ship as old as yours, the pods were made to last. They don't build things like they used to." Fletcher's heart fell. She knew the superior truth of Merrickson's words.

"I can get back to *Aten* in an hour. Then we will find out whether our friends are both alright."

* * *

Lance had had no hope of a signal actually appearing, but that did not stop him from remaining at his post while he waited to die. He knew when his own suit ran out of oxygen he could still switch on the pod bay's system and seal himself in, but why bother?

Already his mind began to replay the moments in his life he regretted, that he might wish to relive. There weren't many. He was a simple person. Maybe he wished he had pursued other careers. He'd qualified for several high-paying positions both at Aurora and for the government, but had instead settled for a tech job at SASH. But he'd been happy enough there. Maybe he should have asked Becca to marry him before that opportunity had passed; but then again, Lance was philosophical enough to realize life alone was no worse than life with company.

He was a little afraid of course, but the fear was surprisingly not a specific dread of being dead. He was going to die in outer space, after all; what more could a computer tech and self-admitted nerd hope for?

Then the signal came through. All thoughts of death, of a life half-lived, vanished as his heart jumped into overdrive. He sent the recall command.

The gap that followed until the signal repeated took perhaps five minutes but for Lance it contained the combined eternities of heaven and hell, along with the hope that the signal would lock and the terror of the same.

Then the signal did lock. His recall command went through, and the pod began to rise.

The monitor began to flicker as the video feed came through, and Lance flinched as he prepared to see Traver or what was left of him. It only flickered: not a shape to be seen. Either the camera or the camera's transmitter had been damaged for good.

The elevation climbed. -400, -200, -50…it pierced the surface and shot upward. As before while crossing the lower atmosphere the pressure readings rose dramatically, crossing the threshold of danger. As before, the sensor readings died.

They didn't come back on.

If the transmitters had been crushed, if the signal had been totally lost, then the pod would not continue its flight – it would be caught in the crushing pressure and finished off for good. Lance hoped and prayed that only the sensors were dead.

Then he hoped and prayed for the transmitters to be dead. For Traver to be dead.

Please, let Traver be dead.

There was a dull thud.

Lance opened his eyes. Then he realized they'd been closed.

P-02: DOCKED, the monitor screen read.

The blood rushing floodlike through Lance's head prevented him from thinking, from feeling. He went blindly to the port as quickly as he could, bumping his arm – protected by the cast but nonetheless in pain – against the bay's door. He didn't care.

He felt the dull impacts of the pod locking in, sealing.

He shut the door behind him and switched on the room's power. Heat and air rushed in at once.

He tugged on the pod's port door. It didn't open; the lock light still displayed red. He tugged incessantly anyway.

It turned green. The port opened.

A cloud of steam rushed out at Lance, momentarily blinding him.

Something lay inside the pod, visible as the steam cleared. At first it was difficult for Lance to make out its shape (his suit lamp being the bay's only illumination).

Then he moved closer.

The figure's skin was seared, from head to toe wrinkled from heat. Its hair was nearly all melted away. It wore an oxygen mask, one of the ones with which the pods were equipped. The eyes were closed and nothing moved.

Lance moved closer still.

The clothes, synthetics as they were, had burned or melted away. Around the waist they had fused with the skin. The fingers on the sole remaining hand had lost their definition, and the fingerprints had melted to smoothness.

Lance pulled himself in, looking closely at the face as he hovered inside the dilapidated pod.

The oxygen mask filled with a fog. Then the fog dissipated. Then the fog returned.

Traver was alive.

CHAPTER FIFTEEN
EARTH

Weston received a call. The cell where he was held was not high-security, as he was only awaiting trial for tech crimes. He was allowed open communication with the outside world, though the calls were monitored.

"Are you in a sound-proof room?" asked the female voice on the other end.

He looked around. The cell neighbors were all out on exercise time. "Yes. But there will be somebody listening in to the call."

"We knew that, which is why the guards are hearing a pre-recorded message we made just for them. In it, I play your long-lost cousin who's devastated to hear you've been incarcerated."

Weston knew that voice, but even better he recognized the attitude.

"Callie, you know I'm the one who's going to get hit with a worse sentence if they find out their line's been hacked. I'm ending this call."

"There's a new Traver video."

Weston couldn't bring himself to push the red button to end the call, even though his finger hung poised in the air above it.

"And you know this how?"

"Oh, great! You're still on the line. Thought I was gonna lose you there."

"How do you know?" Weston had all the time in the world to spare and he knew it, but he lacked patience for Callie. He was well aware that she was the most direct reason behind his incarceration, the most recent after a long litany of unfortunate occurrences for which he'd excused himself of any responsibility.

"There's not a lot of time to explain, since your cousin's call only lasts two minutes."

"Then get to your damn point."

"Ooooh, testy! Prison's supposed to be good for some people, but I remember you being jollier before."

Weston cleared his throat in such a way as to try and sound menacing. The result was a sound that resembled the clearing of a throat and not much more.

"Anyway," continued Callie, "Laffy's been picking up a lot of chatter at Aurora. They're sending twice the usual number of messages, making three times as many calls, and your boss' name keeps turning up."

"So?" Weston tried his best to remain unaffected. "What does that have to do with me?" And then he quickly added: "It's probably just another Lucy message anyway. They're just going to keep forcing status updates until they figure out what the hell is going on out there."

"Nope." Her response was immediate and confident. "This is a bona fide *Traver Talk* broadcast. Nobody's saying what it's about, but it sounds like a doozy."

Weston had to sit down. He tried once to say something, but his words failed him. He began again: "Why are you telling me? What do you want?"

"Me? Why would I want anything?"

Weston's bitter chuckle lasted only a few seconds before it turned into a quiet sob.

"Cheer up ol' Wes. Listen. Consider this a courtesy call. Me returning the favor you paid us before. I know it won't get you out of the legal troubles, but it might go some of the way to restoring your good graces with your old friends at SASH. That's got to count for something, right?"

"How would it do that?"

"Okay, we've gotta hurry because there's only twenty seconds left to go. You remember that little contract that Traver signed, and SASH signed, and Aurora signed?"

"Yes. Yes."

"Well, anything Traver sent back for the purpose of public distribution – *anything* – legally belongs to SASH. So yeah, I blatantly stole the content when I aired it, but people loved me for it so nobody really cared. Point is, SASH can claim the new video. Aurora can't keep it a secret without being sued. People are gonna go bonkers over this one. And it's up to you now, to get it out into the world. Oh, look at the time. I love and miss you, cuz, but I need to get going now. I'll give Aunt Alicia a kiss from you. Bye!"

The call ended and Weston laid back in his bed. His mind raced with the thousand things a new Traver broadcast could mean, if it even existed. He was disinclined to doubt Callie's word on this – what could she hope to gain from simply causing Weston more pain? But even she could be mistaken. It was only vague chatter she and Laffy were interpreting, after all.

Regardless of his doubts, his mind soon turned to the logistics, should he decide to take the bait. Any call he put in to SASH headquarters would be rejected. Who else could he contact?

Karen. He knew her personal number. She would be as eager as he was – more eager – to go back home to SASH. A new Traver video was an instant foot in the door, since SASH could only grind its teeth in hopes for the opportunity to right the wrong it had committed in the public's eyes.

He lost sleep over the decision for exactly one night, and then he called Karen.

"They'll deny the broadcast's existence. They've kept it hidden so far; they must have a reason for that," shrieked Karen Tiplins.

"Then make threats. Press charges. Sue to see their transmissions." Weston felt more alive, more present than he'd felt in the days uncounted he had spent in that damn cell. He had a purpose again, even if he didn't know for sure what that purpose was.

"And if they ask how we know? Hell, Weston, I don't know how *you* even know. Couldn't they press their own charges if the information was gotten criminally? I don't want to go to prison. I can't go to prison." Karen's typically nervous chatter had not lessened over the course of her unemployment.

"It doesn't matter. If the information is valid, if the transmission is there, then it won't matter how we know, because they broke the contract first by holding onto the data illegally."

Karen was silent.

"Call Brucker, or call Bruckner. They'll tell you exactly what I just told you, except they'll say it fancier."

* * *

After that conversation Weston heard nothing for two weeks. His feeling of purpose slowly wore away in the face of the day to day routine – eat, exercise, read, exercise, eat, read, sleep, repeat. These days he exercised more than he ate, since cell food was comprised of a mash of misprinted faux-foods that had been thrown out of the factories. He was no longer a squishy blob of a man, a fact which had given him some small self-fulfillment upon looking in the mirror every day. But he'd gotten a taste of real hope, real usefulness. Now that usefulness slipped through his fingers as every passing day he grew more certain that Karen had grown cold feet and given up on him.

One morning he woke up unusually cheery. He couldn't have

explained why. His breakfast mash tasted as good as any upper-class fare he'd once been used to, his conversation with the boorish and introverted cell neighbor proved stimulating, and his exercise time yielded his best weight lifts and run times of his life. Something was different in the air (which he also believed smelled sweeter than normal).

What he didn't know was that at approximately 5 AM, Earth U.S. Eastern Time, a ship called *Iris* had made the jump from the star system containing AMA-712. Under the frighteningly efficient piloting of Captain Merrickson, it had fallen into the Solar System impressively near to its target: within the radius of the asteroid belt between Mars and Jupiter, a scant two months from home.

Weston, in his unusual jollity, had no way of knowing any of that. But just after lunchtime, when he'd settled in to his hard steel cell chair to read a recently uncensored science fiction novel, a call was directed to his cell.

He nearly fell over himself, dropping the book in his rush to the audiophone. He couldn't pick it up fast enough.

"Yes? Hello. This is Weston. Who is this?"

Karen's voice was shaking. From fear or excitement? It was impossible to tell with her. "Weston...do you have a slidescreen or a monitor in there?"

"I have a chair, a hard bed and this audiophone. Why?" He felt his own voice starting to shake in anticipation of what might be coming next.

"Well then, just listen. It's on the air in sixty seconds."

Weston's legs gave way and he collapsed, aiming for the bed but missing and hitting the floor with a thump. His cell neighbors gave him a confused glance, muttered comments and laughed, but Weston didn't care. "You...you got the recording? It was real?"

"I talked to Ariel and Chad. It took some maneuvering but they pulled the right strings. We got it."

"Have...have you seen it?"

"No. Not yet. This is the first I'm seeing it."

"Are you back at SASH? And, they approved it?"

"I'm back in! SASH was so desperate they'd put even Traver's ass on the air." Karen with a sense of humor? This *was* a good day.

"But shh," her tone hushed. "It's starting. I'll hold my slidescreen recorder up to the display so you can hear."

"Describe it."

"Huh?"

"I don't have a visual. You'll need to describe it."

"He's...it's just his face. It's not the regular recording cabin. Hard to describe. He looks cramped. Like he's sitting in a little box. He's just looking...at something. The light on his face is green."

The mental picture Weston constructed was nothing like the reality and it confused him. But the context didn't matter just now. He was about to hear Traver's voice again. So was the rest of the world.

How many billions of people went silent in the tense moments before Traver spoke? How many families sat in their living rooms, how many crowds watched from public forums and squares as Traver's face appeared on multiple massive monitors? How many arguments were paused, how many woes were forgotten, suspended by the unexpected sight and the long anticipatory silence? The planet Earth itself must have taken a soft breath of relief in that split cosmic moment of stillness during which humanity had offered a reprieve from itself.

"I have somewhat lost track of time..." the broadcast began. Weston held his breath as long as he could, fearful of missing even a single word. But as the message went on and Traver's words grew stranger, Weston began to breath unconsciously. He was puzzled. In the long pauses between Traver's statements, Weston began to say something, to ask if the broadcast was over or whether there was more, but he was lost for words.

"Don't be angry with all of us. I'm not mankind. I'm not mankind.

I'M NOT MANKIND.

"*Are you angry with me?*"

It stopped.

The silence went on.

"Karen?"

"That's it."

"What?"

"It went to static. And it cut out."

"He sounded…he sounded…did he look the way he sounded?"

"Yes. He did. He looked agonized."

....

10/26/2160

Galina,

I received the news this morning about the planned large scale testing, and I only have this to say: DON'T.

While the Pytheas *findings were eye-opening, they were by no means conclusive enough to carry on experimentation in a non-controlled environment. Yes, I'm sure Abrahim has told you that we will see absolute success if we proceed, but I am writing now to tell you differently.*

David Gandy's blood did yield organic growth of the calcium crystals in trace amounts. That the planet evokes that response in the human body has been confirmed. But the toll the process has taken on his mind is irreversible. When he woke from stasis he remembered neither his name nor his position nor his own species. He is a blank slate and has not shown any signs of recovering nor any interest in relearning. What good do the calcium crystals serve if the host is unresponsive? If we are hoping to connect a human mind to a heavenly body via natural transmitters, what good will it do if the mind is corrupted?

Even more concerning to me is that you plan to continue with the experiment before we even know the human body's longterm behavior with these crystals in the bloodstream. If they are artificially inserted, how might the body react? Your model for duplication of the crystals is limited to Gandy's specimens as a blueprint: what if his body's crystals are unique, rejected by others?

There are big questions to ask here but let's still operate under some code of ethics. The impending meteor strike is NO justification, since it is NOT a heavenly body that will produce results similar to those of Zilly and AMA. Be wary of Abrahim's claims – he is using the meteorite as an excuse to test the mass effect of concentrated calcium crystals on a population.

I did NOT intend for this result when I sponsored the Pytheas mission. I know I've worked around sanctions and crossed ethical boundaries before, but Gandy was a volunteer for his position, a consenting participant. This has turned into something else completely.

Before the week is out, I plan to go public with the project. The Co-operative will hear about Gandy, the Department of Health will hear about this large scale experiment, and Aurora will be fully audited and operations will cease. I'm sorry. I suggest you nip this in the bud before I release the information.

If you bring the crystals to Cairo you're going to end up with blood on your hands.

With professional regret,
Eduardo Aguilar, PhD

[Dr. Aguilar's date of death: 11/01/2160]

....

September 17th, 2177, a year to the day after *Aten's* departure, the *Iris* made landfall at Aurora's desert headquarters.

To maintain any shroud of secrecy around the arrival was a logistical impossibility. As with any ship landing, the *Iris* made four laps around the globe as it decelerated on its way into the atmosphere, providing a spectacular lightshow for the fortunate hemi-sphere that lay shrouded in night. Rumors led to speculation which led to anonymous tips and leaks, and by the time the vessel touched down, the whole world knew it was the *Iris*, and that the *Aten* had been abandoned as inoperable. What the public didn't know was the current passenger manifest.

The media was there, clamoring at the facility's perimeter fence. They sent their camera drones as high as they dared – some dared more and sent theirs beyond the fence, but those drones were shot down before they'd proceeded five meters.

For all the shouted questions, months passed without any answers. Dana Graff was tracked down and ruthlessly interviewed, but she hadn't seen or heard from Traver at all. As for SASH, they had enjoyed an incredible surge after that last transmission, but it was the last information they had.

Nobody officially knew what to make of Traver's final breakdown. The numbers, however, argued for its resounding success. It had become the most-watched recording – *of any kind* – ever to hit the networks. That viewership never declined, right up until the arrival of the *Iris*. And then when the ship landed, the video spiked in popu-larity once again. Discussion in the media was limited on the subject; Traver supporters and detractors alike chose to focus only on the phenomenon of the broadcast's success and its odd place in Traver's compendium, rather than on the strange nature of the content itself. Few, very few dared to speculate on the context of Traver's flight. Had it ended in death? If the question was on everyone's minds, the mass populace maintained an unspoken agreement to postpone such discussions until after the details were made known.

* * *

One morning in January, Chad Brucker, attorney, stepped off an aircab. His destination: the Aurora Southwest Region Headquarters in Denver.

The security checkpoints were bothersome; he went past four of them: one at the front gate, one at the entrance to the basement elevator, one at the entrance to the containment section, and then one in front of the quarantine cell. Each time, Chad was required to strip to the waist and endure a thorough pat-down below. Humiliating, even if it was standard procedure for something like this. He didn't know for sure whether it *was* standard procedure; he'd never been in Aurora's basement before.

Traver was there inside the glass cell, sitting in a latex armchair. Or at least, Chad was told that this was Traver. One arm terminated in a stump. The man's visible skin, including that on his face, was deformed, wrinkled and yellow. The hair, once dark and luscious, had only grown back in white patches.

Chad stopped for a moment, eyeing the figure with a combination of disgust, suspicion and sadness.

But then the figure sprang up. For being such a deformed thing, it was surprisingly light on his feet. As it moved, Chad realized that there were fully formed muscles beneath its elastic jumpsuit. A set of exercise machines sat in the room, and they had clearly been put to regular use.

"Chad! Chad! By god, do you know how good it is to see a familiar face? *Any* familiar face! Talking on the phone was fine, but face to face. I'm finally starting to feel like I'm home."

When their eyes met through the glass barrier, Chad accepted that this was Traver. The bright blue eyes were unmistakable. They were full of life.

Traver spoke again. "You look well. You don't need to return the compliment; I'll see right through the lie. But I feel great."

"Good. Um, good. What can I say? It's good to see you too. Have they been treating you well?"

"For a rat in a cage, I can't complain. But from what I hear, I'm getting out of here soon."

"You are." Chad pulled up the chair that had been set up for him outside the quarantine. Traver dragged his own chair across the floor and sat in it, facing his lawyer.

Chad tried to smile, but struggled. "Can I just start with business? It's just…there is a lot to get through."

"Of course." Traver's smile through warped lips, on the other hand, was genuine.

Chad pulled out his slidescreen and began to swipe through multiple slides worth of notes.

He started to say something, stopped, and stared at the screen. He looked up at Traver, his mouth agape. "This isn't business, but…the Eams. Is that true?"

"Gone. Not a trace. Not a single bone-eating bug."

Chad smiled his awed approval. "Congratulations on that. That's the first win. Now, let's talk about the next. The trial dates have been set."

"I've been told."

"It starts in a month. It's unfortunate that you'll be transitioning from one cell to another, but this whole situation is anything but fortunate."

Traver's eyes caught his. For the briefest moment, Chad felt a strange impression that he was being scrutinized by Traver, or by something that looked like Traver. But the feeling passed as quickly as it had come. Traver smiled at him, and he managed a smile back.

"Of course, the timing of your last recording was pristine, really pristine for us. Let's not pull any punches here; after watching that, nobody looks at you and says, 'that guy is in his right mind.' *Nobody.* It's not for me to judge; I'm just saying that's the general mindset. So we use that. We argue insanity."

Traver squinted. His wrinkled face folded even more. Now he really was scrutinizing Chad. "Insanity? No. I can't argue that I was insane. That's a lie."

"Insanity is the best plea you have. The first-degree murders… well there're two of those, not counting everything else…"

"And I was perfectly in my right mind."

"Don't say that to me, Traver. Please? You can't say those words to me, you can't say those words to the court. You can't even say those words to your wife, when you see her. A guilty verdict means the death sentence. And if you get the zap, I lose the case, so we're both out of luck."

"Chad, I know what you need from me. I know how it all looks from down here. But...the insanity plea?" Traver leaped out of the chair and started to pace the room. Once, twice, three times he moved its length. Yes, this was Traver alright, the Traver everyone had known and – loved? Loved.

"Let's take things slowly, then, shall we?" Chad was eager to appease his client, but equally eager to win the trial of the century. "Together we can work out the best course of action. I know we have a winning case here. All it'll take is a little cooperation and some rational thought."

* * *

When the trial was publicly announced, the reaction was anything but rational. That Traver was alive and had arrived with the *Iris* was the big shock, of course, and with that came the inevitable rush of delayed speculation about those last moments of the transmission. The second surprise, the one that nobody had anticipated, was the peculiar set of details about the trial that began to trickle out from the official sources.

Multiple counts of off-world homicide, the loss of the majority of the *Aten's* crew, attempted jettison by a captain of her passenger, coercion by captain, suicides resembling foul play; the details were vague but as the unconnected pieces of the puzzle reached the public they were reassembled into a thousand different narratives, some nonsensical and some surprisingly close to the truth. The media outlets, usually so ready to present a constructed narrative, dared not speculate at all for fear of facing a lynch mob later on if proven wrong. To await the trial was all anyone could do.

* * *

In February it began. It lasted five days.

The location of the trial was undisclosed, but that did not stop the mobs from crowding every courthouse and law office in New York until process of elimination revealed it to be the Department of Space-Transit Law Building (though a very small amount of guesswork would have provided the same answer).

The trial was a global governmental one, as were all off-world related hearings. The Honorable Margot Halpern presided, under the oversight of a Space-Transit Safety committee.

The charges brought against Traver Graff by the Pilot's Cooperative were two counts of first degree murder, one count of mutiny, and attempted destruction of a manned vessel. But Traver's crimes were not the only focus of the trial; as per government regulations, Fletcher was to be examined by a Pilots' panel separate from the main jury, her leadership actions put under scrutiny. Fletcher was assigned to be represented by Cooperative Officer Steffan Lumley, a longtime pilots' attorney.

In a broad stroke, the trial was not much of a trial at all; it was a hearing meant to construct an accurate account of events as they'd taken place, then to assign blame accordingly.

Captain Merrickson had been summoned to relate his version of the happenings. He arrived late on the first day of the trial, appearing shortly after court officers had been dispatched to fetch him.

"I only have an hour. Try not to interrupt me," he began. His account had little to say about Fletcher, and even less about Traver. In his remote, uninterested way he recounted the incredible jump he'd made, during which he'd allowed himself no margin of error and arrived only a month's flight from AMA ("a risk without which I would have arrived too late and found no survivors at all"). He related the plan to boost the signals and retrieve the pod ("my plan, and the only plan that would have worked"). Finally he touched on the return journey during which Traver had remained heavily sedated and the two others, Lance and Fletcher, had been pleasantly inconspicuous.

Questions were directed toward Merrickson from both sides; Chad Brucker demanded whether Fletcher had shown any malicious intent toward Traver, while Cooperative Officer Lumley, on Fletcher's behalf, delved for Merrickson's intuitions on whether the state in which he'd found the *Aten* had indicated a methodical, pre-planned mutiny.

To both questioners, Merrickson replied: "I can speak to no intent but my own. May I be excused?"

The captain was released from the stand, his testimony useless to either party.

* * *

Later the same day, Lance Lanka was ushered into the courtroom, accompanied by the heavy SASH security guards who refused to distance themselves until court officers had flanked the witness. He walked with a barely noticeable limp but otherwise looked recovered, if slightly thin and pale. He recoiled a little at the sight of Traver, seated behind a thick glass wall on the right side of the room. Traver looked back, his blue eyes connecting with Lance, providing comfort and horror.

Lance's testimony was central to the trial, and his story had not been tainted by personal bias or the passage of time. He remembered the details of key events, right down to the words spoken in conversation. The marathon of broadcasts, the slow unraveling of Traver, the terror of the mutiny and the numbing months that followed were all faithfully recounted.

His version of events was taken so seriously that the rest of the day as well as the entirety of the next was dedicated to questions and clarifications. By the end of that lengthy process Lance had begun to nod with exhaustion.

Despite the vivid and monstrous image he painted of Traver, Lance's story proved a victory for the accused. Chad Brucker directed the final two questions to the witness. The first was "Can you verify the part of your story where you indicated Captain Fletcher *stated* an intent to execute – or murder – Mister Graff before his entry into the pod was conceived?" to which Lance replied "she did." The second question was phrased with brazen delight by the lawyer: "Would you say that Mister Graff committed these atrocities while mentally unstable?"

"Without a doubt. I think – I know, he went insane."

* * *

Those first two days, Traver sat and listened. To all observers it appeared he had nothing to say.

* * *

Though the media cried and clawed for details on the proceedings that stayed behind closed doors, only one publication, one known for its unbiased reporting and refreshingly honest search for the truth, had weaseled its way into a prized courtroom seat. *Debunker Daily* released day-by-day synopses of the courtroom revelations as they were written down faithfully by Callie Vargas. The public followed along with riveted attention, making the nightly publication of *Debunker* the most anticipated market in the world, with numbers higher than any other media outlet for the length of the trial.

* * *

The third day, Fletcher spoke.

Her senior officers at the Cooperative, to whom she had delivered her full, unfiltered report, strongly advised her to avoid mentioning the white blood flakes or her suspicions regarding the injections. "There is not a lick of proof," had blustered Lumley, a large and loud old bureaucrat, "and it will weaken your case. Your case is to deliver justice to Graff and to convince the panel that you did your best. That's all. Aurora isn't your target. Aurora needs to stay your friend here."

At first she heeded his advice. Her testimony began with the discovery of Akachi's corpse and proceeded through the many offenses of Traver. The details were consistent with Lance's account, but her version of Traver was cold, calculating and thoughtful. His murder of Akachi had been preplanned beyond the shadow of a doubt. The process by which he gained the upper hand and successfully enacted his mutiny was not a collection of rash, emotional actions; there was careful, masterful structure to it all.

"Would you, then, call Mister Graff mentally unstable?" puffed Lumley.

"No I would not. And from what I've heard, he's perfectly rational at the present. I suggest you speak with him now and have him mentally examined. I suggest you'll find evidence of a strong mind."

Judge Halpern interjected: "Mister Graff has been under careful psychological examination for the last several weeks. In due time the findings will be brought before us. Thank you, Captain. Mister Brucker, any questions?"

Chad stood energetically, with the relish that had become his trademark whenever preparing a question to which he already knew the answer.

"Miss Fletcher. *Captain* Fletcher, that is. Did you on not one but *two* occasions attempt to carry out an execution onboard your ship? Off-world execution without due process of law has been illegal since 2122, as I'm sure you know. Your first attempt was to jettison my client, and the attempt was so mishandled that four *other* passengers died as a result. The second attempt was to strand my client inside a remote pod. Can you deny either of these allegations?"

Fletcher looked around the room, seeking for someone to target with her eyes. Traver was there, but he was not the Traver of her hated memory; this was a melted, disfigured Traver, not worth her hateful stare. She looked at Chad, who met her eyes with a sadistic lawyer's grin. She looked at the judge, who was yawning. She looked at Lumley, and she gave him a curt, meaningful nod. Lumley nearly jumped out of his seat, his saggy face wagging back and forth as he shook his head, his eyes widening.

Fletcher stood up. "Permission to speak, Your Honor."

The judge's yawn was cut short. "It's your turn to speak; you don't need my permission at this time. Please."

"I wish to request a blood test be done on Mister Graff."

The courtroom buzzed. Judge Halpern tapped her gavel. "Extensive medical tests have been performed on the accused. Please answer the defense's question."

"Those tests have been carried out *by Aurora*. I request that further tests be performed by a third party."

The murmurs in the room grew louder, so Fletcher raised her voice. "I have questions of my own, relating to Mister Graff's behavior. I've been looking for the answers since before we left the *Aten*, and I will withhold discussing my own actions until my demands are answered."

The whispers and gasps in the viewing audience built into a ruckus, requiring a series of heavy gavel falls before Halpern could be heard. "There will be order!"

Traver sat silently, his eyes unsettling in their unblinking watchfulness.

Officer Lumley stood indignantly and shouted over the hubbub: "Captain Fletcher should not be asked any more questions. Captain Fletcher should be excused from the stand for the remainder of the day."

A few more requests for order, then silence was mercifully returned to the courtroom. Halpern looked over the room with a weary eye. She settled on Fletcher. "You have one minute to make your argument. I cannot guarantee any requests will be met. After one minute, you must answer the defense's question."

Fletcher's internal clock began to tick. "Your Honor, I do deny that Mister Graff acted on impulse or through impaired judgment. But I do *not* believe he acted without outside influence. Upon the loss of his arm I observed microscopic white crystals in his blood.

When the scientists, notably the late Doctor Zhang, put these crystals to the test, they found them to be lab-grown and directly reactive to the gas collected from the planet AMA-712. I believe Traver Graff was not truly a random passenger on my ship. I believe I was lied to by the Aurora Corporation, that Graff was a test subject for some unknown science project, and that the crystals were administered along with the medical injections purportedly used for the treatment of his Eams. It's a secret to which only the Aurora medical staff were privy, and that Doctor Marin died to protect. If all this is true then Traver Graff is as much a victim as anyone onboard, and justice should be sought against the Corporation for their clandestine actions resulting in thirteen deaths and the loss of a ship." Her minute expired as she inhaled.

Now the courtroom's silence was more overpowering than the ruckus had been. All eyes were trained, awestruck, on Fletcher's rage-filled, twitching face – all eyes, that was, but two. Nobody saw how intently Callie Vargas was writing in her notepad, her shorthand accurately capturing every word from Fletcher's mouth.

Halpern dryly responded. "If the representative from the Aurora Corporation would like to offer a response, you may do so. Otherwise, Captain Fletcher will answer the defense's question."

Mr. Gladstone stood up from near the jury stand, his lanky, stiff frame giving him a towering aspect over the other inhabitants of the room. A laughing smile twisted the edges of his mouth.

"I don't know that Captain Fletcher merits a response, but I will indulge her. Is it our Corporation that is on trial? While accusations are being thrown around, perhaps it should be the good captain who is considered for an insanity plea." Some slight giggles ran through the room, extinguished quickly by Halpern's (by now fully awake and alert) stare.

"We are more than happy to provide samples of Doctor Shurovsky's Eams treatment formula, which has been approved by the Global Department of Health, by the way. But I don't think the captain would be satisfied. We would bring Doctor Shurovsky in to speak about her life-saving compound, but she unfortunately passed away late last year. So if the captain would like to provide her own proof, I invite her to do so. Anything that could corroborate her story – the vials of formula used to treat Traver onboard, the planetary samples, the monitor footage and scientists' logs – was abandoned with the *Aten*. Her ship is not expected to be salvaged at any time in the near future due to the expenses incurred by the rescue. Would she care to provide the funds for another journey to retrieve that evidence? We've already bankrolled one mission more than was planned, and that was purely for the sake of saving lives. The story I'm hearing is that Captain Fletcher was unable to defend her own ship from an unraveling madman with no skills except his public speaking ability. To compensate for her shortcomings, she's invented a host of otherworldly attributes for her adversary which, truthfully, are the stuff of science fiction."

With a grunt of disgust accompanying his last words he sat down, his nose held aloft while his set jaw still held the remnants of a smug smile.

"You will answer the defense's question, Captain Fletcher."

Fletcher had nobody left to look at, nobody to turn to. She wished that even Merrickson was still here; at least his brand of adversity was without bias or malice.

"I cannot deny any of these accusations." Her heart sank.

"No further questions," beamed Chad.

CHAPTER SIXTEEN
TRAVER

Callie Vargas found Fletcher that night, after the day's proceedings. She tracked the captain to a hotel near the city center, in a penthouse suite on the eightieth floor.

"May I come in? I'm a reporter with *Debunker Daily*."

There was no response. She knew Fletcher was in there; Laffy had accessed the hotel's logs, which reported the room's occupant had not gone anywhere.

"Might I buy you a drink? Pick your brain? If nobody else wants to listen to what you have to say about Aurora, then consider me a breath of fresh air."

A moment later Callie heard padded footsteps coming toward the door. Then it opened. "I don't talk to reporters." The captain was still wearing her uniform from the day's trial, but it was wrinkled and unkempt, the usual pristine straightness of her hair disheveled. Callie thought she smelled a hint of alcohol.

"Then you don't have to talk. Just listen. And if you do say anything, it won't be on the record unless you want it to be."

In the penthouse living room Callie found herself staring out the window overlooking the whizzing, colorful lights of the city. Fletcher sat sternly behind her on the couch, a rum in her hand.

"Captain's salary, huh?" Callie waved her hand to indicate the room and view around her. "Here I thought I was doing alright for myself, but I've never been able to afford to so much as glance at a picture of a room like this."

"I don't enjoy small talk," Fletcher droned after swallowing a hearty gulp of liquor.

"Alright, I'll get to the point." Callie turned from the window and faced the Captain. "Do you know about the *Debunker?*"

"I don't give a shit. If I'm going to care you'll need to make me."

"Five billion people know what's going on inside the courtroom because of me. My transcriptions are the news that everyone hears, and I have been relating every testimony accurately and without bias. People are getting the straight truth. But when you started talking – when you started yelling – it struck a chord with me. I don't think the full truth is being served like it should be. I think you believe what you're saying, and I want to believe it too. But…" she reached into the pocket of her long coat and pulled out her handwritten notebook, holding it up as a prop, "*this* isn't enough. I'm worried that sly Aurora snake-man is a little bit right; when people hear what you said in the court, some of them are going to think you're crazy."

"And?" Fletcher sipped down the last drops in her glass and her face remained stone. "What people think doesn't matter. I spend most of my time billions of kilometers away, and thank god for that."

"All I'm saying is that it doesn't *look* good. But hear me out. It doesn't look good, because Judge Yawnface only gave you a minute. It wasn't enough time. Now, I reach a billion people on a bad day. Yesterday it was more than five billion, tonight it might be more. I'll give you more than a minute. I'll give you an hour. Two hours. Whatever it takes. Make your case. Make it convincing. Make people want to believe you, like I want to believe you. Five *billion* people. If even half of those readers rant against the Corporation and demand answers, you can bet something is going to happen. Something's gonna have to happen."

Fletcher stared past Callie and out the window for a long moment. She stood up and refilled her glass, then returned to her seat.

Callie patiently waited for a response. She knew that to interrupt Fletcher's consideration now might be damaging.

"No."

"No?"

"No. Get out."

Gingerly Callie whipped out a calling card and left it on Fletcher's drink table. "If you change your mind, here is how to find me."

"I won't."

"I'll go. But I can't go without just asking: why won't you even consider it?"

The glass filled with rum flew out of Fletcher's hand and smashed against the window. It shattered, and the city lights danced and swirled in the liquid that now splayed across the window glass.

Callie jumped back, startled. Fletcher rose from the couch slowly as if nothing had happened. But her voice was trembling.

"Because, everyone wants something. I lost a ship, and I lost thirteen people; but nobody cares, because everyone is too busy wanting something."

Callie lowered her eyes. Fletcher made a noble silhouette against the bright traffic lights flying past outside, but this was no time to admire her tragedy. With a small, timid nod, Callie turned and left the penthouse.

She published her transcription later that night. Six billion people read it. In the popular opinions of the day, Captain Fletcher was the loser.

* * *

The fourth day was Traver's day.

His glass box was wheeled to the witness stand and plugged in to the room's sound speakers. Front and center as he was, it was difficult for those entering the courtroom – jurors, officers and audience members alike – to keep from staring at him. He sat eerily still, his eyes tilted upward but rarely blinking. Perfectly composed, he kept his left hand gently laid on his left thigh, while his right stub stayed firmly pressed to his side. The sensation that passed unspoken through everyone's minds was that they, not he, were the ones on trial and that he was an alien god of judgment, watching their every move and reading their thoughts.

The trial proceeded and all eerie sensations faded from memory.

Traver gave his own account of his year in space. It was surprisingly brief and to the point, coming from a man so well known for his elaborate and lengthy use of words. What was most surprising was how terse and unfeeling he was in the telling of his own deeds. "I used the needle and stabbed Officer Akachi in the neck" – "I pulled the trigger and killed Friedrich" – "I took the ship's controls and pushed us downward toward the planet surface." Very little in his testimony was new information – he told the story as would a third party observing over his shoulder. He stopped just after telling about his entry into the pod.

"Can you elaborate on the reasons for your actions?" Chad seemed a little frustrated, despite his best attempt to appear confident. "Before each killing, before each action you took pursuing control of the ship, you were – urged? – coaxed? – by a voice inside your head?"

"No."

Chad whipped around to look at Traver with a badly-hidden scowl. "Your actions were not your own then, because, from your perspective, someone or something was – puppeteering you – for lack of a better term?"

"No."

Chad was stranded, standing in front of the court with his celebrity client throwing away the trial without so much as an emotion.

"Okay. Okay." He had another card left to play. "I'd like to direct everyone's attention to the monitor here in the front of the room.

Surely this is not the first time you have all seen this, but if this is new, it may come as a shock that the figure in this video is the same stoic man who's sitting in front of you now."

The final pod recording played for the court. It was the fascinating seventeen minutes of Traver ruminating, rambling, shouting and sobbing all while being shaken nearly to death. Truly, every soul in the room had seen the video before, some many times, but it remained a bizarre and sublime vision to behold and hear.

"How can you describe what took place in this recording, Mister Graff?" Chad asked, his confidence restored fully after the final moments of the video.

"I can't describe it, Chad. I don't remember it."

This *was* news. News for everyone but Chad, and Gladstone.

"Can you repeat that?"

"I don't remember saying any of that."

"At what point does your memory stop?"

"I remember up until the point I've just told you about: when Captain Fletcher helped me into the pod."

"So there was a point in time when you may not have been in control of your own actions?"

"I can't say. I don't remember."

"Your Honor, Members of the Jury, I believe that Mister Graff's behavior in this video and his complete lack of memory concerning those moments is definitive proof of mental instability. We cannot hold a man responsible for his actions, when that same man believed...believed he was speaking with a planet."

"I *was* speaking with the planet."

The hush in the room was so absolute it formed a thick substance of its own.

"Didn't you hear me, right there in the recording? My temporary lapse in memory is not relevant to whatever it is that went on there." Traver stood up inside his box, but he still did not raise his voice beyond the steady, rhythmic tone he always used. "By saying that my claim was incompatible with the truth, you are calling me either a liar or a madman. By all means, accuse me, imprison me, study me, but don't insult me."

Chad couldn't help himself from smiling. Traver was officially a loose cannon now, but he was firing in the right direction. "Take careful note, members of the jury. Mister Graff *was* conversing with a planet."

The audience was peppered with snickers of laughter, which Halpern swiftly quashed.

"I'd like to go on, if I may," Traver's strong voice resounded through the glass, proving the sound amplifiers to be an unnecessary redundancy for him.

Chad glanced hopefully at the judge: *please let him keep talking.*

Halpern nodded. "Go on Mister Graff."

"Good. Thank you." Traver again seated himself, more comfortably than before. Lance, sitting in the audience, recognized the relaxed but upright posture best of all; it was Traver's broadcasting position. Lance smiled a little in spite of his distaste for the whole proceedings; the court had better prepare itself for whatever was coming next, because it would be neither short nor predictable.

"I can't help but continually find myself in surprise at the lengths to which you are all going – to prove what exactly? Half of you want to finish the job of shriveling me up with one quick electric pulse to the brain, while the other half of you want me to be a raving lunatic. Half of you want Captain Fletcher to go on enjoying her fruitful career as a successful pilot, while the other half want her stripped of her rank right here and now. But why? Why should you, *you*, care? Either way, the captain is going to be out of your lives within a week, whether that means she's alone half a universe away from you or living in a basement somewhere, just as alone and just as removed from you. Either way, I'm going to be a forgotten blip on the world's radar, whether that means I'm dead or rotting in an asylum. What is any of that going to matter to you – what is it going to *prove?*

"And, for heaven's sake, how much *effort* you've all put into this! You have a judge, you have at least four gigantic organizations represented, you have a full courthouse, you pulled Captain Merrickson – goddamn Merrickson – off an assignment so he could testify. And I'm not even going to mention the hundreds of security guards you must have outside the front doors, holding the crowds back. There *is* a crowd. There's always a crowd.

"It's all so unnecessary. The facts are the facts. And it's your problem, not mine, if you choose to mangle the interpretation of those facts or downright disbelieve them. It's clear that you prefer a resolution that is neither simple, efficient nor factual. If you had, you could have simply listened to me in the first place.

"Because the truth – the truth is this. I killed two people on the *Aten*. I did so with full volition and an awareness that murder is generally frowned on. I killed them because it was the only choice I had, and then I took control of the ship because it was the only way to reach the planet. I had to reach the planet because I knew by getting close enough I could speak with it – a goal which, apparently, I achieved. Though, I do wish I remembered.

"Captain Fletcher's truth is this: she did what she had to do to protect her ship and her crew. As my intentions were alien and un-friendly, she acted as a captain must always be expected to act to suppress a danger to livelihood and order.

"You've accused her of two attempts on my life, both of which I must beg to dispute. On the first occasion, it was the unexpected power outage that caused the ship's doors and ports to open. The power outage was the result of a burst from the planet's surface. Captain Fletcher has verified as much. I claim responsibility for it, because it was the first time I had reached out for help, and it was the first time AMA answered me. The results were unexpected and tragic for all involved; Karl was more than my assistant; he was my friend. The tragedy would not have occurred had the planet not intervened, so do not assign that responsibility to the captain, who was busy doing her best to keep me out of the cockpit.

"As to the second event, my journey inside the pod was completely my own plan. Lance's story has already corroborated this fact. If the captain had refused my request, I would have insisted. I would have done whatever I needed to do – and that includes further violence – until she allowed me to undock and descend to the planet.

"To sum it all up, friends, I am guilty. *And* Captain Fletcher is guilty. But she is only guilty in the light of the cosmic laws that demanded I follow Doctor Misleh's path to AMA. In that light, I'm the most innocent of all. But last I checked we're on planet Earth, and you are judging the pair of us based on the old precepts that have kept civilization relatively bearable for the past few millennia. Given the laws of that system, you *need* to find me guilty and have me killed, and you *need* to determine Fletcher free of misdeeds. There's no interpretation to be done. It's merely science.

"Was that so hard?"

* * *

Callie actually hesitated before sending out the day's account when the time came. She'd enjoyed the humongous success this ordeal had brought her, but the impact was about to grow beyond what her imagination, even at its most nightmarish, could conjure.

Then she stopped thinking and pressed the command. Whatever might happen, it wasn't her responsibility. She was only a messenger, and the information that rightfully belonged to the public was in the public's hands.

* * *

The public responded with all the rational understanding of a tidal wave.

Within the hour, Judge Halpern's home was surrounded by a small army of security guards and public safety officers after thousands of death threats had been received, threatening everything from arson to poisoning should she deliver Traver a guilty verdict.

"Fletcher fan clubs" sprang up out of nowhere. Where just twelve hours before she'd been a subject of ridicule on a vast scale, hers was instantly the new household name, replacing Merrickson as the "space captain" who came to mind when children played and adults imagined.

Most insidious of all was the rapidly-spreading belief, unspoken at first but shared more and more often through whispers, that Traver (though he *must* be declared insane to be spared the capital zap) was indeed the most rational person out of the whole affair. That he was not only telling the truth, but was hyper-aware of his circumstances, past and present. That he had been speaking to the – no, nobody's whispers would admit so much. Not yet.

* * *

On the fifth day, the psychologists brought in their findings.

Having questioned Traver over the course of several weeks, analyzing his responses and his brain waves, their decision was quick and unanimous.

"While he has suffered at least one memory gap, there is nothing in his current behavior, his speech, his brain patterns or his thought process that would indicate he is anything but a mentally healthy forty-four year old male. He is sharp, quick-witted, easily solves complex problems requiring pre-planning, and displays none of the usual symptoms generally found in sufferers of mental illness. It is our professional opinion that Traver Graff is mentally sound."

Chad, disheartened, offered up an angle of his own. "*Is* mentally sound? Present tense. You can only study him as his mind stands currently."

"That is correct."

"The events we are discussing took place more than seven months ago. It is entirely possible that, while his body recovered, so did his mind."

"Of course, it is *possible*. But we've all come to the conclusion that a recovery so complete and so quick, without treatment, would be an anomaly. We consider it unlikely."

Theirs was the last testimony.

* * *

"The Jury will retire to consider their verdict."

Those twelve individuals, randomly selected from diverse walks of life from all around the globe, disappeared together.

Nobody in the courtroom spoke for the entire hour for which the jury was absent. But unlike before, the silence was no longer overwhelming; it was filled with a hollow, constant boom, like distant thunder. It was not a natural noise; it was the sound of thousands of people gathered below and around the Space-Transit Department Building, overwhelming the guards, slamming their fists and protest boards and bodies against the cold steel walls, screaming words that were lost in the geyser of screamed words.

And inside, the audience listened to the roar. Judge Halpern listened. The court officials listened. Nothing could stop the roar, just as nothing could make the jury come to a decision faster.

* * *

Finally the jury reappeared.

Not a single one of them looked to be lighthearted as they reassumed their seats. All gloomy, some of them trembling, all of them with their eyes cast down.

Then, "Have you reached a decision?"

The jury foreman stood. "We have."

"And what is your verdict?"

"Not guilty, by way of insanity."

....

Personal Letter, by Dr. Galina Shurovsky from her bed in Knoll Heights Hospital
9/3/2177

Mr. Gladstone,

I had repeatedly asked for an opportunity to speak with your superior, but I've been told he is unavailable. I can't help but feel I've been cut off from the usual channels, now that my usefulness has run its course. Without access to those channels, I'm going to just go ahead and apologize for communicating like this without confidentiality. This morning I feel particularly badly, and I suspect I'm not going to make it through the night. I trust you to forward this message to him, but by the time it reaches him I'll likely be dead.

So what message is so important that I bypass all our security protocols? Well, I have had plenty of time to myself to think. I've decided that the experiment should be called off. I don't know how far it has gotten, but the last I had heard was that Abrahim had suffered a fatal accident. Without him present as an overseer, how can the project possibly be monitored? Philip and his boys don't know enough of this science to be really useful. If you let the experiment go on then you are putting more lives at risk. If Abrahim was anywhere near correct, you could be risking much more than that. If anyone or anything receives signals via crystals outside of a controlled environment, there's no knowing how the body might be provoked. That's not anywhere within my purview of study, but perhaps it's good advice.

I know that you will disregard my suggestions. You've put too much into this experiment to not see it play out. I hope that you get results, but I also hope that you don't. Discovery is a high cause, but human life is higher. Perhaps it has taken my being on my deathbed to realize that.

As an addendum I'd like to say something that is fully within my realm of expertise. The crystals are not, by any means, to be used as a cure for Eams. Though a condensed and constant dose of the crystals may, as a side effect, demolish the bacteria with which they share blood, there are still too many other effects we can't predict. Remember that the crystals provoked the existence of Eams in the first place, not the other way around. One imbalance leads to another. If I didn't use it on myself, to cure my own case of Eams, be sure that I would not dare use *it on anyone else. If the temptation crosses your mind to put it into a wide release as a cure, consider this: what would happen if ten million Eams patients, their blood filled with crystals, were to all broadcast at the same time? What if one of Abrahim's "alien bodies" were to pass by then? Nobody knows, because not even one conscious human has been subjected to those parameters aside from the current subject whose experiment I beg you to suspend.*

But of course you'll consider this, because it's your purview and not mine.

That's all I have to say. I won't add that I regret my previous part in the experiment, because I don't. My contributions to science overcome any harm I've done. But with the intention of preventing further harm, let the record show that I stand firmly against the continuance of my efforts. Let Abrahim's work die with him, and let mine die with me.

Sincerely,

Dr. Galina Shurovsky

....

Traver Graff was committed to Grassy Hills Mental Hospital, a lavish and roomy institution generally populated by individuals whose families were able to pay substantially for their crazy loved ones' room and board. The Secular Alliance for Social Humanities, in its infinite goodness, happened to be one of its prominent donors.

The newest member of the Grassy Hills family received its largest, most comfortable quarters. The rooms housed exercise apparatus (Traver was not deemed a self-harm risk, after all), full media library, and a false window. The false window was, of course, not a window at all but a screen simulating the sights and sounds of a beach, or a grassy hill at night, or as Traver tended to prefer, a starry sky.

He was allowed regular visitors, and he received many. Hundreds per day at first, and thousands on some. Small crowds would gather in the waiting area just outside his room to ask him questions, to listen to him talk, or just to look at him.

The hospital staff rejected as many as they could but were often overwhelmed. They had no legal recourse to call officers to dispel the crowds, since no laws were being broken and Traver never turned his visitors away.

Only on one occasion did Traver abruptly ask for the crowds to be shuffled away, and that was the day Dana came to visit. She came alone; Damian and Allie were too disturbed and frightened to see their disfigured father in person, especially after they'd been subjected to the nightmare of his final broadcast.

Dana's visit was short. Not much was said. She asked about space; he asked about the kids. She assured him that everything was well taken care of by Aurora's insurance payout. When she left, Mr. and Mrs. Graff never saw one another again.

"He's not the same," she murmured over her untouched coffee, weeks later when Callie had caught up with her. "I don't mean that he's changed. Of course he's changed. I mean – I know he was the same man standing there in front of me, but he's not actually Traver anymore. Don't ask me how I know. Only a wife can know, I suppose." She sipped the coffee. Callie scratched on her notepad.

* * *

Weston, who had only followed the trial through the hearsay of guards and cell neighbors, was again pleasantly surprised one May morning when one of his guards opened the door to his cell. "What? Did I oversleep?" Weston hoped he hadn't missed breakfast. He needed the protein for his workout. He had muscles now.

"Nope. You're free."

"Sorry? What?"

"Free. As in, you can get your belongings and get the hell out of here. If I were you I'd do it before the Secular Alliance people change their minds about dropping the charges."

Weston was half-certain he was dreaming. "SASH dropped the charges?"

"I can't stand here holding this door open all day. Are you gonna go, or not?"

Weston did not waste another moment. He ran out of the prison, a free man for the first time in over a year, while running as a free man for the first time in his life.

His slidescreen, in prison storage for so long, had since run down on power or he would have received his messages right away. As it was, he did not find out the reason behind his freedom until he entered his old apartment building and bounded up the stairs, hoping that his bank account had held out for the intervening months of rent.

It had. But he wouldn't find that out until after he met Karen Tiplins, who was waiting for him at the door.

"Karen?"

"Wes! Wes Wes Wes, I'm so glad to see you!" Karen wrapped her arms around him. Karen was not somebody from whom he had ever wanted a hug, but this was a good day so he tolerated it.

"Wow, look at you. You're…you're…looking good!" She looked his proportional body up and down with an intrigued gaze that wasn't very subtle.

"What are you doing outside my apartment?"

"None of my calls went through. I've been trying to get in touch with you all day."

"I've just come from prison."

"Right. You know why, right?"

"I'm innocent, for one thing. That's a good reason."

"I'm sure you are. I had to make so many calls to get those charges dropped. The legal team, the Data Security people, you wouldn't believe…"

"Okay. Well, thanks. But why did there need to be a reason?"

"You have Traver to thank for that. He requested you to be his producer. Imagine that!"

Weston knew he'd woken to a dream that morning, and the dream had still not ended.

"Traver's...broadcasting?"

"Ssshhhh, it's not really big news yet. Don't go telling the world, even though the world's going to find out soon enough. Isn't it so exciting?"

Weston couldn't look at Karen anymore. He would have preferred not to hear her either. He stared off into the blank greyness of the apartment hallways. His mind went equally blank. "Yes. Exciting."

* * *

"Why the World Wanted Traver Back. Is that a good title?" Callie looked at Laffy, whose bulk blocked out the light of his monitors, creating a shadow over half the room. He didn't turn around, but Callie mostly only talked to him as an excuse to talk to herself anyway.

"I'm not sure about this part. Listen: 'The most mystifying aspect of the trial is the one that went completely overlooked. While the two main stars of the trial get a happy ending – Traver Graff returning to broadcasts and Louisa Fletcher to her post – the rest of us have been distracted from the real questions: why were Captain Merrickson's orders so explicitly centered around rescuing Graff? Why did Aurora storm heaven and earth to save the *Aten* only when it seemed apparent that Graff was at risk? Was there more to Fletcher's oft-overlooked emotional contribution to the trial's third day? Perhaps the greatest victims of the tragedy of the *Aten* is us, the public, who in the end must put up our shoulders and admit: *we'll never know.*'"

"Yeah, I like it." Laffy's voice rolled softly through the old house, this one located several kilometers from Sable Valley Drive.

"You didn't even listen to it. I just don't know if I should mention Fletcher at all. That might be too suggestive, too pointed at that particular narrative."

"Speaking of that narrative..." Now Laffy swung his projected head around. "When are you going to publish the big one?"

Callie froze. She licked her lips and tapped her fingers together, old nervous tics that resurfaced whenever she felt she was in over her head.

"I thought we weren't going to talk about this."

Laffy's huge eyes, usually so dull and insect-like, adopted an earnest intensity. "You already know all the answers your headlines have been asking. We've been compiling the letters, the memos, the articles for years. Now seems like as good a time as any, so what have we been waiting for?"

Callie stared at the floor. "I'm still not comfortable with it."

"Why?"

"Who's going to believe it?"

Laffy looked at her for a long moment, and frustration appeared on his boulder of a face. "You have the family members. You have all the proof. What more do you need me to get for you?"

"The family members won't be enough. Zweicker and Gandy only have personal testimony and that's not the same thing as proof."

"You're scared, aren't you?"

Callie looked up from the floor. "Aren't you? Doctor Fraunen, Doctor Aguilar, Doctor Shurovsky…there is a pattern of deaths, and we're nowhere near as noteworthy or death proof as they were. Why do you think I didn't release my Cairo documentary? Even ten years ago I knew not to poke the bear."

The large man's flat face stared bluntly at Callie for a moment, before the head swung away. "You want me to delete them all? I'll delete them. It's just a pity, after all your talk about bringing justice to Aurora, that you're too scared to do anything about it."

Callie turned around and around again, pacing in place, the article in her hand forgotten. "You can wipe over any footsteps? Get rid of any trace that you hacked them at all?"

"What do you think I do every single time? Of course I can."

"Wait. Don't get rid of it." She pivoted on her heel to face him. "It's good that we have all this, so let's not throw it away. Someday the time will be right."

Now Laffy didn't look up from his computer. "When will the time be right?"

"I don't know. All I know is that if we can try to get these facts out into the world, we should. But it can't look like it came from us."

* * *

Lance sat at the bar of the *Downed Eagle*, bitterly looking up at a screen. Karen's face had just appeared a moment before. She couldn't be heard here over the murmurs, grunts and clatters of the bar, but he knew she was announcing the brand new run of *Traver Talk*, live from the Grassy Hills Hospital. Just like nothing had changed. Lance chugged his pint of beer, choked at the end and spat a little.

"You okay?" asked the bartender.

"Yes." Laughing at himself. "But I'll take another one."

This was the reason he'd left SASH once and for all, the moment the trial had ended. He could feel this moment coming; Traver's public resurgence was somehow inevitable. But could he blame Karen? Could he blame the SASH board? Could he blame good old Weston? Perhaps all of human nature was to blame. Once Traver had you in his cockpit, it was difficult to get out.

"Oh I heard about this," came a small voice from beside him.

Lance turned and nearly jumped in his seat, startled to see that a soft-spoken giant had sat beside him while he'd been intent on the screen. "*Traver Talk*. You don't look happy about it. You look pissed." The giant's head swung toward him. Lance dodged to avoid collision with its shallow chin. "Say, I recognize you," the stranger's disproportionate voice continued. "You're the Lanka guy from the trial. I followed all that on the news. Pretty cool stuff."

"Yeah, that's me."

"You should be excited about this, huh? Didn't I read you used to work on the show?"

Lance reached for his drink. One gulp in, he changed his mind about chugging the whole thing.

"I did. But things got pretty weird for a while. I can't go back."

"I can't say I blame you. Didn't he almost kill you a couple times?"

"Yep. Yep he did."

The large man received a drink and together they watched the screen in silence. Images flashed, showing bits and pieces of various Traver shows. Most of them Lance recognized too well. The segment that showed Traver inside the pod was one Lance would have liked to never see again.

"What do you think he's gonna talk about now?" asked the big man.

"Beats me. But you can bet it'll be more of the same that we heard in the trial."

"Well that was pretty interesting. People'll listen to that."

Lance took his glass in both hands and stared at the tiny rising bubbles, focusing on them to prevent himself from looking back at Traver's cursed face. "That's the problem. People will listen. They listened before, when his message was all about staying home and fixing our own problems instead of worrying about what happens on other planets. Now the same people are going to listen when he starts to say the exact opposite. And they'll never even notice the difference."

"Hmm," came the voice from somewhere inside the big head. With a well-intended action, the giant patted Lance on the shoulder, disrupting him enough to spill his beer onto the counter and onto himself.

"Oh, shit."

"Sorry."

"It's okay. Excuse me. Be right back."

Lance ran to the restroom, where he dried off his soiled pants as best he could while still failing to remove what appeared to be evidence of an overzealous bladder.

When he returned to the bar, the big man was gone.

"Where'd he go?" he asked the bartender, more interested in *how* the giant had vanished so quickly.

"Left. But he said he found your slidescreen under your chair." The bartender set the device on the counter in front of Lance.

"Thank you. That's weird. I thought I had it in my pocket."

As he wandered into the darkness after seven beers, he slid open the screen to cursorily scan for messages. Jobless and homeless, he now spent most of his time perusing the worlds that could be found inside that screen.

But now there was only one thing to be found. A file sat on his home screen, front and center. It was a file he was certain he'd not downloaded.

Curious, he opened it.

Sober awareness swam into his head more quickly than most people think possible, and he sat on the sidewalk to read in disbelief. He was a quick reader and was able to gather the gist of the content by skimming for five quick minutes.

It was a collection of notes, memos, letters and reports dating all the way back to the Zilly mission. Many of the files were personal messages from notable scientists, some were unpublished articles, but the majority were highly classified internal communications.

Lance started to feel sick to his stomach. The beer hadn't sat well.

When he reached the end of the file he found two sentences tacked on after the closing letter. The sentences read:

This is everything needed to expose the truth behind Aurora, Eams, AMA and Traver. Now it's in your hands.

Lance vomited on the sidewalk.

* * *

Weston put the finishing touches on his transmitter setup in the waiting area outside of Traver's cell. It was refreshing to be once again assembling a recording array, and this time never having to call for help hauling in the heavier pieces of equipment.

About a half-hour remained before the transmission was to go live. Traver had been promised privacy, so neither SASH executives nor onlookers would be allowed in the waiting area during sessions; Weston would be alone with him. Now that Weston had gotten over the shock of Traver's appearance and reconciled himself with the other circumstances, he was excited. He'd be working again, doing what he loved. That was all that mattered.

His preparations were interrupted by the one person in the world he could not order off the premises. It was the Aurora man with the five o'clock shadow still brushed on his jawline. Accompanying him were two scientists.

"We're going to be on the air in just a few minutes. Nobody else is really supposed to be in here…" For all his restored confidence, Weston still trembled in the presence of this unassuming and unmemorable individual.

"We'll only be a few moments. We need to take a small blood sample. We've been doing this monthly and it will continue on the same schedule."

He nodded to the two scientists, who went inside. Traver looked up at the shadow man and nodded in greeting. The shadow man nodded back.

"How has he been?"

Weston was surprised the question had been directed toward himself of all people, but he answered as best he could. "Good. At least I think so. He doesn't talk about himself much, or about…any of the stuff that happened. But his energy is good, and I think he's looking forward to broadcasting again."

"Perfect." The man didn't seem to be responding to Weston at all. He was too intently watching the scientists as they pricked Traver's good arm and began to draw blood.

"Are they checking for Eams?" Weston asked.

"No. The Eams is gone." The man said this without any note or fascination.

"Then what are they looking for?"

Again the man didn't seem to answer the question. He went on in his steady but normal voice as he watched the scientists. "The significant moments in history go unnoticed until after the fact. Some are never recognized at all. Isn't that sad?"

"I don't know. I guess it's sad."

"The first monkey who opened his mouth and started to speak could not have found his own action remarkable. He likely only did it to call for food, or warmth, or a mate."

Within, the scientists produced a vial filled with a thick blue fluid. A drop of Traver's blood was deposited inside and the men watched it intently.

"The saddest thing of all is that, when the truth is right there in front of people, they'd rather find something petty to worry about than open their eyes and see something amazing is happening. Columbus only wondered where the gold was. The moments happen, but they slip past us."

A minute passed, then one of the two scientists looked toward the shadow man and discreetly shook his head, "no."

The shadow man did something Weston hadn't thought possible: he lost his composure. His shoulders sagged; Weston thought he suddenly seemed old and tired well beyond his apparent, unguessable age. He took off his glasses, carefully but distantly cleaning them with his tie though they'd been perfectly spotless.

"We were so close. The moment slipped past us, as moments do."

The scientists emerged from the room, carrying the blood samples with them. They passed by Weston and left the lobby.

"Still," the shadow man's energy seemed to return as he raised his shoulders, replacing the glasses on his face, "the moment happened. We made it happen. I'm going to ask a favor of you, Mister Hillquist."

"Yes?" Weston was not a little bit confused by now.

"If Traver remembers anything more, particularly about his time broadcasting from the pod, I'd like to know about it. We will still be dropping in once a month, but he may say something in private."

"Of course."

"Good day to you, and best of luck on the maiden broadcast."

The man turned to go. Weston stopped him with one last question, a desperate attempt to try and clear up his own confusion:

"But, what more do you think he's going to remember from inside the pod? You already know he believes he was talking to the planet."

"That's because," the shadow man said without turning or pausing, "he was."

The man vanished from the room. Weston tilted his head, trying to understand.

There was a knock on the glass of the cell. Traver stood upright with his face nearly pressed against the clear wall, looking intently at him.

Weston shook off his confusion. He knew he would forget all about it soon enough anyway. Nothing the shadow man ever said was easy to remember.

Traver had gotten Weston's attention. He sat down in the seat that had been prepared for him, outfitted with microphones and cameras. "Are we ready to go?"

Made in the USA
Las Vegas, NV
18 February 2022

44151010R00215